BRITANNIA
THE INVASION CHRONICLES (BOOK I)

BY
JOHN WAITE

Original edition © John Waite 2015
This edition © John Waite 2016
All rights reserved

Follow news for the series on Facebook:
https://www.facebook.com/pages/John-Waites-Britannia/1641114536120731

For my soul mate and the love of my life:

Helen Waite.

Semper Amemus.

Before I go any further, I really need to thank the following people for their help in getting this book of the ground:

I know my wife got the dedication, but I also have to thank her first because she is the one who has put up with me and 'it' for so many years. Helen, thank you so much for your patience, I owe you so much.

Thanks also to my friend, former comrade-in-arms and fellow author, Craig Emms, for showing me that there is a way round the great stranglehold exerted by literary agents and publishing houses.

Lastly, I am indebted to my test audience, so many of whom have kept faith in my writing for many years. So, thank you:

Primus Aebutius
Carole Ayre
Sam Pepper
Andy Scott
Steve & Karen Sinden
Brett Thorn
Emma Tyler

You guys rock!

AUTHOR'S NOTE

In 2005, I published my first book: 'Legionary – a Call to Arms'. In truth, this was to prove to be quite a painful experience for me, some of the shockwaves from which still resonate today. In my eagerness, not to mention naivety, to see hours of isolation at a keyboard bear fruit, I opted to go down the author funded publishing route. Something irrational in my head kept telling me that I would enjoy overnight success and that my dream of becoming a full-time writer would be magically fulfilled.

You can see where this is going, can't you?

Suffice to say; my faith in my publisher was badly misplaced and my own expectations were set unfeasibly high.

So, what do you do with an experience like that? Do you tell yourself that you really should have known better and sweep the whole thing under the carpet? Or, do you take it on the chin, pick yourself up and start over?

Well – here I am.

I now have a couple of non-fiction titles to my name and a modified sense of perspective. In truth though, I'll always be convinced that handled a little more professionally, 'Legionary' could have done a bit better than it did. Though, for my part, I was so wrapped up in getting the historical details right, I missed the now plainly obvious fact that the book would never really achieve a significant readership. Why? Because it was too niche and had little or no story to it. It was, essentially, taking a very basic story of a young man's life and using it to tell people what it was like for a young soldier in the Roman army of the 1st Century AD. A total 'No Frills' read. Well, that's great if you're a fan of Roman history or a re-enactor, as I was at the time, but not really the stuff that mass appeal is made of.

Ah, well - as we're always so fond of pointing out after the event; we'd all be geniuses with the gift of hindsight.

That being said; you can still find the odd copy on Amazon.co.uk. You can also still read the reviews which allowed me to draw comfort from the fact that this long out of print book did actually provide a few people with what they said was an enjoyable read.

So, you may ask, why am I talking to you about a book that the vast majority of people have never heard of, when what I should be doing is talking about this one? Well, here's the thing, you see. This book is essentially an evolved version of that book. Not really the same, but recycled both in terms of historical context and main characters. Although this time, it has a much more compelling storyline. Something which I now know was so conspicuously lacking in the original. I Must also confess though, I did directly pinch a few scenes from the old book, simply because I really liked them and thought they deserved a second go.

Now, I'm sure at this point, people are going to be inclined to ask why I didn't just scrap the characters and start afresh, instead just doing something different against the backdrop of the same historical context. It's a fair point but, as anyone who knows me and why I used those old characters will tell you, it's just not possible for me turn my back on them. In the main, you see, they are, or were, real people.

As re-enactors, I and my group took the names of real Roman soldiers and civilians from sources such as tomb stones and other inscriptional archaeology. Then, in tribute to that person, we adopted it as our own Roman name. We felt that in some fashion, it would give them some semblance of life once more, as we created new personas to fit the names of those who had lived and died so long ago. It was, if you like, our attempt to bring a little bit of immortality to a handful of the millions of anonymous souls who lived within the Roman Empire without ever achieving fame – or notoriety for that matter.

So, you see, by using those names, I had a ready reference source of faces and personalities to refer back to and build on.

As I've already suggested, my ultimate failure was in placing those names in a book which was not capable of doing them justice. Consequently, I recently took the decision to try and put that right. I've therefore carried them forward into a work which, hopefully, is a more suitable vehicle for the purposes of allowing their names to be heard again – even if the lives I had given them were entirely of my creation. As you read the book then, you may come across names which you may not think ring entirely true, perhaps most notably our hero, Vepitta.

I admit, it's an odd sounding name for such a centrally important character, but he lived. His name was recorded on a tombstone which stood for many years outside the gates of his former fortress home of Carnuntum, now modern Petronell in Austria, where he served with the XIIII Gemina Legion. Despite how these names may sound and their obvious literary appeal, I didn't want a book entirely populated with old favourites like Maximus or Brutus. I wanted somebody real, to take forward in an adventure. I wanted to place him in a world which, if he were here to critique my work, he would be instantly familiar with. I'd want him to say that he recognises my characters, perhaps adding with a nod and a grin that he knew somebody very similar when he was alive.

Sentimental, I know. But these characters are a part of me now. I could never leave them behind, just for the sake of trying to convince any readers of my work that this was an entirely new book. I freely admit it is not – but for what I feel are good, honest reasons.

As for the history - well, it seems that these days, many authors feel compelled to add historical notes to their work. Not least it seems to convince their readers that, actually they do know what the known historical facts are, but that they've purposefully changed things in order to make their story more appealing. I'm not entirely sure why writers of historical fiction insist on doing this as I'm sure most of their readers know they are picking up a work of fiction. They realise therefore that it is not always a precise commentary on a specific time, event or place. Consequently, I'm not going to go down that road as I don't really see the point of it.

Of course, this is a totally mercenary and a shameless plug I know, but if anybody wants to discover a little more about my non-fiction take on the Roman world then it might not be such a bad thing to read the two non-fiction titles I wrote since my opener with 'Legionary'. The first was 'Boudica's Last Stand', an examination of the Boudican revolt and my suggestion as to the site of her final battle. This last being derived from a close examination of tactical and practical considerations applying to both the Roman and rebel forces. My second title is 'To Rule Britannia', which focuses in the main on the Claudian invasion of Britain in 43AD. The book also contains a detailed discussion of Caesar's landings of 55 and 54 BC.

For now though, my greatest wish is that you immerse yourself in the story I have to tell. After all, it is my intention that there are many more adventures in store for Vepitta and his friends. It is also my hope

that, after this first instalment, you will want to march with them, all the way to the end.
John Waite
Bedworth, England
April 2015

Forget not, Roman, that it is your special genius to
                    rule the people;
To impose the ways of peace, to spare the defeated,
and to crush those proud men who will not submit.

                            Virgil, The Aenid.

PROLOGUE

My story begins where I think any good story should - in the place I call home. Though, before I begin its telling, I need you to understand something important about me. The truth is; I was neither a king or prince, nor a knight or general. I was just a soldier. So, you may well gather then that mine is not one of those tales of greatness, power and fame that everyone is so fond of.

Mind you, if you are content to settle for the reminiscences of someone a good deal more obscure than any of history's notables, then I'll be more than happy to share mine with you. Although, I'll lay good money on the fact that if you do decide to stay for the telling of my tale then, sooner or later, you'll begin to judge me for what I have done.

Well, I suppose that's only natural. Though at some point you may do well to remember that as people, you and I are very different. So, always try to keep in mind then that your morals are not my morals, your code is not my code and your world is certainly not my world.

Still, now we have that out of the way and now you know what I am, then perhaps it might be useful if I next tell you who I am.

My name is Marcus Sulpicius Vepitta, although Vepitta will do. I was once a legionary who served under the standards of one of the greatest of Rome's legions; the mighty XIIII Gemina. Now, you may begin to think me guilty of an excess of pride at this point. Particularly when I boast that I was steadfast in my oath to my emperor, and that I also won out over the ambitions of many others to achieve my position. Well, you may be right. The fact is, I am glad I can brag of beating so many aspiring hopefuls, by winning my place in the elite bodyguard that protected the legion's legate. I might also add that it was because of that honoured duty that I was bound too by another solemn oath: To defend at all costs, both the person of the legate and his administration. Anyway, before we go any further down that road - and to avoid my getting carried away a little too early - perhaps I should try to explain instead just why it is that I want to share my story with you.

Look at it this way: In your time, the ordinary people from my world probably amount to little more than insubstantial shadows from the past. For the most part, our names are no longer even a whisper on the breeze. Well, I want to change that. I want to fill your thoughts instead with pictures from my lifetime, to awaken those who have lain silent for so long. I want to allow you to know us.

Of course, this may be starting to strike you as somewhat sentimental. I can understand that - but let me ask you something. Have you any idea just what this means to me? For you to actually see us for who we once were and for you to know us, as you would a living person. Well, I'll tell you. It would mean no less than to grant us what only a privileged few enjoy. It would grant us immortality, because we would have finally escaped from the shadow world of obscurity where we have dwelt for so long. Then, with our names alive once more, our restless ghosts would be ready once more to obey the call from war horns which last rallied us so long ago.

And when I have finished – when I have told you all there is to tell and you have experienced my world for yourself - then our eternal souls will rest a little more contented. Because you see, even if my world only comes alive again in the closed universe of your thoughts, I and my comrades will have at least experienced a taste of that immortality I spoke of.

And what's more; I will also have the extra pride of knowing that it was I, Vepitta, who caused the glorious golden eagles of the legions to rise once more above those ancient battlefields.

CHAPTER 1

It was on a freezing cold morning in the second year of the reign of Claudius. Just as the last of the snow storms of late winter were threatening to bury the fortress and town of Mogontiacum under a thick blanket of white. That was when I had stolen my very last opportunity to spend a night under the same roof as the small young family that Salviena and I had managed to create together.

I distinctly remember the weak, flickering light from the smoky flames of the tiny oil lamps. Though insubstantial; their light was still capable of providing the small and sparsely furnished home with a feeling of warmth.

The comforting glow of the lamps adorned the walls with drapes of gently swaying shadows, picking out Salviena's features with subtle shades of light and dark. The fine contrasts further enhanced the sensuousness of her expressions as; closing her eyes she moaned soft responses to the pleasure of our love making. Her muted sighs and the strands of dark golden hair crisscrossing her face served only to heighten my own passions further as we moved rhythmically against each other on the creaky little bed.

She kissed me passionately and called out my name, wrapping her legs tightly around me, pulling me deeper into her warmth. My lips locked onto hers once more as my movements took on a growing urgency, hastening our union towards the peak of pleasure. My mind filled completely with the intense physical sensation of my climax and a feeling of joyfulness. It was a feeling which I only experienced in the arms of the one woman I had ever really loved. It made me gasp with the release, shuddering with its intensity; I flopped down breathlessly, kissing the soft skin of her neck and throat.

We lay for a while, breathing deeply in time with each other as the heat of the moment gradually transformed itself into a feeling of deep wellbeing and a lazy, reassuring warmth. I savoured the moment, eager to remember the entire time that I had shared with her that morning. For only the Gods knew when we would share such precious time together again.

Slowly, I rolled to one side and lay there on my back. Almost instantly she had rolled on top of me, her face suspended above mine, framed by a loose cascade of golden hair.

"You know you need to be outside the fortress by the sixth hour?" she reminded me in a low voice.

"I know it." I replied assuredly, tracing my finger down the smooth skin of her back, following the curve of her buttock. "And I will be there on time, as will the others."

"Does it not matter then that you did not spend the night in barracks Marcus? Surely, Fatalis will punish you if he finds out?"

I placed my hands behind my head. Smiling, I looked into her eyes for a few seconds before lightly stroking her cheek with the back of my hand, hoping I suppose to brush away the worry evident on her face.

"Not even Fatalis would deny those of us with families one last night to say our goodbyes." I assured her. "After all, who knows how long we will be gone? Besides, he knows full well we'll all be where we need to be when the time comes."

"Tell me again, where is Britannia?" Salviena asked, sitting herself upright. I groaned as her weight shifted and she positioned herself above my loins.

"You keep sitting there my lady and it won't be a geography lesson you get." I assured her, feeling myself begin to stir once more.

"For the love of Venus." Her expression lightened as laughing, she swung herself off the bed and picked up a linen shift. "Don't you think of anything else?"

"Not when I'm with you." I growled, swinging my legs off the bed and wrapping my arms around her waist. Laughing, she pushed me away.

"Please my love, where is it?" she asked again.

"Why, it's right here." I grinned, cupping my hands around my groin.

"Please." her face quickly took on a sad expression. "When you're away, I need to at least be able to try and imagine where in the world you might be."

It pained me to see her face drop. I began to feel clumsy and foolish at my crude joke so I tried instead to tell her what she needed to know. In her too, I sensed the growing uneasiness that had rapidly spread through Mogontiacum, since the day we had first learnt of our new mission.

"We will have to march west, I reckon for at least a month, to reach Portus Itius on the far coast of Gaul." I explained. "That is where we will eventually take ship with the northern fleet and sail further west to find the shores of Britannia."

"But my love, everyone says it is a cursed place, far beyond the edge of the world and peopled by fierce and sorcerous savages." The composure that Salviena had maintained for the last few days was beginning to crumble. My heart went out to her as I watched a solitary tear slide down her cheek.

"I'm frightened. This is like no war you have ever fought before. They are asking you all to march off into the unknown and even fight demons maybe."

I felt an urgent need to comfort her so I quickly grabbed her up in my arms. I held her tightly, trying to both reassure her and set aside my own private misgivings.

"Whoever it is that awaits us on that island, you can be sure that they've never had to take on anything like us. You know that if the Emperor commands it, we will fill the whole world with the widows of his enemies, demons or no." I kissed her tenderly on the forehead, reminding her of just what we were as she smiled uneasily up at me.

"Have you forgotten my sweet? I march with the Fourteenth Gemina Legion. It's not us who are accustomed to doing the dying. You know that too."

"I know, I know. But, I've heard such stories I…"

"And stories are all that they are." I cut in, placing a quieting finger over her lips. "Wait and see. Once the Emperor has what he wants then we can all come marching home. Then I'll be able to tell you and those two boys of ours just what it was like to fight these blue skinned barbarians beyond the edge of the world, you'll see."

Salviena smiled briefly, though I could tell that she wasn't convinced. As I drew away from her, picking up my under tunic and pulling it over my head, I resolved to give up trying to convince her that everything would be as I had said. It was the place of politicians to convince people of the need to go to war, not mine. And besides, I didn't have the tongue for it.

As I began to gather my equipment, Salviena came up from behind and wrapped her arms around me. I relished the feel of her embrace but wondered just how long it would be before the Gods would allow me to feel the comfort of her touch once more.

"Will you look in on the boys before you go?" I felt the warmth of her breath on my neck and then she kissed it lightly.

"Of course." I replied. "I don't want to wake them at this hour though, so promise that you will be sure to bring them to see the column march out won't you?"

"Even if the snows are as deep as I am tall." she assured me, stroking my arm. "We will be there for you."

"Good. That's good." I said, squeezing her hand.

Quietly, I crossed the floor, parting the heavy drapes dividing the room. Peering into the dark space on the other side of the curtain, I could just make out the pale shapes of my two boys faces. Salviena stepped up behind me. She raised a small oil lamp close to the gap I had made in the drapes.

At five, Gaius was the eldest. He was fiercely protective of his younger brother, little Marcus, who had just turned three. As usual, he had curled up as close to his big brother as possible. Their faces seemed so perfect and pure in the insubstantial light and, as usual, just a glimpse of them filled me with pride.

Though they would grow up to regard themselves as Romans, it was not hard to see their true pedigree. After all, they had inherited the same blonde locks and Germanic features of both I and their mother. Time was; we would all have lived our lives within one of the wild tribes who used to rule Germania. But that was all gone now, for we were now part of the biggest tribe in the world, Rome.

"In another age and another time, they could have been born princes." I spoke quietly as I shared my thoughts with Salviena.

"In this age, they are loved." she replied. "And that is all that they need."

I stepped into the dark space and knelt by their bed. I felt the warmth of their bodies through the blankets and smelt the sickly sweetness of their breath. As gently as I could, I leaned forward and kissed each of them on their forehead, pausing briefly to admire their perfection before pulling slowly back and whispering:

"Honour your mother and the Gods. Be strong and remember me. I will return to you my sons. I swear it."

I turned and stepped back out of the dark space, standing before Salviena once more.

"You and the other women will all be fine. Just be strong and trust me when I say: I will come home to you."

"Then trust me when I say: I will do my duty, to you and our boys." she said, quickly wiping an errant tear from her cheek. "And who knows, what we have just done may even bear more fruit. After all, the time was just about right."

A wide grin broke across my face and I grabbed Salviena up once more, planting a firm kiss on her forehead.

"What a joy that would be." I exclaimed. "There could be no better welcome home than to find another little bastard running around and swelling the numbers of my own small tribe."

"Then wait and see soldier." said Salviena as she smiled up at me. "And one day, when you are done with war, perhaps you will finally make it legal between us two?"

"I could not ask for a finer and sweeter wife than you." I responded. "And when the soldiering and fighting is done and the Legion owns me no more, I swear, we will be joined before the gods. Then we can share each day they give us together. For now though, we must be strong and I must be gone."

We lingered over a tender kiss until finally I pulled away, throwing my cloak around my shoulders. I pulled open the door, letting in a cloud of swirling snowflakes that invaded the room on a freezing cold blast of wind. Stepping into the doorway I turned to face Salviena once more.

"Just come home safe to us." were her final words to me.

"Not even the gods themselves will bar my way." I promised, as I pulled my hood around my face and stepped out into the snowstorm.

* * * * *

We had finally marched out from the great fortress in the middle of that same swirling blizzard. The wind's baleful howling that day had intermingled with the wailing of the women and children, gathered in the freezing weather to see us off. Men folk too, either too old or too young to take their chance also called out their goodbyes. These were the less foolhardy, who had wisely chosen not to follow the military column on a journey so arduous that it could well prove to be their last.

For some though, the pain of separation was far too much to bear and the risk of falling by the wayside was much more preferable to being left alone. For others, the chance to become pioneers and follow the Legions over the sea to what could potentially be vast riches was too much to ignore. Packing provisions and shelters on mules and carts, they had offered yet another prayer to Fortuna and tagged on to the rear of the column.

Those who remained behind now looked solemnly upon the great marching column. Women hugged each other, or cradled babes or small children in tight wrapped arms. Now and again they would catch sight of the face of a loved one. Briefly, the sadness on their face would melt as they shouted and waved frantically. They yearned for one last glance into a loved one's eyes before the men marched out, knowing that the prospects for their return were bitterly uncertain. Fathers, brothers, sons and lovers were prayed for one last time as those who knew them called out for a safe return; but only the Gods knew when. Their lamentations mixed with the cheers and salutations of the many others who had come to wish us well in our quest.

Despite the best efforts of the Gods to belittle our mighty formation with their storm, we marched out in good order, loudly and lustily singing our marching songs. Though, at the same time we maintained a quiet hope that someday we would return once more to see what we now regarded as our true home.

As we pushed our way into the swirling white flak I did my best to keep alive in my mind's eye the recent image of my two sons as they stood with their mother. Salviena had kept her promise and she had been there for me, with Gaius and Marcus at her side. The three of them had stood motionless as I marched by, close enough for me to see the heavy flakes of snow building up on their winter clothing and sticking to their eyelashes. As I passed, I caught one last kiss from the frozen air as my greatly beloved released it from her palm into the wind. With a heavy heart; I had smiled briefly back at the ruddy, snotty faces that huddled either side of her skirts. I saw the expressions on the boys' faces. Their look spoke more of their discomfort in the bitter cold and did not quite convey the notion as to whether they actually understood that this may be the last brief seconds of my time with them. Perhaps that lack of realisation was for the best as I allowed myself one last look at my family - my world. Then I smiled at them once more, swallowed my pain and faced the front.

Gradually the cheers and excitement of our send-off were swallowed up by the blasting winds. Soon they became nothing but a hazy memory. Minutes stretched into hours and then days. As day after testing day passed, the accumulated pain and privation of the long winter march began to bite down hard on us. Before long, the hushed mutterings circulating amidst the mile long column of soaked and frozen soldiers began to erode any last vestige of enthusiasm for our mission that still remained. We pushed on though, wrapped tightly in our hooded woollen cloaks, fighting against the bone chilling winds that combined with the all too frequent snow and rain falls.

As we marched ever further, the talk that originally grew from the growing need to divert our minds from the harsh reality of our circumstances caused the first seeds of dissention to be sown. Slowly at first, the mutterings became much more serious talk. It percolated steadily through the entire column, eating at the men and feeding on their doubts about what we were really marching into.

As the men endured the sapping march, they eventually came to do nothing else but exchange the many stories that spread through the column. Tales about what kind of land Britannia really was; creating a creeping dread that soon touched us all.

I and my own small group of comrades were no exception.

"So let's hear it, what do you lot make of all this stupid talk that's doing the rounds then?" Surus growled, making his own position clear, setting his jaw against the stinging snowflakes which were being lashed into his face by the biting winds.

"You can't just say it's stupid and dismiss it that way." Marinus grumbled from behind us, rebuking Surus as we trudged on. "What do you know of

Britannia? None of us has any idea what we're getting into here. What they're saying is right. This is nothing but a damned fool's quest. Mark my words."

"You shouldn't talk like that Marinus." Aebutius berated him. "It's bad for morale, especially when it comes from an old hand like you."

"Bollocks to your morale, boy." snarled Marinus. "Where's your morale going to be when you're lying dead and rotting in a field with the rest of us, eh?"

"Hey, watch out." muttered Pudens as he nodded to the side of the road, drawing our attention to our Optio, Mestrius. He stood there, unmoving, watching the passing column and glaring malevolently at us from out of the swirling snowflakes. We quickly fell silent as we tucked our chins down and marched past him, taking care not to speak again until we were sure he was well behind us.

"That bastard will roast our arses over a slow fire if he gets wind of this kind of talk." warned Pacatianus. "Fair do's though; he'd be right too. It's already having a bad effect amongst the men as it is."

"Bad my arse." snapped Marinus. "The talk is right. The sensible thing would be for us all to turn round and tell the big cheeses to stick their invasion plans right up their arses, cos' we're not going anywhere."

"And that's exactly the sort of talk that'll get us all in the shit, especially if Fatalis gets wind of it." came the disembodied voice of Zenas from just forward of us. His remark prompted us to contemplate just what would happen if our Centurion came to hear of the talk amongst us.

"You of all people should have more sense, Marinus. Now take a spot of sound advice and just shut your flapping maw and push on."

On hard marches such as this you could do nothing but push on, trying to ignore the oozing pus that half-filled your eyes, as the biting cold wind threatened to blind you completely. You had to try, as well, to ignore the stinging pain as you sipped your ration of freezing cold, watered down wine, wincing as its sourness bit hard into the cracks of dry and blistered lips.

In the bitter weather, your finger nails throbbed as though they had been hammered with iron and the creases on the skin of your knuckles cracked and bled as the wind dried them out. In those conditions, the last thing you needed to do was to allow your mind to dwell on what you were expected to endure. You needed to talk, to shift your focus. But in the end; that was precisely how the rumours had been able to take such firm root in the minds of the men.

The information and opinions on Britannia were by now rife amongst the men. They were generally always qualified by the fact that the soldier telling the tale knew it to be true as it had come directly from a trusted source. Sometimes a sailor who had been to trade there was hailed as the source of the knowledge. Sometimes a soldier would refer to the tales passed down by the long dead veterans of Gaius Julius

Caesar's two failed attempts to conquer the distant land. Always, the talk harkened to a wild and terrible sea populated with monsters that no men knew the name of. And of a strange people, who wielded potent magical powers, awaiting us in a forbidding and unknown land.

Steadily, the imagination of the men had started to run amok with the dread images that the idle marching gossip had conjured up in their minds eye. Eventually an all-encompassing superstitious fear grew steadily with each new tale exchanged. Incredulity and dread had now encroached on the place in their minds which had once been occupied by consciousness of the agony of tolerating heavily blistered and almost permanently wet feet.

Who would have thought that such things, which sensibly could only be regarded as little more than a child's bedtime terrors, would foment such dread in so formidable a war band? Who would have thought that such a mighty force, with many veterans amongst its number who had fought the most savage of enemies, would baulk so at nothing more than ghost stories? Though the notions were seemingly ridiculous, it was nonetheless the truth. To compound matters, as we had slogged along endless miles of road, scaring ourselves to the point where I thought we would all begin to squeal like nervous girls, the march began to claim its first victims.

As the cream of Rome's military might, the Legions would march anywhere, over all distances and, if need be, in all weathers. After all, it was our lot. It was what we were created to do. We were meant to be the hammer of the Emperor, striking out anywhere at any time, shattering all of the enemies of Rome. It was not, what we all knew from the outset, what women and children were meant for, especially in the foul and brutal conditions that we had endured on this march.

As the distance between our great marching column and Portus Itius grew ever shorter, so the straggling line of wretched, frost bitten, and half-starved hangers on that trailed behind us grew longer and thinner. In our wake lay too many filthy bundles of clothing that now served as shrouds for the pathetic and wretched scraps of skin and bone that lay within them. These were the men, women and children who no longer needed the meagre, protective warmth they provided. Not since gnawing hunger, sinking exhaustion and perishing cold had finally freed them from enduring such a gruelling march. An ordeal that if truth be told, they always knew in their hearts they could not possibly survive.

More than once I had witnessed a soldier steal away from his unit in the cold light of dawn. More than once I had witnessed an all too brief reunion with a sobbing woman who cradled a lifeless bundle in her arms. I always watched quietly, perhaps in the company of other silent men, as a grieving comrade tried to comfort the woman, whose unshaking yet fatal loyalty had brought them to this. They always took their opportunity to make a small offering on a makeshift altar and then quietly offer a prayer for the soul of their dead child, trying their best to salvage some scrap of dignity for their grief. And yet it was always so cruelly brief.

With no more time to spend than a passing moment before forming up to march, the soldier in question would always give the woman a last brief but heartfelt hug. Then they would tenderly lay the small bundle in the bottom of the marching camp ditch. Always the soldier would then hurry back to his unit, not once looking back as the lonely woman wailed her pain and beat her fists on the cold hard ground. Then the work party would quickly fill in the ditch, unceremoniously covering over the sorry source of her grief before leaving her to her misery.

It was at times such as these that always, I would remember my words to my family, that they should stay home and wait, and always I would look at my bereaved friends and think without any trace of shame:

'Better your children than mine.'

*****

Even by our own standards, the march that we had endured to reach Portus Itius had been punishing. Eventually, we had pushed our way through more than 900 miles over what turned out to be a month and a half of the foulest weather that the late winter could throw at us. In any normal year, we would have over-wintered in the great fortress of Mogontiacum. There we would make the preparations for the coming year, making good use of the time it took for the snows to pass and for the raging waters of the great river Rhenus to subside.

This year it had been different. With the coming of the new orders from Rome the much hoped for possibility of spending the rest of our service in the province had dissolved before our eyes. Instead we had set out on a march over what seemed to be nearly halfway across the imperial map. Our objective had been sold to us as the greatest chance of glory since Caesar had first subdued the wild tribes of Gaul. We had answered our Emperors call; that the XIIII Gemina Legion should join its brothers in arms in Gaul by early spring to prepare for the most prestigious of military undertakings. We were assured that it would be a venture which would clothe us in glory - one that would cause our name to ring down through the annals of history. We, it had been proclaimed, were fated to be remembered as no less than the mighty conquerors of what would become Rome's new province of Britannia, the strange and fabled island on the very edge of the world. But, by the time the march was drawing to a close, the gnawing rumours had shrivelled any common desire for glory. There were now very few of us who still set any store in the heady promises of greatness, or stirring speeches that had set us upon this path. Even as the march finally drew to a close and our spirits rallied.

We had first seen it from some miles out. A great oily grey brown layer of smog in the western sky that thickened and spread as it was fed by smaller columns of smoke from many scattered fires of many different sizes.

As we grew closer, the scudding clouds, sullied by the presence of so much smoke, eventually began to take on a more appealing colour. They gradually fought off the drab colourings of the thick, polluting smoke. The clouds became imbued instead with the warming shades of red, orange and gold. Shades that changed in their intensity as the dying sun fell below the horizon, while Luna began to rise once more to cast her silvery light over the world of night.

Dusk was beginning to fall as we reached the outer limits of Portus Itius. Here, finally, was journeys end and a return to civilisation, if such is what you would call it. In truth, one Roman town is much like another. You make your approach through dumps, and the houses of the dead before you eventually pass through the town gates and into every country boy's worst nightmare.

For myself; I was born in a town which had grown up around a fortress. I was used to the foul stench of what I suppose could be loosely termed as urbanity. However, those amongst our number who had come from more rural backgrounds always had something to say about life in the filth ridden towns and cities of

Rome's vast empire. Seldom, I must admit, were their opinions on town life all that positive.

As we marched towards Portus Itius in the half light of the approaching dusk we passed by great holes and vast, stinking piles of shit. These were the dumping grounds for all of the unwanted detritus of life in the port town. The hollows and pits lay either side of the road, filled almost to capacity with decaying piles of refuse; steaming languorously as though their very stench seemed to be slowly building to boiling point. Here and there vicious, skinny dogs and desperate vagrants competed with each other for rotting table scraps. Scores of sleek but well fed brown rats flitted in and out of the filth too, gorging on an abundant and constant source of food.

Lying clothed in a miasma of the foul stench of rot was also the less fortunate of the port towns' inhabitants. Here and there could be seen a freshly dumped corpse of an executed criminal, keeping company on occasion with the distended and decaying carcass of a low value slave. Like a broken possession, they would be stripped of their clothing by either master or executioner, then flung unceremoniously onto a cart and wheeled out to the dumps. There they would be tossed onto the piles of filth with the rest of the debris of humanity. Here, the criminal who had forfeited his right to life and dignity now rotted anonymously as he shared a last squalid resting place with someone who never had any in the first place.

Finally, our spirits were lifted as we sighted journeys end and the walls of the port town hove into view as we made our way through the dumps and into the area of the town Necropolis. The crunch of thousands of iron studded boots on the road surface shattered, as if with indifferent insolence, the peace of the towns more fortunate dead. Having left the mortal world behind, they now resided in the vast collection of tombs and mausoleums that lined either side of the road. The ornate sarcophagi and vaults of the wealthy dominated the simple stones and markers of those less able to afford a more ostentatious memorial. As we strode out over the last mile of our journey I glanced idly over to the tombs and read the lines that celebrated yesterday's people. Here and there, amidst offerings of food and simple sprigs of winter flowers, a heartfelt sentiment for a lost loved one would contrast with a business-like but well-meant endorsement of a once purposeful life now ended.

I enjoyed the distraction from my aches and pains as I strained in the half-light to read a few of the words cut deeply into the stones as I passed. Small oil lamps flickered away in niches, adding a spark of warmth to the growing gloom while the carved and painted faces of the departed watched our passing. They stared out from their monuments, striking a perpetual but dignified pose in stone as they lounged on couches, or stood proudly with voluminous Toga's draped over arms and shoulders. Here and there a couple of solitary souls walked slowly back towards the town gates. And a new widow, seemingly oblivious to the great host noisily marching by her, knelt cowled in her black mourning attire and wept softly at the side of her husband's stone. She seemed to be rooted there in her grief, unwilling to leave, even though the blackness of night would soon descend. Then the restless or evil dead would be free to roam the darkness and do who knew what to her?

"Go home widow." shouted a voice from the column. "The dark Lemurs of night are close now."

The warning fell on deaf ears as the woman remained by the stone, not even bothering to cast a glance at the passing troops as she maintained her vigil.

"Poor old girl." growled Pudens lecherously. "It looks like she won't be getting any tonight then, what with the old lad croaking an' all. Wonder if she likes soldiers?"

"Where's your respect, you fucking goat?" Surus castigated him.

"I was only saying…"

"Well don't." ordered Zenas, cutting Pudens short. "Just face the front and keep marching."

At last, we passed through the main gates of the port and crammed ourselves shoulder to shoulder into the narrow, stinking thoroughfares of Portus Itius.

The good citizens had seen it all before. Two Legions had arrived before us and a fourth was expected any day. Auxiliary forces had been camped close to town for most of the winter and the town had quickly learned to both despise the military presence and exploit the increased trade opportunities in equal measure. Children ran in and out of the column and tugged at our belts, dodging the sweeping backs of hands as they went. Amidst the chatter of the street, the shouts of soldiers mingled with those who tried to ply us for trade, even while we still marched.

Here and there Centurions and Optios ahead of us could be heard snarling at the bystanders.

"Make way you scabrous bastard. Get out of it will you?"

"Stand aside, clear the way for the Imago, the Imperial Eagle and the sacred standards of the Fourteenth Gemina Legion. Show some respect you idle, useless swine!"

"Ere, ere soldier!" I heard a prostitute calling to no man in particular from an upper storey window. "Bring that cock of yours back into town tonight. I'll ease them balls o' yours for yer. Lollia is who yer ask for - the best fuck on the street an' no mistake - cheap an' all!"

A brief bout of seemingly knowing laughter rose up at this last and an unseen man called impertinently back up to the garishly painted and haggard looking old bawd, shouting gleefully:

"What yer gonna do Lollia, pox all this lot an' all, you old crab?"

Guffaws burst from the crowd as the furious hag screeched back down at her tormentor.

"You wizened old half cock, Rufio, I see you. I'll stab you in the fuckin' face when I catch up with you. You see if I don't!"

This seemed to amuse the assembled crowd even more. As we left the banter behind I could hear further exchanges between the raddled old whore and her tormentor, rising above the hoots and guffawing of the crowd.

"Good lads, good to see you all." an Innkeeper shouted from his door as we passed by. "Get your tents up and make your way back to Fulminatus' place on the Street of Three Fountains. I've had a load of Greek wine in today that needs sampling…And you can bring your own dice too!"

He quickly added the last, as though the afterthought would do the trick and clinch our future custom.

Almost as soon as we entered the town, we passed through the forum and headed out to the north gate, taking us out of the town once more and on to the coast road. When we had left Portus Itius it was as though we had entered another town. Only this one was made of leather and comprised of vast temporary camps, housing the units that had arrived in the area in the days and weeks before us. Row upon row of goatskin tents seemed to cover the fields as we reached our destination. Finally, we had joined the great invasion force that was assembling to invade Britannia, the island that now, we had been told, lay just beyond the western horizon.

Though for all of its closeness, to all of us it still seemed to be on the other side of the world.

CHAPTER 2

If the march from Mogontiacum had been where the seeds of dissent had been sown, it was Portus Itius where they had germinated and put down deep roots.

We did nothing for nearly a month, other than doss in the squalor of freezing cold, wind-swept camps, inundated with filth and mud. There the tempers of the men had finally started to fray and a thick air of menace had begun to pervade the lines. Some cautionary advice I recall, and which any general would do well to heed would be this: When large assemblies of fighting men are left to their own devices with little to do but talk, the ones whose bad planning first caused their idleness should expect nothing but trouble to come calling.

To be fair of course, the commanders had made some efforts to ensure that the vast army was kept occupied as much as possible. But, it was only with gradual improvements in the weather that the men could at last devote their energies to more time consuming tasks such as regular large scale battle drills. The problem was, much of the army had been assembled in the fields around the port town far too early in the year. Consequently, by the time conditions had improved and the men were finally being made busy, it was all really too little, too late.

On those frequent occasions when spare time was abundant, many of the men would sit around amongst the tents and either tell yet more sinister tales about Britannia and the northern seaways, or grumble incessantly about their grim living conditions. Very often, the talk of a growing number of individuals amounted to nothing less than rabble rousing. Then it soon came to pass that the entire camp was teetering on the brink of mutiny.

When the talk got too much to stomach, I often felt the need to get away. I had no desire to either join in or to sit listening to the snarling, resentful voices which lived in almost every tent. They constantly offered opinions as to whether sailing to Britannia was really worth the risk.

When I was able to get away, I always walked alone, gladly wandering far away from the area of the camps to walk the coastal paths leading towards the harbour at Portus Itius. Alone with my thoughts, I would console myself with memories of home and my family. Often wondering just what they would be doing at that moment in time, doing my best to conjure up a picture in my mind.

With so little to do for most of the time, one day seemed much the same as another. Though, I do recall one day, during the time of the storms, when for once my thoughts were occupied by more than secretive yearnings for home.

With time to kill once more, I had strolled along the coastal paths, looking out to sea and marvelling at the rapidly growing power of a rising squall. As I watched, the storm winds built in strength, furiously whipping the ocean up into a wild state, while the sky itself seemed to boil and writhe in torment as the tempest darkly menaced the coast with its approach. Realising I would soon need shelter; I had quickened my pace and made my way to the outskirts of the harbour, arriving just as the full fury of the storm hit the port. Truth to tell, I was all for making for the nearest hostelry when my attention was caught by something at sea, just beyond the safety of the harbour.

It was neither duty nor concern that held me there. After all, I was free to disappear down into the cramped streets that led away from the docks and find myself warmth and a fortifying drink. Yet instead, there I remained, completely unable to tear myself away from that which had caught my eye.

As I looked out to sea, for a few brief heartbeats I found myself pondering just why it was that the impending spectacle of death and destruction always seemed able to capture the attention of men so entirely. Was it perhaps because this was really just nothing so different to experiencing the thrill of the games? In those places I could say with certainty that, of all the thousands of people that packed the arenas around the empire, there were few among the audience who would gladly fill the shoes of those who trod the sand before them. Yet, while none of the audience ever really cared to participate, they were all so very eager to see blood spilt - to witness death swooping in to claim the weak and unwary.

What unfolded before me then was just the same. Even though I could think of no worse place than to be out there, I still could not tear myself away. I needed to be part of the audience, to be there at the final outcome. This was after all just another contest in another arena. Different in some ways perhaps, but the consequences were the same because the contest that absorbed me so fully would still end in a triumph for either life or death.

I looked on with an almost shameful eagerness, watching expectantly as the sea churned below the iron grey sky. Then the storm began to unleash its full fury, hurling muddy waves ever harder at the stout bulwark of the harbour wall. The rolling breakers filled the rain slaked air with the noise of their power as they pounded relentlessly against the dockside, a loud hiss accompanying their transformation from a rolling wall of water into a salty wash of stinging white spray. For a brief, uneasy moment I wondered if the sturdy oak-built wharfs on which I stood would survive the assault. Nevertheless, I continued to peer through the thickening rain and spray, out towards the floundering transport barge as it pitched and rolled on the heavy sea.

As the vessel seemed almost to claw its way closer to the safety of the harbour, I could just about hear the anguished shouts of the doomed crew. Their voices became mixed up in the noise of the storm, along with the thin, terrified screaming of the cavalry mounts that had been loaded on board the vessel earlier that day. Nobody else who bore witness to the scene before me could now possibly think that those men, struggling so desperately out there on that ship, could still regain control of their destiny and save their vessel from the deadly fury of the tumult.

For me, there was no doubt; the crew were all dead men by now. They just didn't know it yet. It would take just a little while longer, as they were forced to endure a little more panic and terror, then it would all be over. Then the vessel would finally be lost to the wild waves. Then, all on board would cease to be as they became no more than memories, drowned and damned as their lifeless flesh and lost souls were claimed by Neptune, as he dragged them down to the ocean bottom. Arrogance and ignorant presumption had led men to believe they could survive in a realm that they could never hope to tame. It would be through the deaths of these men this day that Neptune would once more remind the world of man that his kingdom had only one ruler.

As I watched the ship's struggle for survival and continued to draw my conclusions as to its fate, I began to ponder how Neptune would mark his victory this time. After so much time camped out on the coast, I had witnessed the fleet suffer the loss of a ship before. So, the spectacle that was unfolding before me now was not unfamiliar. I had become accustomed to the sea's moods and ways. I had come to know that eventually there would be something, a bloated corpse perhaps, or some wreckage or cargo, which would later be returned back to the world of the living. The sea nearly always gives something up and such things were always seen as a message from Neptune. It was his way of flaunting his victory palm. To remind us of whose domain it was and whose it always would be.

As I continued to peer out through the blinding rain and spray, I held absolutely no doubts that the wallowing ship and its crew would soon be obliterated as its sturdy timbers failed and were smashed to splinters by the raging waves. Once the sea had begun to crack her open, the end would quickly follow. She would break apart and the men who served on the vessel would sink into the depths with her. All would be condemned to eternity with no grave to speak of but the cold grim sea, as it claimed them for its own.

After all; no ship out there, alone in the maelstrom, could ever have held out any sort of hope that it may yet stand some chance of mooring up in the storm lashed harbour of Portus Itius. That was where the many vessels of the Classis Britannica, Rome's great northern fleet, now sheltered. The unrelenting force of the storm would not possibly allow the crew to get the ship in close enough. The great swells and howling winds would deny any opportunity to tie off safely against the other ships that now lay at anchor, rolling and bucking on the heaving surface of the harbour.

The crew had only one slim chance left now; to beach the ship on the nearby shore and take their chances, trusting to the fickle will of the Gods as to whether or not they survived the perilous leap from ship to land. Though, as I continued to watch, it seemed plain enough to me that even being a mere bow shot away from that one last chance, they may as well have been a hundred miles out to sea. All of the other Gods must have realised that on this day, they held no sway over Neptune's affairs. One by one it seemed, they turned their backs and abandoned the unfortunate ship and crew to its ultimate fate.

When it came, the end was heralded by the sharp report of the main mast snapping. The loud crack was clearly audible over the noise of the storm as the intolerably stressed timber failed at just above deck level. I looked on, even more deeply engrossed by the scene as the great spar fell across the deck. Mercifully, it flattened some of the crew, killing them outright, yet cruelly it snared others with a heavy drape of tangled rigging, pulley blocks and sodden sail. Those men trapped by the falling mass could do nothing now but await the inevitable as all hope of salvation was instantly lost.

Almost at once, the shattered mast seemed to signal the vessel's surrender as the sea seized its chance to make the kill, tossing the boat like a child's toy onto its back with a surging wall of foam whipped water.

The faint screams that indicated that some of her crew still lived, ceased immediately as the stricken hull was swept along and hammered into the end of the harbour mole. It hit with a force that almost seemed to shake the base of the Pharos that loomed indifferently above the scene, bathing the doomed ship in the flickering glow from its great beacon of fire. How those sailors must have yearned for the warming comfort and safety of the light that lay so tantalisingly close, and yet so impossible to reach.

The sound of more shattering wood heralded the breaking of the ships back as, almost at once; it broke into three large pieces under the relentless battering. I took no pleasure from the accuracy of my previous prediction as to how the ship would die as, quite rapidly, the once sturdy vessel began to be reduced into smaller fragments. The ruined pieces that remained afloat swirled around on the seething waters, before being dragged beneath the waves.

As I held my vigil, I realised that when she had been launched and named, a sacrifice had been performed and prayers had been said for the ship, asking that the gods grant her safe passage as she sailed the seas. To aid the ship in her voyages the shipwright who built her had painted a pair of eyes on her prow so that she might see any evil ahead and take steps to avoid it. Now, those same eyes which had failed to keep the ship from harm seemed to take one last forlorn gaze skywards. The unblinking painted eyes stared up to the heavens as the shattered remains of the prow slid backwards, before finally being pulled under the waves.

Here and there the squealing, shaking head of a frantic horse disappeared too as it succumbed to the grasping undercurrent, as along with a last extended arm or terrified face, the waves swallowed all.

Glad of the scrap of warmth and comfort that it offered me, I pulled my hooded cloak tighter around my neck, trying to put aside the intense feeling of dread that had swept over me as I had watched the ship die.

The awful feeling I had experienced wasn't anything to do with witnessing such a dreadful end to so many lives. After all, such things are simply to be accepted. These events are no more than the nature of the world and as such, cannot be changed. No, what did not sit well with me was more the growing concern I now harboured. Perhaps, the many voices of dissent that had grown steadily louder in their condemnation of the great invasion may be right after all. If I had ever needed proof that the Gods were against us in this great scheme of the Emperor, then surely I had just beheld it. How could I not now concede that every critic who had argued that this great plan could never work might just be right? How could I not now see that, what we were mustered here to embark upon required us to blatantly defy powers far greater than any wielded by mere men? That was surely a fact that still held true, even if the man in question just happened to be Claudius, Emperor of Rome and possessor of more earthly power than any other living mortal.

A climate of fear and superstitious dread had spread through the great army that had assembled in Portus Itius on his orders. That fear had steadily gnawed at the men and eventually flourished as it was voiced in the protests of so many of us assembled there in the area of the great sea port. At one level or another, most were now becoming convinced that what was planned could so easily bring about the end of us all.

The dissenters argued that Rome was growing too ambitious in its expectations of its armies. All powerful Rome and its Emperor, Claudius, now expected its glorious Legions to achieve nothing less than the crossing of an unknown and hostile ocean in which who knew what terrors lurked? Then, if the men survived that, they were fated to engage the wild natives of a largely unknown and reputedly haunted isle. This strange land of Britannia was a place which not only resisted two attempts at conquest by the great and divine Gaius Julius Caesar himself. It was also the place where the accursed body of the barbarian priesthood of Druids was supposedly spawned from. They, all Romans knew, were a dark order of shamans. Their black rituals and seditious teachings had seen their activities forbidden in Gaul and beyond since before living memory. Yet this distant island that Claudius now so sorely coveted was their ancestral stronghold and where it was said that they would send immense blue painted mad men to fight against us.

How then could we prevail? When so much of what we needed to fight lurked in the shadow world and beyond the northern sea. The possession of immense military power was one thing, but what good was that when it was measured against dark and sinister forces that spawned the Druids beyond the western horizon?

Putting the tales of superstitious dread to one side; what most of us did know was that the isle of Britannia had largely only been visited by trading vessels from around the Roman world. With the exception of Caesar, Rome had been content to keep the island beyond the fringes of its northern borders. It was seemingly satisfied to simply maintain tenuous diplomatic links, preferring more to engage in trade for the wealth of natural commodities that the land was rich in. Then, two years since, Caligula had resurrected the Divine Caesar's ambitious plans for conquest. The entreaties of certain exiled nobles from the island pricked what were then unattainable ambitions into life. Then the mad Emperor had briefly settled upon a plan to conquer the wild tribes of Britannia.

Caligula's scheming had come to nought, earning him nothing but grumbling contempt from the soldiers who he had marched to the coast of Gaul. There he had sorely humiliated them by having them assault the waves with great barrages of catapult missiles. He had then ordered them to scour the beaches like children; plundering the shore for thousands of sea shells to carry back to Rome, where he would proclaim them to be the spoils of victory over the sea.

After the bloody assassination of Caligula, it was shrewd old Uncle Claudius who had then seized upon the plan as a perfect vehicle for bestowing upon him the military triumph that he so desperately needed in the early years of his reign. This would be the victory that would consolidate his grip on the ultimate expression of mortal power, as Emperor of Rome. We, his Legions, would seize it for him.

And so it was that a vast army of 40,000 men converged on the town of Portus Itius, the great sea port which lay at the narrowest point between Gaul and Britannia.

There, we would-be invaders waited for the blustering coastal storms of late winter to subside. Once the weather had improved sufficiently, a great fleet had been assembled and boats such as the cavalry transport I had seen go to the bottom were prepared for their journey. They would be regularly loaded and off loaded, sailed out to sea and then sailed back in to shore again. Time after time their crews and living cargo rehearsed what they needed to do when they reached the shores of Britannia.

At first they diligently practiced these drills close to the shore. Beginning with one or two ships, as the weather slowly improved, they would go further out to sea in ever larger flotillas. They were training the men to lose their fear and mistrust of the deep and eventually acquire a more rational and soldierly appreciation of what was to come.

Ironic then that however efficient the soldiers and crews became; the weather was still unpredictable enough to throw the most detailed planning into chaos. I had just seen what happens when the weather catches the navy off-guard. I had witnessed how one ship, having steered too far from its proper course, suffered the ultimate penalty for not beating the storm back to port. Its companion vessels had only just made it home, lashing themselves tightly together before the drama had unfolded. All of the occupants of the safely moored vessels had scrambled ashore. But, rather than take cover from the blustering storm, the crews of the ships remained by the churning sea, held just as I was, by the compulsive nature of the spectacle that unfolded just beyond the harbour .

At first they had cried out their encouragement for the battling crew of the stricken vessel. They seemed to use every last ounce of breath to bellow out their support. But, as the hull finally broke up and every scrap of hope was lost, the men on shore wailed in lament and cast their prayers into the wind, offering a mariner's requiem for the lost before they slowly turned their backs and quietly dispersed for their quarters.

CHAPTER 3

"I'm telling you Vepitta, that's what he said he definitely saw!"

Crispus was emphatic as he explained to me all that his brother, who served in Cohort III, had seen in the skies above the vast encampment.

"He wouldn't lie about this. It was the day of the big storm that came in off the sea." said Crispus insistently, waving his arms in some strange attempt to visually recreate the devastating storms that had recently blown in off the ocean.

"Lupus told me he saw a great eagle flying west towards the storm clouds and, flash, the lightening knocked it straight from the sky."

"Was it killed?" I asked, gravely.

"You would think so, but I can't say for certain." he replied, in more subdued tones which contrasted with his earlier enthusiastic recollections. "My brother looked for the bird but found nothing where he saw it fall, not even as much as a feather."

The eight of us sat huddled around our camp fire and each of us wore the same grim mask of concern and uncertainty as we listened intently to news of the recently witnessed portents. Our fire popped and cracked as the damp kindling dried out. Steam whistled briefly from one of the freshly placed logs as we all drew closer, attempting to fend off something more perhaps than the creeping chill of the cold, damp night air. After a brief shared spell of troubled thought I resolved to seek an answer to the question that was quietly disturbing us all. I turned to Zenas, passing him a cup of hot spiced wine that I had filled from the small iron cauldron suspended over the fire. Then I asked him:

"What do you think? It sounds bad. Is it?"

Of the eight men of our Contubernium, Zenas was the one in charge. He passed on orders, berated us for our mistakes, delegated duties and generally kept us in check. He also ministered to our spiritual needs. As the oldest and most experienced soldier amongst us he was the natural choice for leader of our small band. As such, he kept the small, bronze effigy of our Genius, the guardian spirit that watched over us.

Zenas sat there for a moment, occasionally emitting the odd thoughtful noise and massaging the greying stubble on his chin. We remained poised and silent, eagerly awaiting his appraisal of just how to interpret what Crispus' kin had seen. After some further ponderous rubbing, muttering and peering into the steamy wine that he swirled round in the cup, he finally shared his thoughts with us.

"Hmm, now although I have received a fair bit of instruction, I'm not a trained Augury, so I can't really say for sure whether I've read all of this just right."

"Shades of my poor dead parents, never mind all the babble, just spill your guts will you?"

Like us all, Pudens was eager for an answer and, just like Pudens, he was the first to tell us so.

"Shut your big fat hole!" said Aebutius, mumbling through a half chewed mouth full of bread. "Let the man speak will you?"

Pudens shot Aebutius a petulant look and choosing to ignore him instead, he concentrated his gaze once more on Zenas.

"Well, if I have this right, "Zenas continued. " I'd judge the eagle to represent our invasion force. That at least, is the easy bit. After that it gets a might trickier."

He paused momentarily, nodding his head as if to affirm his own view. He swigged from his cup and then placed it down in front of him, once again seeming to contemplate the portents a little more.

"The eagle was seen flying west, out to sea. That was when it was hit by the lightening."

He sighed heavily, rubbing his temples and then pulling his palms down his cheeks until he was again absentmindedly rubbing his chin and gazing up into the night sky. Abruptly, he stopped and looked towards the wine cup once more.

"I'll warrant you won't like this over much, but, for what it's worth, here's how I see it."

The expression on Zenas' face grew very solemn as he continued with his interpretation of the newly sighted portents.

"As I said, the eagle represents us, the Imperial invasion army. Flying west out to sea indicates the path that we are all ordered to take towards Britannia. So, it can only mean that the Gods have indicated that they will not allow this venture to succeed, hence the lightning strike. If such is the case then I may only conclude that, if we proceed with this plan, we risk certain destruction."

"Lupus said he couldn't find the eagle's body." said Marinus quietly, pausing from polishing his dagger and pointing it idly towards Zenas. "What about that bit then, eh?"

"Again, I'm not absolutely sure, but Crispus' kin said the eagle disappeared without trace. I judge that to mean that whatever happens to us all, might well happen out at sea. After all, what else is capable of swallowing us all up without trace if not the sea?"

Marinus was the second most senior soldier in our band and, having spent over twenty years serving with the Legion, he was almost inevitably imbued with a heavy dose of cynicism concerning most things. One thing he seldom scorned however, were the signs sent by the Gods.

"By the shades." he growled, spitting into the small camp fire and ramming his dagger into the scabbard on his belt. "That just about settles it as far as I can see."

"Settles what?" Zenas asked pointedly. "Now look - If you start that rabble rousing shit that's been doing the rounds again then you're only going to bring big trouble down on us all."

"Trouble, you daft old bastard?" Marinus spread his hands and looked at Zenas in mild disbelief. "By the words from your own mouth, you calmly tell us that the Gods are sending signs that we could all end up drifting around on the sea bed with our lungs full of salt water. Then in the next breath you're worrying what the top folk might do if we refuse to go. In the name of Dis, how much more trouble beyond that do you think they could cause us, you idiot?"

"Hey, hey. Remember who runs things here will you? Show some respect you stupid pig!"

Zenas' finger almost ended up in Marinus' eye as he stabbed it towards his face, underlining his sharp reminder of just who was in charge.

"If you don't start to listen to sense soon Zenas, then the only thing you'll be in charge of will be seven floating corpses!" spat Marinus as he slapped Zenas' hand away, glaring at him. Both men sprang to their feet and squared up to each other over the dancing sparks of the fire. Instantly, the rest of us stood up too and Surus placed his body between the two men, eyeing each of them and waiting for that first punch to be thrown.

A stonemason by trade, Surus had been with the Legion for four years. He was a massive man, built almost as solidly as some of the walls he erected. His awesome talent for casual brawling was largely down to his unfaltering ability to throw some of the most accurate and devastating punches seen outside of the Pugilist battles of the arena.

"Let's not go down this road again, eh comrades?" he growled. "This bollocks has followed us all the way from Mogontiacum and I for one am sick of all this talk of refusing orders. We're soldiers. We don't refuse orders and we don't fight each other. That's what we all decided, and that's what we're all sticking to, right?"

In the flickering light of the fire I could see that Surus' eyes had narrowed to slits and that his jaw was set hard. I recognised the look I'd seen so often before and knew from it that his brain had fully committed his body to the fight. If one of the parties didn't back down now, then the matter would probably be ended with a thunderous punch. Enough to fell an ox never mind a man.

"Sounds like good advice to me." A disembodied voice growled from beyond the light of the fire. "Can't say I heard all of what the talk has been about, but I'll guarantee it's dangerous. Mark me though, when I tell you that I'll personally nail all of you bastards to crosses if what I suspect is going on actually comes to pass."

Fatalis materialised from the darkness next to the group and glared at us as we snapped to attention. He carried his cloak draped over one arm and his Vitis was held firmly in his other hand. He tapped the short vine staff absentmindedly against the side of one of the silvered greaves that covered his shins. Piercing grey blue eyes regarded each of us with acute suspicion. He walked up behind Zenas and leaned towards his shoulder.

"Stand them easy Zenas," said Fatalis, growling in his ear.

"At ease!" Zenas snapped the order, touches of relief but also trepidation evident in his manner. Immediately we loosened up but remained standing. Each of us stared expectantly at Fatalis, wondering what would happen next, now that our own Centurion had caught us openly discussing what could amount to conspiracy to mutiny in the ranks.

Again his eyes glittered as he quietly scrutinized us all.

It was difficult to tell what was going on in the mind behind the eyes. The man seemed to have a head as solid as catapult ball, topped off as it was with close cropped silver hair. Even that seemed as though it could injure you by perhaps sticking pin-like into your fingers if you touched it. The leathery and scarred old face seemed to speak volumes about Fatalis' years of service under the eagles, but also exhibited a considerable amount of cunning and intelligence. It gave away little else.

"That's the good thing about prowling the lines at night," he observed casually as he looked at us, each in turn. "You pick up so much from fireside chatter, sometimes without even being noticed." He paused momentarily. "Of course, as soldiers in my Century, I'm given to remind you all that it just happens to be in the most senior Cohort of the Legion. It also forms the Legate's bodyguard and you should therefore be mindful of your privileged positions. I also expect you to choose to avoid indulging in the sort of disruptive and seditious talk that I've heard is doing the rounds at the moment."

Fatalis turned to face Zenas before offering the old Legionary some further observations

"You know, all of what I just said aside, what troubles me most about all this is that it's a cold night and none of these men have drawn guard. Yet I see they're all still here, wasting valuable leave time, stooped around camp fires and rattling like a bunch of old hags."

The last sentence was delivered with a look to all of us that suggested that he was perfectly aware of what was going on. It also roundly challenged any notions that we may have harboured towards disobedience. Fatalis paused, gazing at each one of us now in a seemingly more impassive manner. Each of us knew though that the battle hardened old Centurion was weighing us all by his own standards and constant mental notes were being made of any deficiencies that he perceived in us.

We watched quietly as Fatalis stooped to poke at the small fire and then dip a spare cup in the small cauldron of simmering wine. He sniffed the contents then took a sip, nodding and grunting approvingly as he blew off the steam and swallowed the warming liquid.

"I don't imagine that the Britons, whoever they are, have such cordial places as the hostelries of Portus Itius," opined Fatalis, surveying the night sky as he took another swig from his cup.

"I suppose too that I shouldn't dwell too much on the question as to why, when you will soon be on a ship bound for war, you are all still sat on your rosy fat arses round here, clucking away like a bunch of old hens."

"In fact, if I were you," he added in a matter of fact tone, while flicking the dregs from the cup into the fire. "I wouldn't be sitting round here banging on about idle gossip at all. Instead I'd be in town drinking, gambling and fucking while I still had the chance."

With that, he turned and walked off up the lines, disappearing behind the cloud of pinkish steam that rose hissing from the fire.

*****

"You really are a fucking halfwit!" I chided Marinus as we entered the north gate of the town. "I'd rather volunteer to clean the shit out of Cerberus' lair than bring Fatalis' wrath down on us."

"Watch who you're calling a halfwit, Vepitta," he snapped. "You don't have enough under your belt to take on an old bear like me."

Marinus began to trot sideways next to me, spitting on his knuckles and drawing them up in a pugilists defence as he thumbed his nose and nodded at me, playfully goading me to fight.

"Under my belt?" I replied. "Oh no, Marinus. Down there is for the girls only. If I was going to take you on it would be with my fists, or would you prefer me to mount you like a whore and ride you into submission."

The others laughed out loud, slapping the old Legionary on the back and urging him to respond as he quickly barred my way and squared up to face me.

"Tread careful, Vepitta." Pacatianus added his voice to the banter that surrounded the mock scuffle that Marinus and I were now involved in.

"Remember what your father should have taught you," he laughed. "Youth and enthusiasm will nearly always fall foul of old age and treachery."

"He's got a point there, arse wipe." growled Marinus. "I'm going to give you a ride like you've never had before, you mouthy young game cock!"

Marinus swung a meaty fist towards the side of my head as I laughed and ducked the blow.

"You're certainly an old bear," taunted Pudens as Marinus rallied for another swipe. "A younger one would have much quicker paws."

Again laughter rose from our group as I dodged Marinus' flying fist once more and we circled each other, grinning as we made jabbing feints at each other's bodies.

"Quickly", mocked Pudens once more, "Somebody find musicians, the dance of the prancing arseholes is about to begin!"

"Hey, hold everything!" shouted Aebutius, shouting out above the rising uproar, trying to alert us to something much more interesting.

"Comrades, lets dispense with the horseplay for now. I believe our evening may start here." he said as he jumped in front of a building, spreading his arms wide and grinning broadly as he nodded over his shoulder at the structure behind him.

As we stopped and looked at the building that Aebutius had indicated, we all began to grin as one and Surus voiced all of our thoughts as he puffed out his enormous chest, cracked his knuckles loudly and announced;

"He's right, by the gods. I reckon it's time for weapons drills men."

We approached the raised walkway that separated the frontage of the brothel from the filth of the street surface and made towards the iron bound double doors of the building. It was a three story timber framed frontage that looked as though it had an open courtyard beyond the doors. Stepping up on to the walkway and approaching the doors, we attracted the attention of the small fat man that squatted on a stool, next to the doors.

He heaved himself up from the stool, spreading his arms as we reached the doors. A yellow toothed grin split his oily dark face as he prepared to pitch us for our business. I looked him up and down, trying to work out who, or what he might be as his Eastern appearance conflicted with the freshly laundered toga that he fussed over as he stood. However, I didn't have to wait over long before he obligingly solved the mystery for me.

"Ah, yes please!" His face lit up as he greeted us with a practised geniality.

"Great soldiers of the Empire," he enthused as he invited us in with a gravelly, thickly accented voice, "I am Aziel, lately of Nabataea and more recently a full citizen of your excellent and great empire." He grinned widely running his hands over the toga, nodding at us as though we now understood the significance of the garment.

"Great gods, a real live Nabatean," exclaimed Pacatianus. "I've never seen the likes of you before. What are you doing in this shit tip of a town?"

"Ah no, great fighter," fawned Aziel as he shook his head slowly. "This shit tip as you call it is full of the most excellent and wondrous opportunities for a good businessman such as me. I have supplied the most excellent and wonderful women to men such as you for many years now. My services have even won me my Roman citizenship. So, soon, when I am tired of making lots of money, I will finally go home and feel the hot and passionate kiss of the sun of my homeland once more."

Pudens leaned over to Aziel and grinned as he muttered into his ear.

"Always assuming nobody slits your fat throat for all that money you've made in the meantime, eh?"

Pudens tapped the dagger on his belt and gave an evil grin as Aziel gulped loudly and gave out a nervous laugh before recovering his thread.

"Please, such talk sets a poor tone on your evening, I think," said the whoremaster, sweating nervously now as he quickly diverted the conversation round to business once more.

We stood and listened, grinning broadly at his obvious discomfort as he fought to keep business on track and divert any new talk away from slit throats and incautious mentions of plentiful coin.

"Ah yes, yes, the excellent and happy things you may have heard about my house are all true." Aziel assured us as his enthusiasm began to bubble once more. "My women are the cleanest in town and you can make your own price with them too. This is a very excellent and good thing for you as I have my own arrangement with them, so you do not have to trouble yourselves with dealing with me, I think. I ask only that you enjoy yourselves, pay fairly for our excellent hospitality and then go in peace when you are done, yes?"

The last comment was delivered with a hopeful tone as Aziel clasped his two podgy hands in front of his face and seemed to pray for an agreement.

"Of course! We're not barbarians you know?" huffed Crispus as he stepped towards the doors, the rest of us following on behind.

"Ah, excellent, excellent! My kind and noble new friends."

The Nabatean rolled his eyes and chuckled gleefully at first, realising that his pitch had paid off. Though, even his professional hosting skills could not disguise the nervous look that appeared all of a sudden on his round, sweaty features as we made towards the doors.

"Relax." said Surus planting a large hand in the middle of Aziel's flabby chest and pushing him back down onto his stool. "We are men of honour."

"What a champion arse licker." commented Marinus as he walked up and pushed past the fat little man on his chair, causing him to wobble unsteadily.

"Excellent, excellent!" declared Zenas as he threw his hands theatrically into the air, parodying the now profusely sweating whoremaster before passing through the doors.

I stifled a laugh as I followed on behind our group and caught the look of blessed relief on Aziel's face as he clasped his throat protectively. He beckoned me in with another forced smile, impatiently waving a podgy hand while he dabbed his forehead with a fold of his toga.

"Excellent, excellent. If you hurry you will perhaps catch the end of the play, I think!"

The thought of what lay inside instantly reminded me of my growing need to feel the touch of a woman once more and with Salviena so far away, one of Aziel's whores would be substitute enough. My grin broadened as I saw Aziel's shoulders slump visibly with relief, then I walked past him and stepped through the doors into the revelry beyond.

CHAPTER 4

As expected, the sturdy double doors had led us into a spacious open courtyard that was surrounded by a sloping veranda around the level of the first storey. Above that rose another two storeys where dim lights flickered behind half open wooden shutters.

The courtyard itself was bustling with off duty soldiers, sailors, merchants and sundry townsmen, the presence of whom seemed not only to justify our choice of establishment but also to endorse the popularity of Aziel's hospitality. Our fellow guests paid no heed whatever to the entry of eight more off duty soldiers. They were far too busy being entertained by an abundance of women, either in gaudily coloured and sparse clothing, or in various states of undress as they unashamedly paraded their wares for all to see.

It really was a sight to induce a feint in even the most worldly of respectable Roman matrons. Yet, to men far from home such as my comrades and I, it was just what we needed. The night outside the courtyard was turning frosty but, in here, braziers, cressets and oil lamps burned with a warm and welcoming glow, warding off the uncomfortable chills from outside. The opportunity to spend time in warm solid buildings was always appreciated when far too much time was spent under cover of tents.

The 'play' that Aziel had referred to was indeed in full swing on a small stage on the far side of the courtyard and certainly appeared to be reaching some form of climax at least. A small group of musicians played at the foot of a low stage, resolutely ignoring the goings on just above them as they accompanied the performance. We all stopped in our tracks, each of us grinning with our eyes wide and our mouths open as we watched the scene unfold before us. An actress wearing a painted mask and dressed as some sort of woodland nymph was pleasuring two masked males while taking up position at the centre of the stage on her hands and knees. As a faintly ridiculous aside, an absurdly grim faced orator stood to one side, clearly absorbed in his own role and determinedly reciting an accompanying dialogue that absolutely nobody was listening to.

The first of the males waved his arms in time to the wild rhythm of the music while the actress took his engorged manhood through the mouth of the mask, pleasuring him with obvious enthusiasm. An equally enthusiastic performance was simultaneously being delivered by the second male who crouched behind her and thrust frantically into the girl for all he was worth. A small group of men stood around the stage clapping enthusiastically and nodding approvingly while a brightly dressed young boy stood by the side of the stage, about to lead a large wolf hound fitted with some bizarre looking false horns onto the stage.

"Yes! By Vulcan's balls, you've surpassed yourself this time, Aebutius." Surus enthused. "This has got to be the best idea you've had all winter."

"Absolutely, you lot definitely owe me for this one." Aebutius replied with a smug grin on his face and adding as an afterthought: "Even if I do say so myself."

"Hmm, lucky bastard at dice as well," observed Crispus, sharing his thoughts with nobody in particular.

"Hadn't you better go find some food, stick man?" quipped Marinus to Aebutius, thumbing over his shoulder in the direction of a table full of food. "Your skinny frame is going to need some nourishment before you go into battle here."

"Right, I'm in," announced Pacatianus as he clapped his hands together and pushed his way through the bodies, shouting back with his final words of advice.

"Get neither robbed nor poxed, and for the sake of the Gods themselves, enjoy."

Aebutius grinned, making towards the table Marinus had indicated earlier. It was then that I suddenly noticed that most of the group had also mingled with the crowds of revellers in the courtyard. The only one left was Surus who stood grinning at the stage as the large, bizarrely accoutred hound was now led reluctantly on.

"Well, that's it then," said Surus in an almost matter of fact tone.

"That's what?" I asked.

"This is the night when Mars gets to lie with Venus," he growled. "Now, be off and do what you have to. I have a spear I need to cast."

With that he was gone, ploughing his way into the gathering and intercepting a plump and gaudily painted girl whose exposed breasts were instant targets for his great rough hands. I watched briefly, grinning broadly as I saw him utter something in the girl's ear and bite lightly on her shoulder. She squealed and spun quickly around, throwing her arms around his thick neck and locking her brightly painted lips onto his own.

"Now I need a drink." I said to myself, turning from the stage and making my way through the milling bodies, towards a slave in charge of a large collection of wine amphorae. Moving through my fellow pleasure seekers, I was only dimly aware of the squeals of delight and a low growling emanating from the direction of the stage.

The slave serving drinks was surly and ill mannered. I exchanged a coin for a large cup of wine and I was about to offer him some good advice when my attention was drawn to a girl a short distance away. She stood, propping up a pillar of the portico and smiling at her surroundings, lost for the moment it would seem in her own thoughts.

She was the one. She was what I wanted for myself that night, and I would have her.

I took a deep gulp from my wine and walked over to her, flushing with annoyance as a sailor from the imperial fleet made his way over, beating me to her by just a few feet. Her smile widened as, parted from her thoughts, she effortlessly turned on her charm and gazed up into his eyes. He spoke to her as she leaned casually against her pillar, toying with a small ringlet of hair next to her ear as she listened. Within a heartbeat I had reached them both, brushing his arm away and slipping quickly between them. She turned to me with a brief look of mild surprise and slightly raised one eyebrow.

"I have the drink you asked for," I announced, passing her the cup and turning to face the sailor.

"So it would appear," she said with a slightly indignant, yet slightly amused tone, as I turned and addressed the leathery faced mariner.

"Many thanks for keeping her safe during my absence friend, but I can manage from here."

"And bollocks I say…friend." The sailor rolled his shoulders and nodded towards the girl, ready to affirm his claim to her.

"I been watching her for a bit now. You ain't been near her and that ain't no lie."

"Then that must mean you're calling me a liar, friend." I replied coldly.

By now several of the other customers had detected a threat in the air and a small clearing had formed around all three of us. The girl still leaned against the pillar, sipping lightly from the wine cup I had previously handed her. She seemed to be enjoying the impromptu show unfolding before her as the sailor slowly cocked his head to one side and looked me slowly up and down before delivering his response.

"I speak as I find and yes, I do say you are a damn liar."

Before the sailor even had an opportunity to consider the weight of his words I had seized hold of his genitals and leaned towards him, a cruel smile breaking large on my face.

"Now, I think it would be fair to say that you are definitely sailing in dangerous waters with a serious risk to your precious cargo, yes?"

I breathed the words into his ear and he nodded frantically in agreement as I continued.

"As a member of the legate's bodyguard of legion XIIII Gemina, I aspire to the highest standards of the soldier's code. I feel my honour is now slighted in light of the accusation you make and if you choose not to walk away this night, I will seek redress for the insult. What say you?"

I squeezed the delicate handful more firmly and raised my eyebrows, waiting for the reply. The sailor flinched and quickly nodded his head as he panted rapidly, not even daring to pull away or draw a concealed weapon for fear of what the firm grip could do.

"Honour will be satisfied then when you turn and walk away." I advised him. "That said, should you choose to take the matter further then we will take a walk outside of here and you and I will find a quiet corner. Then I will happily send you on your last voyage, and I vow to you now that it will definitely involve your accompanying the boatman across the Styx, yes?"

The sailor nodded and I pushed him clear with the palm of my other hand as I squeezed just firmly enough to be painful with the other. Instantly the sailor pulled his tunic down and nursed his aching parts. I fixed him with a glare which would have been plain enough in its unspoken intent.

"Then be with her." he spat. "There are plenty more cows in this midden. No doubt she will give you a little something to remember her by in the days after you rut her!"

With that, he turned and stormed off towards the other side of the courtyard while I turned to survey my prize.

I immediately felt my insistence with the mariner justified as I beheld her more closely. She was around twenty years old and, as far as I could tell, native to the northern Empire. I could not say that she was stunning in a complete sense but, what really set her apart were her eyes. Piercing green eyes that had caught my attention from afar and that seemed to be home to her very spirit.

"Is this how you normally get your women on their backs?" she questioned me directly. "By the force of your threats?"

The pointedness of her questions threw me somewhat but, when she spoke, her eyes flashed with that fire and sent a surge of lust through my loins. Her glossy dark brown hair was put up in loose ringlets contained within a woven hair band. Thick black eye makeup enhanced the edges of her eyes and lashes. It created the perfect frame for those flashing green eyes, whilst a pale saffron colouring was carefully dusted onto the eyelids. Sharp contrasts created prominent cheeks as the rouge she wore stood out from the delicately whitened skin. Finally a seductive smile came from a pair of full lips carefully enhanced with the application of a blood red colouring.

"A military man knows no better than to challenge for those things that are to be won." I replied. "A battle is a battle, after all. Be it the siege of a great city, or fighting for the charms of a woman such as you."

"A woman such as me?" the reply was delivered almost bitterly. "I am a whore, a slave to my master, Aziel. You could just have waited your turn and paid like the rest."

"Where is the satisfaction in that?" I countered. "Who knows when the shades will call me? I could die while I wait for what I want."

"Then take it soldier, if you have the coin, I'm yours for the hour."

My eyes traced a path down her body as I admired the slender elegance of her neck, which spread finely out to her soft skinned shoulders. I was minded to think that this had surely not been her life for that long as my eyes moved down to her modest cleavage, covered for now by the low neckline of a soft linen dress in a deep scarlet colour. The dress hung in light folds, tied just under her breasts by a braided woollen belt of a bright red and cream diamond pattern. The material then dropped over her thighs, vaguely outlining their shape in the plush scarlet colour before terminating around her ankles. At the top the dress was fastened together at the shoulders by a pair of delicate circular brooches of silver. A simple chain of round silver links hung around her neck and silver pendant earrings finished the adornments off, set with small red garnets glinting with a fiery flash in the flickering light. No doubt, they were gifts from admiring suitors yet she wore them with an air above that of the whore she claimed to be.

The chatter rose again, as everyone sensed that the chance for violence had passed. I brushed my lips on the lightly scented skin of her neck, speaking quietly of what it was I wanted from our time together. She sipped on the wine and laughed occasionally; flashing those eyes, heightening my arousal yet further. I indulged myself in courting her, though I knew it was unnecessary as the simple exchange of a few coins would secure my ultimate pleasure.

Naturally, she held no inhibitions and, as my soldierly bravado subsided and the wine I shared with her relaxed me further, I began to feel at ease with her. Surely this must be the same reception that had been given to many a man before me but it still felt somehow special and unique to me. Clearly she had developed a talent for her profession and I was now benefiting from the experience of all those other men before me. Still, it did not matter as far as I was concerned. Along the violent path that my life led me, an uncommon moment of tenderness was always welcome. In a perverse kind of way it reminded me of home, and it comforted me.

"Does the soldier have a name?" Again the eyes flashed alluringly and my thoughts returned to her.

"Vepitta. My name is Marcus Sulpicius Vepitta." I informed her. "And yours?"

"Perhaps later, Vepitta." she replied

The emphasis she placed on my name sent a shiver down my spine. My lust for her was now growing by the second as I stared, almost like some stupid, naïve young boy, into those amazing eyes. My mind had gone beyond the need for a painted trollop to throw coin at. I had found a rare pearl in a place it seemed not to belong and, for a while at least, I would possess it.

"Why do we waste time talking?" She seemed to breathe the words into my ear, as she leant into my neck, the warmth of her breath on my skin arousing me yet further.

"Time is short." she added. "As you said, you should take what you want before the gods steal you away from the world of the living, for ever"

Kissing me lightly on the lips, she took hold of my hands and pulled me slowly with her, smiling enigmatically and fixing me once more with those eyes. I felt my blood surge. Thinking I would burst, there and then, if I could not take her soon. She turned and pulled me along by the hand until we reached a door leading to the stairwell. As we entered the darkened passage I pushed her against the wall and roughly pressed my lips to hers. Instantly she pushed me away and mounted the stairs.

"Do you wish to spend your coin on a staircase, or in my chamber?" The question seemed almost to be a rebuke. I said nothing, following her like some obedient hound.

Occasionally she would glance back at me, smiling seductively, biting her lower lip, fixing me with those eyes from a lowered brow. We followed the balcony above the veranda to her chamber where she silently pushed the door open and stepped inside. I followed and stood, watching her as she stood momentarily with her back to me, bathed in the warm glow of the light of four small oil lamps. Then she spun to face me, a girlish giggle danced in the quiet air as she reached up to pull away her hair band. With a gentle flick and she tossed it onto a small stand near to the bed. A further swift tug and a carved bone hair pin was also removed, causing lustrous twisted locks to fall. Tussling them, she gave a final flick of her neck, loosening the hair and allowing it to fall onto her shoulders.

My ability to control my soaring lust was almost non-existent now as she turned sideways to me and began to release one of the silver brooches from her shoulder. As she freed it so the two halves of the dress fell away, revealing a tantalizing glimpse of a small, ivory breast. She turned her attention to the other brooch and soon it too was free. Using her arm to hold the dress in place, she bent to place the brooches on the stand.

She stood before me then, the smile now gone and her mouth slightly open, gazing provocatively at me as she released the dress. It slid silently down her body revealing the soft globes of her small, firm breasts. Her flat stomach and trim waist appeared before me as I was engulfed by yet another wave of intense desire for her. In the half-light the shadows danced on her naked body, creating a soft dark area between her legs and shading the small, perfect circles of her nipples. The dress lay around her feet like a dark scarlet pool as she stepped from it and crossed to the bed as I watched, captivated. She lay down, reclining on her side and raising her head with her elbow. One leg drawn up to her waist to reveal the sensuous round curve of her buttocks. Slowly she extended her hand towards me and flicked her head, throwing the long hair over her shoulder. Once more the light picked out the details of her form in shadows and the garnets and silver twinkled in the half light.

"You won't be needing those I think." she said softly, as she gestured to the scabbarded sword and dagger belted to my waist.

I discarded the weapons and dropped them to the floor with my cloak as I unlaced my boots and pulled my tunic quickly over my head, eagerly approaching the bed. Almost instantly she took hold of me and began to pleasure me with her hands, smiling seductively up at me then giggling mischievously once more, as I stood before her, utterly powerless to resist her attentions. It was no time before I could take no more of her teasing and I roughly pushed her flat on to the bed, almost forcing my way into the most intimate part of her. She groaned and dug her nails into my chest as her soft flesh yielded and I urgently began to fulfil my lust for her.

She allowed me my moments of wildness as I moved frantically against her, slowing me now and then for more sensuous moments. She kissed and caressed, nipping me around my neck and upper body. We moved through many of the positions that Venus had shared with man before I finally groaned loud at my release.

Spent now, I slumped beside her as she lay beside me panting softly, her skin glistening with a fine sheen of perspiration.

After we had lain together for a while, she dressed me. Once more I looked into her eyes and still the green fire of emeralds glittered in them. I watched her as she gathered her dress up, taking the opportunity to survey her slim beauty for one last lingering moment. Her pale flesh glistened in the half light, the light layer of perspiration still glistening here and there on her skin. I watched carefully as the dress, now moving up her legs and veiling her body, covered her beauty as she pinned it in place with the two brooches. Once covered, I immediately strove to recall every curve.

She quickly scraped her long dark hair, slightly dampened by perspiration now, into a tail, before deftly winding it into a tight bun on the back of her head. She reached into a small wooden box on the stand and took out a pair of bone hair pins which she used to secure the bun. Smiling, she crossed the room and opened the door, standing in the doorway and holding her hand out to usher me from the room.

As we traversed the balcony towards the stairwell she held my hand and pulled me along to the doorway. Once in the darkened stairs she gently pushed me back against the wall. Pressing her warm lips to my mouth once more, she gave me another taste of her sensuous touch, laughing softly as she nipped at my ear.

I felt the leather purse being slipped from behind my belt. She turned her back to me then and pushed her body back, slowly rubbing herself up and down me as I sighed in pleasure. I heard the feint chink of coin as she giggled and turned round once more to face me. Gently she placed her hand against my face and stroked my lip lightly with a finger as she replaced the purse.

It was no matter to me how much she had taken; I wished only to know her name. If I never saw her again at least I would have a name.

As we emerged from the door of the stairway into the courtyard I opened my mouth to ask, just as she touched me on the lips with a finger.

"Julia," she whispered. "Will you remember that I wonder?" she asked as she stepped away and melted into the crowd of revellers.

"Oh, finally he decides to show up!" Pudens loudly appeared by my side. He clapped his hand on my shoulder as I strained to keep sight of the girl, fading away into the mass of revellers in the courtyard.

"What happened? Did you get your balls stuck in there?"

Close behind him, the others hooted with laughter as a wide grin spread across Pudens' face.

"Just making the most of it," I said, craning my neck in an attempt to catch one last glimpse of her. "No law against that, is there?"

"Was she a good ride then, or what?" sniggered Pacatianus.

"Who said it was a she?" mused Zenas.

"It's Crispus that likes the pretty boys, that Greek stuff isn't my thing" I replied quickly.

"That's outrageous you bastard, I never did," Crispus countered furiously as the others laughed and teased him further.

"Well, whatever the truth of it, I think that enough time has been passed here," I said, failing to convince myself adequately that I did actually want to leave. "What we need now is a place where we can drink our fill and give Pudens a chance to throw those funny dice of his."

"Now that's just plain wrong." Pudens responded

with mock indignity. "My old grandmother carved those dice herself from the foot bones of the family's favourite cow. Just before Charon came and took her to the ferry."

"Took who?" mocked Pacatianus. "Your grandmater, or the cow?"

Laughing loudly we made our way out of the courtyard as I took one last look back. Unable to see who it was that I sought; reluctantly, I placed her to the back of my mind and walked out of the doors. As we left, Aziel was busy pitching another group of soldiers and missed our departure. We boisterously made our way along the street, moving towards the town forum as we bragged to each other of how we had just spent our money.

CHAPTER 5

Darkness had descended on Portus Itius many hours ago. Although, we still had to weave through large crowds and dodge heavy carts as we made our way to the forum area. The carts carried everything; from imported goods, to corpses bound for the town dump. Beggars of all ages pleaded for coin and street hawkers sprang out with tiresome regularity, asking for a few bronze asses in return for the pointless junk they generally offered.

Food sellers' kitchens added to the thick, rancid odour that pervaded the almost claustrophobic streets. Inevitably, the food became the centre of Aebutius' attentions and he pestered us frequently to stop and eat.

"Oh, look at those meat skewers over there," he drooled. "I could murder a few of those and I bet they're only cheap too."

"They're probably putrid you stupid arse." Zenas offered "Now, stop gobbing off about food for a second, or it'll be us that murder you."

"Listen," said Marinus, "Fat Decius from the Century of Proculus was talking to me this morning. He said if we followed the forum road from the north gate then we should find a tavern called the Capricorn about two street corners away from the forum. Apparently the keeper is a fellow named Batiatus.

He's ex XIIII Gemina and came here after drawing his pension pay off. Proculus reckons we'll get a warm welcome and some good food too. Hopefully that should make us happy and maybe even shut him up for a bit."

Marinus's suggestion seemed agreeable. We began to make approving noises amongst ourselves and then turned to look at Aebutius.

"What? For the love of the gods, I've just finished rutting. I'm famished. What's the problem here?

"What's new here more like?" grunted Surus as we continued on up the street.

After a short walk we found the tavern easily enough. We saw the sign hanging on an iron bracket over the door and were instantly cheered by the painted image of the Legion Capricorn, swaying in the light breeze.

However, just as we approached the tavern, the doors burst open and a shortish, thick set fellow in a stained brown tunic burst forth. He grasped the hair of a young and plainly very drunk soldier in one meaty fist and propelled the lad in front of him with the other.

"Make way!" shouted Zenas as we halted in our tracks. The young soldier flew forward, landing just short of our feet, with a sickening splat into the filth of the road.

"Didn't I shagging well warn you?" bawled the hulking tavern keeper. "Don't keep touching up the serving girls says I. They moan on and on to me and it gives me a shagging headache, so don't do it. But did you listen? Did you bollocks!"

The rant continued as the man stepped forward, thrusting a thick, stubby finger at the young soldier who was lying face down, burbling in the filth of the gutter.

"Boys who can't take their piss shouldn't come and drink with old Batiatus. Look what it's got you. Spark out in the street, sucking shit for your troubles."

Batiatus finished the tirade by raising his huge hands and gesturing as though to wash his hands of the boy, terminating the performance with a loud "Pah!"

"By Jupiter!" shouted Zenas, "Surely not that Batiatus?"

"It is, and no mistake there." confirmed Marinus with a surprised laugh.

"What?" Batiatus turned and looked the eight of us up and down. Beady little eyes peered out from a battle scarred, puffed up old face that bore more than a little resemblance to a wild boar without its tusks.

"By the shades of the lads I lost," he roared, laughing. "Zenas and Marinus? I'd have put good money on some hairy arsed German tribesmen doing for you pair years ago."

The three of them approached each other, embracing with much back slapping as they gripped each other's forearms in the traditional greeting of the Legionary.

"I still can't credit it" exclaimed Zenas. "It must be nigh on twenty years or more since I last saw your ugly puss. Word was you got attacked by bandits heading out here with those merchants you left with. All the old sweats think you're long dead, which is why I never thought twice when the name Batiatus came up here."

"Zenas, old lad." Batiatus shook his head and placed his hand on his chest, surveying Zenas with a fake look of surprise. "Even if the merchants couldn't fight for pennies, did you really believe that old Batiatus could be bested by a gang of country bumpkin robbers?"

"No, rumours of my demise were greatly exaggerated as you can see. Me and that old sword of mine made short work of those mincing idiots and once I got here it suited me not to correct anyone regarding my fate. I'd made a fresh start, but that's all gone out the window now that my old legion has turned up on my doorstep."

It crossed my mind briefly as to why Batiatus may have preferred the anonymity of the fresh start he referred to. But the thought quickly left me as we were beckoned in to the tavern with promises of good food, plentiful drink and genial company within.

As we made for the door Surus reached down and hoisted the young soldier out of the filth by the neck of his tunic, dumping him on the cobbled walkway in front of the tavern.

"Don't eat that shit boy." he advised the muck coated and still unconscious lad. "It really will kill you."

The interior of the tavern smelled heavily of rotting wood and stale wine. A thin cloud of oily smoke hung in the air, rising from the many lamps and braziers that provided light and warmth and making the place eminently suitable for our purposes. Groups of soldiers and sailors sat around drinking, throwing dice and dipping large chunks of thick, doughy bread into steaming bowls of thick meat broth. Talk of anything from old battles to women bedded hummed in the air as we settled into the feel of the place.

As we all sat round a large table, Batiatus crouched down next to us momentarily.

"Lads, make this your home for this evening," he gestured around him. "One rule though. The girls are out of bounds so that means no tit grabbing, arse feeling or sticking your fingers where they don't belong. The noise I get off them when it happens is just more than I can bear sometimes, so don't do it – understand?"

Batiatus stood and gestured for one of the girls to come and serve us.

"That counts for you too, tiny." Batiatus nodded curtly at Surus and then pointed to a small empty table in the corner.

"You two old war dogs had better come over there with me for a proper catch up in private." he nodded to Zenas and Marinus and turned for the table just as Surus began to rise with that look on his face.

Marinus clapped a hand on Surus' shoulder, pushing him back down on the bench as he rose from the table and leant into his ear.

"No man can win every fight you great ox. Trust me; you don't want to go there."

Whilst the three veterans remained in their corner, deep in conversation, the rest of us enjoyed the hospitality on offer. The prices were reasonable and the food and drink was good honest fare, which we managed to enjoy whilst limiting ourselves only to cheeking the serving girls and not actually touching them. They for their part seemed to enjoy the banter and became more relaxed with us, even sitting on occasion to steal some drink and poke fun when it suited them. Obviously we must have been deemed to be sticking to our boundaries though, as Batiatus had not approached with a mind to launch any of us from his tavern.

After an hour or so three more off duty Legionaries came in that we recognised from our own Cohort, from the Century of Lucillius. They seemed oddly on edge as they made their way over to our table and asked to join us. We called for more drinks as the soldiers sat and spoke to us. The news they brought was disturbing.

The oldest of their group, Lepidus, seemed to elect himself as spokesman while the other two sat quietly, their faces grim masks as their comrade passed on the news.

"I don't know what we've marched into here lads, but it doesn't look that good." He shook his head as he looked around the table at us.

"You know that the XX and II Legions were here a month or so before us and that the IX has just arrived?" We all nodded, waiting expectantly for more.

"Well, it seems as though ours is not the only Legion beset by talk of what waits for us over there. Word is that the two legions that got here before us are on the point of mutiny and it won't be long before we get caught up in it."

"What? How so?" asked Crispus.

"Rabble rousers within the units are convening illegal gatherings anywhere within the town or camps. They're giving speeches to anyone who will listen about refusing to sail. It's catching like wildfire and a massive crowd is gathering in the forum even as we speak to listen to a Centurion from the XX who refuses to commit his men."

Lepidus paused to collect his thoughts then added:

"One other thing, apparently the authorities are now using troops from a Praetorian Cohort based in this area to break up or deter the gatherings whenever they get word of them."

"Praetorians!" Crispus exclaimed. "Now that is interesting."

"Why?" enquired Aebutius, his words muffled by a mouthful of bread and broth.

Crispus groaned and reached over the table, bouncing the flat of his hand off Aebutius' forehead.

"By Dis, a light burns for sure, but only dimly I fear."

"Huh?"

Exasperated, Crispus thumped his cup down on the table top and spelled it out.

"There is no chance that a Cohort of the Emperors personal army would be here; unless they hadn't travelled directly from Rome under the command of somebody very important."

"Exactly brother," confirmed Lepidus. "We've been here nearly two weeks now but, as I said, the XX and II Legions were here way before us. They've been doing nothing much but living in muddy fields and complaining bitterly while they waited. Rome has obviously got wind of unrest spreading amongst the troops. Even the auxiliaries are rumbling now."

"Anyway, word is the news quickly got back to Rome and, seeing as how Claudius wants this invasion so badly, he despatched his secretary Narcissus with a Cohort of troops directly from Rome. Apparently they sailed across from Ostia and then directly up river from Massilia about a week ago. They are now camped out on a Senators country estate a few miles from town."

"Narcissus you say?" asked Pacatianus.

"The very same." replied Lepidus.

"What's his story then?" asked Surus as he drained a cup of wine and finished with a loud belch.

"Very rich, very powerful," added Crispus. "He's a former slave who now carries an awful lot of weight with old Claudius. The Emperor trusts him unquestioningly. Apparently this freedman has really made good and is dripping with money and favour. In fact; word is he even offered Claudius a loan when the treasury coffers were a bit run down."

"I heard something like that too," I put in. "You know what it's like. You pick up on gossip when you're guarding the Legate. I had heard tell that Claudius was desperate for this venture to succeed so that he can consolidate his rule with a big triumph. It must be true if he's sending one of his most trusted ministers to deal with this."

"Do you think we should take a look at this carry on in the forum then?" asked Aebutius.

"I'll remind you once more who you are." snapped Zenas, as he appeared at the end of the table with Marinus and Batiatus. "You are troops of the most senior Cohort in the legion and bodyguards to the legate, Titus Flavius Sabinus. Any involvement in the goings on in that forum tonight could see you all executed for sedition."

"You'd do well to listen," added Batiatus as Marinus stood by, saying nothing but glaring at the floor with a face like thunder. "Now is the time for keeping site of your duty, not for running with the mob. You are different from the rest and you should show it. Sabinus will need you in the days to come."

Zenas turned and clasped Batiatus by the arm, smiling and nodding his head at his old friend.

"Batiatus, it was good to see you again and I thank you for your hospitality but we should go now," said Zenas. "I have a feeling tomorrow will bring its own trials and we really need to be ready."

"May the gods go with you all and keep you safe until the next time we meet," said Batiatus as we stood and made for the door.

CHAPTER 6

"Up! Rise you lazy pigs. I want you in armour and ready to move now."

I squinted at the first weak trickle of sunlight penetrating between the leather tent flaps, briefly considering pushing my head back under my blanket. I realised there was no point. Just as the thought had crossed my mind I had heard the dull thud of feet on the ground and accepted that my brief but deep sleep was at an end as Mestrius shouted for us to rise.

The rest of the occupants of the tent began to stir, groaning and complaining as they awoke. I made for the tent flaps and rubbed my face, squinting in the pale light and ignoring as best I could the bitter taste that remained in my mouth from last night's wine.

"Is it just me," grumbled Pudens behind me as I left the tent, "or would anyone else like to stab that loud mouthed whore monger in the throat?"

As Optio to Fatalis, it was generally Mestrius who mustered us and made us ready for whatever it was that we were required to do. In time, Mestrius would take over from Fatalis as Centurion. Though he was at times somewhat unpopular, we all regarded the old warrior with a healthy respect. As with Fatalis, he had proven himself many times over and had won his position through his skill and excellence as a soldier. For that, we would always follow his lead.

As I gathered my armour together I looked around and saw other men rising and moving around in the mist of the grey dawn. They too were part of the Legate's bodyguard, responding to the morning call by Mestrius. Aebutius appeared beside me as I began to don my equipment. He farted loudly as he hitched the front of his tunic up and let forth a steaming river of piss onto the ground.

"May Mars and Mercury blight that man," he complained. ""What's so important that I don't even get time to break my fast?"

"Whatever it is," observed Pudens, "You'd do well to cut that piss short and get some armour on. If he comes back and finds you in just your tunic he'll cut that maggot of yours off and shove it down your throat."

Aebutius was just about to respond when Zenas emerged, lacing the front of his armour up and cut in.

"Enough! Forget all the talk and armour up quickly," he snapped. "I'm not aware of anything but general duties for us today. Something's definitely afoot."

"What do you think it is then?" asked Surus.

"How hard can it be?" said Crispus in an exasperated tone. "All this talk going on in camp has obviously borne fruit. I reckon there's real trouble on the way. You see if I'm wrong."

The conversation was just about to continue when Mestrius reappeared from behind a row of tents, confirming instructions as he made his way back towards the camp centre.

"Full armour and weapons for all Legate's guard," he barked. "Form up outside the Legate's compound immediately!"

With that, Mestrius stalked off into the morning mist, repeating the order to other troops as he went.

Having equipped ourselves as ordered with shields, javelins and helmets we formed up on the muddy track way running between the tent lines. We then set off at a brisk run towards the compound. Other Contubernia joined us on the track. The metallic clank and jingle of armour and equipment filled the air, along with the rhythmic thud of our iron studded boots on the ground as we made our way to the muster point.

As we reached the compound, Mestrius was there to meet us. He ordered each Contubernium in turn to take their position in escort formation to await the Legate. Once in position we quickly composed ourselves and waited silently for our charge to appear. As we waited, the cavalry contingent of the guard arrived and formed up next to us, ready to receive the Legate into their midst.

Finally, the gates of the wooden stockade around the commander's area opened up and the Legate's party rode out. Fatalis too was on horseback and heading the small column of horses. As they emerged he immediately indicated for the waiting cavalry to be ready to receive the Legate. As the formation split to either side of the road the party emerged. Ademetus the Camp prefect rode out behind Fatalis, closely followed by the six legion tribunes. Behind them came the legate, Sabinus, and his aide.

In his early forties, and with a strong squat frame and rugged but shrewd look about him, Titus Flavius Sabinus cut an imposing figure. As with his younger brother, Vespasian, who commanded the II Augusta Legion, he was clearly every inch a soldier as well as a politician. The gleaming armour and purple ribbon tied around his breast plate marked him out as a Senator of Rome as well as a Legate. Nevertheless, there was no mistaking the posture of a man who was as comfortable on the battlefield as he was in the Senate house. As he made his way into the ranks of the cavalry escort he halted and cast his eye over us all. After a short pause he addressed us.

"Though you did not expect to be mustered here this morning, this is perhaps a day I myself had expected to come about for some time now."

Sabinus shifted in his saddle, carefully considering his words.

"Some men can afford to give way to their fears and concerns. In doing so, they choose not to confront that which baulks them so. You and I are not such men and cannot therefore pander to such self-indulgent whims."

My fellow legates and General Plautius, are charged by the emperor himself to embark on a mission that will clothe Rome in ever greater glory than that which she yet wears. Even so, my mission and theirs will fail without such men as you. Of all men of the legion, you are my most trusted. It is you who lead by example and hold positions such as your brother legionaries would one day aspire to. Nevertheless, I tell you now that their courage fails them. There are many who openly refuse to go where the emperor directs."

A brief murmur made its way through our ranks as Sabinus confirmed the now almost universally held suspicion voiced earlier by Crispus; that the whole army around Portus Itius was on the brink of mutiny.

"You men have fought and bled many times. Even more perhaps than most of those who refuse now to do their sacred duty and abide by the oath they swore to their emperor. That is why you are what you are, trusted above all others and charged with my safety, because you have proven your courage and loyalty time and again. You should not therefore be offended when I ask you my next question, because I do not question your loyalty. All I want to hear is what is in your hearts."

At that moment I realised that Sabinus too must face whatever awaited us across that sea. His courage was not failing him. His resolve to fulfil his duty was plain as he addressed us, calling now for our loyalty to support his courage. If such a man as this could face the will of the Gods with strength and fortitude, then why not I?

"Rioting broke out in the town last night and Praetorians put a number of your brother legionaries to the sword," announced Sabinus grimly. "This morning I go to the town forum to meet with the emperor's envoy, Narcissus. It is the sacred duty of I and my fellow legates to bring this dissent to an end and to stop any more killing of Roman by Roman."

Sabinus paused once more and bowed his head slightly before finishing his address to us.

"So I ask you then. Will you then stay true to your oath and come with me to Portus Itius - so that I can show the servant of the Emperor and your brothers in arms what loyalty and courage really looks like?"

"Aye!"

A hundred and sixty mouths roared out the answer. Sabinus looked over to his officers and nodded, assured by the knowledge that he could still rely on the soldiers he had placed the utmost trust in. With a further nod from Sabinus the cavalry commander moved his men off and we fell in directly behind the party, marching out towards the town.

As our column passed through the camp we were watched buy our fellow legionaries. Not even bothering to stand for their legate, a change seemed to have happened almost overnight as they silently watched our passage through the camp with an air of surly indifference. As we watched like hawks for any threat amongst them, Sabinus rode on, not even bothering to cast a glance at his men for the time being.

As we made our way into Portus Itius it was readily apparent that we had returned to a very different town to the one we had frequented just a few hours ago. The streets were empty of civilians. The shutters of many of the windows remained firmly closed. Here and there, gangs of soldiers loitered on street corners. None wore armour but all wore a look of extreme resentment and all carried at least a sword.

As we approached the forum at the heart of the town, the atmosphere was thick with the eye watering reek of smoke from the burned out shells of several buildings that had been put to the torch. The grumbling crowds of soldiers began to thicken as we approached the forum, until we were finally forced to barge our way through them. We pushed into the wide open space where the town market should have been doing brisk trade by now. Passing through men, some of whom we could identify as being from our own Legion.

None spoke to us, but equally, none seemed inclined to offer violence either. They just stared impassively as the Legate passed by under our protection. It wasn't until we had almost reached the far end of the forum, where the Praetorian cohort was formed up in a great block, that we noticed the dead.

Piled at the corner of the forum were around sixty bodies, all slain by blades judging from the congealed pools and runs of blood that had puddled around the base of the pile, and from the injuries that we could make out. Though, what was making the atmosphere truly oppressive were the makeshift timber frames close to the corpse pile that supported the bodies of around twenty crucified soldiers.

"Great Gods!" murmured Marinus. "I tell you, if that's the work of Praetorians this could get very bad. Field armies won't stand for palace fops nailing their pals to pieces of wood."

"Marinus, if you don't close that big stupid hole in your face," warned Mestrius, "I'll nail you to a piece of wood."

The crowd closed around us as we passed Sabinus through our ranks and the Praetorian formation opened up to allow him access to the town's senate house behind them. Sabinus dismounted and climbed the steps to the platform overlooking the forum. I glanced over at the crucified men, wondering if the still audible groans and weak movements from those who still lived may yet prompt their comrades to attack and attempt rescue. My attention was drawn away from the scene as Mestrius ordered us to face the crowd.

Within an hour all four legates and the various commanders of the auxiliary units had arrived in the forum and joined Sabinus in the senate house. While we waited outside, I eyed the growing crowd of soldiers with rising suspicion. I wondered too what it was that such powerful men could be discussing in the senate house by way of resolving the dangerous situation that they now found themselves in.

By mid-morning, after what seemed like an age facing down the grim faced and largely silent mass of soldiers packing the forum, the great doors swung open. Then the party inside the senate house began to emerge into the spring sunshine. An excited ripple of chatter seemed to work its way through the crowd and I looked briefly over my shoulder to see what was happening.

As well as the four Legates and their aides, I instantly recognised Aulus Plautius, the supreme commander of the invasion army. Plautius had visited our camp on several previous occasions to meet with Sabinus and I formed the impression that he too was a soldier's general. Albeit his faith in his men was now sorely tested as he stood before them in the company of another man whom I certainly did not recognise.

Plautius stepped forward and addressed the assembly before him. An obvious look of anger and perhaps an element of shame too clouded his face. He spread his arms as though in appeal to the crowd, addressing the assembly with an obvious passion in his voice.

"Can any of you men tell me why it has come to this?" he asked of them. "Why has such a great army faltered - failing in the face of nothing more than tall tales?"

He gestured towards the grim scene to his side, whilst at the same time disdaining to cast his glance in the direction of the spectacle.

"Is this really why your brothers yonder bleed on crosses and suffer so terribly? Because you really believe that shadows and ghosts can stand in the way of force of arms?"

Shaking his head, he turned and pointed to the silent group of sullen faced superior officers behind him.

"For many days now, I have met with your commanders and puzzled with them as to why you speak as you do. And how it may be that we can turn you back into soldiers once more, rather than the mewling children you would clearly have us take you for."

An angry rumbling rose from the crowd at this slight but Plautius was righteous in his anger and continued.

"They say that such harsh truths bring their own kind of pain. I certainly have no kind truths to sooth your sensibilities this day. In continuing this disobedience you shame us all. I came here to lead a great and powerful Roman army, forty thousand strong. Seemingly, I now find myself in the company of thousands of old women. All of who are content to do nothing but gossip and agitate. Shame on you all, say I!"

Plautius let out this last barb with an impassioned shout and the crowd responded with a low rumble and briefly shuffled forward. Instinctively we all reached for our swords. The hiss of them being drawn half from their scabbards managed to restore order as Plautius gave way to exasperation and fell silent.

"By Nemesis!" hissed Pudens. "Is he trying to get us all murdered?"

Plautius stood by, his face a mask of anger and his fists clenched until the knuckles had gone white. But, as the angry mob settled once more, the unknown man standing next to Plautius made his way to the edge of the senate house steps.

Narcissus was a man of unremarkable stature. He had no distinguishing features and, had it not been for his opulent attire, you would not have looked twice at the man. He wore a pure white tunic and toga, which was trimmed with a rich crimson band and gold embroidered laurel leaves. Even at a distance, you could see that the clothing cost more than some earned in years. He wore scarlet boots and a thick gold chain encircled his slim neck, from which hung his Imperial seal of office. Bejewelled rings adorned perfectly manicured hands and fabulous gold bands decorated his wrists. The man positively stank of wealth.

Two Praetorians advanced with him, flanking him as he surveyed his audience. A gentle smile began to break on his face as he settled on the centre of the crowd and slowly spread his arms, as if to embrace all.

"Soldiers of Rome." Came the cordial but surprisingly firm voice. "Your emperor sends you his greetings!"

The politicians smile grew wider. With upturned hands, Narcissus gently bobbed his hands up and down and nodded affably towards us. All at once it seemed as if the man was now possessed of a smug superiority. He appeared to be looking down on the assembly before him, as though preparing to talk to them like errant children. The assembled crowd was in no mood to be spoken down to by a man aspiring to be his master and, as if possessed of the same mind, the gathered crowd bellowed with one voice.

"Io Saturnalia!"

The shout seemed briefly to freeze him in his tracks. His guards suddenly exhibited the first outward signs of nervousness as yet more resentful noises spread through the gathering. I took a tighter hold of the hilt of my sword and glanced between him and the restless crowd. The self-assured smile, however, never left his face as he composed himself to address them once more.

He must have been aware that he, his Praetorians, and all of us could be torn to pieces if he provoked the mob too much. The right choice of words would be crucial now if he and his men were to leave Portus Itius alive, let alone succeed in ending the mutiny, as he had clearly been tasked to do.

"Yes, yes I do wear my masters clothes on this day." he declared, nodding his head and defiantly placing his balled fists atop his hips. "And what of you, soldiers? Whose clothes do you wear this day?"

A hush fell over the crowd and Narcissus steadily began to regain his composure further as he began his campaign to re-secure the obedience of the disgruntled army.

"There should be no need for me to ask this of you, but I must truly confess that I stand before you a confused man." He cast another long glance over the assembled troops. "Your emperor and my master sent me to come and see just what it is that goes on here. He knows very well that a mighty force of Rome's best soldier's stands poised to conquer her enemy but, he too is now confused."

"Whenever news arrives from this great army, all he hears of are the bleating of superstitious old women and the gnashing of weak willed souls frightened of dark places. Where then, he wishes to know, is this mighty army?"

The last, shouted question, prompted loud replies from the men. They berated Narcissus loudly and jeered him. Proclaiming that the army he sought stood there, before him.

Slowly Narcissus shook his head and silence descended once more as he threw a fold of his toga over his shoulder, strolling slowly across the top of the senate house steps, surveying his audience.

"No, no. This cannot be it." He swept his arm across the men before him. "Any army of Rome that I know is dutiful and ever ready to do its Emperors bidding. This mass of scruffy, unwilling men that I see before me now has forsaken their sacred oath to the Emperor and to the sacred standards of their units. Now, where once stood a great and formidable army, there stands only a hoard of renegades. A rabble, aspiring only to terrify innocent civilians and disobey the proper authorities. This is no army!"

Instantly a rumble of angry voices again shot through the crowd as the assembly rankled at the slight that Narcissus had just delivered upon them. The man was deliberately inflaming the crowd, but he was cunning, for I could see his game now. He was gambling with the fact that honour still counted for a lot with the men present. Without doubt, it was a dangerous game, but he was going to play it. Slowly, I started to admire him for his courage. He was risking his very life to bring about his masters wishes because he knew, if the crowd turned, he would certainly be torn apart. Slave he may once have been but he had heart, and I had to credit him for it.

"What then do I tell the emperor when he asks me why the mightiest Roman army of recent times will not do his bidding? How can I return to Rome and tell him that his beloved soldiers languish in sodden, muddy fields and grow fat and lazy? That they chase whores and drink themselves unconscious every night. Should I really tell him that his finest warriors are now too frightened to move, and all this because they have terrified one another over the campfires with ghost stories?"

Narcissus spread his arms, looked down at his feet and slowly shook his head in a deliberately theatrical display which conveyed his apparent sadness and disappointment in the men before him. Grudgingly, slowly, my admiration for him grew a little more as I realised that he was also reaching out to those soldiers who could not hear his words. Clearly, Narcissus was adept at manipulating even large crowds as he continued his delivery of such a consummate performance that any skilled actor would have been proud to present it.

My eyes darted back and forth as I did my best to keep an eye on both him and the crowd before me. Slowly, they quietened down and started to look around at each other, faintly ashamed now that the envoy's words had, after all, the ring of truth. Thousands of soldiers had marched here. Many of them were vastly experienced in the art of war and conquest. All of them now stood, ragged and pathetic. Now that they had put aside their discipline and courage they were without honour. Now they were scorned by their masters; for being afraid of rumours that they themselves had built up beyond any semblance of credibility.

As the plain truth of the situation dawned on them, Narcissus sensed the change in them and pressed home his advantage. Stepping forward he thrust his finger towards the crowd and played on their shame further.

"So, after all of this, if you would still call yourselves soldiers, then answer me this. In the ages to come, how will history recall this army?"

He spread his arms wide once more and raised his face to the skies, as if to appeal to the Gods for the right words to use. After a short pause, he continued.

"The divine Julius made not one, but two thrusts into the unknown land of Britannia. True enough, he did not succeed in conquering the land, or bringing its people to heel. But he showed the uncivilised barbarians beyond these shores the might and courage of Rome. He and his brave soldiers did their duty and returned home with honour. To this day the natives of Britannia remember their taste of Roman power through their fireside stories. They pass their memories on in the songs they sing of their history. They know in their hearts that one day Rome will return and finish what Caesar began!"

Narcissus' head snapped down, the smile gone from his face as he stabbed his finger out once more to the crowd before him.

"Have no doubts, the army that languishes here today will certainly be remembered in years to come. So the question I ask then is this: Will you be remembered throughout time as the army that was beaten by nothing more than ghost stories?"

A thunderous 'no' echoed across the forum as the men present bellowed their answer. Narcissus thrust his arms down at his sides, knowing now that victory was his, spreading his fingers wide and turning his palms up he shouted to the sky.

"Then are you telling the Gods that you will instead embrace Caesars legacy and do honour to his shade? Do you now choose instead to be remembered by generations to come as the great army of Claudius, conquerors of Britannia?"

"Aye!" shouted the assemblage as one, fired now by the recovered pride that Narcissus had stirred in them and roaring as if to shake the gods themselves and to make them hear their pledge.

"Then do this for honour and glory, and for your Emperor," directed Narcissus, smiling triumphantly. "And prepare to take your rightful place alongside history's heroes!"

The entire forum shook with the noise of the thunderous cheering. Weapons were waved wildly in the air and grubby fists thrust high as renewed pride and a fresh wave of confidence flowed openly through the assembled force. Men whooped and yelled as they began to turn and hurry back to their camps, eager to galvanise their absent comrades for war and to prepare for what lay ahead.

Narcissus remained standing on the steps of the Senate House. The soft smile had returned to his face and he stood with his left hand extended and his right hand over his heart, slowly nodding as the crowd dispersed. He knew that he had placed his head in a lion's mouth and had lived to tell the tale.

* * * * *

In the space of a week, the invasion fleet was ready to sail. The vast assembly of vessels were loaded with supplies and equipment and, as if blessing the invasion itself, the Gods even sent fine sailing weather. The temporary camps that had become vast, filthy tracts of well-trodden mud had been all but broken down. The tents had been stowed on ships for the crossing. The next time they would be erected, gods willing, it would be on the soil of Britannia. Huge columns of troops filed into the port area to embark upon the invasion ships, each unit preparing to board their allocated ships in precise adherence to the orders that had been issued by the commanders.

Before we boarded our own vessel, Sabinus summoned our Century to the end of the wharf where we gathered round a great white ox that had been tethered to one of the thick timber uprights of the moorings.

"Now the hour is at hand, you need not fear what lies ahead," Sabinus addressed us.

"You can see with your own eyes that the Gods show favour by sending the right wind and a calm sea."

As Sabinus spoke he quietly drew his Gladius and walked towards the magnificent ox. The great beast stood impassively, distracted by an attendant with a handful of fodder.

"We are soldiers, and the sea is not our realm. We are the children of Mars, but we shall do honour to Neptune this day. We ask the great lord of the waves, for the sake of our entire legion, that you grant safe passage across your kingdom."

The lethal blade licked out and sliced across the throat of the ox, giving only the briefest opportunity for it to emit a low grunt before its steaming blood spurted out over the boards of the wharf. Within seconds the beast collapsed to its knees, heaving and convulsing as its throat filled with blood. An Augur, waiting with the attendant knelt and opened the ox's stomach with a long slim knife, delving into the animal before swiftly cutting the liver free. For a few short moments he gazed at the organ, probing it with the tip of the knife, inspecting it.

"The signs bode well, Legate" the Augur eventually announced. "Neptune will grant you safe passage."

As we cheered loudly, Sabinus hacked through the tether securing the beast and a group of men shoved the hulking carcass off the edge of the dock. As a loud splash rose from the waters of the harbour Sabinus shouted out to the waves.

"Take this magnificent animal as our thanks for your protection, oh Neptune, great lord of the seas."

With that, Sabinus turned to face us and raised his reddened blade high in the air as he cried out the traditional call to the Legionary.

"Are you ready for a war?"

It seemed as though the very dock we stood on shook as, three times, we bellowed out our answer.

"Ready, aye!"…"Ready, aye!"…"Ready, aye!"

CHAPTER 7

As dusk descended on Portus Itius, the bustling dock area was filled with the noise of men loading the last of the equipment onto the ships that would take us across the water to Britannia.

Ours was a sturdy old Trireme called Sea Snake, which was moored against the side of the wharf like some great wallowing whale. She creaked and groaned, her thick timbers flexing with the gentle rise and fall of the swells as we worked alongside her, completing our preparations to board. I hoped then that my apprehension for actually boarding the vessel was not too evident. Instead, I did my best to put from my mind the memories of the transport barge I had seen wrecked just beyond this very harbour.

Captain Cornelius, Master of the Sea Snake, bellowed out orders to his crew and shouted up to us from the deck as we made the last of our equipment ready to load aboard.

"Two hours and we push off with the night tide." he announced. "If it's not on board well before then, it's not going anywhere."

"Vulcan's balls," observed Surus. "He's a salty version of Fatalis, and no mistake."

We laughed and joked, poking fun at each other as we passed packs, weapons and supplies down onto the deck of the ship, stifling our laughter abruptly as

Fatalis appeared from below decks and stared up at us.

"You animals had better not be wasting time up here," he growled at us. "I want nothing going wrong at the last minute so keep your wandering minds on the job at hand."

"See?" muttered Surus quietly.

Quietened by Fatalis' chastisement, we turned our attentions once more to our work when a new voice broke in abruptly from behind us.

"Ah, come now Fatalis, what could possibly go wrong now that I'm here?"

The words were enough to instantly stop Fatalis from going back down below and for us to momentarily stop what we were doing. As one, we turned and looked towards the direction of the voice as the unmistakeable figure of Batiatus the innkeeper appeared amongst us, looking down to the deck where the old Centurion now stood. There was a rare look of mild amusement crossing his face.

"Somebody did mention that Sabinus had gone and hired some reliable ex-soldiers for this little outing." Fatalis said in a matter of fact manner as he turned towards the hatch once more. "Obviously, they must have been sent somewhere else."

"Still got the tongue of a viper then?" Batiatus replied.

Fatalis paused and glanced briefly back, his grin growing slightly more evident as he looked up from the deck.

"Make sure you bring some wine with you when you board Batiatus. I won't be able to listen to your tall stories once more without at least having something to numb the senses."

With that, Fatalis disappeared back down the hatch while Batiatus stood there grinning at us all.

"Well," he quipped. "I see the old mountain bear is still as cordial and welcoming as ever."

He laughed to himself and rummaged in his large leather pack. Presently, he pulled out a small wine skin and nodded at it with a smile, as though in approval of its contents.

"And you lot, you were all like an old farmer's cart the last time I saw you. All rattle and shit. Now look at you, struck as dumb as a virgin facing down her first prick."

Batiatus strode towards us and thrust an ancient looking bronze helmet towards Aebutius who duly took hold of it, examining it carefully as Batiatus approached the edge of the dock.

"What on earth are you doing with this old piss pot then?" queried Aebutius, grinning as he continued to cast his eye over the old helmet. "This thing looks old enough to have been around in Varus' time."

"It was." growled Batiatus. "It belonged to my older brother and he, along with it, were two of the few things to emerge from that forest in one piece."

"Vulcans balls." Surus whispered reverently. He stepped forward to admire the old relic, suddenly awed by the helmets impressive history, as were we all.

"Look at you all, standing round gawping like a bunch of village idiots. " Batiatus chided. "That thing has seen more fighting than you younger ones put together. Old and battered it might be, but at least it won't get thieved because nobody with any sense would take something so recognisable. Particularly when people get to know me and come to realise that I'd saw the fingers off anyone sniffing round my stuff."

He scowled at us all briefly before giving a brief but loud laugh as he threw his mail shirt and pack onto the deck. He followed it down with a leap that carried more spring and finesse than one might have expected from one of his age and build. After landing with a good solid thud on the deck, he turned to us and shouted back:

"We'll reacquaint ourselves later I fancy. Meanwhile I've a crusty old bastard I need to catch a few years up with. Now, nice and careful like, drop that old lid down here to me."

As Batiatus had instructed, Aebutius carefully dropped the helmet down for Batiatus. Catching the battered old helmet, he grabbed the rest of his gear and disappeared down the hatchway, dragging the bundle behind him and leaving us there on the dock above, puzzling over what had just occurred exactly.

With our collective curiosities aroused we questioned Zenas and Marinus as we worked. It was they who had sat with Batiatus in the tavern that night, speaking privately on another table for most of our stay, and it was they who knew him from all those years ago. Steadily, we managed to coax from them some of the story of how a rough old innkeeper who once served under the same standards that we did now, had since decided that retirement did not really suit him after all.

Though reluctant to divulge specifics, we learned from the pair that, just prior to leaving the legion; Batiatus had been a junior Centurion serving with Fatalis. Marinus and Zenas were then just youngsters serving in his Century. It seemed that, with the arrival of the invasion force in Portus Itius, and in particular the XIIII Gemina, Batiatus had taken the view that perhaps the goddess Nemesis had taken a hand in his life once more and that his fortunes now lay back with the army. Rather than re-enlist in the legion, Batiatus had chosen instead to take pay as a mercenary scout in the direct employ of Sabinus. Apparently, Batiatus had once been commanded by Sabinus when the Legate was just a young tribune on the staff of a previous Legate, Valens. The young Sabinus had been so impressed by Batiatus' talents as a natural soldier that he had aspired to reach such standards himself one day.

When Batiatus had re-emerged from retirement and presented himself to the Legate's compound, Sabinus had wasted no time in offering him the post of chief of scouts on his personal staff. As a mercenary scout commander, it would not only be Batiatus' role to find the enemy. He would also to act as messenger, emissary, assassin and spy when needed. Only a man taking coin directly from the purse of Sabinus would be completely trusted to this role and, as for Batiatus personally, his credentials were excellent and Sabinus knew it.

Though we had now gleaned a little more about Batiatus we could draw no more knowledge from Zenas and Marinus about his actual service with the legion. Whilst they were happy to confirm that he had been a decorated soldier with a proud service record they would not expand any further when pressed. We were merely told that, if we wished to learn more, we should ask Batiatus himself. After all, they reasoned, it was his business. It should therefore be his decision as to whether or not to tell us more.

Eventually, Captain Cornelius had ordered us all aboard. As the sky had blackened with the onset of night the scene in Portus Itius had changed. Everywhere had become bathed in the flickering light of hundreds of torches, burning both on the vessels at anchor and on the sides of the docks.

For over an hour, we sat aboard the Sea Snake while she rose and fell on the gentle night tide. My stomach began to churn and cramp as I watched the endless numbers of ships slowly rising and falling around me as we waited for the great fleet to get underway.

Moored close to us were some large, broad beamed

transport barges that had been loaded with scores of mules. The stink that emanated from them was thick enough to cut. I yearned to sail just so that I could get some fresh air into my lungs once more. I was aware that it wasn't just me and that others too felt that the fetid atmosphere amongst the closely packed ships was now becoming hard to bear. More and more soldiers seemed to be coming up to the rails, heaving the pits of their stomachs over the side as they tried to get used to coping with the unfamiliar experience of life on a ship. The sour smell of their vomit added to the thickening stink as I listened to the baleful braying of the confused and distressed animals, crammed below the decks of the transport barges. How could anyone choose to be a sailor? This was such a wretched existence and what was worse, we hadn't even put to sea as yet.

Finally, the waiting came to an end. Cornelius began to bellow out his orders, prompting his crew to begin running in all directions over the Sea Snake. Now I had something to divert my attention from the stink and misery of the animals and men as I watched the sailors. They moved quickly over the deck, casting off and hauling in mooring lines. Others shoved off against the dockside, pushing the warship out of her berth while those high aloft in the darkness prepared to unfurl the sails as the Captain sought to capitalize on the light night wind. Finally, our vessel slipped out of harbour, gliding towards the open ocean.

As we cleared the harbour mouth, I suddenly became aware of the vast blackness of ocean around me. Briefly, my mind harkened back to the idle chatter that had circulated, both while we were on the march and once we were in camp. It had started as little more than a trivial seed which had since germinated into something outlandish and which had briefly caused a great army to falter. I remembered once more the talk of the dreadful monsters that waited in the deep, lurking below with their huge, scaly bodies. Armed too with wicked, sharp, white teeth, waiting to shred the flesh of mortal men.

Briefly, a shiver shot through my spine and raised the hairs on the back of my neck, and then all at once the feeling was gone. Man was right to fear the unknown, I reasoned quietly, but a Roman soldier should never let that stop him from carrying forth Rome's greatness.

As Sea Snake slipped effortlessly into the blackness I felt the fine cold spray of the sea on my face. My lungs filled at last with the fresh crisp air that I had so longed for in port. Invigorated now, I felt heartened and I found myself taking in the scene around me, marvelling at the size of the enormous fleet of ships that had put to sea around us.

What man could not be astounded by this sight? It was the most amazing of spectacles as the torches on the decks of one of the biggest fleets of our times sailed forth. Gradually, the twinkling lights of Portus Itius faded from view as we forged on, cutting our way through the Stygian blackness for Britannia.

I remained on the gently rolling deck, choosing to enjoy the air, rather than descend below decks where many of the others now vied for a space to sleep the journey out. I listened to the sound of the sea, the hiss and slap of the bow cutting through the waves and the sail billowing and flapping over the ever present rhythm of the ocean. It was a sound that could only be the steady breath of Neptune, sleeping below us and dreaming of whatever it was that such a mighty god might dream of.

With little to see but the reflected light of torches flickering on the low waves my mind began to wander, back to Mogontiacum. As clear as could be, I saw once more a humble but welcoming house in a street on the edge of the town. There stood a woman - a good, honest woman. Coping alone now, but still doing all the things needed to keep a home as it should be. My mind cast an eye over the two young boys wrestling on the floor. I smiled briefly, wondering once more whether or not the home which I quietly longed for was a place where I could ever expect to set foot again. The images though, were no more than insubstantial wraiths. All it took was Aebutius' voice and they were gone, retreating back to a place in my mind where only special things were locked away. There they would stay, to be released once more when I could appreciate them on my own, and in peace.

"How goes it Vepitta?" Aebutius asked "How do

you like Neptune's great kingdom then?"

Surus had accompanied Aebutius and stiffened visibly at the last question.

"Gods protect us you stupid arse wipe." cursed Surus nervously "Don't set out to go making light of a god in his own domain will you?"

"What? All I said was…"

"Come now brothers," I smiled at them both. "This is a fine night. Let's just enjoy the air."

"Aye, perhaps this may be our last night of peace for some time to come." Surus observed.

"Perhaps that is so, but we are after all nothing if not the hammer of the Emperor. Men such as us were not made for peace," Aebutius pointed out. "Tomorrow, we will do what the gods set us on the earth to do. We will make war."

"Your words ring true enough friend," I replied. "But for now we do have a little peace to enjoy. And I for one am grateful for it."

"What do you suppose drives a man to give up his peace for the promise of more war?" Surus asked the surprise question to nobody in particular as Aebutius and I gave each other a puzzled look.

"No, I mean, when your fighting is done and you have at last found peace in your own small patch of the world, why would you forsake it all to serve Mars once more?"

"Now I'm with you," replied Aebutius. "You speak of Batiatus, do you not?"

Surus gave a confirmatory nod and I contributed my

own thoughts concerning Batiatus' decision to abandon his new life.

"Where's the surprise? When your talent is for killing your enemy, why would you ever settle for the life of an innkeeper?"

"Close," came the voice from behind us. "But you're not quite there yet, son."

We turned as Batiatus joined us. Taking a deep breath, he gratefully sucked in the clean air, purging his lungs of the stink from below as the light wind blew on his leathery round face.

"Drink this in lads," he cast his arms wide about him, nodding at the lights of the other ships all around us. "Don't you know what this is?"

I watched him, noting the spark in his eyes as he began to explain why an inn in a port town could no longer hold him from his true calling.

"Look around you, see the lights of the fleet burning all round? It is as though we ride the head of a giant comet that burns its way through the blackness of night. Soon our light will burn in somebody else's world. Do you think that a man such as I could ever sit back and throw away the chance to become part of something that will be remembered forever? No, if a man does nothing else with his life, he should never pass up the chance for glory."

I nodded to myself as I realised that whatever it was that drove us now, still held a tight grip on the heart and soul of Batiatus. How could he ever be satisfied with rousting drunks, peddling cheap drink and bearing the constant whining of his serving girls? For him it must have constituted only an existence and nothing more. Now that the standards had called him back to arms, a fire burned in his bones once more and he was alive again.

"See!" exclaimed Batiatus, thrusting his finger to the night sky and tracing the path of an exceptionally bright shooting star. We followed its fiery trail in silent awe as it streaked briefly across the sky before burning itself out.

"The Gods favour us. They send a messenger of fire in the night. See how it travelled from east to west? Now you can be sure my lads that we have the aid of the Gods and nothing will stop us!"

After a while, the conversation died away and the need for rest after a long hard day eventually took hold. I made my way below deck and crammed myself into a space I had found between the sprawling bodies and stowed kit. Using my rolled up cloak as a pillow I pulled my old woollen blanket around my chin and in an instant, I was in the arms of Somnus.

CHAPTER 8

I woke just after dawn, rubbing my eyes and wincing at the cramps in my hips and shoulders. Quickly I stowed my blanket in my marching pack and threw the still warm woollen cloak that had recently served as a pillow around my shoulders. Treading precariously between the tight packed bodies, I made my way towards the ladder, ready for the clean morning air up top. The thickening stink below decks of vomit and stale bodies, and of damp leather and wool was now capable of turning even the strongest of stomachs. Even the draughts, whistling through the ship, seemed incapable of purging the rancid air. Men had lain around all night belching, puking and farting, constantly contributing to the foul, gut-churning mixture of odours building within the belly of the vessel. Though, through it all, Aebutius seemed oblivious to the stink. He sat, propped against the ribs of the ship, scoffing great chunks of bread dipped in oil.

"Good morrow, citizen!" He smiled cheerfully as I passed, offering me a piece of the dripping bread. "Here, get that inside you. A man needs to start the day with good food."

I felt my stomach muscles tighten with an involuntary spasm and waved the bread away as I passed him. He may have been right, but to start loading my stomach with food just then may perhaps have been pushing my luck a little too far. I mounted the ladder to the upper deck, clambering up the slippery wooden rungs into the grey drizzly morning. The stout old warship pitched and rolled on the waves, confirming that my decision not to try the bread just yet was perhaps a sound one. Although, I immediately began to feel better as the fresh sea air entered my lungs.

All around Sea Snake, as far as I could see was the vast invasion fleet, spread out upon the heaving, grey ocean. Vessels of varying shapes, sizes and functions each flew pennants on their stern, identifying the units they were transporting. This would be an important detail when landing in the correct order, once we reached our destination. The rolling grey clouds were full of rain but for now, we only experienced a heavy drizzle. The air was of a reasonable temperature for the middle of spring and it occurred to me that, if the day's conditions did not worsen, we would be well placed to make a successful landing without any great loss to shipping or cargo.

Many of my comrades had now made their way onto the open deck, milling around and getting in the way of Captain Cornelius' crew when Fatalis emerged from below decks with Mestrius. The Optio pointed to a small group of soldiers and barked his orders at them;

"Everybody on deck now, go and get the rest of 'em

up here. Snap to it!"

The handful of men scattered and quickly disappeared down hatches. Soon shouts could be heard below us and the remainder of our century began to surface from the hatches onto the rolling deck. Men grimaced against the cold spray on weary, newly woken faces, whilst others went straight for the rails and instantly threw up over the side. The mariners continued with their tasks, grinning at the weak stomachs of some of their passengers as the men assembled, facing the stern where Fatalis stood talking to Mestrius.

"Right men, listen to me," commanded the Centurion, shouting above the sound of the ocean breaking against the hull and the thump of the gusting wind slapping the sails. "Captain Cornelius informs me that in a couple of hours we should reach our landing sites. We can then leave the sailing to the navy and finally get our arses off this old bucket to stand on solid ground once more. Assuming that you haven't all puked yourselves unconscious by then, I expect us all to get ashore like organised fighting men. Not like something resembling a pack of blundering simpletons!"

Although the last remark did raise a few subdued laughs, it also seemed to act as a prompt as several more men made for the rails and heaved their guts loudly over the side of the ship. Ignoring the plight of the stricken men, Fatalis looked out over our assembled heads, bracing his legs for balance on the rolling ship.

"Remember; once the ship beaches you are just to concern yourself with the business of getting ashore ready to fight. I do not expect to see any of you floundering around in the sea and losing equipment as you land." he warned us sternly. "If you are near the Scorpione crew, you will assist them ashore with the weapon. And know you, if you drown amongst all this, then forging new acquaintances with Pluto and Proserpina will not be your only problem. You know I hate men deserting their posts without permission so I assure you; I will track you down in the afterlife and beat the shit out of you when I finally get there."

We laughed more convincingly at this as Fatalis waved us silent once more to finish what he was saying.

"The role of the XIIII Gemina is to immediately engage any enemy that we encounter upon landing," he informed us. "When you are ashore, you will form the Century in extended line and move to join the rest of the Cohort. If we are attacked, then remain calm, look for the standards and listen for the sound of the Cornu. You will not advance until Legate Sabinus has landed behind us and we can protect him, clear?"

"Yes Centurio." we shouted in unison.

"Good, now, make sure your kit is prepared and ready," he told us. "I want all of your equipment on deck in an hour. In the meantime, eat and drink as much as you can. I am sure that yet more of you will want to part company with it very quickly but you must try. Neither Gods nor Generals have confided in me regarding what we will find when we get there. Whatever it is though, I want you all to have the strength to deal with it. Oh, and when you are fully armoured, stay away from the rails while we are in deep water. The sailors tell me it's a long way to the bottom and I don't want any of you men finding out just how far."

With that he turned, speaking briefly to Mestrius, before going back below decks.

Presently, the others joined me on deck, where we ate in the fresh air. For most of us it was the first meal of the day, but for the ever hungry Aebutius it was yet another opportunity to top up his perpetually empty stomach.

A little later, we saw black headed gulls skimming the surface of the waves. One of the sailors told us that it would not be long now. So we sat on the deck, passing the time in idle chatter but fully armoured and equipped by now, waiting expectantly for the word to finally make ready. For a while we were quiet, just listening to the hiss of the spray covering the deck and the crash of the bow cutting the waves. Though it seemed as though we had made a new friend as Batiatus had sought us out once more and sat whiling away the crossing with us.

We talked of the past. We recalled our friends, families and homelands and all the things we had done since joining the legion. We spoke of comrades we had lost and actions we had fought. And yet, I do not think any of us actually mentioned what we were about to do. Our minds were elsewhere, wondering perhaps if we would ever see home again.

"And what of you then Batiatus?" enquired Crispus. "How is it that you came to leave the legion? Had you served your time then?"

The question seemed to prompt a series of quick and uneasy glances, shot between Marinus, Zenas and Batiatus. Batiatus glanced briefly downwards before addressing the question with a long sigh.

"Would that it was that uncomplicated." he paused once more, a vaguely sad look on his raddled old face. "Look, you fellows are a tight bunch and, that aside; you're led by one of my oldest comrades. You also serve with these two old scrappers." He nodded at Zenas and Marinus before continuing:

"After all of my years in the ranks, I know who I can trust and I sense now that I can trust you boys. Secrets are best kept at times, and at others they should be shared, if only to release old friends from the burden of having to keep them for you too. Zenas and Marinus have told you nothing, and I'm grateful to them for it, but perhaps the time has now come for you to know this. I need to feel like I belong again lads, and I hope by telling you this I will gain your trust and you will honour me with your friendship."

By now Batiatus had well and truly captured our interest and we had closed in around him. Like a gaggle of gossiping washer women, we were hanging on his words and eager to know more, sensing that this would be no ordinary tale. Presently, he continued:

"Ademetus and..."

"What, our Camp Prefect Ademetus?" interrupted Surus.

"Yes, yes. That's the one." Zenas answered irritatedly for Batiatus.

"...Ademetus, Fatalis and I were Centurions in the same Cohort and stationed together in Mogontiacum. Well, Ademetus hails from quite an influential family and I'll always maintain that he got where he is today through his family business connections to the then Legate, Valens. Oh I'll not deny he was a good soldier. You can't command men at that level without talent, but I don't think his ability was a great as some folks cracked on it was. More to the point, I never really saw the proof of it either."

Sensing that the story was about to take an even more intriguing turn and drawn by the fact that it involved Ademetus, one of the most powerful officers in the legion, we drew even closer to Batiatus. We held our silence as Batiatus related his story in a frank but matter of fact way. He spared no detail in telling his tale. At its end we knew pretty much all there was to know about how an experienced centurion with many years good service left to go, was eventually forced to choose to leave behind the life he so loved, or die trying to hold onto it.

At the heart of it all was a woman - Flavia Severina. Then twenty years old, she was the daughter of the local magistrate, Claudius Rufus Severinus, and she was beautiful. Severinus had been a centurion in the legion too but had retired some years previously and made his fortune from what were rumoured to be less than legitimate dealings in precious metals. Nevertheless, he had become a solid member of the community and had eventually found his way into local politics in Mogontiacum. Though, despite his new found status, like all old soldiers, he found it hard to sever the ties with his old legion, maintaining social links with the Centurionate in which he once served.

Subsequently, he attended anniversary celebrations with his family for such things as famous actions the legion had taken part in and also the feast days for the various religious festivals. It was at one such occasion that Batiatus had initially met the girl who would first claim his heart and later be responsible for almost breaking it.

Batiatus, it had to be said, was never a popular choice of suitor for Flavia. His family were leather merchants by profession and lacked the heavy weight connections that Severinus would have wanted for a potential suitor of his only daughter. Ademetus on the other hand, had family ties to the local senate that were in turn tenuously linked to influential clans in Rome itself. His family were old established horse traders who had secured some lucrative contracts to supply the military in that part of Germania Superior. However, as a member of a Plebeian family,

Ademetus could never have walked straight into a young officer's post in the legion. But, credit to him, he had joined as a legionary and worked his way up the ranks to the Centurionate. Although, it had to be said that the money and connections backing him would certainly seem to have accelerated his rise through the ranks.

Now, twenty years on, it seemed that Fortuna had smiled broadly on him. He had soared through the ranks to achieve the post of Camp Prefect, second only to the Legate in seniority. While Batiatus had walked away from perhaps what could have been a great career, Ademetus had flourished, with many quietly suggesting that good fortune had only a little to do with it.

It was the summer of the year of the Consuls Gaius Asinius Pollio and Gaius Antistius Vetus. By then love had grown for Batiatus and Flavia and he had asked her father for her hand in marriage, Severinus however had refused the match. As it turned out, Severinus had already arranged her betrothal to Ademetus in an effort to forge political links with the Roman families that Ademetus was becoming connected to. For his part, Ademetus was completely smitten by Flavia and would do anything to have her. Flavia on the other hand, loathed the very ground that Ademetus walked on and flatly refused to marry him.

The family row that had erupted only served to cause Flavia to despise Ademetus even more, driving her further into the arms of Batiatus. Despite the best efforts of Severinus to part his daughter from the rejected suitor, the couple always found a way to meet each other. Inevitably, the thing that would cause things to finally come crashing down around their ears happened. Flavia fell pregnant.

Amidst the subsequent scandal and recriminations it was rumoured that her mother, Rufilia, had taken pity on her daughter and sent her away before her father could punish her. She knew that as Pater Familias, his role as head of the family was absolute. If he felt compelled to do so, he had the right to take her life for bringing such terrible shame on his family's good name.

To this day it seems nobody ever knew exactly what had happened to Flavia. Though most, having no information to the contrary, held the view that she and her unborn child had been done away with. Severinus forbade his surviving family ever to mention Flavia's name again and immediately dedicated himself to ruining Batiatus' reputation and career. The combined efforts and connections of Severinus and Ademetus had soon made his position in the legion very unstable. The loss of his beloved Flavia had made Batiatus vulnerable. He knew that he would not be able to fend off many more attempts to kill him than the two that had quickly followed the disappearance of Flavia.

Batiatus and Fatalis had once been the first men over the rampart of a powerful tribal king's great stockade in the territory of the Suebi. Unusually, both had earned the coveted Rampart Crown for their gallantry that day. Such bravery is a quality which is long celebrated and their actions have lived in the memory for many years. Indeed, it was because Batiatus' record as a soldier was built on deeds such as this that the legate, Valens, was prompted to make the extraordinary decision to petition the then Emperor, Tiberius; to release Batiatus from his service and allow him to leave the legion early.

Valens it seems, had a particular disdain for the toadying and social climbing of Ademetus and Severinus, but he also recognised that he could not intervene in the matter of family honour. As a result, Batiatus was not safe. It seems Valens did not relish the thought of one of his finest soldiers being killed like a dog after such an illustrious career. So, he did the only thing he could to give a loyal and courageous soldier the chance to survive and make a new life.

Batiatus' men hated it. But they would have hated it even more if he had ended up murdered and they would probably have then sought revenge for the death. Valens could not afford to see his legion fractured by internecine score settling. This way, it was better for all.

"You once mentioned being set upon by bandits on the way here," ventured Pacatianus.

"What's your point lad?" Batiatus queried.

"They weren't ordinary bandits were they?" Pacatianus shared his thoughts via the question he posed.

"No, as you suspect, they were paid as assassins and hired by Ademetus and Severinus." Batiatus shrugged his shoulders and gave a short low laugh.

"Those two never seemed to have too much of a clue about what makes a good fighting man," he grinned. "Otherwise they'd have spent their coin on something better than a bunch of piss stinking, wine soaked, Gallic brigands. Those daft bastards hardly knew one end of a sword from another. They all spent far too much time dancing around trying to kill the party of merchants I was with, instead of concentrating their efforts on the real threat, me!"

He laughed again as he briefly re-lived the scene in his mind's eye.

"Once I'd walked away from that I realised that my trail was now cold and I could go where I liked. So, I picked up my things and just carried on until I got to the coast. And there I stayed until you lot washed up on my doorstep."

"What about Ademetus?" asked Surus. "Does he know you're alive now?"

"He knows." Batiatus' reply was delivered in a calm dispassionate tone as we took in the gravity of our association with Batiatus.

"Besides," he continued. "I personally never gave them any reason to think that their half arsed bunch of would-be killers actually did for me like they were supposed to. The thought that those two idiots had maybe spent all these years wondering over just what happened to me has long been compensation for the times when I'd yearned to return and knew that I could not."

"But you're back now." Crispus pointed out.

"What choice did I have? The Legion found me once more and I was granted an opportunity to face things on my own terms. Besides, I ran once in my life. That was more than enough. Whatever happens from here will finish it for all time and I'm prepared to take my chances - especially if I can call you all comrades and friends."

I banished the thought that, by telling us all this, Batiatus had cynically attempted to rope us into becoming his own personal bodyguard and instead addressed what I considered to be the one, as yet, outstanding question:

"And what about you, Batiatus? What do you think happened to Flavia?"

High in the ships rigging a sailor shouted out above the slapping of the billowing sail and the alert instantly ended the conversation as we sprang up to look for the sighted land.

"Land. Land rising, on the western horizon!"

Captain Cornelius was directing the steersman when he heard the cry and responded immediately.

"Gather the canvas, prepare to go to oars!"

Several sailors mounted the rigging and climbed swiftly for the top of the rolling mast while another shouted down the deck hatch to those below.

"Oarsmen to posts, stand by!"

The ship seemed to suddenly swarm with activity. I

became aware of distant shouts echoing over the waves as other crews reacted to the sighting of land and made their own preparations for the approach. I looked out over the side and saw sails being taken in and signallers mounting the high sterns of their vessels, beginning to send messages with their flags. Other vessels too were putting out oars, ready to strike out for shore. Presently I heard clunks and scrapes over the side of our ship as three banks of our own oars appeared on the side nearest me. The blades were then poised horizontally for the order to row, ready to plunge into the water and propel us to shore with powerful strokes.

All of us now peered out to where the sailor had indicated, trying to catch our first glimpse of Britannia. As the flapping sail was gathered in, exposing a better view of the horizon, we glimpsed it for the first time.

'There!' We shouted and pointed.

Gesturing excitedly at the distant stretch of coast and looking backwards and forwards at each other, the misty strip of coastline gradually started to gain more substance in the drizzly haze hanging over the sea. No Roman army had seen this place for nearly a hundred years. Now we were back, determined that it be taken, for the glory of the Emperor and the people of Rome. It began to grow in the distance as I watched. The coast began to rise up before us as the sail was taken in and the triple banks of oars began to slice the surface of the sea with rhythmic strokes.

Our ship was part of a great group of sleek, fast warships that struck out for shore first. As Fatalis had reminded us, we were going to be first ashore in this wave and the rest would follow. I looked behind me, seeing the distance between ourselves and the transports increasing rapidly. A second fleet of vessels followed behind, along with a group of broad beamed barges, which probably held cavalry to reinforce the horsemen already landed with the first ships. Signals were now passing between the ships all the time as the land drew nearer. Fatalis re-appeared and made his way to the front of the ship and shouted back;

"Fetch the Scorpione to the front and as many bolts as you can carry." he ordered. "Make ready. Prepare to give cover, as and when directed!"

The crew of the light artillery piece ran forward and placed the tripod stand on the deck, quickly setting the body in place before setting the weapon up, priming it ready to shoot. As the galley surged forward, the sound of our Scorpione being cranked back was joined by the distant clatter of ratchets from similar weapons being readied on surrounding vessels. The loader placed a stout, iron tipped bolt in the slide, then set about searching for likely target areas on the far off shore, whilst the trigger man waited for his orders.

As the land grew closer, I noticed that we were heading towards a wide inlet. Signal fires blazed on either side of the mouth, directing the approaching ships to the landing area. Already, a large number of Roman ships were already moored in the channel. Fatalis jumped up by the Scorpione and spread his arms wide;

"Form double lines, either side of the ship. Be ready to file towards the front and the gaps on the rail." As he instructed us, the sailors lifted sections out of the rail on each side, which would enable us to jump swiftly from the ship.

"The ship will beach in shallow water. As soon as we hit, move fast and make for the beach." he shouted. "Form the defensive line as soon as you have enough dry beach then look for the standards, understood?"

"Yes Centurio!"

We roared the reply and I knew that I could not be the only soldier whose heart was pounding now. My senses surged with the energy of impending combat as I gripped my sword hilt and faced the nearing shore as we drew closer to the mouth of the channel. In a few brief moments we had entered the inlet, sailing a short way up the centre until we approached another signal fire on a large outcrop of land on our left. Again, I looked either side of me. I was awed at the speed at which we were closing with the land and watched the other galleys slicing through the water, their compliment of soldiers poised on the decks as we were. Soon enough the beach appeared before us, growing more distinct with each oar stroke, until I heard the shout from Cornelius;

"Raise oars!"

Abruptly, the oars completed their stroke and rose horizontally, pausing for the next order. Quickly, the follow up was issued;

"Ship oars!"

At this, all oars withdrew and the ships glided towards the shore under their own momentum. Fatalis placed one foot on the bow, leaning forward to see over the side as the waters grew ever shallower on the approach to the beach. He raised his hand above his head, poised to motion us on as the gap closed between ship and shore. It was then I noticed that the area around the great signal fire was occupied by many men. Roman troops moved all over the outcrop of land, busying themselves in the preparation of defences over a wide area, securing the ground that had already been taken. Deflated, I realised there would be no great battle for the shoreline this day.

"Get ready. Brace yourselves!" warned Fatalis, his hand dropping to his side as the prow drove itself into the soft, silty beach. We lurched forward as one and then recovered our balance, ready to move.

"Off. Off!" Ordered Fatalis, sweeping both hands forward and motioning us to move off the sides of the beached vessel, into the breaking waves.

We surged across the deck and jumped from the ship into the waist deep water, forging through the waves and foam to make dry land. At last, my feet were planted on the soil of Britannia. In an instant, we formed an extended line as instructed and sought out the standards. Three clear blasts from a Cornu alerted us to its presence and Fatalis wasted no time in moving us into formation.

"Battle line," he ordered. "Quick time, advance!"

The whole Century trotted up the beach in extended formation as Fatalis strode out in front of us. As we drew level with the standards he turned us, halting us squarely behind them. In a very short space of time, the whole Cohort was formed up, awaiting orders - eager to battle an enemy who was as yet, nowhere to be seen. There was no time to waste. If the enemy had chosen not to engage us then we were to make good use of the time we had.

We were immediately directed to join troops from the first wave, assisting them in constructing vast defences that would secure our foothold on the coast. We soon found that in the immediate absence of any real opposition, Plautius would make capital from the lack of defenders, sending Vespasian south with II Augusta and a force of Auxiliaries. They would win control of the land along the coast, securing yet more safe anchorages.

Across the inlet where the great fleet was now moored lay a small island, familiar as yet only to traders and sailors. This was called Tanatus Insula. Legend had it, the Greeks knew of it too. They believed that the isle they called Ynys Thanatos was actually the island of the dead where, in the middle of the night, the bodies of the recently departed were rowed across the black waters for burial. The XX

Valeria and accompanying units had landed there now, spreading out from the landing point and pacifying what few folk dwelt on the island so that it could be used as an offshore supply base. Once the island was secure, any attackers would have to cross the narrow channel to retake it. It would make an ideal offshore stronghold that was easy to defend, supply and reinforce.

Now that Rome had set foot on its shores and a powerful army held the island under its boot, any further thoughts of its mystical and dread past seemed to evaporate as fast as the morning mists.

So much for ancient Greek ghost stories.

CHAPTER 9

For five days we remained in the area of the landings. Fortifications were raised and improved whilst cavalry ranged about the area, hunting out enemy forces. Batiatus was given command of a group of cavalry scouts and spent much of his time away from the camp. I for one was glad of this as none of us yet knew what would happen when he and Ademetus finally met once more.

It was a difficult position for us. We were loyal to the Legate and standards, but Batiatus had endeared himself to each one of us. I had modified my earlier view of his motivations for befriending us. I knew now that he was just a soldier who wanted to be in the company of other soldiers once more. We were connected to his past by who we served with and he felt able to trust us because of it. Nevertheless, I knew that our association with him could bring trouble.

Within range of our fortifications lay several small settlements. These belonged to the Cantiaci, natives who lived mostly in simple farming communities. They were made up of folk who worked the land to survive. Caring little for politics or warfare; they could tell us nothing of what we might face, but their elders would recite to us the tales their Druids told of the history of their land. Just as Narcissus had told us back in Portus Itius, they still recalled the time when

Caesar had come to their lands. They warned us that now, as it was then, fierce tribes would attack from the west and try to destroy us if we remained.

It was nothing personal. They had no particular argument with Rome. After all, their chiefs had traded with us for years. No, their loyalties lay more with Adminius, prince of Cantium. He had followed us back over the sea to reclaim his tribal seat after begging Rome for help against his brothers, Caratacus and Togodumnus. Once we had re-installed him in his tribal seat he would keep order with his people, serving Rome like the good puppet he had sworn to become.

A few days after landing, Batiatus and his scouts had captured a handful of native riders which he believed were scouting for a bigger war band close by. We had stood around laughing and jeering as the Quaestionarii had subsequently set to work upon the six captive Britons.

At first the prisoners withstood the kickings and beatings. Then their inquisitors re-doubled their efforts. They began instead to flay the skin off their backs with whips and scourges and break their bones with clubs and staves.

We sank wine and swapped observations as the Britons' tormentors beat the soles of their feet with iron rods, cheering along those captives who we had laid bets on to hold out longest. We modified our wagers to include which of them would die first as their agonised screams rang around the camp. To the disgust of Surus, Pacatianus and Marinus, the three they had bet on were the first to expire from the shock and pain of the torture. The other three finally began to sing like birds and it was then that we solved the riddle of why there had been no army to meet us. Through ragged, burst lips and shattered teeth, the half dead Britons mumbled out their explanation to their tormentors.

In the early spring, a mighty force of united tribes had indeed been present in the area, waiting eagerly to repel any Roman force that attempted to land. Soon though, word had arrived that, although a great Roman army sat just across the sea in Gaul, it was in the midst of a mutiny and refusing to cross the water to their land.

The two warlord brothers, Caratacus and Togodumnus, were commanding the defending army of some one hundred thousand men and were spoiling for a fight with the empire they so despised. Once they had heard of the mutiny in Portus Itius, they had wrongly surmised that the invasion would not come to pass and dispersed their forces inland. Their big mistake though, was that they had failed to wait for further word from their spies informing them of the dispersal of the Roman army.

Now, to compound the error, it was proving extremely difficult to re-muster the forces previously at their disposal. Many of the warriors had split up and made long journeys back to their tribal territories. Recalling them to arms was proving extremely difficult.

Ironic then, to think that we once so feared invading this land and that by voicing that fear so loudly, we had effectively given ourselves the best possible advantage.

The two brothers had made a bad error of judgement but it was certain they would eventually reform their forces and attack us as soon as they were able. Their father, Cunobelin, had seized control of great tracts of land before his death, creating a huge kingdom that he and his sons ruled with an iron hand. Indeed, it was Cantium that Cunobelin had turned over to his eldest son Adminius and which would now be the first of the cantons to be pacified by Rome. Nevertheless, Togodumnus and Caratacus would not sit idly by and let Rome threaten their birthright without a full scale war. For the brothers, the coming storm would not only be a struggle for their survival, but for their very way of life.

Scouting parties were already returning with news that hostile forces were moving across the countryside, driving livestock far away from us and destroying grain reserves to deny us food. Time was now against us and Plautius would have to march us inland or lose his advantage.

Finally, we marched from the landing areas and drove westwards. Legionary cavalry swept the ground before us, hunting for armed opposition and opportunities to seize food supplies. As we marched, we came across farming settlements, villages and isolated homes. Places which were populated by simple people, who had never seen such a sight as that which marched through their homelands now. Those that had remained in their homes regarded us with a mixture of bewilderment and awe. I knew then that Mars the lord of war now walked the land and theirs was an entirely unhappy position. Now they had been cast headlong into the terrible bystanders game of chance and misfortune that came with armed conflict.

These peasants were the innocents; those who would suffer most for the ambitions of powerful men. These pathetic wretches had managed to preserve some of their supplies against the pillaging of their own kind as their army sought out food. Now, they had to surrender it to us. For many of these people death would soon come as a consequence, heralding its arrival with protruding ribs, parchment thin skin and dull sunken eyes. One by one, they would be forced to lie down and give up on a world they had never really had a stake in.

As we passed the small settlements along the way, we saw the children standing at the side of the ancient track ways, watching us as we marched ever deeper into their land. They would stand at the side of the column, staring at the vast army as it marched indifferently past their homes. The innocent eyes of these children, staring from filth smeared faces, had not the first clue about what was happening to their land.

Long ago, it seems, I saw the same eyes staring from the faces of two boys as they watched their father and the legion march out. They, and the rest of the children of Mogontiacum though, had not been watched over by parents who knew that savage, brutal warfare was about to rock their world.

I never questioned for a moment why we were there, or what we had to do to achieve our ends. It was our duty as Romans to bring law and civilization to lands such as these. For centuries it had been so, and for centuries it would continue. This land would benefit from our coming and thrive in the coming generations, just as many other lands had before it. All they had to do was submit.

When I was first trained as a legionary, I was told that we were the weapon wielded by the hand of Rome and the emperor. Nothing had changed since that day. If the emperor ordered us to wipe out such people as these, then so be it. In my time as a legionary I had borne witness to the killing of innocents. I had put to the sword those enemies who opposed the will of Rome. I had driven nails deep into the living flesh of criminals and subversives. Though I had the capacity for compassion, pity and mercy, I recognised always that war was played by different rules. Moreover, in time of war, my actions could not be governed by thought or feelings; just orders, cold, unbending discipline, and duty; nothing more.

Though as the mighty Roman war machine passed

by the gawping children of this new land, this Britannia, I could not help but think that the gods of our world were truly cruel.

CHAPTER 10

The night was clear. A bright moon hung in the sky, bathing the tops of the vast rows of tents with a pale wash of silvery light. I shifted on the soles of my feet, allowing the blood to circulate and shrugged my shoulders to ease the stiffness that comes with standing guard for long periods. Aebutius and I silently flanked the opening to Sabinus' command tent, doing our best to stay close to the braziers that glowed close by. Inside the huge, house-like leather tent, Sabinus, Ademetus and Batiatus discussed what would be our first major battle with the forces of the two brothers. Outside, we each cocked an ear for news of what we were about to undertake.

Batiatus had only just returned from a mission to gather intelligence about the enemy force that had now been located just outside the Cantiaci's tribal capital of Durovernon. The distraction from the monotony of guard duty was too hard to resist. Aebutius and I listened eagerly as Batiatus relayed his observations to the Legate and his Prefect.

"It's as I thought I'd find them Legate. They are massed outside the eastern defences of the town and assembling their army while they wait for us." Batiatus delivered his appraisal in a frank, straightforward manner. "They'll wait for us to go there because they want to fight us on a ground of their choosing."

Although I could only hear and not actually witness the conversation, I was easily able to picture the scene as Batiatus passed on his news. I knew Sabinus and his ways and I knew all of his staff. I knew that now he would be pawing scrolls and analysing what maps he had to try to visualise the ground as he took the news on board. Close by would be Ademetus, sat on a stool no doubt and rubbing his chin as usual as he stared into a wine cup, absorbing every bit of intelligence that Batiatus was feeding them.

"You're sure that there are no other large assemblies in the area?" queried Ademetus.

"I sent eight parties of four in different directions and ordered them to sweep the ground, Prefect. They all returned safely with nothing to report. I'm confident that what I've seen is all we will face if we move on them soon."

I heard a 'hmm' from Ademetus and was again able to picture him in my mind's eye, swigging from his beaker and rubbing his chin a little harder.

"What is their strength Batiatus?" asked Sabinus.

"I would say they number around twenty thousand, Legate."

"Twenty thousand you say?" Ademetus queried the assessment. "We expected them to be able to put many more on the field than that. Indeed, our spies told us that over eighty thousand were waiting for us in early spring alone."

"This is true, Prefect." Batiatus replied patiently.

"But you must remember that the original army at their disposal has now dispersed. Their leaders are having trouble in mustering them again"

"I should, should I Batiatus," snapped Ademetus. "What I do remember is that the intelligence you speak of is now a number of days old and our enemies could by now have mustered many more warriors to attack us with."

I could hear the restraint in Batiatus' voice as he responded to Ademetus' point.

"With respect, Prefect, I do not see that these barbarian princes are anywhere near capable of regrouping their allies that quickly in just a few short days."

I clearly heard the contradiction of Ademetus' assessment of the time scale and knew that even now, Ademetus would be starting to boil. I fervently hoped that Batiatus had not over stepped the mark and rattled Sabinus too with such an open slight. I listened keenly as Batiatus carried on with his assessment.

"Again, with respect, Prefect, I would agree with your view, if it appeared that these people were capable of fielding a tighter army than they actually seem able to. As far as I can see, their armies are no different to formations we have fought in Germania and beyond with only a nucleus of trained warriors, backed by poorly equipped client levy's. If we faced a more organised foe then I would concur with your assessment. But clearly, we don't"

I sensed that Sabinus would now be preparing to

intervene in the debate that was now beginning to bubble between the two. As though confirming my view, I heard his voice cut into the conversation.

"Good comrades, skilled and wise counsel that you both are, there is clearly a difference of opinion between you both but mark me now, the point you dispute is not relevant at this time."

"How so, Legate?" queried Ademetus. "Surely their ability to bring more troops to the field is crucial to how we form our battle strategy."

"Not so, Ademetus," the Legate replied. "Batiatus has already stated that he has swept the land for their forces and found none. Even if there were reinforcements on their way, Batiatus has reassured me sufficiently that they will not reach Durovernon before we can mount an attack."

"But, Legate…" Ademetus was beginning to sound incredulous now. "Whilst I acknowledge that Batiatus has an illustrious service record - that was twenty years ago. Much can be quickly forgotten about the business of soldiering. I fear we place too much reliance on him before he has fully recalled his skills."

"You need not question my competence Ademetus." snapped Batiatus "For the twenty years I have been gone, I have forgotten nothing!"

The last words were delivered like the crack of a whip. I feared that I would soon be called inside by the Legate to part the two men from setting about each other as long dormant animosities boiled up from the past once more.

"Enough!" barked Sabinus. "Batiatus, you forget who you speak to. Ademetus is Prefect of this legion and should be addressed as such. Ademetus, perhaps Batiatus has developed a few rough edges which will need smoothing as we go, but I trust his judgement. If I did not he would not be getting one coin of either mine or the senate's war chest."

"Now, Batiatus, speak to me of their disposition once more. You say they hold their chosen ground. Can we allow them the luxury of fighting them on it?

Instantly the mood had turned. Both men realised that the mutual loathing that had begun to eat away at them once more would have to wait a little longer before it was finally allowed to come to a head. It was as if the tension in the tent had never been as Batiatus explained the position.

"If the Britons remain in their current position, I am confident that we can break them in a morning. They do not fight the Roman way. They are undisciplined in their movements. They cannot fight heavily armoured formations as they have no experience of such and their positions will allow us to hit them like a landslide with a downhill charge. With some refinements to the current battle plan I guarantee that our first major battle with the Britons will bring us victory."

"You are a confident man indeed to make such a pledge, Batiatus. But what of their chariots?" asked Ademetus. "The use of those things even tested

Caesars men. Do they have any at Durovernon?"

"Very few, Prefect. As I mentioned, with a few refinements to the plan we can take care of such things before they are allowed to take proper effect."

"Excellent!" enthused Sabinus. "In the morning we will adjust our plan but for now, we should sleep. Ademetus, you have been planning without sleep for nearly three days now. Batiatus, you have spent the same in the saddle to bring us this news. We have all earned some rest."

I briefly heard the sound of scrolls being re rolled and of other things being put away for the night before the flaps of the tent swung open and Batiatus and Ademetus stepped into the chill of the night air. Batiatus stood next to one of the braziers rubbing his hands as Ademetus turned for his tent next to Sabinus'.

"I'll bid you good night then, Prefect," said Batiatus in a cordial yet insincere tone. "Sleep well, for we have much to do on the morrow."

Ademetus turned; a faintly menacing grin appeared on his face as he reciprocated the pleasantry with his old rival with equal insincerity. In the meantime, I did my best to look utterly disinterested in the two men's conversation.

"Yes, you too, Batiatus."

He turned and began to make for his tent before looking over his shoulder once more.

"Oh Batiatus, you will take care how you go from now on won't you? The enemy is a lot closer these days and I find that I am becoming concerned for your safety."

With that, the Prefect ducked into his tent. Batiatus paused, grinning briefly at me before turning away from the warmth of the brazier and quietly making for his own bed.

CHAPTER 11

The morning after saw our camp bustling with activity. Hundreds of tents were packed up and all of the paraphernalia associated with a legion on the move was either loaded onto lines of wagons pulled by oxen, or lashed to scores of mules and pack horses. The air was filled with the clangour of equipment being moved. Men shouted out both orders and profanities in equal measure as the XIIII Gemina prepared to march towards its first great battle with the waiting Britons.

Sabinus and Ademetus stood around a table, oblivious to the bustle, refining their battle plan with the legion Tribunes and senior Centurions as the great command tent was packed away around them. Batiatus had already left before sunrise to make a final assessment of the waiting enemy.

I knew from the conversation I had heard from inside the command tent the night before that it was now time for the next piece of the campaign plan to be put into place. The Cantiaci had shown virtually no opposition to the landings in their territory. Capital would now need to be made from their apparent acquiescence.

I had already learned that one of our tasks would be to return Adminius to the heart of the kingdom of Cantium, a place where he could best be used to influence his subjects. That heart would be Durovernon and the town now lay very close by, just a little less than a day's march inland. Batiatus' reconnaissance had confirmed this. It was located on reasonably flat ground, close to areas of thick woodland and swamps, limiting the ways that reinforcements could arrive by to strengthen the native army.

The marching itself was easy enough. The countryside rolled gently and we used many of the ancient track ways that had been established by the Britons generations ago. Though, as we marched for Durovernon we had made our first acquaintances with small parties of Britons. Rather than keep a discrete distance and an eye on us, they had preferred instead to test our reflexes on a number of occasions. Predictably, they always emerged from behind natural features at short distances, striking swiftly in an attempt to panic the column and disrupt the formations. Their efforts had seemed almost comic to us, given that they had never encountered anything like a Roman army before. Their futile attempts to inject panic into the column had ended up costing them dear.

They would generally attack the sides of the column in an attempt to break the line, but always without success. The Britons preferred to swoop down using war chariots and horsemen in fast moving raids. The riders would hurtle fearlessly down on us wielding long iron swords, which they flourished enthusiastically above their heads. They also carried long spears that they twirled above their heads as they rushed in, screaming their war cries. Instantly, our lines would react, turning to meet them and closing up as a tight packed formation to meet the attack. For all that I recall their efforts as largely ineffectual; I could not help but harbour a grudging admiration for the wild courage they displayed. The hearts of these warriors must have been large indeed to rush in at over five thousand heavily armed soldiers in such woefully small bands. At least this time the rumours we had heard about the courage of these men seemed to have a ring of truth as we finally came to experience our new foes up close for the first time.

In general, they were tall and robust of build. All exhibited an almost unnerving wildness about them. Many rode bareback and wore only a pair of breeches, preferring instead to clothe themselves in intricate swirling designs which they painted onto their bodies with thick blue body paint. They also sported tattoos of a similar style, etched deeply into their skin. Status seemed to be everything with these people and many of them fought wearing heavy gold ornaments round their neck and wrists. This last feature caused much interest in our ranks as it made us even keener to come to grips with them, so that we might have a chance to cut them down and plunder the corpses for their wealth.

To add further to their ferocious image, they often sported thick drooping moustaches and coated their hair with some foul white mixture which they used to set their long locks into hard spikes on top of their heads. Apart from a few I saw clad in mail shirts and helms, they wore little or no armour in battle. Nevertheless, I never saw any of them shy away from a fight. They seemed always to revel in the glory of combat and once stirred to action, could often only be felled by the most mortal of injuries.

Of course it is true that, when a Roman army marches onto the field of battle, it first seeks to intimidate by a display of discipline and organised strength. But, when closing for battle, it also relies heavily on the intense training of each and every man to carry out their orders to the letter. The Britons, I soon learned, were a different animal entirely

Though seemingly caring little for the discipline we were so fond of, the Britons never wasted an opportunity to demonstrate their fighting prowess to us. Everything about the warrior Briton was intended to convey an air of menace and to intimidate their enemies. Perhaps the only piece of accurate information that we had ever been given about Britannia, were when the rumours flew thick and fast back in Portus Itius about these warriors. They were truly formidable in both appearance and skill and never to be taken lightly. When the time came for combat, these men would fight and die hard.

We had not seen a great many of their chariots as yet, but what we had seen of them more than demonstrated the skill and courage of a foe which I for one had quickly developed a healthy respect for. On the occasions that their chariots had so far been used against us, they had always approached at breakneck speed, with much shouting and flourishing of whatever weapons they had to hand.

The chariots themselves were of a light wooden construction. They were of a very low profile and drawn by a pair of short but sturdy horses which seemed bred to possess incredible stamina. Whilst one man drove, another would prepare to attack his foe in various ways. He could choose to engage with sword or spear from the back of the chariot, or even by climbing up the yoke pole and standing between the two horses. Apart from hurling javelins, the warrior had the ability to discharge slings or strike with heavy wooden clubs. When ready to fight on foot, he would dismount in a flash, engage his foe and then remount the chariot, either making good his escape or directing his driver to circle for another attack.

Though for all their skill and courage, these small raiding parties had made little impact on the column. Generally, when the Britons threw their horses and chariots onto our column the first line of troops nearest the threat deployed the anti-cavalry wall. They would drop to their knees behind their shields while the line behind them would throw their shields over the top of the front rank to create a sloping roof. They would then present their javelins to the shoulder, ready to throw. By then, the front line was already bristling with the points of their own javelins as the needle sharp slender iron shafts protruded from behind the shields in a deadly row, like a sharpened iron fence.

Even the hardy ponies of the Britons refused to gallop directly into such a lethal barrier. But, when they foolishly ventured close enough for the rear rank to throw their javelins effectively, the weapons would be cast at them in one devastating wave, which never failed to instantly break the charge.

Inevitably, for all of the attempts by the marauding parties of Britons to disrupt our advance, the march to battle finally came to an end. By the following morning the legion stood before Durovernon, massed in attack formation and waiting to be deployed against a now very visible enemy.

As we drew up in our formations; a wildly defiant and extremely vocal army of thousands stood directly between us and the town in a single great formation that ranged across the rolling meadow land in front of us. Now that they had at last got their chance to confront us close up, they stood resolute, shouting out their hatred, making every kind of obscene gesture. They goaded us to attack as they continually roared defiance and whirled their weapons above their heads.

Durovernon sat behind them. A random collection of different sized round thatched roofs rising from behind the protection of a wooden palisade that sheltered the population within. Wispy grey tendrils of smoke rose from the houses and, to all intents and purposes, it seemed as though the settlement was living through just another ordinary day. The oddly peaceful image it promoted clashed jarringly with the increasingly violent atmosphere that now boiled just beyond its walls. It was as though the town wished to deny the coming battle. It continued instead to occupy its own quiet space in the world, blending in a perfect harmony with its surroundings as though it had seemingly just grown there.

Soon, Vespasian and II Augusta would join us here and we would then push further inland for the great rivers standing between us and our later objectives. But first, we needed to sweep aside the seething mob that now stood before us, bellowing out their defiance.

Sabinus and Ademetus had now modified our battle plan according to Batiatus' information and had arrayed three Auxiliary infantry Cohorts of five hundred men apiece before us. They had also placed a Cohort of five hundred archers on our right flank. With all of the formations now in place, we stood in extended lines along with the second and third Cohorts of the Legion whilst the rest of the XIIII waited behind us in seven vast blocks of men. Two Alae of five hundred cavalry apiece took up position, one on each flank, awaiting their orders. Then, the carefully orchestrated task of drawing the enemy out began.

Once you join in the thick of battle there is no time to stand back and take in all that is going on around you. Once you are in the melee; there is nothing but the exhausting toil of attack and defence, as you cut your way into the tightly packed mass of the enemy army. It was therefore only at the opening phases of the battle that there was any chance to take in the wider picture, so I always liked to take that opportunity to see just exactly how the army commanders played out their opening moves. Thus it was the day we stood before Durovernon.

As we stood in silence I watched intently from inside our formation as, moving in a dense block, the first of the auxiliary infantry Cohorts began their steady advance. They headed away from the extended lines of their comrades and effectively presented themselves as bait in an attempt to coax the great force of Britons out towards them. I could hear the thud of a thousand feet on the ground, the clanking and jingling of equipment as the formation advanced. The gap between them and the enemy gradually began to reduce.

Now, the Britons saw what Sabinus had intended for them to see. Eager to engage the invaders, they instantly seized on the opportunity to destroy the small force and rapidly began to move forwards in one great formation. Confident of being able to wipe out such a small contingent, they streamed forth, howling and shouting as they came.

As the Britons committed to their charge, I joined in with the rest of the Cohort in yelling out a well-used repertoire of choice insults. We mocked the Britons for their stupid impetuosity, before we began to cheer loudly, striking up a thunderous banging on our shields. Thousands of Britons descended in a hectic rush on the small, tight auxiliary formation, still not realising for even one second that this small force was never going to fight them alone in a suicidal head on clash.

Suddenly, the auxiliaries broke formation and swung sideways, beginning to run hard now for the left flank, furthest away from the Britons. On the right flank, as the native formation faltered briefly, struggling to make sense of the manoeuvre, there instantly rose a great, densely packed cloud of arrows. Seeing their killing ground now clear of friendly forces, our Hamian archers launched a hail of lethal shafts at the shocked Britons. Never before had these Britons seen what a bow made in the hot dusty lands of the Levant was capable of. They would never have known that it could shoot almost twice the range of their own bows, or that the highly trained bowmen wielding it could put as many as another two arrows into the air, before their first had even struck its mark. To their further horror, they would also soon come to realise that they were sorely mistaken in their apparent earlier belief that they were well out of range of the archers as the rapidly rising cloud of shafts hit the peak of their climb before falling down upon them with lethal precision.

In my career I had watched the Hamians deal their own particular brand of death many times before.

Still, no matter how many times I witnessed the carnage that they could wreak on the enemy, I always shuddered as the first wave of arrows tore into their targets. I also always thanked the Gods that I didn't have to experience what the enemy was experiencing. There was just something about the whole thing that filled me with a peculiar sense of dread; to be so appallingly helpless and having absolutely no choice other than to brace yourself as a huge shower of arrows fell upon you. All the time you must be praying that one or more of those deadly shafts didn't have your name on it. No, give me a face to face fight over that every time.

As I watched the swarm of arrows fall upon the Britons, the first agonised screams of wounded and dying men rang out across the field as the projectiles pierced their marks. Soon enough, the Britons started to fall en masse in a chaotic tangle of thrashing limbs. Even then, as the native army began to think about retreating back out of range of the aerial threat, the cavalry poised on the left flank set off at a gallop.

They moved swiftly behind them, effectively cutting off any chance to return to the town.

As the thunderous noise of 500 cavalry commencing their advance alerted me to the next phase of the battle plan commencing, the archers halted their deadly accurate delivery of arrows into the tormented, howling mob. I watched, appreciative of their skill as the mass of cavalry swarmed at their rear. Quickly, they began to drive the whole lot forward towards the waiting Auxiliaries, treating the Britons almost as though they were merely an unruly flock of sheep about to be herded to the slaughter.

Their ill-considered and undisciplined charge soon began to crumble in panic. The Britons started to break away towards the right flank, only to be intercepted by the second Roman cavalry formation.

Instantly, it thundered towards them at full charge, driving the Britons back towards the central killing ground that they had so easily fallen into. As the great native throng surged backwards and forwards, desperately trying to break out of the tightening trap, the two reserve auxiliary infantry Cohorts gave out a great roar and charged into the seething mob of Britons.

As we stood overlooking the battle, I was minded to think that the whole thing had now taken on the appearance of a wave breaking over the shore as the charging auxiliary force swamped the leading edge of the doomed Britons. I watched as the now desperate native army, far superior in number to us, finally lost any control of the battlefield. It was they who had chosen when to make the first charge, and that was all the choice that they would be allowed this day as Sabinus' battle plan fell flawlessly into place.

I looked on, waiting impatiently for the order to join the fight as the tribal standards they carried to the front of their charge slowly began to fall under the weight of the onslaught engulfing them. Soon, the last of their barbarian standards fell as their bearers were mercilessly hacked down, but defending them to the last.

Now it was our turn. Once more I felt that almost elemental surge of energy through my body as Mars took hold of my soul and possessed my mind. It was always the same, in those moments just before joining battle. It always felt like I was even more alive and vital as the gnawing need to fight and destroy overtook me completely.

A long clear blast from the Cornu blared out, starting us off on a slow advance down the slope, towards the mounting carnage in front of us. Steadily, our battle line began to close on the seething ranks of the auxiliaries as they continued to hack their totally outclassed enemy to pieces.

I could hear the calls of the auxiliaries own horns blaring out and knew from them that they would now withdraw from the fight, allowing us to smash what was left. I felt my heart starting to pound as though it would launch itself from my chest as I waited for the auxiliaries to clear from the field. The yelling and screaming of men caught up in ferocious combat now grew deafeningly loud around me as we came ever closer to the massive, seething press of bodies that were now locked in combat. Tremendous surges of energy shot up and down my spine as we drew ever closer to the vast line of bloody murder that stretched out across the field. I clenched my jaw so hard that I thought my teeth might shatter under the pressure.

A further series of flat, blaring notes sounded out

over the chaos and the auxiliaries finally broke off from their withering assault, running swiftly over to the right flank. Finally, that allowed us the opportunity to charge into the now desperate mass of Britons that still held the middle of the killing ground. The badly ravaged tribesmen did not give chase to the withdrawing forces. Instead they stood firm, bracing themselves for the oncoming assault of the three Cohorts of heavily armoured Legionaries now bearing down on them. As they vainly rallied to face us, butchered corpses lay in a twisted sprawl before them. A contorted tangle of arms, legs, faces and the gods knew what else covered the ground amidst a thickening slick of congealing, reeking blood.

With every step closer to the battle line the stink of combat filled my nostrils as I sucked in great lungful's of air, as though fuelling myself for the fight. Largely oblivious to our approach, the wounded writhed around in the filth of war. They screamed out in pain, wailing and moaning as their life essence spurted from them in bold gouts of crimson, bathing the ground in blood. My body surged with incredible energy as I finally heard Fatalis bawl out the order to draw swords. The hiss and scrape of the blades being pulled from their scabbards set the hairs on the back of my neck on end. The order was immediately accompanied by a thunderous shout as the Cohorts bellowed out;

"Iuppiter, Optimo Maximo!"

As we cried our exaltation to Jupiter, each of us

slammed the wickedly pointed blades onto the sides of our shields at waist height. As the weapons bristled from the line of shields, the enemy were at last able to see exactly how we, the Legionaries of the emperor, would deliver them to their Gods.

As we advanced we began beating the sides of the shields with our blades. The rhythmic thumping noise throbbed through the air, matching the fall of our feet on the ground, rising up to let even the gods know that the XIIII Gemina were about to enter the fight. At last, just before I felt I would burst with anticipation, I heard one long note sound out from the Cornu, finally signalling the charge. With one great collective shout; we stormed forward and fell upon the doomed Britons.

I quickly picked my first kill as, in a heartbeat; we closed on the struggling lines of Britons. This would be the only time where I would likely have any choice of opponent as I surveyed the Britons directly in front of me. Once I was in the press, it would be a case of killing whatever stood in front of me. I heard myself let out a low animal like growl, drawing back my sword arm, then propelling it forward with a lightning thrust as our shields finally smashed into their lines.

There was no fear in his eyes, nor any look that betrayed what the man was thinking. The point of my sword soared up past his sweeping shield, biting deep into his neck. He left me with the briefest memory of his head snapping back and an image of teeth in a gaping mouth as the blade tore open his throat, splattering my sword arm and face with hot, red blood. As soon as my first encounter with a Briton had begun it was over. As the ghost left him and his legs gave way, his twitching corpse was lost to sight as it slumped to the ground.

Pressing forward without a further thought for him, I continued to batter my way into the mass of Britons, hammering with my shield, repeatedly plunging the point of my sword into the densely packed bodies before me.

As I recall it, there were no more faces after that. I just remember the dogged resistance from the Britons as they constantly tried to push back against us. Every time I thrust out with my Gladius, it plunged into a body. I was continually twisting the hilt to free the blade, battering the men in front of me with the iron boss of my shield. My streaming sweat mixed with the ever present spray of blood as it lashed through the air in abundance, wetting my lips and stinging my eyes.

My breath came in short rhythmic gasps as I sucked in the reeking air of the battlefield and dug my boots hard into the ground, fighting for purchase as I forced myself forwards. Like my brothers beside me, I gave over every last ounce of my strength into utterly destroying the enemy before us.

Greedily, I gulped in more and yet more of the foul smelling air as my lungs heaved with the relentless toil of combat. I was in the midst of hundreds of men. All around, warriors spilt their guts on the ground, dying in their own filth. Were it not for the distraction of the imperative frenzy of battle, the smell would have made it unbearable to remain there.

Inevitably, the army of Britons could resist no more. Instead they buckled, succumbing under the force of our relentless assault, trampled utterly into the ground by the stamping boots of their attackers. Hobnailed soles kicked out and ground down on upturned tormented faces. Their owners thrashed around in vain, attempting to stand once more after going down in the packed, struggling mass of combatants. The iron boot studs tore great rents in the flesh of their faces as they screamed in their agony before being swallowed up in the seething carnage that carpeted the field. Furious, guttural shouts and animal grunts, combined with the ear shattering ringing of metal on metal. The thunderous din of hundreds of shields clashing together surrounded me as we continued the task of butchering the defenders of Durovernon.

Finally, I heard another blast from the Cornu, accompanied by a distant shouted order to break off and fall back which was loudly repeated by those who had heard it first. As the leading battle line, we were now being pulled out to regroup and recover from the shattering, draining impetus we had maintained in the fray, whilst a fresh wave of Legionaries took over the killing. We moved swiftly to the back of the formation and again formed our attack line, waiting to move forwards once more while the new front line fought with murderous, unrelenting efficiency until it too was eventually replaced by a fresh line of yet more eager killers.

As I waited in the rear lines and watched the battle rage on, my chest rose and fell like a set of smith's bellows. I wiped my face with the back of my hand, only now realising that my nose had been broken and was pouring blood onto my armour. I had no idea when it had happened and to be frank, I did not much care. I had fought in battle once more and for all its savagery, it still felt as though nothing else on earth could make me feel more vital and alive.

Soon after we had moved to the rear, I heard multiple blasts from Roman war horns all over the field, again accompanied by shouts to disengage and cease the killing. As the din of the battlefield finally began to die down, there was a brief moment of peace before the victorious Roman forces raised their weapons to the heavens and erupted into triumphant cheering. The Britons were utterly crushed.

What few native warriors who still stood had now yielded and the way to Durovernon was clear. I wiped the back of my wrist across my nose and mouth once more, looking briefly at the broad crimson smear on my filthy skin before I turned to look at Marinus, standing beside me in the line. I smiled humourlessly at him and spat the congealing blood from my lips to the ground. He looked tired as he cleared the sweat from his eyes with grubby fingers before nodding his head slowly at me. Then, smiling slightly, he turned his face to the front, expelling his own gobbet of spit and declaring;

"Glory days brother," he said as his grin slowly widened. "By all the gods, I swear we are living in the midst of days of glory unmatched!"

* * * * *

The battle for Durovernon was over. Our army moved beyond the battlefield, forming a wide formation on the approach to the town.

I passed the ranks of soldiers as they stood in their formations, quietly watching the passage of Sabinus. Weary eyes stared out from grimy, blood spattered faces. Though the battle had drained their strength considerably, they were still able to stiffen their backs up and pull themselves to order, showing respect to their Legate rode by on his way to the town gates.

As his bodyguard, we accompanied Sabinus toward the gates of the town where he would issue his terms for the surrender of the settlement.

A party of cavalry had approached the gates before us and now sat astride their horses, shouting up to a handful of defenders manning the palisade and gate tower. One of the cavalrymen then broke away at our approach and rode up to Sabinus as we reached the outer defences of the town.

Batiatus reined in, took off his ancient helmet and placed it under his arm as he raised the other in salute to the Legate.

"Now, Batiatus," hailed the Legate. "What news from inside the town? Will they capitulate, or no?"

"They lack the stomach for more fighting Legate." answered Batiatus. "They know that if we are pressed to siege the town then there is no hope left for them. I have told them plainly enough; all will die if we have to take the town by force."

"Do they know that Adminius follows?" asked Sabinus.

"They know this, but they will not speak further with me. They wait instead for formal dialogue with you."

"Who is their captain then?" Sabinus enquired further.

"He is Boduogenus." answered Batiatus. "He waits with his retainers behind yonder gate. He bids you approach and he will walk out to meet you."

"Do we trust him, Batiatus?" asked Sabinus, nodding toward the heavy wooden gates. "Do you judge this man to be honourable and without treachery at this time?"

"I do judge him so." came Batiatus' instant reply.

"I'd advise caution here Legate." Ademetus cut in quickly. "These people know nothing of the proper rules of war. If you give them too much trust you may end up on the point of one of their blades."

"Ademetus, I am truly grateful for your concern but, even after their exertions on the field just now, these men will not allow harm to befall me." Sabinus gestured to us as he began to move his horse on to the gates. "Besides, I trust the judgement of Batiatus. There will be no problem. Now, are you coming?"

Sabinus nudged his horse into an easy trot as we too set off and jogged alongside, forming into two lines either side of him as Ademetus caught up. Batiatus had remained with Sabinus and, as I kept pace with the horses, I looked up just at the moment that Ademetus reined in beside him and shot him a murderous look. It was clear now that Batiatus, if there were any doubts before, was risking his life in provoking the Prefect's ire.

Stout oak gates braced with iron towered before us as we deployed around Sabinus, watching for any threat from the blue painted faces that peered down at us from the timber defences. Presently the sound of the gate being unbarred came from within and slowly they began to swing open.

The man we presumed to be Boduogenus and around a dozen fully armed warriors walked briskly out towards Sabinus and instantly we moved to his front, forming a shield wall from which protruded the still blood stained blades of our swords.

The chieftain halted just a few feet from the wall and stared at Sabinus as though we did not exist. As I watched for the slightest sign of aggression I took the time to briefly apprise this barbarian warrior now standing within easy range of my strike.

The man's face was entirely dispassionate as he stood before us. Not a trace of either anger or grief could be seen as he prepared to negotiate the future of his town and all within. Instead he conveyed a clear air of dignity as he considered his opening words. His richly coloured clothes and abundance of gold ornaments spoke well enough of his wealth. His armour of polished bronze helmet crested with blue dyed horsehair, combined with a shirt of fine iron links, testified to his warrior nobility status. The Latin he addressed Sabinus in said much for his breeding and intelligence as he fluently delivered his opening lines.

"There is no threat to you here now, Lord Sabinus." he began in calm, even tones. "Bid your men step aside that I might talk with you as one man to another. My warriors will not raise a weapon against you and yours, if we can do this like fair minded men."

There came a brief, silent pause as both parties weighed each other, searching for any signs to indicate intent - good or bad.

"Step aside men." Sabinus ordered. "I would speak to this man as honoured ambassador to his people. I trust his words."

The barbarian captain bowed slightly towards Sabinus and, with a feeling of slight unease I did as ordered. Though, I confess that I too then felt that this man, this Boduogenus, could indeed be trusted at his word. As our curtain of armour opened up and nothing now stood between Sabinus and the Briton we watched their party very carefully for the slightest sign of treachery. If anything was to happen, it would probably be now. The tribal chieftain instead made no move to come forward, choosing rather to continue his dialogue from where he now stood.

"In my thirty years, I have learned something of Rome." he began. "I have learned your tongue and acquainted myself with your ways and customs. Your world opened up to me when I left these shores and crossed the sea to Gaul, the ancient homelands of my ancestors. Those are lands that you now rule and as such, it is where I have gone to try to understand you better. I knew that one day, you would cast your eye across the sea once more and the hand of Rome would again reach out to take what is ours. It is the way of your people. Only when you rule all will you perhaps be content."

Sabinus dismounted and walked slowly forward until he was but a few feet away from Boduogenus.

"You say it is we who have reached out to take this place. Yet you forget that it is on the bidding of your own kind that we come here to halt the tyranny of the two princes of the Catuvellauni, and free your people from their oppression."

"I know what you bring Lord Sabinus. As I say, I have seen it for myself." replied Boduogenus, maintaining his dispassionate air, despite the clear meaning of his words. "Even had your emperor not been asked for his help, you would still have come here sooner or later. For years your people have traded with ours. You covet what is ours. But why trade when you can possess it all? So, Claudius at last sends his mighty legions to take it by force. If you succeed, this land will never be free again and the tyranny of the sons of Cunobelin will be forgotten as the tribes of this land labour under the burden of Roman rule."

"Do you fear the coming of Rome, Boduogenus?" asked Sabinus.

"I fear my people and heritage will be lost forever, swallowed whole as Rome makes us all one people. What man worthy of his kind would want to cast aside his own identity in favour of another?

"I hear your words Boduogenus, and I must confess, I do feel the weight that presses hard on your heart now."

Sabinus' tone adopted a business like edge to it as he appeared to tire of the conversation and decided instead to change tack and state his case plainly.

"My envoy here has told you that your Prince, Adminius, will be here directly. He has also told you in clear terms what will befall you and yours if you choose to hold the town against us. You must tell me now what you wish your prince to find when he returns here finally: Will you be here to pledge him your loyalty once more? Or will he find naught but smouldering ash and slaughtered corpses? Your answer Boduogenus, I will have it now."

The decision Boduogenus made now would be crucial to the survival of all within the walls. If he chose to capitulate then they would live and Durovernon would be safe from destruction. Adminius would duly be installed as a client ruler and the people would live under the rule of Rome. If

Boduogenus chose to resist then the town would be assailed by the Roman forces until their defence failed. Then, they would certainly be doomed.

It was common enough practice that any town or city which resisted siege by a Roman army would be summarily annihilated. The besieging Roman commander would allow his troops to enter the city and pillage at will for war booty. While this was happening, almost every man, woman, child and animal within its walls would be slaughtered. After all, it was by far the best way to let the world know that, if you defied Rome, you risked the ultimate penalty of total and utter destruction.

As Legionaries, we reasoned that it was much better if the enemy chose to hold out for a siege. That way we got more booty out of it.

For long moments there was silence as the two men faced each other. Boduogenus had been allowed to share his thoughts and the speaking had been plain enough as Sabinus had pressed for a decision. Neither man's face gave away any trace of what they were thinking until finally, Boduogenus reached for the hilt of the long sword that hung in the polished bronze scabbard, hanging on a thick chain around his waist.

As the brightly shining iron blade slowly emerged from its scabbard, every one of our right hands now tightly gripped the hilts of our own swords, waiting for the one treacherous move that would seal the fate of all of the Britons present. As the chieftain slowly raised the blade and held the sword out horizontally with both hands, I quickly came to realise that there would be no more violence. I felt the tension slowly uncoil from my sinews as Boduogenus dropped to one knee and offered the magnificent sword up to Sabinus.

"Aside from my personal retinue of warriors here with me now, there are another two hundred warriors of my clan that are still armed and awaiting my word inside Durovernon."

Boduogenus raised his face towards Sabinus as he continued with his answer.

"From this moment, neither I nor my men will raise any weapon against you or your army. I ask only in return that you are magnanimous in your victory and spare the innocents inside who have had no say in what has gone on here this day."

"What of the two princes, Caratacus and Togodumnus?" asked Sabinus. "Do you denounce them now?"

"Now and always lord. They left us here to stand and die, deserted us while they made their way back to their own lands to prepare for your coming. We owe them nothing but our contempt."

"Then keep your sword Boduogenus, and wait for the arrival of Adminius." Sabinus placed a hand on the warriors shoulder and gestured him to rise. "Take your men back into Durovernon and prepare to receive your lord, Adminius. He will need the support of your family and retainers. As long as you do not raise arms against Rome then your safety is assured."

Boduogenus rose and acknowledged Sabinus with a further shallow bow and turned towards his men. Without a word they made their way back inside the town, the gates of which remained open.

"Fatalis!" Sabinus summoned the Centurion over.

"At your command, Legate," said the grime coated officer, snapping to attention and awaiting his orders.

"Form my guard up ready to return to the army and set up camp. Adminius will be here by tomorrow morn at the latest. I want you and these men to at least look somewhere near presentable to receive his party. Oh and there will be a Roman diplomat and his retainers amongst them so we'll need an honour guard that doesn't look as though it spent all morning in a slaughter house."

"I understand, Legate." replied Fatalis, as he turned and ordered us into an escort column, to be formed up around Sabinus.

Quickly we fell into place and marched off on Fatalis' order. The sound of our equipment clanking and jingling and the crunch of our boots on the dirt track offered far too good an opportunity for at least one man to quietly add his own thoughts on the day. It didn't take long before I was laughing quietly to myself as I finally heard what I was waiting for.

"Bollocks," muttered Surus. "That's the bonus work put paid to then!"

CHAPTER 11

Though the Legion and its supporting troops had only recently emerged from the first full engagement with the Britons, many good hours of daylight were still left. Essential works needed to be completed before anybody got the chance to rest and eat.

To capitalise on this, the fighting strength of the Legion was split down into separate workforces; each detailed to complete one of the myriad routine tasks before the men could finally rest. The camp areas outside the settlement were already being established. The air was filled with the clamorous sound of men digging the shallow defensive ditch. They swung purposefully at the ground, breaking the chalky soil up with their picks, before shovelling it onto the inside edge of the trench. There it was piled up to form the low earth rampart that would augment the ditch, protecting the tents pitched within its perimeter.

As the soldiers toiled, some of the men kindled the first of the fires for cooking the evening meals and to provide some crumb of comfort to what would then be very weary bodies. Scores of small columns of smoke began to spiral slowly skywards in the still air. While the distant sound of axes striking tree trunks could be heard echoing round nearby copses as fresh wood was cut for building and fuel.

I paused from my work for a moment and cast my

eye over the lush meadowland, out towards the now deserted battlefield. I placed my hand to my brow and shaded my eyes as I squinted out over the fields, while a gently warming sun shone on my cheeks as it slowly dropped from the heavens. Small birds tentatively began to greet the approaching twilight with the first of their songs as I stopped to gaze briefly upon the human cost of our first great battle for Britannia.

And what a land it was. I will admit now to being struck by the lush green beauty of the place and its unspoilt tranquillity, untouched as it yet was by the civilisation that we would soon seek to import. That process had now begun and the hard touch of Rome's hand could be felt here now. The peace and beauty of the scene before me was now marred by the sight of so many hacked and battered corpses, still lying where they had fallen.

A scatter of Roman dead lay amongst the masses of slaughtered Britons. The unequal cost of their defiance was plain to see as the pale and lifeless bodies of the defenders of Durovernon vastly outnumbered the corpses of their attackers.

In the sky, groups of carrion birds continued to circle, just as they had since shortly after the battle had ended. They flapped down from the sky on glossy black wings before landing and disappearing in amongst the sprawled bodies. Then, they would hop into view again as they perched on one of the fallen. On occasion they would flap and flutter around;

cawing and squawking their protests and threats if another bird came too close. What need had they to squabble over one small scrap of flesh, when such an abundance of flesh now littered the quiet field? There was after all, more than enough to go round.

Eventually they would settle down, pecking persistently at the once living flesh with their keen black beaks. Now and again they would stop what they were doing. Cocking their heads to one side, they would look around suspiciously; pausing briefly to reassure themselves that there was no threat before they continued to fill their bellies with the fresh red meat of battle.

Our wounded had earlier been removed from the field before we had begun to make camp. Those wounded Britons who it was considered could not be quickly healed and enslaved were despatched on the spot as groups of us had moved over the ground, searching for our own men.

I myself killed at least a dozen of them as we quickly made our way through the chaotic scatter of corpses. It wasn't a difficult task, thrusting my sword up into the throat to shatter the base of the skull. Or driving the blade upwards under the ribs, bursting the still beating hearts that clung so stubbornly to life.

It seemed that it was the right thing to do, and that I was really conferring a favour on those I despatched. Every time I looked down into a pair of dull dying eyes, it seemed that the only thing I could see that was stronger than the pain they felt was their obvious desire for release. They had fought with ferocity and bravery and ultimately they commanded a soldier's respect.

They had met their end that day, lying amidst the litter and filth of battle, crying out or murmuring their plea for release in their strange tongue. Though their words were unknown to me, I knew exactly what it was that they craved. With the ferocity and malice of battle now gone from my heart and mind, no anger or hatred for my enemy yet remained. It seemed instead to be the honourable and merciful thing to do, to end the suffering of the defeated. It was a part of the unspoken code of the soldier and I can freely admit I was happy to remove them from their pain and confer on them a warrior's death. After all; was that not better than living on in misery and bondage as a slave of Rome? With such a prospect in mind; the dead it seemed should count themselves as the lucky ones.

Ultimately, I reasoned that a fighting man who gives his life over to the good of his people does not deserve to experience such a wretched, agonised passing without there being at least someone there to see them on their way. I knew too, as time and again their eyes met mine and the cold point of the sword pushed deep into their flesh that, in their position, I would have craved the same swift release I had granted to them. One by one, they had greeted the blade without fear of death, and one by one I sent them on to join the shades.

Just before dusk, each affected Cohort sent out a

small party of men onto the field to retrieve their dead and strip them of their weapons and equipment. They worked until nightfall, bringing in the dead and laying them out in lines. The work parties moved quickly and methodically, stripping armour and weapons from the corpses. Soldiers, who only that morning, had risen from their sleep and marched to this very field, taking their place in the line of battle. I watched as their bodies now flopped lifelessly around as their comrades struggled to remove the salvage, their stiffening limbs sometimes making it difficult to part them from armour and equipment. I was glad that the dead had no inkling of how their bodies looked so different to how they did in life.

When it was all over, they were laid to one side, dressed only in blood-stained tunics and their boots and relieved now of the soldierly accoutrements of which they were once so very proud to bear. As I looked upon the faces of those men I once knew, I was briefly struck by the harshness and finality of the image before me. I hoped somewhat forlornly that, if this would one day be my fate, perhaps those who retrieved my body from the field would treat it with a little more kindness. Though the bodies of the former owners lay only a short distance away, the salvaged equipment seemed poignant too in its own way. Having been removed from the corpses of the fallen, it had been placed in piles, waiting to be either repaired or scrapped.

I cast an eye over each separate heap of equipment,

the bloodied swords and dented helmets, the battered shields, the body armour and the mail shirts. I knew that every gouge, dent and bloodstain told its own story. Its very presence in this place meant that perhaps a family somewhere would soon be receiving the worst possible news, as a comrade of the fallen man would send word back home; that their man had fallen in battle for the glory of Rome.

As darkness fell, still other parties remained on the field. Carrying torches now, they scavenged through the corpses of the Britons, removing valuables and weapons alike. What jewellery and valuables that had not been looted from the dead immediately after the battle were placed in boxes and taken back to Sabinus' compound. Particularly fine examples of weapons and equipment would also be taken back to the legate's quarters. Soon they would make their way to Rome where they would eventually be paraded through the streets with all the other booty that we would later win. It would become the finery that would dazzle and thrill the crowds at a magnificent victory procession, a grand triumph to show the mob just how mighty Rome really was.

Eventually, I made my way back to the tent and joined the others. The blackness of night had all but fallen and soon there would be too many restless and vengeful spirits wandering abroad to be out on the field alone. A wise man would be sat with the living at this time, not walking out anywhere near the new dead.

Within the defence works, the whole camp was buzzing with the banter of soldiers, bragging of their exploits on the field as they recalled the great victory we had won that day. Wine was passed around and the rations we carried were being supplemented with local kills of all kinds of animal from hares and waterfowl, to deer and boar. The hunting had been good today. Soon the enticing aroma of all of the different meats roasting over the many fires mingled together and filled the night air in the camp, making the waiting for a share of the food seem almost unbearable.

As I slumped down in front of our campfire I gave a silent prayer of thanks to the Gods that we had all lived through the battle. Zenas had produced the small bronze figure of the Genius of our group and we had offered our thanks to the little guardian spirit that we had all survived the day. And so the eight of us celebrated our good fortune as we sat and talked, ate and drank. Loudly, too loudly perhaps, we laughed and joked as we offered our own comments on the events of the day.

After so much death and killing, it occurred to me that it would be a hard task indeed to explain to an outsider why we were possessed of such apparent cheer. But, those who have never known what it is to stand in the heart of a great battle can equally never know how good it feels to come out alive - with all of your limbs where they should be and with all of your friends by your side.

"Ah, Vulcan curse it. It's going to take an age to get that out!" Aebutius complained loudly as, turning briefly from his food, he ran his finger over a deep notch in the blade of his sword. Muttering angrily he fished around in his pack, eventually pulling out a whetstone before setting to work on the damaged blade.

"I'm sure mine's bent you know." mused Pudens, as he cast his eye down the edge of his Gladius. "I'd just stuck it right in some Britons throat. I was all ready to twist it out when 'smash', this big bastard goes and clouts the blade broad side on with a club the size of a tree."

"What - that little twig?" Zenas mocked him. "Don't forget that I was standing next to you in all that. A child could have stopped that one coming in. I saw the whole thing."

He laughed as he diligently continued to rub an oily cloth over his armour. He worked at the dried blood spatters on the surface of the iron plate, softening and loosening the now dark brown deposits and removing it with a lighter cloth, before finally restoring a dull shine to its surface.

"May the Gods curse you for being a lying old whoremaster!" grumbled Pudens, rebuking Zenas with some mock indignation before returning to his tale.

"Anyway, I'll reason that he didn't like the return tap I ended up giving him with my shield. In fact I'll warrant I could probably find the fellows very own snot and teeth marks if I look close enough." He gave a low chuckle as he began to scrutinize the scratched and battered face of his shield.

"Any more of that stew left in the pot?" enquired Aebutius with a grin. "My belly worms are telling me I must eat more."

"Ha!" bellowed Marinus. "Worms is it? More likely you're just a greedy pig. You'd eat until your guts burst if you could. Now piss off, you've had your share."

Marinus shot Aebutius an evil glance and gave a huff of disdain, slowly shaking his head as he lifted the hem of his tunic and began to stitch a jagged rip in the coarse wool.

At this, Aebutius sprang up, pointing his finger at Marinus who continued with his sewing. "Hey! What's with you and the un-neighbourly talk all of a sudden? If there's more to go round, then what's the problem with me taking a bite more?"

"A bite?" Marinus snapped, "I lost my cousin out there today. He served twenty three years and forgot more about this business than you know. While he lays out there stiff and cold, all you can think of is stuffing your damn face as usual. Now sit down and shut up or I might just cut you a new maw!"

The outburst was as unwarranted as it was unexpected and a quietness descended as it seemed that the surrounding tents had now stopped what they were doing to listen to Marinus's unwarranted outburst. Zenas and the others stopped what they were doing too and began to watch the pair carefully. I saw Aebutius flush with anger and, thinking that things may turn a might nastier, I made ready to part them as he spat his reply back at Marinus.

"This world is for the living Marinus. "Aebutius retorted. "I too lament that your cousin sleeps beyond the black river tonight and that Pluto watches over him now. Though, were he able to hear your words this night, I'd wager that he wouldn't hold with how you speak to me in his name. For sure, he would cry shame on you for your threat. We can all mourn the dead as well as you Marinus. I've said too many goodbyes in eight years of soldiering, but time's wasted dwelling on it too long. It changes nothing."

Marinus gave a dismissive huff and continued with his repairs, not even bothering to look up as he delivered his reply to the rebuke.

"Why don't you come back when you've got some more time in and seen a deal more war? Perhaps then you can sing me some more of your little laments, eh?"

Aebutius was taking things too much to heart, and I knew he was thinking of the brother he lost two summers ago when we hunted out the settlements of the marauding tribes that dwell east of the border lands of Germania. I stood up quickly and took him by the shoulders, steering him away from Marinus' front and pushing him back toward his spot by the fire.

Aebutius had taken the loss of his younger brother

Serenus very much to heart. He was only seventeen when he was killed and in the short time that the lad had spent as a soldier he had become much liked. His loss had been a heavy blow for all of us, especially of course for Aebutius.

I said nothing to him, and instead I just looked him in the eye to let him know that I shared his thoughts, ruffling his hair for him as I pushed him down onto his outspread cloak. He remained silent and grudgingly made himself comfortable again as he retrieved the whetstone from off the ground, continuing to grind the blade of his sword once more, scowling now and then at the seemingly oblivious Marinus. I knelt down next to Aebutius and patted him on the shoulder, speaking quietly into his ear.

"You can have some of mine friend. I'm not that hungry anymore"

"What's the matter with you then?" Zenas enquired of me, pausing and looking up from his polishing.

"Nothing, I'm fine," I answered. "But maybe we should count ourselves fortunate that we eight all sit here tonight and share a pot of stew. I saw some of our own lying out on the field earlier who'll never feel the warmth of a camp fire again."

"Fortune doesn't come into it," Zenas retorted. "It's the divine will of the Gods whether you live or die. If they decree that your time is at an end then nothing you can do will change it. Simple as that."

"Rubbish," Marinus huffed, still busy at his repairs. "I can't swallow any of that divine will business.

Those men out there made mistakes and they paid for it, including my cousin, Decius. None of us were slow enough to get in the way of an enemy's weapon like they did so now we get to have their share of the rations. That's what's simple, Zenas."

An uneasy silence fell around the fire. All that remained was the sound of the wood, cracking and spitting as the comforting flames lit our faces. The noise from the other tents around us seemed to fade out once more as we all paused in silent thought, reflecting on the day's events. Eventually Pacatianus broke the silence as he stared thoughtfully into his wine cup, examining the reflection of the fire on its ruby surface.

"Say what you like, but I'd be happier if they were all still here, taking some food and sharing a drink with us round the fire."

Eventually the warmth of the fire and the comfort of a full belly began to have the desired effect. The surrounding chatter of earlier had died down to the odd muted conversation, which in turn gave way to our sitting ponderously, quietly gazing into the dancing flames as they reduced the wood we had gathered to glowing red embers. Eventually we gave in to the need for sleep and drifted off to our beds. Finally, the encampment fell utterly silent.

CHAPTER 13

I slept soundly enough, until just before dawn. Then, my eyes seemed to just snap open and instantly I was awake. Nothing had disturbed me and the others still slept soundly around me, save for Surus who had won one of the last of the watches and was out at his sentry post. I pushed back my heavy woollen blanket and picked up the rolled up cloak that I had been using as a pillow. Quietly I moved the tent flap to one side and stepped out into the chill of the pre-dawn darkness. I strapped on my sword and unrolled the cloak, pulling it around my shoulders and giving a slight cough as the cold air tickled my lungs.

I silently made my way through the camp towards where Surus stood guard. In the eastern sky the first faint traces of a steadily broadening blue line was beginning to grow on the horizon, heralding the arrival of the new dawn. Even now the still unseen birds were beginning their morning chorus. As I walked through the lines I smiled to myself at the contrast in sounds as the cheerful song of the birds accompanied the constant drone of snoring, rattling out from the throats of scores of sleeping soldiers.

Making my way through the camp, another noise reached my ears. Faint at first, but growing slightly with each step as I approached Surus' post looking out towards Durovernon. A distant and strange noise that I could not place as yet was being carried over the still air, causing me to cast my eyes out towards the settlement as I walked. Here and there I could pick out the presence of small fires in the settlement, their warm yet far off glow gently flickering from behind the palisade. It suddenly occurred to me then, that the sound that I could hear drifting across the field from the town was the far-away wailing of women.

The Cantiaci had not taken up arms against the invasion in any great numbers. But, the warriors who had been present when the other force of Britons had arrived to fight would have been forced by Caratacus and Togodumnus to join forces and defend their territory. The brothers would have played upon their honour as neighbours fighting a common enemy. The Cantiacan nobles, not being able to bear the shame of standing by whilst other tribes mounted a stand outside their capital, had been given no choice but to join battle with us. The outcome of the battle had sealed the fate of many of them, as the two warlord brothers used them to buy time to mount a stronger defence elsewhere. It had been a day of immense woe for the Cantiaci. Most of the dead were theirs and the tribe now bitterly mourned the loss of so many.

There was naught left for the women of Durovernon to do now but to grieve. Practically every able bodied man who had entered the field that day was lost. Those who had fought and died were still lying on the battlefield, cold and shattered. The survivors were now shackled and collared in heavy iron chains, waiting to be shipped to Gaul. For the living it seemed that fortune had turned quickly on her heel indeed, as the proud warriors of yesterday had now become mere merchandise for the ever hungry slave markets of the Empire.

The best they could expect now was a life of cruel hardship and servitude, many miles from the land of their birth and the embrace of their people and loved ones. Many of the captives were fiercely proud and it would take much to turn them to any new master's will. I could see that ultimately, many would refuse to bend the knee and accept their lot and that some would receive the ultimate punishment for their rebelliousness. No doubt others still would catch the eye of a Lanista who would purchase them to fight in the arena.

There, in the butcher's shop that was gladiator school, the weak and disobedient would perish. Only the strong and intelligent would survive the brutal training regime and go on to take part in the games. If they were good enough to stay alive, they had a chance to prosper and become famous. For those fortunate few who did, wealth and adoration would follow. They would also attract the lusts of highborn men and women who would pay well to be pleasured by a great fighter. Ultimately, they may even win their freedom. Perhaps then, they could finally return home.

Such prospects would no doubt be a goal to aim for,

but the price of failure was high. Failure meant your blood spurting over the sands of the arena floor, while slaves smashed your skull with a hammer, then spiked your lifeless body with hooks before dragging your slaughtered carcass out of sight. The spectacle of your violent death would be accompanied by the screaming and cheering of a baying, pitiless crowd. A heartless mob - driven into a rapturous frenzy by the brutality of your passing.

Unless you had died a popular fighter, with the money for a funeral, then even death would not spare you a last indignity. In a final display of careless contempt for your life, Rome would toss your used up corpse aside, dumping it in a vast pit, to rot amongst the carcasses of animals, criminals and all of the other filth of the town which your death had so thrilled.

For now though, those men, once proud and free warriors, sat in defeat on the edge of their own town. Weighed down by the thick iron chains that marked their enslavement, they could have little idea of what a life of servitude to Rome would bring.

After walking for a few more yards I found Surus. He stood, looking out over the camp defences, towards the battlefield now shrouded with a thin ground mist. His breath appeared as small clouds of steam in the chill of the early morn as he leaned on his shield, jabbing the butt of his Pilum idly into the ground. As I approached he turned, ready to issue a challenge but stopped when he saw me.

"Gods Vepitta!" he hissed in a whisper. "Are you

trying to scare me out of my skin?"

"Scared - you?" I laughed quietly. "I didn't think anything bothered a great ox like you."

"You read me wrong; it's not the living that bother me." he smiled. "Anyway, why didn't you tell me earlier that you couldn't sleep? I'd have been glad to have taken your place in the tent so that you could have come out here to shiver your bollocks off as I have."

"You're wrapped up like an old beggar woman." I teased him. "How can you shiver so in just a bit of cool night air?"

"Cool my arse! It's freezing just standing around watching that lot out there sleeping."

He stamped his feet and hugged himself, laughing quietly as he gestured over to the dark shapes lying out on the battlefield. I gave a muted laugh in response and turned away from the field, disinclined now to give much more thought to the hundreds of bodies lying close by.

I held with Zenas on this; man indeed makes his own choices but his ultimate destiny is mapped out for him by the gods. If their great design means that you end up lying dead on a battlefield in Britannia, then that is the inescapable way of things.

Soon, the Britons would come and claim their dead for their funeral rites. As for us; we had the funerals of our own men to see to later that day. Then the dead would be gone from sight and mind, at least until the next battle.

"How long do you think they'll keep us here?" Surus wondered.

"I don't know." I answered him honestly. "No doubt we'll have to wait for that turncoat bastard Adminius to turn up and for a few more reinforcement units to join us before we go anywhere."

"Hmm, I suppose you're right." he replied. "Have you seen this Adminius fellow yet? What a shit he is. Fancy him getting a bunch of foreign troops to do his dirty work. I bet his subjects will love him for that. Especially if we don't piss off and leave them to it after all this."

"The gods alone know how he'll get round that one." I mused. "It's too late for second thoughts now though. Another good win for us against the locals and we're here to stay I reckon."

"Do you suppose we'll take the whole place then?"

I scratched my chin, and casting my mind back to the gossip I'd picked up from around the Legate's compound, I shared what I'd heard.

"Of course we will. This Adminius is not the only one who likes to come snivelling to Rome, but mark me, it's all going to cost them in the end. These Britons seem to be a right little nest of vipers and keen to betray their neighbours at the slightest chance. In fact, it gets worse even than that."

"How so?" asked Surus.

"Because I've heard that these two chieftains who gather the tribes and try to unite them to resist us just happen to be the brothers of Adminius."

"Vulcan's balls!" Surus was outraged. "You're right. What a sordid little nest of vipers this lot are. It doesn't even seem that family, let alone their subjects, mean anything to them. Its small wonder they need bringing to heel. Oh yes, I'm glad we're here now. This mess needs sorting out and no mistake."

We chuckled quietly and I slapped Surus cheerfully on the shoulder. We didn't have much to speak of but it was good to be able to gossip once in a while. Presently, we were joined by Peronis, a soldier from the Century of Lentulus, as he took over sentry for the dawn shift.

"Morning men." said Peronis cheerily. "Did you sleep well Surus? Oh, course, you had no sleep cos' you've been doing this for the last two hours. And here's me, just got out from under the blanket after a full nights rest."

Peronis grinned stupidly as he reached up to the huge Legionary and drummed his knuckles lightly on the crown of Surus' helmet.

"Fuck off, Peronis." growled Surus, doing his best to stifle a grin. "Didn't anyone ever tell you it's impossible to do guard when you've just had your arms ripped off?"

"Never happen, you big ugly bear." Peronis smiled as he placed his shield down and drove the butt of his own Pilum into the ground before pulling a large piece of bread out from under his cloak.

"Shouldn't you two be somewhere else now then?" enquired Peronis, pushing a large wad of bread into his still grinning mouth.

"See you later then, arsewipe. Don't get your throat cut by the way, that would break my heart." I submitted my own contribution to the banter before Surus and I turned and made our way back to the heart of the camp.

The light was still poor and much of the camp was indistinct, either still in silhouette or devoid of any finer detail. Picking our way through rows of tents and moving around weapon racks, for some reason I soon felt myself automatically moving slower, more quietly. Something was wrong, I felt it. Surus felt it too as we gave each other a glance and crouched lower as we moved with increasing stealth, Surus soundlessly ditching his shield and javelin as he went.

With Surus close behind me I moved around the tents until we reached the rows just outside the Legate's compound. I was just about to move across one of the gaps between tents when Surus squeezed my shoulder and pointed very slowly, off to my left. Had I crossed the gap I would have alerted the two Britons that now crawled slowly across the ground, as low as they could get. Silently, they were edging their way directly towards Batiatus' tent, avoiding the view of the sentry who stood guard at the entrance to the compound.

My heart began to hammer in my chest as I considered what best to do about tackling the two Britons closing on the tent that I knew Batiatus was definitely occupying. I turned to Surus and gestured that we should move quietly to get as close as possible before launching an attack that would also alert the camp. Surus gave a brief nod and together we moved from out of the cover of the tent, hands tightly clasping the hilts of our swords, trying to reduce the rattle of our kit. Immediately the two Britons seemed to sense our presence and each looked over their shoulder as we froze for a split second.

"Alarm!" screamed Surus as we both dragged our swords free of their scabbards and ran at the Britons who by now had pulled long knives from the backs of their belts.

Amidst the shouts that rose up from out of the tents and the noise of men clamouring to stand to, I yelled Batiatus' name at the top of my voice, followed by:

"Assassins!"

The nearest Briton immediately took up a fighting stance and raised his blade to engage us as we closed with the pair. Though, it was the other who alarmed me most as he turned on his heel and began to run for the tent, shouting out in fury as he went. I ducked low under the slicing blow of the defending Briton. From the corner of my eye I was just in time to see Surus snatch his heavy iron dagger from its scabbard, hurling it in the direction of the Briton charging towards Batiatus' tent. As I thrust myself upwards at my attacker I saw the hurtling dagger hit pommel first between the Britons shoulder blades, connecting with a loud thud. The impact spun the surprised warrior with the concentrated force of the throw.

As I shot forward I slammed into the midriff of the first Briton and knocked him flying as I brought my Gladius up for a downward strike. The Briton swept my leg from under me and I collapsed on top of him, losing my sword and resorting instead to dealing out short jabbing punches to his face and throat as I pinned him to the ground. I felt his fingers clawing at my face. As he sought out my eyes, I pulled my face upwards and locked my teeth onto his fingers, biting down as hard as I could. The cracking of bone heralded agonised screaming. Then, the screaming came to a sudden end as a boot come hurtling in from the left, connecting solidly with the Briton's head and instantly rendering him unconscious in a sprawling heap.

"Try that on for size, you barbarian scum!" growled Surus as he spat on the chest of the prostrate Briton.

I sprang to my feet, spitting out a mouthful of blood from the ravaged fingers of the now insensible Briton as I sought out the second assassin. I need not have worried. The second Briton lay dead on the floor. I saw a single clean stab wound just under the rib cage where Batiatus had burst from his tent and impaled him on the end of his sword. As I took in the scene and a large crowd of startled looking soldiers grew around us, Batiatus bent to wipe his blade clean on the dead Britons leggings.

"Next time, don't leave it so long, eh?" he grinned. "I'd been watching those two crawling around for a while. Any longer and I'd have had to come out and do them both myself."

"Hey, you three. Take a look at this." amidst the commotion, our own comrades had quickly made the scene and Zenas now stood over the still unconscious body of the Briton I had fought with. He beckoned us over and pointed down at the Briton.

"Look at his neck and wrists." Zenas told us. "See those red marks? I'll lay you any money that man has not long since been in irons. I'll guess his friend has the same marks as well."

He looked over to where Crispus stood over the dead Briton, nodding grimly.

"Hey, what's this then?" Aebutius queried as he pointed out a hand sized piece of birch bark protruding from the unconscious Britons waistband.

Pudens quickly retrieved it and passed it to Marinus. We all were able to see that it had a map scratched on it. The map showed the exact location with an 'X' of Batiatus' tent in relation to the Legate's compound.

"Right." said Zenas. "Scrape that bastard up off the floor and let's take him somewhere for a little talk. I want to know what's going on."

"Hold!" boomed a familiar voice behind us. "What are you doing with that man?"

Ademetus pushed his way through the soldiers gathered round and looked at the still unconscious Briton, now suspended between Pacatianus and Aebutius.

"Does he live"? asked Ademetus.

"He does, Prefect." Pacatianus answered.

"Then chain him and take him into the compound. There's only one punishment for attempting to kill the Legate."

"Prefect." I cut in. "He was…"

"He wasn't ever going to get near was he, Vepitta?" Batiatus cut me dead. "These men are a credit to you and Sabinus, Ademetus. Neither of these Briton scum stood a chance of harming anyone in the compound. The lads sniffed them out in a heartbeat."

"Is that a fact, scout?" Ademetus asked pointedly, eyeing myself and Surus curiously. "Then I must ensure that these men are duly rewarded for their…vigilance. In fact I think you two should have the honour of crucifying this piece of filth later today."

Taken by surprise, we both muttered our dubious thanks as Ademetus nodded to Pacatianus and Aebutius.

"You two; drag that murderous dog into the compound and see he's securely shackled next to the hitching posts for the horses. I'll get the Quaestionarii to speak to him and we'll deal with him properly later."

With that, Ademetus turned and made his way back to the compound. As he went Zenas retrieved the piece of birch bark from the back of his tunic and tapped it thoughtfully into the palm of his hand as he watched Ademetus leave. He turned to address Batiatus who stood there slowly shaking his head.

"Don't speak of it Zenas. Giving voice to your

thoughts will only bring more trouble - leave it be."
With that, he too turned and walked away.

CHAPTER 14

Back inside our tent, we sat with the flaps closed and spoke in hushed tones as we applied the finishing touches to our armour and equipment. Before long Adminius' party would be here and we would be expected to provide them with an honour guard that looked as though it had only just stepped out of a fortress barrack block. The mood within the confines of the leather tent was grim as we reflected on the recent events, trying to make sense of what had happened exactly. It didn't help that each one of us now felt in some odd way as though we were conspiring against Ademetus, one of the most powerful men in the Legion and a man we were bound by oath to protect.

"I tell you, both of those Britons had been shackled to the other prisoners." hissed Pudens. "You all saw the marks as well as I. They had both been shackled, but not for long. Somebody turned them loose, I'm sure of it."

"You can't know that." countered Crispus. "What if they'd just managed to get free and ended up in the camp?"

"Are you some sort of imbecile, or what?" Marinus berated him. "If such was the case then why didn't they just make for the trees and grab their freedom while they could? And why was it only two of them managed to free themselves?"

"Dead right, Marinus. And how come they ended up getting past the perimeter guards armed with weapons and a map of the camp?" I queried.

We all sat there for a moment, silently pondering what we ultimately all knew was the truth of it. The Britons had been released from their chains and tasked with a mission to kill. That could only have been orchestrated by somebody with a lot of influence within the camp.

It was Surus who broke the silence first.

"Look, all I know is it was me and Vepitta who came across that pair and I'll tell you all straight, those boys knew what they were about. We could both see that whatever they were up to, it didn't have anything to do with slipping a knife into Sabinus' guts. They were moving away from the only place that they could have got into the compound. They were heading right for Batiatus' tent, and that's straight up fact that is."

Surus folded his arms and gave a firm nod as if to reinforce what he knew to be the truth.

"I've got a question for all you clever bastards then." Pacatianus put in, attempting no doubt to play devil's advocate. "Why didn't the two Britons just piss off when they got the first chance, eh? Nobody was near them when they were doing what they were doing. They could have just melted away without taking any risks and got their freedom back, easy as that."

Ah, come on man, think about it properly." Aebutius

snapped angrily. "If what we suspect is true, then don't you think those two Britons would have been offered enough gold on top of their freedom to see the job through. Greed can work wonders, especially if their paymaster gave them a tempting little peek at what was on offer first."

"And what do we suspect then, Aebutius?" queried Zenas, finally breaking his silence. "Just who do we think was their paymaster?"

A bright shaft of sunlight burst into the tent, dazzling us briefly as Mestrius' unmistakeable shape filled the gap left by the flap he had shoved to one side.

"You filthy lizards, it stinks in here. Has some scabby old mule been bedding down in here? And what in the name of Dis are you all doing back in this tent?"

"We're just working on preparations for the honour guard Optio." Zenas quickly offered.

"Well why aren't you doing it out here where you can see what you're doing then?" growled Mestrius. "Is it because that instead of spending the night sleeping, you've been up all night farting, gossiping and playing with yourselves? Typical, now you're trying to squeeze in a bit more shut eye on my time eh? Well no chance, now get up and get out where I can see you all, you lazy bastards."

One by one we quickly made our way out of the tent while Mestrius stood by, an evil, self-satisfied grin on his face because he had found us to be somewhere we shouldn't have been.

"I'll deal with this later." he snapped at us. "If it weren't for the fact that you all need to at least look like efficient soldiers later, I'd be working you all until your fucking legs fell off. Now get yourselves in order and you two…" he snapped pointing the brass head of his Optio's staff at Surus and myself. "…Don't you dare make a bollocks of that crucifixion later on today. I want these barbarians to know just what it is they're dealing with, so nail the bastard up good - got it?"

"Yes Optio!" we barked out the response as one.

Mestrius turned to continue his rounds but paused briefly before looking over his shoulder at us, an oddly inscrutable look spreading across his face.

"As to what went on earlier with those two Britons." he said in a low voice. "Maybe you'd do well not to make too much of it. You need to keep in mind that we're here to fight, not to think."

With that, he was gone and we all stood in silence, each one of us wondering nervously just how much the Optio had heard of the conversation.

Zenas blew out a great breath of air, demonstrating his relief that nothing further had happened.

"Right, that's close enough for me."

"What's the matter with you?" Marinus asked him.

"What's the matter? Are you mad? We're all sitting there; just warming up to accusing Ademetus of trying to get Batiatus murdered and in comes Mestrius. What do you think is wrong with me?"

"You mentioned Ademetus before any of us, Zenas." Marinus pointed out in a matter of fact tone.

"Don't play silly word games with me you clever shit, we all know perfectly well who the finger is pointing to."

Again, the atmosphere was becoming thick enough to cut between us and it was becoming plain to see why Batiatus had earlier told Zenas to drop the matter. A conflict was now building amongst us that could threaten not only our positions in the elite of the Legate's bodyguard; it could also cost us our lives. Even so, I was sure the unspoken thought persisted between all of us that it was Batiatus who had been wronged so many years ago, and it was Ademetus who was the aggressor in all this. We had sworn no oath to protect Batiatus and our ultimate oath of loyalty lay with Sabinus. But should we really include Ademetus in that oath of protection too?

Batiatus had won our respect and friendship but Ademetus was distant to us. Could we really protect a man so underhand and scheming; especially to the detriment of a man so like us? Surely a man such as Ademetus would stop at nothing to achieve his ambitions, even if that meant threatening Sabinus to reach his goals. Maybe, to protect him would be to allow a threat to grow against Sabinus.

"Who was looking after the captured Britons after the battle?" asked Pudens.

"The slave traders." Aebutius replied. "Why?"

"Ah, Gods curse it!" spat Pudens. "No doubt they've

been well paid for their silence and too scared to speak against Ademetus anyway. If it was soldiers we could have found out who'd done the watches and maybe rattled a few teeth to get the guards to talk."

"Maybe so." agreed Pacatianus. "But it shouldn't stop Surus or Vepitta from trying to get a bit of sense out of that Briton before they do for him."

"That could work." I agreed. "Let's hope the torture detail hasn't quite beaten the ghost out of him just yet then."

"Not a chance." said Marinus. "Ademetus and Sabinus would have them flogged half to death if they killed him. They would have ruined any chance to put on a little show for Adminius and the locals if he dies."

* * * * *

"Right, listen in. Here is how this will be done."

Fatalis delivered his orders as he walked up and down the front of the parade while we waited in our newly resplendent equipment for what was now the imminent arrival of Adminius and his entourage.

"The party and escort are due to arrive in the next hour." confirmed Fatalis. "The cavalry escort will take the party to the edge of the town where they will be met by you lot who will be forming a barrier between them and the town gates."

"A small tented pavilion has been set up down there so that the party can then dismount and join the

Legate and his staff, ready for the afternoon's entertainment. That will take the form of Vepitta and Surus executing the assassin that was captured this morning."

At the mention of this the whole Century gave a low cheer and drummed enthusiastically on the side of their shields.

"Yes, alright." shouted Fatalis over the noise, waving his arms for quiet. "Your comrades did well and as a reward, they will be executing the would-be killer themselves. What you do not know is that these men will be coming to the personal attention of a Senator of Rome this day."

After a burst of excited murmurs, what noise there was in the ranks quickly died away as the formation instantly became eager to hear more of Fatalis' news.

"Adminius and his close family are being accompanied by Gnaeus Sentius Saturninus. He is a distinguished member of the Roman Senate and now temporary advisor to Adminius' court while he establishes a Roman style system of government in what is intended to be the first of our administrative centres as we push forward into Britannia."

"You have all been chosen for your skill as soldiers and your loyalty to the legate and his staff but few of you have had the opportunity to prove yourselves as effectively as did your two comrades when averting the attempt on Sabinus' life this morning. Well done legionary Surus and legionary Vepitta."

Again our comrades cheered and drummed their

shields and, though I was amazed that I was to be brought to the attention of such a powerful man, I could not escape the fact that it was all going to be for the wrong reason. As I looked across to Surus, I knew he was thinking the same thing.

Once Fatalis' briefing of the Century had ended, Surus and I were instructed to step out and remain behind while the rest of the bodyguard were marched off towards Durovernon. Mestrius remained behind to give us final instructions on what we needed to do.

"So, it seems you two animals have done better than you first thought."

Grudging though it seemed, any praise from Mestrius was well received and we stood and listened as he continued.

"This morning you both foiled an attempt on the Legate's life. But let's see it for just that, an assassination that two good soldiers prevented by their skill and watchfulness. Later you'll have your moment, and you'll receive the grateful thanks of some powerful people. Don't spoil it later by running off at the mouth about what you thought you saw, eh?"

The message was clear as we nodded our acknowledgement of Mestrius' advice.

"You both know that I'm not readily given to throwing out little rays of sunshine but I'll tell you this; you two lads are good soldiers. Just make sure you don't give me cause to change my mind, yes?"

"Yes, Optio." We answered in unison.

The speech was brief and to the point and was taken for what it was: an Optio doing his best to keep his men out of trouble and compliant with their duties. He knew that anything beyond that could bring the worst possible kind of trouble. If things went wrong, it would look bad on him and Fatalis. It would look bad on the institution of the Legate's guard and ultimately, it would be the end of us. In choosing to ignore what was going on with the Prefect, Mestrius was playing the cautious game and he was telling us so in no uncertain terms.

"So, to business then." said Mestrius, finally changing the subject. "Get your arses up to the Legate's compound and get the prisoner ready to be brought down to the pavilion. You'll hear the first blast on the horns, which will herald the entry of all of the important folk, and that's when you should start to make your way down the road. You can take two horses and lash that pig between you on the way down. If he falls just drag him. I'm sure he'll survive long enough to start bleating about it when you finally put him up.

"When you get there, just wait for my signal. I'll give you a nod and you can march him in and lay him on the cross. It's already there and when you've finished preparing him you'll get some help to get it upright, understood?"

"Yes, Optio." We replied.

"When you're done with him and he's secure. Turn and march to the tent where all the big noises are sitting, stop short and salute. When you've done that wait for the speeches and the arse kissing to finish then turn smartly to the right and join your comrades, all clear?"

"Yes Optio." we responded again.

"Right, be off with you, and make sure you get it right!"

Quickly, we turned and made our way to the Legate's compound, eager to get a hold of the Briton so that we could try to extract from him what he knew.

"I hope this fellow speaks Latin." said Surus as we entered the compound. "If he doesn't, we've got no chance of learning anything."

"We'll be lucky if he can speak anything." I said as I set eyes on the Briton for the first time since that morning. "It looks like they've really beaten the shit out of him."

As we approached, he barely had the strength to raise his head. The men who had worked on him had clearly done their job well. The Briton slumped against the hitching post he was still tethered to and looked like so much pulverised meat. His body was blotched with long dark bruises, testifying to the ferocious beating he had received. His nose and mouth were caked with dried blood and his fingers formed unnatural angles. Having been dislocated and broken, not a nail remained in either his fingers or toes, the tips of which were now a just a bloody ruin.

As we reached him I took a hold of his matted hair

and pulled his head back so I could look into his eyes, ruptured and blood filled as they were from the savage beating. A sickening gurgle came from his throat, accompanying the rasping of his short, agonised breaths.

"Right you bastard." Surus roared into his face. "It's time you and us had a little talk, isn't it?"

For a moment, the Briton just gazed blankly into his face and then, slowly, he started to smile, weakly at first before it finally developed into a spluttering, sickening open mouthed laugh as gobbets of congealed blood ran from his mouth.

"Bastards!" spat Surus.

"What? What is it?" I asked.

Ademetus' boys have gone and sliced his tongue out. This old lad won't be telling us anything."

CHAPTER 15

There was nothing to be done now but get the crucifixion over and done with. Any chance to extract information from the Briton was gone, foiled by the simple expedient of somebody instructing the Quaestionarii to cut the man's tongue out. We even tried to ask him questions that he could answer with just a nod or a shake of his head but it was hopeless. Either he did not understand or chose instead not to answer, preferring to set us with an oddly impassive gaze as we did our level best to encourage him to communicate.

Surus and I mounted our horses. A heavy chain trailed from each of our saddles, connecting to a broad iron collar around the Briton's neck. We placed our helmets on our heads, adorned as they were by now with fine parade crests of red horsehair, and waited quietly for the signal. The beaten prisoner made no sound either; he just stood between us, swaying slightly and pushing his foot out once in a while to stop himself toppling over.

"Come on then my lad." I said to the Briton as the blaring of the Cornu's drifted up the road to us. "Head up now and a big smile for your family and friends."

We laughed as we kicked the horses on and set off down the gentle slope at a light trot, the Briton blundering along between us as we went, fighting to keep his balance and to maintain his tenuous grip on consciousness.

In a very short time we had passed through the assembled soldiers on the roadside and reached the area close to the execution site. Once there we dismounted and stood with our Century while we waited with the now badly swaying Briton for Mestrius to give us the signal. As we watched the Optio I heard Surus speaking quietly and with a serious tone into the prisoner's ear:

"Don't fall now. I'm serious, listen to me. Keep your head up and leave this world with as much dignity as you can. Understand?"

The ruined man made no sound of acknowledgement but instead gave a faint smile and set his eyes to the front as he waited, bravely and patiently it seemed, for his end to come.

I could see nothing of the Legate and the assembled party of honoured guests at this stage. I could only just hear the last remnants of a speech being delivered by an unseen orator. The disembodied voice spoke of new friendships and the enemies of Rome. I could tell he was building up to the crucifixion when mention was made of Rome's intolerance of any actions that threatened the lives of those who sought to forge alliances with Rome and Adminius and assist in the battle against Catuvellaunian tyranny.

Eventually, the rambling speech drew to a close as mention was at last made of the treacherous attempt on the life of Sabinus, great friend of Adminius, and that the culprits had been stopped by two loyal and true sons of Rome. One assassin had died in the attempt, cried the speaker; the other would be brought forth now to pay the price of such a despicable, cowardly and low act.

It was then that Mestrius gave a sharp nod.

"Right, let's be having you then." said Surus as he tugged at the chain, instantly over balancing the prisoner who, with tethered wrists, had no hope of breaking his fall and instead lurched forward, falling straight onto his face in the dirt.

"You daft bastard." he muttered. "Don't you know good advice when you hear it then?"

"Up!" I barked, sliding my fingers into the iron collar and yanking him to his feet. "Just walk him Surus, if you want him to go out with a bit of dignity then don't pull him around like a unruly dog on a leash or we'll be here all day."

As we came into full view with our charge for the first time, a great howling and screaming arose, the like of which I had not heard before. The unnerving row came from the inhabitants of the town, either standing behind the assembled troops or lining the towns defence works. They had caught sight of the battered and naked prisoner for the first time. I heard the thump of shields being locked together and swords being drawn from their scabbards as the agitated crowd were menaced to keep order by the closely ordered lines of troops.

I focused my mind on the job in hand and set to my task, ignoring both the watching dignitary's and the baying crowd as we led the Briton to the place of his execution. We reached the cross; lying on the ground next to a deep but narrow hole with a collection of wooden wedges and lay the battered and bleeding wretch down onto the stout timbers.

Close by was a wooden pail containing a couple of heavy iron hammers, some large wrought iron nails, other assorted tools and some thin wooden pads with a hole bored through the centre of each. Surus picked up a hammer and a broad iron chisel. He placed the joint of the prisoner's iron collar against the solid oak of the cross spar and with a clean hard strike he sheared off the head of the thick iron rivet that held the collar shut. Surus then pulled the collar open and tossed it to one side with its accompanying chains. The prisoner would have no need of a slave chain where he was going.

By now, I had begun to lash the Briton's arms to the cross member, securing them in position to take the nails that would spike him to the wood. Meanwhile Surus had tied the Briton's ankles together and bound them to the upright section, just above a small piece of oak that sufficed as a foot shelf. I picked up one of the hammers and grabbed three long iron nails before standing to the side of the cross, looking down at the battered and now suddenly defiant face that stared up at me. Now, as his end approached, the prisoner's eyes finally held a wildness and hatred in them that, in the absence of a weapon, he seemed almost to aim at me, to burn into my mind through his eyes, as though poisoning my very soul with the venom of his hate. I turned my face from his and instead looked towards Mestrius, awaiting the signal to finally start driving the nails home. After a few brief moments, the Optio nodded and the execution commenced.

As a strange silence fell upon the scene, we started with the right arm. Surus dropped down and placed his knees directly onto the upper arm, forcing a low grunt of pain from the prisoner as he took Surus' full weight on his arm muscles. The condemned man continued to glare directly at me but I could see in his eyes that his resolve was beginning to falter as I approached with the hammer and he caught first sight of one of the long iron nails that would ultimately take his life. Slipping the nail through the hole of one of the wooden pads I placed it directly above his forearm and raised the hammer for the first strike.

The initial hammer strike effortlessly propelled the nail straight through the prisoner's arm, deep into the timber. A terrible scream rose up from his tortured mouth and his whole body arched, fighting to break free of the bonds. Again I struck the broad iron nail head as the almost inhuman screaming continued and blood began to stain the clean grain of the newly hewn oak. With a final blow, the muscle of the forearm was flattened grotesquely as the wooden pad did its job, stopping the nail head from disappearing completely into the flesh.

As we moved to the second arm, the prisoner fought hard to compose himself once more. He knew that his people watched and I could tell that he wanted so badly to keep some semblance of his dignity as a warrior before he died.

Before this day, he could never have known that crucifixion was as much about humiliation and degradation as it was about torture and death. Now he was learning the awful truth.

As the second nail tore into his left forearm he gave out one shrill scream then bit down hard, clamping his jaw and shaking his head from side to side, refusing to cry out more as his body shook uncontrollably from the white-hot intensity of the pain. I almost hoped that he would keep up his show of courage, admiring him for his spirit, but I knew from experience that the last nail would be too much, even for him.

We repositioned ourselves and, as Surus turned the Britons ankles side on and sat across his legs, I placed the last nail above his heel. I swiftly drove the spike home, sending it smashing through his ankle bones and into the leg below where another strike ensured that it drove through any further resistance from flesh and bone before finally biting deep into the cross.

The terrible, animal like screaming stung my ears as Surus and I finally stood and I dropped the hammer to the floor. With no tongue and therefore denied even the basic comfort of crying out to his gods, all the Briton could do was scream, and scream he did.

I looked over to Mestrius as he motioned two more soldiers to break ranks and approach the cross. Quickly we positioned the cross over the erection hole. Ropes were wrapped around the cross member and head, ready to hoist the frame and its tormented adornment upright.

With a grunt, Surus lifted the head of the cross from the ground and, with tremendous strength, began to push the cross up into the air until the other soldiers and I were able to start assisting him by straining on the ropes. Once under the timber Surus was able to walk his hands up the length of the back of the upright timber, guiding it into the hole as we heaved it vertical until at last, it slipped into the hole with a great thud.

The weight of his own body now being suspended from three nails caused a fresh round of screaming from the prisoner as we slipped the wooden wedges into the hole and began to knock them in, firmly wedging the cross into place. As we worked I could hear a rapid and steady stream of blood droplets pattering on the ground all around me like summer rain, running freely from the vicious puncture wounds that had now been pulled open by the weight of the body bearing on the nails.

I wondered briefly how long he would last on the cross - a day or two perhaps, or maybe just hours? All I knew was that his last moments in this world would be spent enduring the unimaginable pain caused by the great nails that had torn his flesh. He would fight to prevent his own weight from suffocating him as he sagged forward, constricting his rib cage, eventually causing breathing to become impossible.

The two quickest killers would be shock and blood loss but, if we had done our job well he could survive these, at least until his body was wracked by violent, searing muscle spasms, eventually causing his strength to fail. Then, unable to resist the pull of his own body weight any longer, his limbs would loosen off and his own ribcage would slowly constrict and crush the breath from his agonized lungs as he fought vainly for that last elusive gasp of air.

But that would not be for some time yet, and he would have ample opportunity to contemplate the manner in which his demise came about. There would be plenty of time for him to look out upon the town and people whose bosom he had once dwelt in and to look down at his own family as they gathered beyond the guards and cried out their grief at his living death. Plenty of time, it would seem, for his mind to become as tortured as his body as his last dying sights, sounds and thoughts only added to the misery of his passing.

I took one last glance at the Briton who had now grown a little quieter as the intensity of the pain had briefly turned to a merciful numbness. I looked over to Surus and nodded to him and together we strode over to the front of the tented pavilion that housed such important people. Halting smartly before the assembly, we snapped our right fists up and thumped them against our hearts, saluting the Legate and his staff and the party of Adminius and Senator Saturninus.

Standing rigidly to attention, I waited as the man I believed to be Saturninus stepped forward, preparing to speak. It was at that moment that my mouth almost fell wide open with shock as, casting my eye over the assembly for the first time, I caught sight of a girls face as she stood amongst the women of the Senator's entourage. I doubt I could have been more confused at that moment as I struggled to make sense of why the girl I instantly recognized as the prostitute Julia, now stood in the company of a small group of Roman matrons, richly clothed and with her head veiled, just as a respectable Roman woman should be.

Prostitutes, so lacking in any modesty or self-respect, did not much care to veil themselves in public, and the mere thought of a prostitute breathing the same air as respectable Roman women was intolerable. So wrong was what I beheld that my head spun as I tried to reason it.

Recovering from the shock and quickly regaining my composure, I awaited the address from Saturninus. Julia, with seemingly total unconcern, looked on with a faint smile, setting me with a look of vague amusement. It came as an even greater shock then, as it suddenly occurred to me that she clearly recognized me. Nevertheless, she seemed to be totally unperturbed by the whole issue of my presence there. As I wrestled with my thoughts the Senator approached us and I was forced to focus my mind on the matter in hand.

Senator Gnaeus Sentius Saturninus was a short, stocky, yet noble looking man in his early fifties. He smiled approvingly as he approached us and it seemed as though, when he spread his arms and hailed Surus and I, that he was greeting a pair of old and revered friends.

"So," said the Senator, nodding approvingly. "Here stand before us two fine examples of the fighting men that make up the backbone of Rome, our mighty Legions."

Holding his hands out towards us and continuing to nod in our direction, he smiled professionally at the gathering as he continued his address.

"Though let's not forget that these men also represent the finest of the soldiers under the command of my old friend, Titus Flavius Sabinus," he added, sweeping his arm theatrically in the direction the Legate. "And were it not for these two men of such obvious quality, then it might well have been that we gathered here now at the funeral pyre of our great Legate. Not, instead, to witness the just execution of murderous scum!"

Saturninus seemed to spit out the last words as he thrust an accusing finger in the direction of the Briton we had just crucified. As the pathetic figure nailed to the cross was brought briefly back to the attention of the assembly, I heard once more the low groans of the tormented prisoner.

It seemed somehow perverse at this point to think

that the Briton was dying for the wrong reason. Although Saturninus had correctly apportioned the man's guilt of the attempted crime for which he had been sentenced, his announcement of the name of the intended victim was misguided. The Briton was dying in the name of the wrong man. Saturninus turned to face us again and pointed towards us once more before continuing the address:

"I hold up Legionary Vepitta and Legionary Surus to you all. They are true sons of the Empire, who have done their Emperor the greatest of services by fulfilling their solemn oath of loyalty and saved the life of one of Rome's great commanders!"

With that, Saturninus threw his hands in the air and a great cheer rose up from the ranks of the assembled soldiers as they beat their palms on the faces of their shields, saluting us in their own way for what we had done that day.

Then, as Saturninus called for quiet, he gestured over to another man who sat nearby upon a folding stool, quietly watching the contrived display of admiration put on by the apparently enraptured Senator.

"Noble Prince, Adminius." Saturninus hailed him. "We're it not for these two men; you would have lost a valuable friend and ally in your quest to end the tyranny of your brothers. I ask you now to approach and bestow a fitting reward on these fine soldiers to honour them for their vigilance."

I watched as Adminius slowly stood. As he rose

from the stool he seemed to tower over those around him, his slim but muscular frame adding to his imposing air. The richness of his clothes and jewellery set him out unmistakeably to be the barbarian prince that he was. Adminius was a man who gave nothing away. His clean chiselled features remained totally inscrutable as his face seemed devoid of any expression at all. The thick brown moustache that adorned his upper lip ensured that it was impossible to tell if even the slightest expression had shaped his lips.

I found myself trying to weigh this man as he approached us, attempting to gain a measure of his character. For his own part, I could sense that he too was making his own appraisal of Surus and I as he slowly walked over to us. As he drew nearer, no smile touched his lips and his ice blue eyes seemed to have a cold and almost soulless quality to them. Outwardly, Adminius was doing exactly what was expected of him, inwardly; I knew with unswerving certainty that he hated us.

What was he thinking, this Adminius? Did he really think that Rome would allow him to rule as anything other than a puppet, wielding power that was so far diluted as to make him little more than a local administrator for the Emperor? Did he really judge that his end reward was so great he could accept a bitter and bloody war with his brothers and surrender control of his people and lands to Rome?

His eyes were the key. They were the path into his

mind. They told me that he knew in his heart he had sold out to Rome and that, if that was the only way he could live like a prince and be free of his brothers, then so be it.

Although Adminius was carefully promoting the notion that he held Rome up as his greatest friend, It seemed apparent enough, to me at least, that there simmered an intense resentment that he would have to tolerate in order to enjoy the status he sought. I reasoned that the new arrangement did not sit well with him. No doubt the brutal and merciless way that we had just put one of his former vassals to death in front of his own people had perhaps provided him with a somewhat unwelcome moment of clarity.

"Loyal and true soldiers of Rome." he began, with a cold and distant tone to his heavily accented voice. "Your loyalty to your Legate and your skill and vigilance does you great credit. Thanks to you I still have the support of a great friend and ally as I seek to rid my rightful land of the tyranny of my brothers."

In another life then perhaps I would have been heartened and proud to be addressed so by a prince. As it was, I judged the words to lack sincerity and for my part returned a sharp salute with as much military vim as it would take to acknowledge him, but without any trace of respect for him in my heart as I did so

He clicked his fingers and placed his open palm out to his side as an adolescent Nubian boy dressed in a stark white tunic appeared at his side in a flash, placing two leather coin pouches in his hand. I almost had to fight down the wry smile that rose to crease my face as I looked the young Nubian up and down. The boy stood by his master's side, his body stock still but his eyes darting nervously all around as he obviously still fought to make sense of a world that was very strange indeed to the homeland that he had no doubt only recently been snatched from. Already then, it seemed that Adminius was developing a taste for all the exotic little extravagances that the elite of the empire sought to possess.

The prince held out the coin pouches towards us, one in each hand as he went through the motions and continued with what was expected of him.

"Well done soldiers of Rome. May your courage and skill at arms continue to bring you both good fortune and yet more well-earned reward."

"Thank you, prince." We both responded as he handed us each a year's pay in gold coin then raised his hands up high, eliciting a roaring cheer from the men assembled. Though he nodded approvingly at the enthusiasm of the men, the smile that he then wore on his face was as bogus as it could possibly be. Even though this man had just paid me a small fortune in coin, my dislike of him was now fixed and intense.

"Excellent, excellent!" Saturninus enthused as he called across to Sabinus who looked over to us in approval.

"Legate, Sabinus. Say that you can arrange for these men to stand their watch on our tent as we all dine tonight to celebrate the first great success. Only then will I feel truly safe in this wild place."

"Consider it done." replied Sabinus. "Their Contubernium will stand the watch at the tent tonight and then I will be as sure as you that we will be as safe as we need."

As Adminius made his way back to his seat, I cast a furtive glance over towards the small assembly of women present. As before, Julia remained where I had first spotted her and she regarded me still with a curious smile.

I stopped trying to make sense of her presence as Mestrius called for Surus and I to fall back in with the others and, for that moment at least, I forced her from my mind as I re-joined the ranks.

CHAPTER 16

Were it not for walls made of leather and canvas I could have almost convinced myself that I was somewhere else; far away from the edge of a battlefield in a land that none of us knew.

Bereft of the panoply of war now, we had shed our armour for clean off-white coloured tunics complimented by broad, deep red bands of cloth wrapped around our waists. The opportunity to sport undress order always made a man feel good as it was a rare chance, on campaign at least, to shed the filth of war and look at least half human. Always though, we wore a sword and dagger, because our first duty was to protect the person of the Legate and, for tonight, his esteemed guests too.

The rest of the Contubernium were distributed around the sizeable interior of the commander's tent, ensuring that the evening's entertainment would be safe, as well as pleasant. I had positioned myself in a dimly lit corner where I briefly admired the transformation from its earlier, more utilitarian look into a now richly decorated hospitality area. The tent was far removed from its usual night time appearance of gloomy dark shadows, made less Spartan only by the odd lamp or cresset. Now, it was filled with subtle and cheering warmth, created by the careful placing of small braziers. These were complimented by the more understated light of numerous oil lamps, gathered in groups on iron stands. Their more subtle flames fluttered now and again at the intrusion of the odd, gentle draught, adding their own little something to the ambience.

Richly coloured textile drapes also enhanced the tent's newly found conviviality. While incense burners artfully masked the musty smell of its old identity, putting out languorously wafting threads of pungent, sweet smoke.

Together, the various elements of this carefully contrived deception almost caused me on occasion to forget the events of the day. The strength of the illusion was such that even a hard-nosed realist such as I could imagine, if only for a moment, that I had actually found myself removed to a civilised part of the empire and not instead stood watch in a strange and menacing land, where death might call at any time.

They were here to show the Britons what it was to be Roman, Saturninus and his party. The Senator, his accompanying family members and retainers were here from the very start to guide Adminius and his court, to coach them in the ways of their new and all powerful friends and allies. Adminius would not be the last of the British tribal nobility to be mentored in this way but, for now, here would be where the foundations of a new Roman province would be laid.

I watched with mild interest as they all played convincingly at their game of make believe, banishing effortlessly, it seemed, the reality of the campaign tent for the fiction of an ostentatious dinner party in some rich Roman country house. The lengths to which they had gone to banish for a night the frugal trappings associated with a Legion at war were something to behold.

They had conversed politely as they dined on a variety of game and fine imported vegetables and fruits. They lounged around on improvised couches, even observing the seating etiquette of the houses of the wealthy as Saturninus and Adminius occupied the most honoured places alongside their host, Sabinus. As they washed their dinner down with quality wines, copiously dispensed by amphora carrying slaves and exchanged their social niceties, a quartet of musicians sat at the back of the tent, adding to the faintly absurd illusion with a repertoire of soft, melodic arrangements.

As the sound of the polite conversation mingled with the ripple of laughter I cast my eyes once again that evening on Julia, revisiting once more the odd mixture of bemusement and anger that I felt at her presence. My bemusement was due entirely to what I knew her to be and, because of that, why I should ever have come across her again here, in such esteemed company. It just wasn't right.

My anger was all about her deceit. Yes, it was plain now that she had somehow fooled me but as yet, I had no real clue as to just how – or indeed, why? All of this was compounded by the fact that, with seeming ice cool confidence that I would say nothing, she had not addressed me in any way and had chosen instead to totally ignore me.

But what could I expect? It was now becoming readily apparent that this woman was not Julia the prostitute who had pleasured me for a few coins. This was Julia, woman of substance and wealth who would have no real business addressing a Legionary anyway.

She knew I could not open my mouth and say what had happened. Quite apart from the fact that there would be no reason in the world for anyone to believe me, Sabinus and his staff would think I had gone mad for uttering such things and have me instantly stoned to death for such a blatant insult to a lady of the Senator's party. For now, there was nothing to be done but to keep quiet and wait to see what the lady Julia did next.

After a while the evening began to take on a tedious air. I had moved around the tent, exchanging positions periodically with my comrades, I had become bored now with the glaring pretentiousness of the Senators entourage as, one by one, they had courted Adminius and sought to convince him that he would be a key player in the new Britannia that Rome would build for him. For his part, Adminius appeared gracious enough to their overtures but I was convinced that he was beginning to realise that he had helped pave the way for a Roman incursion into his homeland. This , I was sure, would be something which in time would render him even more powerless than when his brothers sought to exert their will upon him.

"Soldier. Might we disturb you from your duty for a moment?"

Saturninus had appeared in front of me almost as though he had been conjured up in a wisp of smoke. So much for remaining the ever vigilant bodyguard I thought, as I noticed that he also kept company with a young Roman nobleman and…Julia.

Recovering quickly from the unexpected approach, I responded:

"Senator Saturninus, of course, I am your servant." My right hand flashed out in a smart salute as I addressed the small group. "So too am I at the service of the young Dominus…and you too, Domina."

I gave a shallow bow to acknowledge the presence of a lady then fought to hold back a wry smile, avoiding the expression of my scorn and incredulity as Julia played the lady once more and arranged her flowing silk head dress so that it protected her decency. Demurely, she avoided eye contact, just as a respectable Roman matron should when confronted by the likes of common soldiery.

Why so shy, I thought? After all, you fuck like some lustful little wood nymph when you play the whore!

If it wasn't for the fact that it would cost me a very painful death, I would have shouted the thought out to all present. I could have openly shamed her there and then, rather than go along with the bizarre game that

Julia was now playing so adeptly. She clasped her hands in front of her waist and looked to the floor, smiling modestly.

"As I recall," continued Saturninus, "You are the Legionary called Vepitta, yes?"

"You are correct Senator. How may I serve you?" I responded.

"May I present my youngest and only surviving son, Rufus?" said the Senator as I nodded to the young man and quickly appraised him.

He was around fifteen years old and was yet to achieve manhood. His richly embroidered Toga hung awkwardly on his skinny frame and was clearly made for a boy. A finely made Bulla still hung around his neck, complimenting the downy fluff on his cheeks and chin, clearly identifying him as one yet to be formally recognised as a man.

"I am honoured young Dominus." I said, addressing the boy directly, flatly refusing to even glance at Julia.

"Young Rufus here was very impressed with the tale of how you and your honoured comrade thwarted the attempt on Sabinus' life." said Saturninus, clapping the boy on his shoulder. "He was too, as were we all, equally impressed by the way you demonstrated Roman justice earlier today. We are all very proud to have soldiers such as you in our great Legions."

I smiled and saw that the boy was just about to open his mouth and speak when Saturninus decided he had got his second wind and cut the boy short.

"Rufus here has always declared his intention to take up military service when he is old enough. Indeed, it's one of the reasons why he is with us in Britannia, so that he can see first-hand how Rome wages war against the barbarian. Then he will see what it is he is letting himself in for."

"Father I…" As the boy began to speak, Saturninus cut him dead once more, laughing and clapping him on the shoulder again.

"Mind you, if his sister in law here were a man, I would worry for the safety of any of Rome's enemies who had the misfortune to get anywhere near her."

Saturninus wafted his hand in the direction of Julia who smiled demurely back at him.

"Now Julia here is the widow of my eldest son - may the Gods watch over his immortal shade - and I say she is possessed of more spirit than some of the so-called fighting men that I have come across in my time. What a pity she cannot be a soldier, she would be an Amazon reborn, I am sure."

"Domina." I spoke to her and nodded once more. "I am sorry to hear of your loss."

As I acknowledged her, I hoped that my insincerity was not so readily apparent, For the first time since Portus Itius I was addressing her again, only this time it was nothing if not totally unexpected and more than that, it almost seemed as though to be in another life. Why would you ever think that some whore that you bedded on leave would ever turn up on a far off battlefield, and in the company of such important people? My head was almost beginning to spin with the effort of attempting to reason it all out.

As I sensed that Julia was just about to reply, Saturninus spoke once more.

"Well, let's not talk of that tonight eh? The honoured dead can be remembered another time I think."

"As you say, Senator." I nodded and waited for him to continue.

"It is strange I know that we find ourselves here with boys and women trailing after battles and generals but Rome has its reasons for doing such things. For my part, I try also to be a good father, as well as a good politician."

The Senators openness surprised me as I waited for him to get to the point of why he was spending his time talking to me, an inconsequential soldier.

"Julia is very much her own woman and Rufus is eager to spend time in the company of fighting men. Both of them need a little diversion from the boredom of the political world that I must inflict upon them. Say that you and your comrade Surus will escort them on a ride tomorrow, that they may blow off the cobwebs and see a little of this land in safety."

"But Senator…I…Legate Sabinus…he…"

"My friend Sabinus has already consented to releasing you from morning duties. He is happy that I feel I can entrust the safety of my family to his bodyguard. He appreciates that trust and would like to demonstrate that my faith is justified, I think."

"Then if the Legate so orders, I will instruct Legionary Surus to attend with me at the appointed time."

"Excellent. Be here tomorrow morning by the sixth hour. The mounts will be prepared and Rufus and Julia will be sent to join you."

With that, Saturninus placed his arms around the shoulders of Rufus and Julia and began to lead them away. As he did so, he addressed Julia.

"And no arguments, my child. Bucco will come with you too."

"As you wish, father." Julia replied as they made their way back to the party.

CHAPTER 17

A light film of moisture lay like a fine shroud over the ground and on the tents as we made our way towards the Legate's compound the next morning. The post dawn sky had all but lightened now and was crystalline blue, unblemished by clouds and conveying the promise of a fine day, a perfect backdrop for the gradual rise of the sun into the heavens. Here and there, drops of dew caught the steadily strengthening light of the sun and glinted like scattered handfuls of tiny diamonds in the grass.

As Surus and I walked, the sound of the vast camp rising to a new day carried on all around us. The clunking of wooden spoons stirring round in cooking pots sounded amongst the metallic scrapes and clanks of armour and weapons being taken up and readied for some light maintenance.

The noises of the morning routine carried on the same as ever. Scattered cracks and thuds sounded from all around as wood was chopped or snapped for use in reviving the fires that had died down to smouldering piles of ash during the night, glowing hearts waiting for the careful attention that would coax them back to life once more. All around men yawned and coughed, farted and groaned as they filled their lungs with the smoky air and stretched out their arms, ready to set about their allotted tasks for the day. Some pulled on their armour straightaway in preparation for operational tasks. Others collected the tools of the many different trades and professions that could be found within the ranks of the Legion, readying themselves to set about another day's work which would see Rome's physical presence in Cantium becoming ever more tangible.

"Hail Batiatus," called Surus as we came across him making his way out of the Legate's compound.

"A fine morning fellows." he responded. "I thought special duties kept your Contubernium late from your beds last night. So what's happened, did you shit the bed or something?"

I couldn't resist a return quip as he stood there grinning broadly at us.

"Don't be soft. We leave the bed shitting to infirm old boys like you."

"Well, I'll maybe agree that I must be getting soft in my old age." Batiatus countered with a growl in his voice and a slight grin still on his face. "Though, time was, for trapping off at me like that I'd have kicked your bollocks so hard they'd have landed up on Claudius' breakfast table. Now, how come you're moving about so early?"

"Were playing nurse maid to the Senator's young lad and his pretty little daughter in law." droned Surus without a trace of enthusiasm in his voice. "They want to go and see the sights on horses this morning. Pah, I ask you!"

"Ah, I see. It looks as though you're paying the price

of fame then, or is it notoriety?" said Batiatus. "Take it from one who knows; make sure the only thing you try and ride today is a horse. Rutting rich folk can cost you dear."

"Which one exactly?" queried Surus. "Him, or her?"

As we laughed at the joke I did my level best to make sure that my laughter at least sounded convincing. On any other day, that remark would have been funny, but today it was just a little too close to the mark for my liking.

"So where are you going then?" I asked Batiatus, swiftly changing the subject.

"A ways northwest for a day or two." he replied. "Those two brothers are out there somewhere with a very big army. I get the job of finding exactly where, then you lot get the job of coming and stamping them into the ground. That's exactly the way I like it these days."

"And what of this business with Ademetus?" asked Surus in a voice far too loud for my liking.

"Dis pass by us you great loud fool!" I hissed. "Do you want the whole damn Legion to know of that business, you stupid ox?"

"Why, what of it? I only asked." Surus replied, an unconcerned look on his face.

"Don't trouble yourselves about it." replied Batiatus. "I only spend as much time in his company as I need. Nothing more has happened, and I doubt anything more will for now."

"Why so?" I asked.

"When I find those two brothers of our fine host Adminius it'll be like the gates of Hades have opened and all of the nasty evil bastards of the underworld have been freed on the rampage. As I said, theirs is going to be a big army and I hear we might even end up going at them with at least three Legions and all of their auxiliary support. It's going to be one big battle and Ademetus is well taken up with the planning of it, just like all the other staff. He's so pre-occupied he probably can't even remember my name just now."

"Well, if you're sure." replied Surus, dropping his hand on Batiatus' shoulder and giving it a friendly squeeze. "Good hunting, and may Diana watch over you and keep you safe."

"Enjoy your day with your new friends. Don't worry about me." smiled Batiatus. "Perhaps, if I have the blessing of Mercury too, I'll see you again when I return with news of the enemy."

With that he turned and set off between the tents as we made our way into the compound.

Once inside we made our way towards the Legate's tent and marched smartly in, snapping to attention. Sabinus stood in front of a low table scattered with despatch scrolls, wax tablets and maps. The tent had already been cleared of the fine decorations of the previous evening and had now returned to its usual functional appearance. Now it provided a fitting backdrop for Sabinus, Ademetus and the rest of the Tribunes and staff officers to paw over the stream of constantly arriving intelligence and decide on a plan for the coming campaign.

"Legate Sabinus, Legionary's Vepitta and Surus reporting as ordered for morning protection detail of Senator Saturninus' family members."

I delivered the report in a sharp and clear tone, chin held high and avoiding eye contact, as was the protocol with senior officers.

"Very good you two." replied Sabinus as he wandered over to us, casually glancing over a report as he confirmed our orders.

"You'll find five mounts in the far corner of the compound that Saturninus' people have prepared for the outing. Make sure you both equip yourselves with lances. If you do find any Briton's when you're out there, get out of it quick with the two family members. There'll be an attendant slave but you can leave him to it for much as I care. Don't fight unless you absolutely have to, I don't want to have to explain to the Senator that two of my boys let members of his family get killed or kidnapped by a bunch of marauding Britons just because you two decided you were up for a fight, right?"

"Yes Legate" we both replied as one.

"Give them about an hour's ride and, not that I should need to tell you this, but on no account venture beyond sight of the outer sentry ring. Brother Vespasian is due to arrive in camp later today. The last thing I'll need then is the compound full of Saturninus' people running round like headless chickens and making me look like an arse because

I've lost two of his brood. Now go, and if you lose them make sure you kill yourselves too, because if I catch either of you alive after that I'll personally cut your heads off and shove them up your arses."

I caught the light grin on Sabinus' face as we turned sharply and exited the tent. I knew that he would have been given scant choice by Saturninus but to arrange this little outing but I knew too that the safety of Julia and Rufus was vital to the success of Saturninus' own mission here. Sabinus would not hand the job over to anyone other than his most trusted and competent men. That was something I could take pride in at least.

Before collecting the mounts we made our way to the armoury tent within the compound and collected two lances, as ordered. We were wearing no armour as the extra weight would only encumber the horses if we needed to flee and we would need to be able to move our charges out of trouble as fast as possible.

"So, what do you think of that then? " I asked Surus. "Legate Vespasian is due in camp today then."

"What am I supposed to think?" Surus responded. "Another Legate in camp with his people is all. It seems there are more important people in these parts at the moment than you'd give a nod to on the Palatine hill by the sounds of it."

"Don't be dim, you stupid ox. It means there's at least one other Legion close by if their Legate is able to just amble over on a social call. With the Second Augusta in the area too now I reckon we'll be set to go into battle again very soon."

"Maybe." said Surus thoughtfully. "And don't keep calling me a stupid ox or I might have to knock your teeth in, you bastard."

We laughed as I swung a playful swipe to his head then ducked the slow punch he returned.

"Better ditch your Gladius for one of these if we're going to be on horses." said Surus as he broke off from the horseplay, drawing a Spatha out of a sword rack and casting his eye critically over the long slim blade of the sword.

"I don't hold with these things," he grumbled. "Nasty, imprecise things, that force a man to slice his enemy to bits rather than just stick a nice neat hole in them. What sort of way to carry on in a fight is that?"

"I know." I replied. "But we'd have no chance without them against a Briton with his long sword. Those barbarian dogs would have your ears off quicker than Jove's lightening if you tried fighting them on horseback with a Gladius."

"I suppose so. Just don't ask me to like it, eh?"

"Fine, now let's go and get this over with shall we? Then we can get back to some proper soldiering."

As promised, five horses were tethered in the corner of the compound, all equipped for the morning ride out. Surus and I shared a few jokes and checked the horses over while we waited for our charges to appear. We didn't have long to wait as Julia and Rufus soon appeared, walking towards us across the compound in the company of a man who was probably the most formidably large and solid looking figure I had ever seen in my life.

"By the arms of Hercules." I exclaimed under my breath. "Will you look at the size of him?"

The man stood fully one hands span taller than Surus and was built with the same frame of heavy, solid muscle. His head was completely bald and looked as though it had been roughly fashioned from a lump of polished oak. While, beneath a pair of thick black eyebrows, darted a pair of keen and deeply set dark eyes, constantly surveying his surroundings as he walked. As the trio approached us the man began to look us up and down. I could sense that the evaluation he was making of Surus and I was anything but friendly. For our part we scrutinised him too and I concluded that he was maybe from somewhere around the region of Dacia or Moesia, given his distinctive features and swarthy skin tone.

"Fucking Dacian." growled Surus, concurring fairly well with my own assessment of his origins. "Can't stand them, they fucking stink."

"Don't talk bollocks." I replied.

"It's a fact. Every one that I've come across has stunk like shit." Surus confirmed.

"That's because the one's you've come across have all been dead, you stupid animal."

"Yeah? Well if he keeps eyeing me up like that then I'll guarantee there'll soon be yet another dead Dacian that I've come across."

"Greetings, good soldiers." Young Rufus hailed us

cordially as they neared the horses. "Julia and I have so been looking forward to a mornings ride out, even more so given that Legate Sabinus has entrusted our safety to two such redoubtable Legionaries."

"Good day to you, young master..." Surus responded.

"...And to you too, Domina." he added as he bowed lightly in her direction.

"Has the Legate mentioned to you that Bucco will be accompanying us this morning?" asked Julia, addressing the question straight at Surus and then nodding in the direction of their enormous companion.

"He has, Domina. And the Senator's staff appear to have already prepared five mounts for us to use." Surus answered her.

"Excellent." Rufus cut in. "Then let us be away, shall we?"

"Of course, young master." replied Surus.

"Your pardon, young master." I interrupted. "And to you also, Domina. But I must tell you that I have grave concerns for the safety of the Lady Julia if we are forced into taking flight at any time."

I could almost sense Surus cringing as I asked the question, but I had never seen a well-to-do Roman lady sit a horse before , let alone ride one properly. Julia wore a full length light woollen dress with a long cloak and a mantle pinned over her hair. I could not reason out how she could even stay on the back of the horse, let alone remain in the saddle over anything other than a gentle trot.

Rufus laughed as he turned to look at a smiling Julia, shaking his head whilst smiling and turning to face us once more with a sigh. As I watched his reaction it seemed easy to forget that the young noble was actually only fifteen summers as yet when he conversed with such self-assuredness.

"I understand that you are only doing your duty as protectors and good soldiers." said Rufus, smiling still as he swung himself up into the saddle of the horse he had chosen and beginning to adjust his position between the four horns of the seat before he continued.

"But let me assure you that my dearest Julia here will, if the need arises, leave us all behind in any gallops we may need to make. Not only is she loved by and blessed of Juno and Fortuna, but she has also been riding since she was but six summers. In fact nobody could keep her from it I am told."

He concluded with yet another fond smile towards Julia, blowing her a kiss from his palm as she approached the smallest of the remaining horses.

"Perhaps, my dear young Rufus, you make too much of my skills with a horse." she observed, as Bucco stepped forward. All at once he closed his great hands around her waist, lifting her high above the horse as though she were nothing more than a sheaf of wheat, before gently lowering her onto the saddle of her chosen mount. "But, modesty aside let me assure you soldier that on a horse, I am more than capable of holding my own against any man."

As she had descended she had hitched the material of her dress high to take away any tightness in the fabric as she settled and then hooked her legs around the horns of the saddle, bracing herself into a sideways riding position. Only now did it become apparent to me just how securely she could seat herself. For a moment, I forgot who she was, nodding my head approvingly at the skilful way she had adapted the shape of the saddle to her own ends.

"I am glad that you approve soldier. Now perhaps you and your comrade will mount your own horses and we can get on with things,"

"Of course, Domina." I replied, smarting slightly from the sharpness of her tone and swinging myself up into the saddle of my own horse.

Surus and Bucco mounted up too and together we rode out of the compound and off towards the outer perimeter of the camp.

We stayed close to Rufus and Julia, our lances resting diagonally across the front of our saddles while Bucco rode close behind, in a position where he could see all of us. So far as I could tell, he remained totally disinclined to utter a word, even to respond with a courtesy when Rufus asked him to pass a water skin. Once we had cleared the perimeter defences by about fifty paces, Julia turned in her saddle and looked directly at me as she smiled wickedly.

"So, we know that our Gallic cavalry Auxiliaries are beloved of their Epona who blesses them with great skill, but just how well does the Roman army train it's Legionaries in horsemanship?"

With that she gave a loud 'hah' and jabbed her heel into the ribs of her mount. As the horse snickered and shot forward Rufus too gave out a loud whoop and set off down the dirt track after her.

"Ah, Vulcan's balls." groaned Surus. "Like we need all this carry on!"

"With that, the three of us kicked our horses on and sped off after our two madly laughing charges, fighting to close the dangerous gap that was opening up between us as I scanned the area, noting the position of watch points and the nearest defence works as we went.

The reckless gallop was but a swift one and thankfully over after about two thirds of a mile. When Rufus and Julia reined their mounts in, I had looked around and noticed to my relief that we were still well within sight of the camp defences.

"Young master, Domina…Please." I addressed them both, still catching my breath. "That was not wise. This area is not considered fully safe as yet which is why you require an escort. There could still be native war parties looking at the camp and you would both make excellent hostages if they were lucky enough to take you."

"Oh really, some chance." said Rufus flippantly. "I'm sure you and your friends murdered most of the locals in the battle. As to what few were left alive, well we all saw the column of slaves on the way in."

I bit my tongue at the boy's observation that we may be nothing more than common murderers and ventured to continue with my advice.

"Nonetheless young master I…"

Julia cut me dead.

"For pity's sake, soldier, I am sure not one of us feels the breath of Pluto on their neck just yet. Can we not just enjoy the ride?"

"My apologies, Domina. Your safety is my sole concern. That is all."

"No, it should be we who are sorry for putting you both in a difficult spot." said Rufus genuinely. "I regret our recklessness caused you alarm. It has been hard for us here, away from home, living in pigsties and tents and dying of boredom. We know we need to support our father with our presence but we just needed a little distraction. Will you forgive us?"

"Young master, please, there is nothing to forgive and no harm is done." said Surus, smiling almost benevolently. "As my comrade says, we think only of your safety, as I am sure your man here does. Isn't that right my friend?" said Surus, nodding affably to Bucco, only to be greeted with an impassive stare.

"A race!" cried Julia excitedly, breaking the new and uncomfortable silence.

"Domina?" Surus questioned.

"A race, to the dead Elm, over yonder," Julia continued. "I wish to blow off the cobwebs a little more."

Surus gave a puzzled look in my direction and was

just about to make comment when Julia continued with her suggestion.

"Bucco will ride to the tree and cast his eye further out to see if it is safe to proceed, then when he is satisfied it is so he will drop his hand and I will race one of you to him while the other remains here with Rufus."

"But, Domina ..." I began.

"Don't waste your time protesting soldier, Julia always gets her way in the end and I for one do not wish to ride against her as I do not like to lose." Rufus smiled broadly as he turned towards Surus.

"It must be you who remains with me, Surus; Vepitta is the lightest of you both and therefore the only one who stands any kind of chance. Will you take a wager?"

Surus gave a thunderous laugh and shook his head.

"Young master," he replied. "I am sure it would be wholly inappropriate for me to take the wager of one so young and besides; I have seen Vepitta ride many times and I confess; I cannot afford to lose the money."

Both Surus and Rufus were laughing now as I scowled at Surus and reluctantly agreed to race against Julia who then quickly dispatched Bucco off to ride up to the gnarled old tree.

As we waited for Bucco to reach the tree, I readied myself for the gallop as Julia set her mount beside mine, twitching her horse's reins and coaxing it to restlessness as it snorted and whinnied, ready for the off. Handing my lance over to Surus I wound my own horse's reins tightly once around one fist while I dropped the other hand to my side, ready to kick the horse off and slap at his flanks at the signal from Bucco.

Presently, Bucco arrived at the old Elm tree and I watched his every movement as he first cast his eye around to check that all was well before turning to face us, his hand held high.

"Be ready now, soldier." Julia breathed as she waited for the signal.

Even as Bucco's hand had sliced downwards and I had jabbed my heels into my horse's sides, Julia let out a high pitched shriek and her horse catapulted forward. The noise and sudden motion caused my own mount to become startled and rear up as the advantage of a clean start was lost to me.

"Hah!" I bellowed as I quickly regained control of my startled horse and set out across the field after Julia. I was frustrated by the dubious lead she had created for herself and was goaded by the jeering from Surus and Rufus that quickly faded behind me as the hooves of my mount hammered on the ground, fighting to catch up with Julia as her horse tore like a thunderbolt through the long meadow grass.

The race was over almost as soon as it had begun and I watched as Julia reined her mount sharply in and swung it round expertly next to Bucco to face back towards me. Awaiting my arrival with a triumphant grin on her face and laughing through deep breaths, she re-arranged her clothing which had been blown about during the gallop.

As I pulled my own horse up next to her she continued to smile broadly and lent forward towards me as she addressed me.

"My compliments soldier, you did well to bring the horse under control so quickly. I am sorry that my conduct was not very fair. Do you forgive me?"

I was angry at being beaten unfairly and by a woman to boot and it was this that caused my response to be incautious to say the least.

"It would be something at least if I knew which conduct it was that you were apologising for - madam."

As soon as I had said it, I instantly regretted my words and wished that I had kept a calmer disposition. Where could this conversation go? Even if Bucco was only a slave, slaves still talked. While I hastily reconsidered my position it was Julia whose response resolved the issue of how the matter would be handled between us.

"You wish to speak plainly I see." she said, with a slight smile on her face. "Then do so and say your piece, for what passes between us will stay between us."

I was somewhat shocked by the candour of her approach to me and looked from her to Bucco. He sat impassively, constantly eyeing the terrain around us. Julia picked up on my unease at the presence of Bucco and continued with further reassurance.

"You have no need to be concerned for Bucco. He is my servant and gives his loyalty to me alone and, as you may have noticed, he does not tend to engage in idle chatter."

"Can't he speak then?" I asked her.

"You can be assured that he will not speak." She turned slightly to smile at Bucco as he sat astride his horse, making it look more like a small donkey as it supported his massive frame.

"Then I must confess madam that I find myself in very strange circumstances and I am most eager to be able to make sense of them."

"Of course you are." Julia replied "So what is it you would wish me to help you with?"

"I want to know why it is that a whore I paid to bed in some cheap town brothel across the sea in Gaul suddenly turns up on a battlefield in Britannia in the company of what I now know to be her very important family. Further; why am I now talking to a woman who, by rights I should have never have seen again but who appears to have more faces than Janus himself?"

"So many questions, Vepitta." The deliberate use of my name was accompanied by her best disarming smile.

"For now they must wait as we cannot keep Rufus and your comrade waiting longer as they will wonder over the delay. I will find out when next you guard the Legate's quarters and I will send Bucco with instructions on where to meet me. Then we will talk."

The conversation ended at that as Julia kicked her horse on and began a gentle canter back to where Rufus and Surus waited for us to return. I cast a brief glance at Bucco, only to be met with a cold, unreadable stare as he set off after his mistress. I resigned myself to the fact that I would have to wait a while longer before I got answers and followed the two of them back across the meadow towards our companions.

CHAPTER 18

"Plautius is clear on this point, brother. We attack as soon as the bulk of their force is located by your scouts."

Sabinus glanced up from the maps and papers spread across the table. The insubstantial glow of the flickering lamps cast his features in light and shadow alike, making him look almost demonic. He set his brother Vespasian with a hard stare before responding to the order relayed from Aulus Plautius, supreme commander of the invasion force.

"I hear you, brother," he answered. "And my scouts are following up on intelligence leads now, in order that we may soon know of the precise location and disposition of the main enemy force. If I am right, we will find them not far from here in the next largest settlement in the land of Cantium."

"Durobrivae." said Vespasian nodding; realising where it was that Sabinus was referring to.

"Just so." confirmed Sabinus, pausing to sip on a cup of wine and to consider his next words before he spoke once more.

"The settlement sits an easy two days march west from here on the banks of a large river and I am certain that the army that awaits us there will outnumber us by at least five to one, even if we can use three Legions with full auxiliary support."

"Which is precisely the force that we will have at our disposal," Vespasian confirmed.

"General Plautius has already despatched Gnaeus Hosidius Geta with the IX Hispana to move across country to the north of us and to locate and track the river that you spoke of inland. Geta awaits our messengers for word of the battle plan that we are to establish before committing to any fight. In the meantime the XX Valeria will also move west but they're to sit this one out and act as support Legion should we need them."

"Excellent brother." enthused Sabinus. "Then I suggest that this is how we will play our game."

I listened intently as Sabinus outlined his plan to Vespasian who stood and absorbed the details, nodding approvingly as the strategy took shape. Vespasian was of a stouter, stronger build than his older brother. His thick neck, bald crown and strained features almost made him look like some sort of rough farm hand in a Legate's armour. Although, anybody that knew him also knew that his looks were extremely deceptive. Far from being the cloddish country bumpkin that he appeared, Titus Flavius Vespasian was a shrewd tactician and a brilliant artillery officer who was beloved of his men.

I knew from past experience of their meetings that if he felt Sabinus' plan was flawed, there would be no hesitation in bluntly promoting his own strategy or opinion, even if it meant conflict with his experienced and ambitious older brother. As it was, the plan tabled by Sabinus was clearly sound and Vespasian embraced it in its entirety.

The intention was simple enough. XIIII Gemina would march to the river and take up a position on the opposite bank to the settlement of Durobrivae, there to goad the native forces and draw them into believing that our Legion would be the force that intended to cross the river and engage them in battle. We would use our own artillery, and that of II Augusta to inflict as many casualties from our side of the river as possible, while II Augusta would skirt wide around the back of us and avoid detection by the force of Britons as they made for a fording point further upstream. There, the entire Legion would then cross the river and head for the settlement.

While II Augusta marched to position it would be the responsibility of Geta to make a crossing further downstream with a large force of Batavian Auxiliary Cohorts who were now advancing with the IX Hispana. The Batavians would then ford the river at a point further downstream from the settlement, moving under cover of the diversion that we were to create.

The Batavians were excellent at fording difficult waters in full kit and then emerging ready to fight. Once the Britons finally realised they were there it should cause a panic, hopefully making them split their force as they reacted to the new threat. That element of surprise and momentary confusion should then allow II Augusta to commence their attack from the opposite direction while we maintained our presence on the far bank and harassed the Britons with missiles.

This last part caused me much irritation when I realised that our Legion would not be involved in the bulk of the fighting and were to be little more than spectators. It appeared that, like XX Valeria, we would only initially be supporting the assault on the settlement. Still, I thought, at least there might be an opportunity to get involved in the later stages if the Britons decided to put up a good fight.

"Did you record it as it was said?" Sabinus turned to a scribe who had been sitting at a writing desk close by, scratching away furiously with ink and nib as the plan was outlined.

"The record is as you said it, Legate." The scribe replied.

"Good, then waste no time in drafting Geta's copy of his orders from the record. Have it ready for me to place my seal on first thing in the morning. I want it away with a dispatch rider before breakfast."

The scribe nodded and reached down by the side of his seat, drawing a clean roll of parchment from a box of writing supplies before he pulled his oil lamp a little closer and began to scratch away once more, drawing up the instructions that would inform Geta and the IX Hispana battle group of what they were required to do.

"It's a good plan," remarked Vespasian. "Now, take the advice of your little brother for once and let's turn in for the night and get some sleep eh? Tomorrow we'll leave a caretaker garrison in each of our camps and then we'll march the Legions west with their auxiliary support."

"I must admit," Sabinus conceded as he slowly rubbed deep at his scalp and neck. "The thought of a decent night's sleep holds much appeal just now. Ademetus, has there been any word back from Batiatus yet?"

"Not so far, Legate." The Prefect answered.

"Who's this then?" queried Vespasian.

"Gaius Vettius Batiatus, brother. He's a former Centurion with the Legion from when it was under the command of Valens and he's now my chief of scouts."

"Good then is he, this Batiatus?"

"As good as the best of them. No question." replied Sabinus, without a moment's hesitation.

I cast a cautious look and watched Ademetus' face as Sabinus endorsed Batiatus' skills. I felt no surprise when I saw the Prefect shoot a fleeting but poisonous glance in the direction of the Legate. It could not be more obvious how he hated Batiatus so, and because of this how potentially dangerous it was to be associated with the old veteran. Ademetus was a powerful and an influential senior officer. No matter though, Batiatus was a friend now, a brother under the eagle, and it was becoming readily apparent that he was a worthier man than the Prefect who loathed him so.

Vespasian's rumbling voice interrupted my thoughts once more.

"Then do not fret over the whereabouts of your man Batiatus, brother. If he is as talented as you say then I am sure he will find the column on the march and make his report to us as we advance west. Now, let's finish these cups of wine and turn in."

"As you will." Sabinus sighed in resignation and swiftly drained his cup, banging it down heavily onto the table top before wiping his mouth with the back of his hand.

"Fatalis, place guards on the sleeping quarters and then get the night watches to pass word round camp that we march soon after morning muster."

"I'll see to it, Legate." said the Centurion, emerging from the shadows at the back of the tent. "Sleep well, sir. First Cohort will be awaiting your orders as soon as you are risen and refreshed."

"I'd never doubt it even for a heartbeat. Good night, Fatalis." said Sabinus as he and Vespasian turned and stepped out into the night air to retire to their sleeping quarters.

"Vepitta!" barked Fatalis, spinning on his heel to face me. "You've been on duty since dawn. Stand down now lad and turn in for the night. Oh, and pass it on to that great knucklehead Surus if you see him on the way back to your tent eh? He's posted to guarding the outer perimeter of the compound so he should be out there somewhere."

"Yes Centurion." I replied and turned to leave the command tent, relieved now that the opportunity had finally arisen to snatch some sleep. Though, just as I had reached the doorway of the tent, Ademetus appeared before me, setting me with an unfathomable look before addressing me.

"Legionary Vepitta." the Prefect began to smile unconvincingly. "Senator Saturninus has expressed his grateful thanks for the escort you and Surus provided to his son and the lady Julia this morning. He felt that they had been forced to remain too close to camp for some time now and wished to give them a little time to stretch their wings. This morning was apparently quite a tonic for them."

"The duty was my privilege, Prefect." I replied, wondering to myself why he would bother to let me know such news. After all, I had followed orders, nothing more.

"Oh, one more thing, Vepitta." continued Ademetus, gently wagging a finger around in the air before looking directly into my face. "I've noticed that you and your Contubernium seem to be forming quite a close association with the chief scout of late."

"Batiatus, Prefect?" I responded, stating the obvious.

"Er, quite so. Perhaps it would be better if you and your comrades were to take my good advice and tone down your association with this man. His personal reputation is not the best I fear. I for one do not wish to see the character of good soldiers who hold such high responsibility being tarnished by keeping bad company. He is after all a mercenary, nothing more than a hired hand, if you will. Do you follow?"

"I understand you, Prefect." I replied, taking the inference of his words very well.

"Of course, Legionary Vepitta, I have no doubts that you are a loyal and obedient soldier. One in fact who holds a position of great trust. I am sure that the Legate and I can always count on you and your comrades to do the right thing and maintain the high standards that you have set for yourselves. Is that not so?"

"Just so, Prefect." I answered him clearly. "May I take my leave now?"

"You may."

The reply was brusque and he had turned and gone back towards the table with the maps and dispatches before the last word had even left his lips, but the thinly veiled warning he had just given me was unambiguous enough. Stay away from Batiatus.

I stepped out into the cool night air and my mind turned over the Prefects words again and again. Things were now becoming very dangerous and Ademetus was using his personal clout to part Batiatus from the close associations he was building with the Contubernium. I was going to have to speak with them all to share what he had said. Decisions would need to be made.

Presently, I attempted to put the matter to the back of my mind and was just about to set off to look for Surus when, all at once, I became aware of a presence nearby. My attention had not been taken up with a noise and it was nothing I had caught a glimpse of, it was just…something.

Soldier's intuition prompted me further as I reached for the hilt of my sword, turning slowly and silently on the spot. I listened intently, carefully scrutinising the shadows and dark nooks lying beyond the flickering torchlight of the compound as I obeyed my instincts and sought out what it was that troubled me so.

As my gaze settled on the armoury tent I peered harder into the gloom, almost unaware of the fact that my right hand was slowly starting to draw my Gladius from its scabbard, creating a low metallic hiss that even I could only just hear over the night breeze.

Abruptly I halted the draw as, from the shadows by the side of the armoury tent; there slowly arose a hulking great shape, instantly identifiable as Bucco. It was almost as if he had materialised from the shadows and I briefly marvelled at how well a man of his immense size had managed to conceal his presence so well. Noiselessly, he skirted the edge of tent, deftly avoiding the guy ropes that radiated from the sides before he reached the entrance flaps and parted them just a fraction to allow the weak glow of a lamp to beckon to me from inside the tent. He said and did nothing, merely setting me with an impassive stare as I silently crossed the compound. I knew full well that I was expected inside and that Julia awaited me there.

I reached the tent and gave Bucco a long stare as I passed him and stooped to make my way through the leather flaps into the dimly lit interior. Totally uninterested, he broke eye contact straight away and without a sound he gently closed the flap behind me.

She stood in the light of a single small oil lamp. Its flickering glow highlighted the folds of a simple woollen dress and painted soft shadows onto her face, giving her a new beauty that I had not seen before. Quietly, I removed my helmet and placed my equipment on the floor of the tent before I tossed the edges of my cloak back over my shoulders.

I made to speak but instantly she raised a finger to her lips and, in the blink of an eye it seemed, she had crossed the space between us. Almost at once she was gazing into my eyes, reminding me once more of the beauty of her own eyes as she reached up. Catching me completely off guard, she kissed me fiercely on the lips, urgently probing my mouth with her squirming, darting tongue. Before I could recover from the shock of what she had done, I could feel her hand pulling the hem of my tunic up as my body instantly responded to the unexpected arousal. She gripped my engorged flesh, massaging firmly and eagerly with her soft warm hands, causing me to groan briefly as I responded to her outrageous boldness by lifting her onto a table, part covered in weapons inventories.

A few of the scrolls scattered and rolled off the edge of the table as she hitched herself a little further onto the edge of the sturdy little table and spread her arms to support her weight, fumbling to find a space amongst the documents. Our lips remained clamped together and we breathed noisily and sharply through our noses as I hitched the warm wool of the dress up around her hips. Eagerly I parted her soft, pale thighs, supporting them with my forearms as I pushed myself towards her.

Again, I felt her hand take hold of my almost painfully pulsing manhood as she guided me urgently into her. Once more I felt her soft intimate warmth yield to me. Our lips parted and I briefly gave out a low groan as I savoured the feel of her silky wetness, beginning to move more urgently now as I thrust deep inside her once more. I felt my passion rise rapidly as I looked upon her face, eyes closed with flushed complexion and pleasured expression. Gently she bit on her bottom lip as she wound her legs further around me, drawing me ever more tightly into her welcoming sex.

The noise of my now rapid breaths began to rise and, as my body began to tremble with passion, I thrust harder towards my climax. She quickly leaned forward, nipping my earlobe and gripping me around the neck with one hand while she held the other over my mouth, burying her face into the folds of my cloak to muffle her own passion as I almost cried out with the shuddering release of the moment. I felt as though

I had burst with the ecstasy as Julia's body stiffened and she dug her nails into my neck, pushing herself hard onto me one final time. I knew then that she had also reached the peak of her own pleasure.

My chest rose and fell deeply and my body still shook slightly with the intensity of the brief but incredibly sensual encounter with Julia. As I stepped back from her and pulled down the front of my tunic she seemed to recover the poise of a lady as she smoothed down the folds of her dress and brushed away errant ringlets of hair from around the front of her face. I tried once more to speak, remembering that, since I had entered the tent I had uttered not one word to her, but again, she had the better of me.

"So, soldier," she said quietly, her voice coming now in low breaths. "Let me give you some of those answers you seek."

CHAPTER 19

"It's all just a game you know, Vepitta?"

I looked around uneasily as I raised my hand in a cautionary gesture, uneasy at the fact that Julia had chosen not to speak in a whisper any longer. The look on my face must have made it plain to her that I was fearful of being discovered in her company in what could only be construed as such obviously compromising circumstances.

"We can speak clearly enough," said Julia in a self-assured tone. "Bucco will alert us if there is a chance that any may overhear our conversation."

"If you are so confident in his vigilance then why did you feel the need to stifle the noise of our…liaison?"

Julia smiled mischievously before she answered; draping herself in a folding chair whilst looking me up and down. She idly twirled her hair around one slender finger of an immaculately manicured hand.

"Surely it would be unfair of me to expect such a loyal and lifelong servant like Bucco to have to bear to listen to such things? After all; he has watched over me and been my protector since I was but a child. To him I am no doubt still just a silly little girl. Sometimes it is wise to be discrete I think, even if it is only to save the feelings of a mere slave."

"Your sensitivity and consideration does you credit,

madam," I replied sarcastically. "But I care little for the sensibilities of your... house boy, and instead desire only the answers you have promised me."

By now, my own tone of voice had risen. In delivering my reply in such a challenging and provocative tone, particularly whilst directing the jibe about Bucco, I wanted her to think it obvious that, despite the unexpected gift of sex that Julia had chosen to pleasure me with, I was in no mood for tricks and deceptions and that I would not be dismissed by her.

"Straight to the point, Vepitta. I like that."

As she said the words, a dark look briefly crossed her face as she too set out her stall, leaving me then in no uncertain terms as to whose agenda would be the one that would set the tone of our meeting.

"That aside though, you would do well to remember what you are and who I am. Think about it, you are in no position to dictate instructions to me."

My temper briefly rose up within me and I was almost ready to respond to her threats in my usual manner when the truth of her words hit me. For the same reason as to why I did not wish anyone to discover us, I chose to keep my own counsel, for now. I opted instead to straighten my back and stand looking down at her. In what I see now was a faintly ludicrous gesture, I crossed my arms and satisfied myself with scowling deeply at her, offering instead a visible but quiet token of defiance. Though inside, I actually felt totally impotent.

As I continued to set her with my frosty glare she remained seated, preening herself and idly perusing the contents of a few of the scrolls on the table before her, totally disinterested in my wasted attempts to impose my looming presence on her as she prepared to set about telling me what I wanted to know. She did not even bother to look up at first. If it was a game of the mind that she played then I must freely confess, she had beaten me hands down.

"Surely you know, Vepitta, that the life the gods have granted to us is nothing more than a divine joke?"

Her face took on a much more serious countenance and she continued to ignore the icy stare I set her with, instead browsing further through the scrolls as she chose her next words. I for my part decided not to ask what it was she meant and instead remained silent, waiting for her to explain further what it was that she wished to share with me.

"Consider this," she continued. "I am of the mind that we are all nothing but players in a great game. It is a game that the gods make us play every hour of every day, using us as their entertainment as they while away eternity. As they watch, they shake their heads at most of the players and laugh at the pathetic attempts of mortals to succeed in what for the most part are inconsequential and wasted lives."

As I listened, I thought I detected just a hint of sadness or regret as she explained herself further. Though, it was clear that whatever it was she was thinking was capable perhaps of disturbing her, it seemed easy to recognise that it was also something that she embraced fervently.

"You see, while most of the players in the game will never amount to anything, there are also those who are beloved of the Gods. They are the ones who are ruthless in the pursuit of their goal and who make their own luck as they scheme and plan their next move. Though there are but a mere few of these players in comparison, they are the ones whom the Gods will favour the most. As such, they are the ones who the Gods will gladly return to the world after death claims them, to take another turn in the great game. It guarantees the Gods their sport in times to come, you see?"

"This is all very interesting," I observed. "But I am not a man who pretends to understand religion or philosophy. Your theory of the Gods' grand plan means little to me. Nor does it supply me with any of the answers I seek from you."

"Patience, you have a part to play in the game and the answers you seek are tied into that. Do you wish to hear more?"

"Go on." I prompted her, beginning now to feel somewhat uneasy. As she continued, I realised my instincts had served me well once more and that my reservations were entirely justified.

"That night in Portus Itius." she reminded me. "How natural it must have felt for someone like you to just stroll into that brothel and bed yourself a whore for a few cheap coins. The irony is delicious, you decided you would use me by spending a few Sesterces, and all the time it was actually I who had spent my coin to use you."

"What do you mean?" I asked, my sense of unease deepening by the second for some as yet unknown reason.

"Do you think that a whoremaster would limit his opportunities for earning coin to just selling flesh? That grasping Nabatean was more than happy to hire out one of his chambers, and fix a price to keep his silence about the well to do woman who had rented one of his seedy little rooms. Much good it did him, given that he ended up in the gutter with his throat cut the following night."

"You?" I asked, astonished by what I was hearing now.

"Bucco, to be precise." Julia confirmed. "Money is always capable of buying silence, but a prettier purse can also loosen the tightest of lips. As you will soon learn, the stakes are high and I was not prepared to take any chances."

"But why?" I asked her. "What is it that you wanted?"

"Oh I have it, Vepitta." Her tone was openly mocking now. "I have you."

I dropped into the chair opposite her and sat staring at her with my mouth open, still unable to comprehend exactly what it was that Julia was telling me. As though she had detected my rising confusion, she obliged me by continuing to explain herself further.

"It is as I told you; the best of players in the game make their own luck and are ruthless in the pursuit of their goals."

"Do you then consider yourself to be one of these players?"

I made my enquiry while all the time, a queer feeling in the pit of my stomach told me that I would probably regret such a closed question as the answer was more than likely to result in grave consequences for me.

"And why not, Vepitta? Your skill as a soldier has brought you admiration, luck and good fortune. You are known by important people now. Even the Gods themselves must surely be watching you with interest by now, so why not I too? Do you think that a mere woman cannot aspire and then succeed to greatness?"

Her tone was earnest now as she briefly stopped toying with a scroll she was examining and leaned forward, setting me with a hard stare.

"I know nothing of you." I answered. "I know only that it is plain to me now that you are certainly a schemer who enjoys her little deceptions and tricks."

"Deceptions and tricks, is it?" she snapped. "For certain, it is true that you know nothing of me but, as I have a part for you to play in my schemes, then perhaps I should paint you a better picture of just who it is you are now in bed with."

"I do not serve you I ..."

"Enough!" Julia snapped once more. "You have asked the question. Now you will know the answer. Be warned though. What I will tell you now will not sit well with you."

I realised then that it would probably be futile to raise any objections and chose instead to choke back the angry response that had formed on my tongue, waiting instead for the unwelcome enlightenment that I was about to receive.

"As I told you," she began. "It is the Gods themselves who place their favour in the better players. I know now that I was blessed by the Gods from the very beginning of my life to play the game better than most."

As I listened; she explained it all to me. She was firm in her belief that, from the very beginning of her existence, everything had happened to equip her to compete with ruthless skill and cunning in this great game of the Gods that she was so convinced that she played.

She began by explaining that the tragedy that had surrounded her very creation had actually tempered the core of her being and imbued her with a remorseless and ruthless drive, allowing her to realise very early on in life that she could actually use the money and power around her, either as a powerful weapon or a versatile tool. While those others who were fortunate enough to be in her position were aware of the potential power and influence they could wield, they never embraced its true potential as Julia had done. They just chose instead to just savour the comfort and security that their privilege afforded them. As I listened to her, I soon came to realise that perhaps it was fortunate for us all that there were not too many more people in the world like her. Life was after all, cruel and harsh enough. It seemed Julia wanted me to know it all, she was proud of how she had risen and her eyes gleamed with a fire as she laid her life bare before me.

As I listened quietly, she explained how her mother had fallen pregnant with her out of wedlock and although her disgraced mother had managed to flee the family uproar that followed, this had not spared her grandmother who Julia's mother had always regarded as innocent of any wrongdoing. With not a trace of emotion apparent on her face Julia told me of how her own mother had later learned that her grandmother had swallowed poison, unable to cope with the loss of her daughter and the terrible shame on her husband and family name.

Pregnant and alone, Julia's mother had eventually made her way to northern Gaul and had been taken in by the family of one of her oldest friends, Livilla, who had by then married Gnaeus Sentius Saturninus, an extremely well to do young man who had quickly risen to become an extremely influential Senator, despite the apparent disadvantage of hailing from the provinces and not being a native of Rome. He was in fact the very same Senator who now headed the entourage accompanying Adminius home.

Fortune had indeed smiled on the as yet unborn Julia and her mother. Livilla persuaded Saturninus to give them a home, allowing them to live as part of the family while offering her mother the chance to live comfortably as a close companion and lady attendant to Livilla. Once Julia had arrived, Fortuna blessed her again as Saturninus eventually agreed to become her legal guardian, effectively providing the baby Julia with the father figure that she would otherwise not have had.

Though, for all their good fortune, as the young Julia began to thrive, her mother had never let up in reminding her of why they lived the way they lived and the fact that this was not their true family. Julia's mother never took a husband, preferring instead to stay within the bosom of her adoptive family and drip venom into her daughter's ear, priming her for the day when, just possibly, she might be in a position to avenge the terrible wrong of being driven away from their true family.

Julia, for her part, took it all in. As she grew into a young woman, so the gnawing and bitter resentment grew inside of her, as she adopted her own mother's bitterness, allowing it to fester inside her. Eventually, she came to embrace it, nurturing it like it was her own.

Taking the place of the father she never knew, Saturninus had treated her as one of his own, loving her as a daughter and equipping her for a life of power and privilege. So much so that he had celebrated her thirteenth birthday by arranging for her betrothal to his younger brother, Marcus Sentius Balbinus.

It was at this point, Julia explained, that she believed the Gods had finally decided her path and showed her their great favour by creating a match which would eventually equip her with the means to act independently of others. By fifteen, she had married Balbinus who by that time was a wealthy and handsome twenty seven years old with the world at his feet - destined to follow his brother into a successful career as a high flying politician. Even at such a young age for a senatorial hopeful, Balbinus was steadily accumulating money, power and influence. The keen eyes of the Senate were watching his ascendancy with benign interest. It seemed that he too was blessed of the Gods.

For three years, Julia finally knew what it was to love properly and shared in her husband's success, devoting herself totally to him as he began to carve a niche for himself in the elite but bear-pit world of Roman politics. There was nothing more that the Gods could give to the bright young couple, apart from an heir to what would someday be a truly great legacy. So it was then that what the Gods did next would provide the final piece of Julia's make up and set her on the road to her destiny, once and for all.

Again, Julia showed not a trace of emotion, as she told me of how, two winters ago, Balbinus had fallen ill with a flux on his lungs. At thirty years of age, the shining light of his success and ambition had finally faded and died as she sat at his bedside and watched him choke to death, drowning in a bloody froth of his own fluids as her heart broke and she cried her prayers out in vain to all the Gods for his salvation.

She had loved him as she could love no other and, as she had mourned his loss, it was her mother who had fanned the embers of her resentment once more. She made Julia realise that she had now been bequeathed the money and power to take on the world and win. Even to the extent of visiting her vengeance on those who had denied her the love of her true family before she had even been born.

As she began to finish her story I knew then that while her mother had no doubt given thanks to the fates for finally delivering her an opportunity for vengeance, Julia had now totally swept aside her desire to love. Instead, she filled the void in her heart with selfishness and a dark purposefulness that she would push without respite until she had achieved everything she had set out to.

For an instant, I almost pitied her.

"So, here I am." she concluded her tale. "Balbinus is gone over to his ancestors now and in return I have been given a powerful family to protect me, money to cosset me and a purpose to drive me. How many others can say that?"

"You haven't told me what that purpose is yet." I reminded her, "Or, exactly where I am supposed to fit in for that matter."

A faint smile returned to her face once more and I knew also that there was the hint of some sadistic pleasure within the smile as she finally began to tell me what I needed to know.

"My interest lies with the XIIII Gemina, and from the moment the Legion marched into town I was certain that I could make the acquaintance of a member of the Legate's bodyguard. It was almost child's play to make it happen. All I needed to do was to trust in the fact that soldiers will always take the opportunity to wander abroad, whoring and drinking. Simple enough then to place myself in one of the larger brothels set on the road leading directly out to the Legion's camp."

Julia laughed softly and her next words were pregnant with scorn and contempt as she verified just how easily her plan had begun to fall into place.

"How much easier could it have been? I would have waited for days if necessary, but there was no need. It wasn't so long after you all pitched camp that you fell slave to that twitch in your loins. Your cocks pointed the way and, blindly obedient to your own lusts and wants; you followed on in a straight line, right to where I knew you would come."

"My unit, but why?"

"Because, as bodyguard to the Legate you and your comrades have more chance to achieve what I want than any other unit in the Legion."

For a moment I was torn. I wanted to hear what it was that Julia wanted, but I also wanted to know why it was that she chose me. Straightaway, I chose to voice that question which concerned me most.

"Why then did you choose me?"

Before she spoke, she took a moment to appraise me once more, she looked me in the eyes as though reading me and a thin smile shaped her lips before she finally answered.

"You can thank Fortuna for that. The choice was not mine, though it is easy enough to tell what unit a soldier is from. As soon as a party of the Legate's guard entered the brothel I was made aware of the fact and I left my room to come down and make my move. My plan was to approach one of you and do what I did with you. However, you very obligingly saved me the trouble when you decided to challenge that mariner for my attentions."

As I took in the words, my confusion only thickened and I was forced once more to ask her for yet more answers.

"But why? What would you want with any of us?"

"Why, a face of course. A face I could recognise later, when I finally followed the Legion to war as part of the diplomatic entourage. Ah yes, Fortuna's kiss could have been no sweeter when I learned that it would be none other than Saturninus who would accompany the invasion. Oh how I bless our Emperor for his ambition."

She smiled briefly and gave a quiet sigh, as if savouring the way fate had accommodated her schemes.

"As for you, I needed a face to remember me and I needed that face to realise that I had a hold on him. Besides, in such a dreary town as Portus Itius I also needed a little entertainment of my own, so the work was fun, as well as important."

"What? Are you insane?" I hissed. "I am no face, as you call me, to be used in your stupid schemes, whatever they are!"

Julia's eyes twinkled in the dim light of the lamp but the low laugh that she gave out held anything but mirth as she leaned towards me over the table.

"Be calm now, did you not enjoy yourself? Surely, if the Empress Messalina can rut her way through half of Rome then I should at least be allowed to mix business with a little pleasure. After all, I must confess, you are an able swordsman."

The back handed compliment was lost on me and I boiled at the thought that I had been nothing more than a means to some as yet unknown end. It seemed that she spoke of me as though I was nothing, a mere commodity, a tool to be picked up and used only when the need arose. As my anger surged I finally reacted in the way that Julia had probably goaded me towards. My arm shot out like a striking viper and I clutched her by the throat. The words that she gasped next ensured that I at last came to realise that she was in absolute control.

"All I have to do is scream."

She hissed the words as she reached up and sank her nails deep into my wrist. As my blood slowly began to stain the tips of her fingers she began to outline just how it would be between us.

"When I scream, it will take but a heartbeat before we are joined by Bucco and your comrades on guard. They will see us alone in this tent and they will see the marks on my throat, even as they notice the marks I have left on you. When I cry rape, as I surely intend to, I will make much of the fact that I am in pain and I will ask for a physician to attend me immediately. He will discover the seed that you have left inside me. And that, my brave soldier, will see you executed in as hideous a manner as your Legate and Saturninus can conceive. All of the favour and admiration you enjoy now will blow away on the wind, as though it were smoke. Now, will you release your grip and listen?"

I snatched my hand back and sprang up from my seat. It was all I could do not to roar out my anger out as loud as I could.

"You scheming, evil witch," I snarled under my breath. "If your plan is to see harm done to the Legate then…"

"Be calm," she snapped. "I wish no harm to Sabinus."

Julia cut me dead as she began to outline further just what plans she had for me.

"But you are right in assuming that I wish harm to befall someone. That someone holds high office in the Legion and you will be the one who I put to good use to see him dead."

Now, as it finally became clear to me that she intended to use me for a murderer if she could, I reminded her of my oath.

"Then both your time and your scheming have been to no avail. I gave an oath sworn on blood to protect the Legate and his staff. Yes, your accusation will surely see me executed as you say, but I will still have my honour as a loyal soldier and I will meet my ancestors with a clear conscience. Cry out rape if you wish woman, but I will not break my oath."

Even though my life was now at stake, it felt good that I was finally back in control of my own destiny and that I had thwarted Julia after all. She had failed in her plan. She knew now that she would not be able to break my oath with the vile lie she was threatening to tell.

"Is your honour so important that you would forfeit your life then?"

She was calm as she asked the question and her manner was almost casual as she awaited my response.

"There is nothing more important to me!" I snapped.

"Such a pity." said Julia, as she idly rolled one of the armourer's scrolls back and forth on the table before looking up and staring straight into my eyes. "I had hoped that you might at least place a little more value on the family you left behind in Mogontiacum."

"What...? You know nothing." I clutched at what I knew in my heart was a forlorn hope. "I'll warrant that all that you know is that soldiers keep unofficial wives sometimes. No, your speculative little bluff will not work on me."

Again she smiled mirthlessly, as she leaned back in her chair and began to tell me what she knew. As shock and anger caused my body to tremble I felt an uncontrollable sense of dread spread through my body, accompanied by an overwhelming desire to launch myself across the table and beat Julia into a bloody pulp. It was a yearning I knew I had no chance of satisfying.

"You see Vepitta, if you pay people enough money, they will travel to the ends of the earth for you. Though, I didn't need to spend that much money as I only needed to send somebody to go back to Mogontiacum."

There was nothing I could say now, other than stand and listen as she demonstrated just how thorough she had been in ensuring my co-operation.

"When you yourself gave me your name that night, I was able to tell my agent who to ask questions about when he reached the fortress at Mogontiacum and made his enquiries with the military clerks there. It wasn't long before he found out all about the woman Salviena and the two boys. What were their names again? Oh yes Marcus and Gaius. Fine young boys I understand."

She smiled, though no mirth shone behind those eyes as she nonchalantly ran her finger over the surface of the table. Just cold triumph.

I thought my hands would shatter into pieces under

the pressure that I exerted as I clenched my fists and clamped my teeth together, fighting against the rising rage inside me and the overwhelming desire to tear Julia limb from limb, but I knew that it was useless as the truth of the situation became starkly apparent.

"Those old timber buildings where they live are so prone to fire are they not? It would be a tragedy indeed if they were all to perish in a tragic accident."

There was a brief, silent pause before she stood and smiled. She pulled her long cloak around her shoulders and walked around the edge of the table, standing before me then with an almost sympathetic expression on her face. She reached up then and slowly, softly caressed my cheek.

"Is your honour still not for sale, Vepitta?" she smiled once more. "Perhaps we can discuss it again soon. In the meantime, I'll bid you goodnight."

With that, she breezed silently out of the tent, leaving me with my thoughts.

For a few moments I just stood and fought with the enormity of the situation I now found myself in. After what seemed like a lifetime I gathered my thoughts enough to collect the equipment I had discarded earlier and stepped out of the tent. The shock of almost walking straight into Surus almost made me shout out as he stared at me, a look of utter incredulity on his face as he asked the question:

"What in the name of all the Gods are you doing brother?"

CHAPTER 20

What could I say? Surus had chanced across the meeting and confronted me there and then, seeking no doubt to find out whether I had actually gone stark raving mad. Of course, I had made the effort to throw in a few weak and half-hearted denials but I knew it was useless from the very start. I could see it in his face that he knew the real truth of it.

After the token attempt at deceiving him it seemed as though he regarded me almost with contempt. My lies had forced him to demonstrate to me that he knew the real truth of things. He told me of how, having been relieved at his post slightly early, he had set off across the compound in search of me or any of the others. It was then that he had caught sight of Bucco, skulking in the shadows by the armourer's tent and as it turned out, totally unaware of his arrival in that part of the compound.

He told me of how, instantly suspicious of Bucco's furtive behaviour, he too had concealed himself in shadow and watched. Puzzled at first by the odd conduct, he had watched curiously as, after a while, Bucco had seemed to give a start and moved swiftly to the entrance of the tent, all the while casting surreptitiously around the compound. A dagger had been clutched firmly in his hand and it seemed as though he was waiting for something to happen as he listened intently, so intently it seemed that he was totally unaware of the fact that he too was being watched from the shadows.

Surus had explained further that he had watched Bucco slide back into the shadows for a short while, lurking there until the tent flaps had eventually parted. Then, Julia had breezed out into the night, heading off towards her own quarters as Bucco had emerged from the shadows and fallen in behind her like some faithful hound.

I continued to experience yet more pangs of shame and stupidity for my attempts at deceit as Surus explained that he had been perplexed at what could have been going on. Resolving to find out more, he had approached the tent, only to be confronted by a blindingly obvious truth as I had stepped out into the night.

There really was no point in issuing denials any longer because, whichever way you looked at it, I had been caught out in circumstances that held absolutely no chance of being passed off with any innocent or legitimate explanation. There was no room for anything but the truth, and in the end the truth is what I told him.

"You've got to tell Zenas and the others. There's nothing else for it."

"What?" I exclaimed incredulously. "Have you lost your mind? By now I'm almost a walking dead man as it is. Zenas will take me before Fatalis if I tell him about this and before you know it you'll all be under orders to beat the ghost out of me at my execution day."

"You know, brother." Surus sighed. "If you think that of Zenas, then it's almost as though you have never known him all this time. Yes, maybe your life could be forfeit because of this, but you are one of us. Do you really think that Zenas will condemn you out of hand without even giving a thought to helping you?"

I remember thinking then that maybe Surus was right. I was too busy thinking with my emotions. I should have been staying more focused and thinking more clearly. For one thing, if it all came out then as well as my possible execution, it could also mean that there was every chance of the rest of the Contubernium being dispersed throughout the rest of the Legion as they would no longer be trustworthy enough to hold their current posts. Through association with me they would always be followed by the suspicion that all knew what was happening, yet none did anything about it.

Julia was a member of a Senator's family and, as a guest of the Legate; she was entitled to the protection of the guard. As such, Saturninus was also entitled to believe without question that as well as protection from attack, neither would she be the subject of the unwelcome molestations of a mere common soldier. The men of the Legate's bodyguard had to be beyond such doubt and therefore they would have to be replaced. The surviving members would not only be the butt of constant baiting by their new comrades as failures; but it would also be unlikely that they would ever be placed in a high position of trust again. For the rest of their service they would be tainted by my stupidity. No, Surus was right, telling Zenas and the others was the only way to handle the matter, regardless of how uncomfortable things were about to become. I had created the situation, but they should have the right to decide on what happened next

The next day, just prior to morning muster, I steeled myself for what I was about to do and called for the others to join me in a quiet corner of the Legate's compound. I saw the initial expectation in their faces turn one by one to expressions of mute dismay as I laid it all out for them, from Portus Itius to last night

"Great Gods, man. You have caused Fortuna to do no less than spit on us all with this little episode, and no mistake"

Zenas was positively seething with anger as he delivered the rebuke. I could see that the consequences of my actions had begun to percolate through into each of the minds of the others. They stood around me, quiet for now, but all of them were stony faced and obviously in deep contemplation about what I had just told them. I shuffled uneasily, waiting for Zenas to add to his last comment, or for one of the others to add their own contribution to my growing discomfort. Finally, Marinus obliged.

"So, you get caught dipping your bread with some crazed witch linked to Saturninus and now you want us to help you out because you can't lie in the sorry little bed you've made for yourself. Is that the way of it?"

"No, Marinus, I…" He cut me dead as he continued.

"That's exactly it Vepitta," he snarled. "But, for what it's worth, I'll tell you the rest of how I see it, shall I? Neither I nor any of this lot should be expected to stand with you on this one. There's only you and your cock to blame in all this and I'm damned if I'm going to lose everything that I've clawed my way out of the shit for just because you can't reign your urges in."

"Hold your tongue a while, Marinus," Zenas told him abruptly, his faced etched with deep lines as he continued to think hard about the situation.

"Hold my tongue you say? If you think for one heartbeat I am going to be dragged into his sorry mess then you have it very wrong. Far better that he gets what's coming to him than we all end up winning a piece of the Senator's ire as well."

"There's the real Marinus for you, and no mistake," hissed Pudens. "You shame yourself in the way you turn your back on your own."

"Hey, go fuck your mother!" snapped Marinus. "I've been in the Legate's guard for years. I might as well go and drown myself in the latrine pit if I fall in with him because everything I've worked for will be over with when word of this gets out."

There was outrage written all over Marinus' face as he finished his bluster and stared at me hard, crossing his arms and breathing heavily through his nose as though he were some sort of angry bull.

"You know, Marinus, I'm not sure we haven't already thrown in our lot with Vepitta without even knowing it." Zenas suggested.

"What?" snapped the angry veteran. "How so?"

"Gods on high, yes, I too see it now." Crispus said, nodding in realisation and throwing his hands up. "Zenas is right if you think about it with care. The point is that it doesn't matter whether we knew about it or not you see? All that Sabinus and Saturninus will see is that Vepitta is one of ours. If that's the way of it then we're all bound together anyway. In a matter such as this they will judge that the conduct of one will affect us all. In other words, we are all complicit anyway."

"Precisely." Zenas confirmed.

"Piss of Jupiter!" Marinus snapped. "So, you mean to accept that he's fucked us all just as well as he did that over privileged harlot? I really don't believe I'm hearing this."

"Why not, Marinus?" Aebutius stepped into the discussion. "We're tight. We stand together and we're willing to fall together. We've sworn an oath to each other as well as to Sabinus and the Legion. Do you really think that they won't judge us all by those loyalties? You know in your heart the truth of it. They don't need proof, just suspicion. That's enough."

"That's right," agreed Pacatianus. "And besides, if not for Vepitta, then we must do something to save his family from Julia's threats. Those boys are like my own kin and I'll not stand by and watch while they and their mother are murdered at the whim of this scheming harpy. We're in this now, like it or no. It's up to us whether or not we keep our oath and help our brother. If we don't then we are choosing to just throw ourselves on the mercy of the Legate. We risk having one of our own executed and then spending the rest of our service digging shit holes. So brother, what's it to be?"

"Alright!" Marinus snapped. "But you can't blame me for my anger."

"True, the anger is righteous enough." Crispus conceded. "But maybe we should all thank the fates. After all, any one of us could have been snared in Julia's little trap in Portus Itius that night, because that is where all this started. Vepitta has done no real wrong here; we must help our brother through this. It's the right thing to do."

"Yes indeed!" Pudens put in, his customary grin beginning to return to his face. "And to be fair, after the sorry old time we've had on this rotten island so far, which one of us would have passed up the chance to rattle that bitches bones if the chance had come our way, eh?"

"Oh, Vulcan's balls." Surus groaned. "I'm heartened by the fact that we all seem to be in accord here, but let's try and focus on finding a solution for now. Later perhaps we can relax and try to make light of this."

"Brothers, I too am heartened and I shouldn't need to tell you just how grateful I am that you will help me in this." I decided at last that I could add something to the discussion. "For involving you all in of this, I am truly sorry. But you have my word; I would lay down my life for any one of you if you needed my help."

"We know, lad." Zenas clapped his hand on my shoulder. "We'll do our best for you, as you would for us, so you can rest a little easier for now. Still, we now need to decide exactly what that best may be. So, what do we do?"

"Nothing." Crispus said flatly.

"Nothing, what do you mean nothing?" queried Marinus.

"Precisely that." Crispus confirmed. "We have all now resolved to throw our lot in with Vepitta and that is really all we can do for now. Julia has not yet said what it is she wants from him, other than to show him that she holds the loaded dice in this game and also to say that she wants someone dead. Until we know just who she has marked for a trip with the ferry man, we are not in a position to make plans."

"Makes sense to me." Pacatianus sniffed. "When will we get to find out though?"

"She'll find a way to let me know, I'm sure." I told them. "No doubt I'll get another cosy invite from that walking tree trunk that follows her around. That's what happened last time."

"I don't like that fucking Bucco." snapped Surus. "I'll be looking to slice a new arse hole open for him, first chance I get."

"Hmm, Julia uses him because she trusts him implicitly. It looks as though we may need to tolerate his particular talents as some sort of go between for now, so your kind offer of surgery may have to wait." said Zenas.

"It's agreed then." confirmed Aebutius. "We wait to see what her next move is."

"As far as that goes, then I suppose yes, though there is more that you should all know." Feeling more at ease with the situation, I confided in them still further, casting my eye around once more to ensure that nobody was close enough to overhear before I continued.

"Last night, I was confronted by Ademetus as I left the Legate's command tent. It would seem that the Prefect does not hold with our close friendship with the Chief of Scouts."

"I was afraid of this." said Zenas, shaking his head slowly. "What's been said?"

"Very little." I confirmed. "But what he did say was enough to make me realise that he is prepared to use any means to see that we do not offer support and friendship to Batiatus."

"Are you sure about this, Vepitta?" Pacatianus asked.

"You all know that he means to kill him and that he has already tried once." I reminded them all. "I am also of the mind that he will go as far as to kill or ruin any of us if we stand in the way of that goal again."

"It's a bad thing to have to accept, but I believe it is as you say it is, brother." Zenas acknowledged. "But here is another truth for you all. By tomorrow, we will all be servants of Mars once more because then we will march to fight the Britons again. Batiatus is still out on his mission to gather intelligence on our foe. I'd say it is highly unlikely that he will return before we break camp. So, it follows that we should not have cause for concern over how we take the old bear into our company just yet."

"That's right." Marinus gave a mirthless laugh. "After all, in a couple of days' time we could all be in Hades playing dice with the old bastard, and then none of us will have to give a damn for either Julia or Ademetus again."

"Oldest first, Marinus." Pudens grinned.

"Kiss my hairy white arse, Pudens." came the reply.

CHAPTER 21

Though our stay in the area of Durovernon had been quite short, I still felt inclined to spend a little time on our last night there, reflecting on what the town had once been and what it was soon to become.

With the arrival of Vespasian and II Augusta in the area, our Legion had been able to devote more time to construction work. The old tribal capital was now beginning its transformation from a random collection of thatched native roundhouses into an entirely new incarnation. It would eventually be a fitting seat indeed for Adminius; wielding such power that Rome would trickle down to him as he played at being king, ruling only under the direct consent and control of the new military governor and a procurator.

With extra men providing additional labour, and newly acquired native slaves being put under the lash, productivity increased immensely. Durovernon was now beginning to experience a rapid series of sweeping and irreversible changes. It was changing from a rural backwater into a new Roman style town with order and form, the first of many to begin the metamorphosis into somewhere worthy of its place in a new Roman province.

News had quickly reached us that a road was being pushed through from the original landing areas and that construction was complete on massive double ditch and rampart defence works, protecting the great docks and quays that were now under construction. It would be completion of this work that would establish a fortified port, rivalling even some of the busiest in the Empire. It was to be known as Portus Rutupiae and its immediate role would be as a key re-supply port used for landing goods, equipment and reinforcements from Gaul.

The vast quantity of supplies and equipment they landed there would be transported inland or shipped around the coast to be landed close to the army as it pushed its way further inland. In these early days of the invasion the port was key to everything, for it was to here that the army looked to sustain its push into Britannia as daily, it swallowed up thousands of tons of food and equipment that it needed just to keep itself moving.

Local resources were nowhere near plentiful enough to sustain the insatiable appetite of the permanently hungry force of tens of thousands of soldiers. Instead, the great army principally relied on a constant stream of heavily guarded oxen and mule trains, streaming back and forth like great columns of continuously busy ants between the port and the forward units.

The supply columns ferried everything that the army would need to maintain their forward momentum. They shipped grain for bread and fodder to sustain both pack animals and cavalry mounts. Weapons and equipment also travelled along the supply lines. Everything from new swords and javelins to spares for artillery pieces and hob nails for boots. All were meticulously itemised and listed. And all, down to the last strip of salted pork, were duly signed for on arrival at their destination.

Right from the start the port would also be shipping goods and cargo out as well as in. After all, now that Rome had finally sunk its teeth into Britannia it would waste no time in bleeding it of the many resources it had previously been compelled to trade for. This strange land was rich in much that Rome had coveted. The more territory that fell to her, the more she ripped from the grasp of the Briton's, satisfying the ever more insatiable demands of her subjects and armies.

More slave traders arrived in the area of Durovernon daily, taking advantage of the abundance of new labour that languished in chains since just after the battle. They visited the lines of shackled men to cast a discerning eye over the goods, examining the vanquished warriors meticulously for their quality and saleability. They closely considered every aspect of their bodies for strength, fitness, and signs of disease. Plenty of time was taken in the assessment; after all, there was no hurry. The traders had no need to worry about competition. They had been given first refusal on the goods because they were the ones who had secured an imperial contract to purchase wholesale as many of those captured by the Legions as they could afford. The money the slaves realised would then be split between the capturing Legion and the Imperial treasury.

When the slave traders were finally finished with their appraisals, they retired to the command tent to conclude the business of the day by agreeing a price for the merchandise, before drawing up a bill of sale with the Legion quartermaster.

The slavers had eventually set off for Portus Rutupiae late on the last day, escorted by a unit of cavalry. Their new acquisitions shambled along in a ragged dispirited column, silent but for the chink of the chains that chafed their necks and cut into their wrists and ankles. These miserable men had once been proud warriors. Now they walked with heads hung low, an emptiness of spirit plainly evident on their filth caked faces. As yet, they were still covered in the dried gore of the shattering defeat which had unexpectedly sealed their fate. After the battle they had sat in their own filth for days, stinking and humiliated as they ruminated on just what their shameful defeat at the hands of Rome would really mean to them. I recalled facing them, when they were part of a fearsome and determined army, ready to push us back into the sea. They were all very different men now.

The slave traders herded them off. Harshly delivered shouts accompanied the stinging lash of whips, carefully administered though, so that the merchandise was not devalued by the presence of thick weal marks on the flesh. Whip marks were after all the hallmark of a disobedient slave. Nobody liked an insubordinate slave; they were always more trouble than they were worth so they were always hard to shift at the markets.

The captive Britons must have known that they were taking the first steps of a very long journey, leading them to who knows where? They shuffled off along the road to the coast, war trophies strung out on forged iron links. Now and again one of them would cast a glance over his shoulder, probably muttering his own farewell to a home and family he was never likely to see again. For myself, as I watched the ragged column slowly disappear into the distance, I found myself quietly thanking the gods that it was not I who had been on the losing side that day.

As the column moved out, the terrible wailing rising up from Durovernon was nothing I had not heard before. I realised though that it would be the last sound that the shackled men heard from the settlement. Their women, still mourning the men fallen in battle, once more felt their hearts being torn apart as they watched their surviving men folk being driven away from them, like a herd of dumb cattle. The women mounted the tops of the town palisade and thrashed around making the most baleful of noises, all the while tearing at their hair. Eventually, troops were sent up to clear them off the defences and drive them back to their homes.

For myself, I don't suppose I have ever been quite at ease with attacking people who didn't pose a threat to us, but I had nevertheless stood and watched silently with the others as soldiers had swiftly mounted the ramparts and set about their task with relish. I reasoned that all the women wanted to do was to show their grief, mourning their losses in their own way and according to their own customs. Although, the actions of the troops made it plain that Rome gravely disapproved of such conduct. Neither I nor my comrades said a word, choosing instead to acknowledge with our silence that the brutal display was an absolutely necessary display of strength and brutality by the new masters of this place. Stone faced and impassive, we watched women carrying small children thrown from tall ramparts, weapon pommels and shields bludgeoned away any resistance. The long, well-kept hair that many of the women prided themselves on was grabbed up in great handfuls by the soldiers and used as a convenient handle to fling the women around like children's toys.

I, like the others, understood that all these women wanted to do was to show their grief. Instead, all they got was more pain. Judging by the gleeful shouts and mocking laughter of their tormentors, it was gladly given too. It came as no real surprise to learn later that they had come to nurture an immense hatred for anything Roman after that.

Despite the resentment of the surviving population towards Rome and her soldiers, Adminius had soon got what he wanted and had been appointed as client ruler. The elders of the tribe spoke on behalf of the people and the Cantiaci duly declared itself to be a loyal subject tribe and ally of Rome. They had pledged non-aggression to Imperial forces, agreeing instead to assist efforts to establish a Roman government, whilst the tribes that resisted the occupation of Britannia were subdued. Of course, all this meant nothing to the voiceless women of Durovernon. It was merely the political posturing of very powerful men. All that those women understood now was that they had lost everything the day Rome had invaded their world. It would take more than the language of politics and diplomacy to quell the burning hatred that they now harboured for us.

As we prepared to spend our last night camped by Durovernon our Century had been mustered and Fatalis relayed the orders we would follow on the march towards Durobrivae.

"Tomorrow morning we begin the march to our next objective." he informed us curtly. "You will make final preparations now and be ready to move after breakfast tomorrow."

He paused, collecting his thoughts to pass all of the recalled detail of his own briefing onto us.

"Further to the west lies the inland trading settlement of Durobrivae. Rome has known of it for many years and Roman merchant ships have traded with it regularly as it is accessible from the sea via the great river that it sits on. General Plautius and the Legion Legate's know that it will suit our purposes to capture it and establish a new supply point, allowing us to push yet further into this land."

He paused once more to look up and down the Century.

"So far, we have done well, with only three of our number injured and none killed. We did a good job of work by capturing this place but the next step is going to be that much harder to achieve."

He stood facing the middle of the formation and leant with both hands on his Vitis.

"We know that the settlement of Durobrivae is now an armed camp and the largest force of Britons we will meet so far is massing there to await our arrival. As we speak, they are forming a large army on the opposite bank of the great river known to them as Medway. It is this waterway that we need to cross to further our own objectives. Already, they have dismantled the bridge that crosses to the settlement in an attempt to prevent us traversing the river. We must now move swiftly to prevent that army from growing any bigger and to prevent them from doing anything else that will hamper our crossing of the river."

"Because this objective is so important, General Plautius is going to throw as many men into this as he can spare. We will therefore be part of a much larger force comprising II Augusta, IX Hispana, four Cohorts of Batavian Auxiliaries and an accompanying cavalry force. When there is more news concerning our role in all this I will give it to you. Now, fall out to your duties and finish your preparations."

We moved out as planned the next day, our massive column of armoured troops snaking through the countryside, marching westwards and slight north across the chalk downs to our new objective. A steady stream of Legionary cavalry constantly galloped back and forth, maintaining communication with the other Legions as our own column pressed on inexorably to its next objective.

Although the weather had been fine and dry with the sun spending most of the day free of cloud, the wind had been very blustery and slowed down the progress of the formation somewhat. We carried heavy packs and large shields which caught the gusts and impeded progress, tiring you quicker than normal, which meant more rest stops. Nevertheless, at days end we had achieved the required distance and reached our planned camp area. All we needed to do now was establish a marching camp for the night and prepare ourselves to assemble for an assault the next morning.

We quickly threw up the usual defences around the immense camp. A ditch topped with a low earth rampart bristled with sharpened wooden stakes, lashed together with lengths of light iron chain. Sentries were placed on the defences while we quickly erected the tents and dug shallow fire pits in preparation for the evening meal. The wind eased a little and allowed us the opportunity of establishing the cooking fires without having kindling brush blown all over the camp. Soon, the air was filled with the smell of wood smoke. The aroma of stews and broths wafted from countless cook pots while men moved in and out of camp, collecting wild herbs and vegetables to add to their pots.

Now and again the fortunate forager would return triumphantly with a hare or water fowl, ensuring that the evening meal that he and his immediate comrades would enjoy would be just that little bit more tempting than the usual ration of dried pork with iron hard biscuits.

Despite the fact that the Legion was at rest for the evening, the camp remained ever vigilant, as though it were some lightly slumbering beast; at rest but always ready to strike out if disturbed. Those who went foraging always ventured out in groups and always wore full armour, knowing always to remain within sight of the sentries. Even at night, our boots stayed on and weapons were kept close. The only concession to a decent night's sleep was the removal of bulky body armour to facilitate much needed sleep, regenerating you for the efforts of the next day.

As we sat down to our meal outside the Contubernium tent, we watched the sun dropping down behind the low hills, its dying rays lighting up the sky with a blend of wondrous shades of gold and russet tones, signalling the departure of Apollo and his fiery chariot from the sky for another day. Eager by that time for sleep, we quickly finished our meal and turned in for the night.

In the field of battle it is considered most unwise to waste opportunities for sleep. Conditions were often arduous and a lack of sleep could cost a man dearly so we did not wish to delay overlong in taking to our beds. There would be other opportunities for small talk on other evenings. The Gods knew, there was much we had to talk of. For now though, we savoured the fact that none of us had drawn guard duty and we all looked forward to the one last thing that needed to be done before we slept.

As we sat silently on our outspread bedding rolls, Zenas took a small object covered in cloth from his marching pack and carefully began to unwrap it. We sat waiting expectantly as the small bronze figure was reverently placed on its wrapping and then all present bowed lightly to it as it again stood before us once more. A lightly moulded but comfortingly familiar smile was visible on its small shadowy face as it seemed to draw the warmth of the flickering lamplight to it. It was easy to imagine that the figure was glad to be free of its dark, safe hiding place once more and that it was savouring the warming lamp light, as well as the pious respect of its mortal companions who had gathered to pay their respects to it.

As leader of the Contubernium, it was Zenas who was the keeper of the Genius, the guardian spirit that watched over us eight comrades. It was always he who officiated over this small ritual, every night before we slept. It was always something from which we drew great spiritual comfort. As always, the ritual was conducted according to our own traditions and it was Crispus tonight who placed a small earthenware bowl containing hot coals from our fire before the figure. After blowing gently into the embers to brighten their glow, he withdrew while Zenas began the prayers.

"Sacred Genius, benevolent and generous protector of we eight servants of the highest Gods of great mother Rome." he began solemnly. "We greet you once more at days end and thank you for the protection you have afforded us this day. We wish you to share again our meal this evening and we ask once more that you bless us with your protection for another day."

In silent reverence Zenas then broke a small piece of bread from one of our small round loaves and placed it on the glowing embers. As the vaguely sweet smelling smoke curled upwards into the still air of the tent, Zenas continued with the rite:

"Blessed Genius, spirit of our band, take this bread to sustain you and drink also of this wine to quench and refresh you."

Zenas tipped a small amount of wine from out of his beaker onto the coals and a small cloud of pink steam erupted with an angry hiss as he finished the prayer.

"We ask with one voice that you watch over us while we sleep. Grant that we live through tomorrow's battle, that we may continue to be faithful to the Gods and the Senate and people of Rome."

Placing his finger lightly to his lips, he next touched his heart, then the head of the small figure. Quietly we copied his actions then, as the precious little figure was wrapped in its protective cloth once more, the lamps were doused and we finally settled down to sleep, comforted now that the protection of the Genius had been invoked.

*****

"Alarm, alarm. Stand to, we're under attack!"

It seemed as though I had been asleep for a mere moment when the shouting snapped me straight back to full consciousness. The first shout of 'alarm' seemed to echo across the veils of sleep, but the second shout registered loud and clear in my brain as I sat bolt upright and began grabbing for my weapons. There was no panic. Well-rehearsed drills clicked into action as we rapidly prepared to leave the tent and man the defences.

The tent flap was flung to one side and my eyes began to adjust to the contrasting light levels. I peered from the pitch black interior of the tent, taking in the pin prick brightness of stars in the clear night sky, along with the dull, slowly pulsing glow of a dying cooking fire. The improved light instantly created silhouettes within the tent, rapidly moving towards the opening. In an instant, we were out, throwing on belts and weapons and grabbing up shields. Other men emerged from their tents all around us and swiftly began to equip themselves as they raced for the outer defences, their minds almost working subconsciously as they repeated the endless drills about where to go if the camp was attacked.

Screams began to pierce the air from the direction of the southern defences as the raiders were engaged by sentries, then the killing began. Nobody detoured from their pre-arranged places. Men ran instinctively to cover all points of the defences, regardless of where the main attack was taking place. It so happened that our assembly points were on the southern line so we ran to defend that side of the camp.

Although none of us had donned our body armour we had all equipped ourselves with helmet, shield, sword and at least one Pilum each. As we fell in behind the defences I caught sight of one of our night sentries lying dead in a spreading black puddle of blood, a spear transfixing his neck. His eyes were open, still bulging with the shock of the mortal blow, while his tongue poked grotesquely out of his wide open mouth. I snapped my head to the front once more and peered out into the dark field beyond. Out there, human shapes ran around, shouting wildly in the blackness beyond the defences. Over the chaos, I heard Fatalis' familiar voice bellow out;

"Double shield wall form! Archers, light the ground up!"

At that moment I felt something fly past my cheek at a great speed, startling me as it passed before hitting something behind me with a thud. Again I felt something else shoot through the air close to my head. An instant after I heard what I could only describe as a wet 'smack,' followed closely with a shrill scream of pain from our ranks.

"Shields up, they're using slings!"

As soon as the shout went up, the shield wall rose higher and the deadly swift little missiles could be heard all along the line impacting with the faces of shields with a series of loud, sharp cracks. All the time, the lethal hail was accompanied by the crazed screams of unseen attackers that assailed us from the blackness beyond the camp perimeter.

Just than a wall of light erupted behind us as a flask of lamp oil was thrown onto a smouldering fire and a group of Legionary archers began to use the bright new flames to ignite arrows wrapped in cloth and pitch. As soon as the arrows began to blaze, the bowmen sent them streaking out into the blackness. They shot them along flat trajectories so that they skimmed just over our heads and ripped across the darkened field, hitting the ground in front of the defences at varying distances. As the fiery trails zipped through the air like miniature comets, the darkness began to diminish rapidly as the fire arrows lit up the night and fell onto the field, setting light to the surrounding undergrowth. As the flames took hold in the dry summer meadow grass, sparks shot up into the night sky, dancing like fiery little sprites on the light breeze as a flickering orange glow illuminated the ground beyond the camp. Now we could see them!

About two hundred Britons were assembled in a loose formation just short of the defences. All were on foot and were armed with a mix of slings, spears and long swords. Many carried lightweight shields. They seemed shocked that the cover of night that had aided their assault so far had been so quickly and effectively denied them. Quickly they realised that it was they who were now presenting glaring targets in the newly illuminated field. Their momentum faltered with the shock of the initial response and we quickly seized the opportunity to react further.

The nearest Britons to us were around ten yards away and almost ready to recover their wits and charge the defences when Fatalis quickly bawled out another order;

"Ready Pila!"

As the thunderous command carried above the chaotic shouting, each man quickly hoisted his javelin into throwing position on his shoulder. Then, immediately after the first instruction;

"Throw!"

As one, we cast a deadly rain of needle sharp iron at the Britons who had by now recovered their wits and were bearing down on us in a wild, screaming charge. The rushing, haphazard advance faltered instantly as the wickedly pointed shafts sank deep into their targets. I don't remember seeing any one of those weapons missing their mark as the entire front row of attackers fell to the ground, screaming with the shock and pain of being skewered by the deadly iron shafts. By now, around a dozen Legionary archers had placed themselves behind our ranks and Fatalis shouted the instruction for us to move to open order so that the archers could shoot between us.

As we moved to accommodate them, the bowmen began to loose their shafts at random into the native raiders. The madly shouting Britons were now running back and forth in fear and confusion as swiftly delivered arrows repeatedly struck down their targets with unerring accuracy. Very quickly, the sound of bowstrings twanging was joined by the familiar sound of ratchets clattering, followed by the meaty 'whack' of a pair of Scorpiones unleashing their deadly, heavy, iron tipped bolts into the hapless attackers. The terrifying power of the weapons bolstered the rain of missiles that the archers were bringing down on the howling Britons. I watched as, one by one, the tribesmen fell to the deadly shower of precisely aimed projectiles that beset them like angry hornets as they struggled to get away from the betraying light of the spreading flames.

Dead and wounded lay scattered before the defences and here and there agonized screams and groans could be heard as the wounded cried out in their anguish and pain. Scattered fires lit up the night and grew in intensity as clumps of scrub began to go up with the dry grass as the flames spread. Swirling clouds of rising smoke glowed light orange as they were illuminated by the flames. The grass smoke that drifted through our lines made me cough as it stung the back of my throat, causing my nose and eyes to stream as the light wind blew it into our ranks. Then I began to detect other smells carried along with the smoke. The spreading fires were also charring the bodies of the felled attackers and now the stink of burning flesh, singed hair, and smouldering wool assailed my nostrils, slowly beginning to intensify until it became a sickening, somehow corrupt stink.

It wasn't long before the marauding Britons' assault collapsed and they fled in disarray leaving us peering out into the night, watching intently for the first signs of their return. We hadn't even drawn our swords; the enemy had never got close enough for that. Behind us, soldiers moved around and planted more javelins into the ground at our backs, preparing us for another wave of attackers as the archers quickly replenished their stock of arrows.

We learned later that about eight Britons had managed to clear the defences and actually gain entry to the camp. They had entered via the track that crossed the ditch and killed another sentry before the alert had turned out the soldiers that would prevent them going any further, or killing anyone else. Those eight had been swept up in the running wave of Legionaries responding to the alarm and their heads had quickly been separated from their bodies. Four had been stuck on the defensive spikes whilst the remaining four were in the possession of soldiers who had waved them around in the air during the defence, shouting crude insults in the direction of the fleeing Britons.

Eventually, the men holding the gory trophies had

thrown the heads contemptuously into the defensive ditch as the Britons called off the attack and fled, leaving no one to taunt.

We held our positions until the first pale rays of light began to herald the dawn. The weak light slowly began to strengthen and, in turn, it slowly started to reveal the results of the nights work in all of its stark detail.

Corpses lay scattered in front of the ditch, pale and bloodless. Many of the bodies had more than one shaft stuck in them, while a cursory look at a few others seemed to reveal nothing wrong at all until you noticed the clean hole left by an artillery bolt which had punched its way straight through flesh and bone. No doubt travelling onwards with enough deadly momentum to claim another victim before its violent energy was finally spent.

Large, ragged black patches of scorched ground still smouldered from the grass fires which had started as the fire arrows had been deployed. A light grey smoke drifted lazily around at ground level, sending curling fingers here and there into the pale dawn sky. It also rose lazily from the charred and blackened bodies which had been caught up in the fires. Often, you could actually tell if the Britons had been alive or dead when they burned by how they looked. The ones who had died before being burned lay in slumped or flat shapes, but the ones who had suffered the torment of the flames were arched and contorted. Their gnarled hands and fingers and exposed, snarling teeth gave testimony to their agonising demise. The site of them caused me to recall again the terrible screams that had penetrated the air, mere hours ago, reminding me once more of what the sound of men burning to death was like.

I rubbed my eyes, which only now did I begin to notice were tired and sore from a sleepless and smoke filled night. I cast a glance up and down the front rank, taking in other weary faces. They were streaked with the grime from the smoke and made even filthier in appearance by the tracks of tears and trails of thick snot brought on by the stinging acrid fumes that had swirled around us. Pudens stood next to me, loosening the ties on his cheek pieces and slowly rubbing his face with his fingertips.

"Well," he sighed. "So much for a decent night's sleep eh?"

I nodded wearily and exhaled loudly, turning round to acknowledge the man on my other side. Marinus leaned on the top of his shield, watching me with a pair of red rimmed, bloodshot eyes. He straightened up and arched his back, groaning loudly with the pleasure of the stretch before sniffing the air lightly in my direction, looking me up and down. I regarded him curiously, unable to work out what he was thinking until at last, he shared his thoughts with me.

"You could do with a wash, friend Vepitta." he observed casually. "You stink!"

CHAPTER 22

It was around two hours after sunrise that Batiatus rode into the camp with his small party of around twenty dishevelled looking scouts, just a short time before the execution of Lucius Fortunatus.

I, along with the rest of the Legates bodyguard were in the compound, preparing to receive the Century of the condemned soldier as they came to perform their onerous duty in front of the Legate and his staff. Fortunatus himself was already being held in the compound under guard as Batiatus and the scouts rode in.

"Welcome back, Batiatus." Fatalis greeted the chief of scouts as he took hold of his lathered horse's reins. "Your timing is impeccable."

"Centurion, don't tell me you've actually managed to find some pretty little virgin who wouldn't mind anointing my aching arse with some soothing balm, perhaps?"

The grimy faced veteran grinned cheekily, wincing as he eased himself out of the saddle before swinging off the back of his exhausted mount. He landed heavily on the ground and groaned loudly as he arched his back and slowly rotated his hips, relishing the sensation of feeling his own feet on the ground once more.

"Now if I had managed that Batiatus, do you really

think you'd be the one to get first go on her?" Fatalis smiled wryly. "No old friend, the less exotic truth of it is that I reckon you've got just about an hour to put your report in before we carry out his execution."

The old Centurion nodded slowly in the direction of Fortunatus who sat cross legged on the ground in a corner of the compound. At just sixteen years old, Fortunatus looked more like a boy who had stolen a soldier's uniform as he sat with his head bowed, chained at the wrists but still fully armoured, between two grim faced guards.

"What's to do then?" Batiatus asked; his tone matter of fact as he continued to stretch out his spine and groan with the pleasure of the restored mobility in his lower back.

"The lad fell asleep on guard duty and the camp ended up on the receiving end of a raid by about two hundred Briton's. We recovered things well but his need for a good night's sleep cost us about ten more men than we would have lost if we'd been ready."

"Fair enough then." growled Batiatus. "If I'd been his Centurion I'd have kicked the little bastard to death myself by now."

Batiatus slowly rubbed the back of his neck and rolled his head around as he turned his gaze away from the hapless young soldier.

"Two hundred you say? When was this?"

"Probably just after the third hour." Fatalis responded. "Why?"

"Because we've been tracking a big war band of

around five hundred for the last two days who have been shadowing the IX Hispana a bit further north of here. Just last night I actually thought they were going to go have a go and do what was done here. I was having a right old time of it, trying to get round them and warn the camp. Then, all of a sudden like, they just turned and went back west, towards Durobrivae. I'm telling you; that lot in the IX don't know just how lucky they were. A surprise attack by that many could have done them a fair bit of damage. After all, the Britons had the right idea; if you're going to have a crack at a whole Legion, you might as well try it while most of them are snoring and farting in their beds."

"Hmm, right enough." Fatalis agreed. "Fortuna definitely smiled on the IX last night then, I fancy."

"Bollocks did she." snorted Batiatus. "It was me and my lads who saved their arses. I reckon those blue skinned bastards knew they were being watched and realised there was no chance of a surprise party last night. Shag all to do with good fortune and everything to do with good honest soldiering I'd say!"

Fatalis ginned again at his old friend and slowly shook his head in a gesture of mock despair.

"Oh, absolutely Batiatus." Fatalis retorted in a tone heavy with sarcasm. "Why, you'd even shame Mars himself with your military prowess. For now though, perhaps you can spare us all from being dazzled by that shaft of brilliance shining out of your arse and consider instead getting your men stood down and giving your report."

Batiatus smiled again and nodded before turning to the group of scouts, still sat wearily astride their mounts.

"Right, dismount you lot, and get the horses seen to."

He then called over to his second in command. "Cordus, take my mount with you and see if you can't get all of the horses changed over for fresh ones. I get the feeling we won't be stopping too long."

Cordus, looking every inch as filthy and exhausted as his comrades, responded only with a nod as he took charge of Batiatus' mount and walked off with the rest of the riders as they slowly dispersed.

Batiatus then turned towards the eight of us as we stood nearby watching and listening to what had been said between him and Fatalis. He grinned as he eyed us all up and down and then started to open his mouth, no doubt to shower us with a collection of good natured profanities, just as Ademetus appeared at the entrance to the command tent. The Prefect scowled as he clapped eyes first on Batiatus, and then registered the fact that we were also close by.

"Chief of Scouts." he barked. "You have your report?"

"Yes Prefect." Batiatus instantly shot to attention and thundered the response back, his tone and mannerisms seeming to be more mocking of Ademetus than indicative of obedience to the Prefect as he turned and grinned at us once more.

"Then may I suggest that you grace the Legate and I with your presence so that we can find out just what in Hades is actually going on in this shit hole."

"At once, Prefect." Batiatus sent the response back like a whiplash before quickly turning to us and muttering from the corner of his mouth:

"And I'll be sure to see you whoremongers later."

With that, he turned and strode off towards the command tent. However, the look that Ademetus shot in our direction as he turned and went back inside the tent told me everything I needed to know about what the man was thinking.

"I'm thinking we're going to need to have a quiet word with our friend the Chief of Scouts before too long." said Zenas, to none of us in particular.

Fatalis had been about right in his estimations when, just over an hour later; we found ourselves formed up in the compound, opposite a Century of stone faced and silent soldiers from Cohort V. Standing in front of us, dressed in the stunning full regalia of his office, was the impressive figure of Sabinus. He stood stock still and as straight as a rod of iron as Fortunatus was brought before him by the two guards who had stood watch over him earlier. Sabinus seemed almost statue like. The only things about him that actually moved was the rippling fabric of his rich scarlet cloak and the deep blue coloured plumes of Ostrich feathers that adorned his silvered helmet and waved lazily in the light wind that blew across the camp.

With his back to us, it was impossible to tell what

Sabinus's face was like. But, as Fortunatus was now facing him, I could clearly see the young Legionary's face and I found myself thinking, albeit briefly, that at least his mettle was doing him credit now, given that he must surely know what was to follow.

Every soldier knew that if you fell asleep on your watch, it was as though you were telling your comrades that your comfort was more important than their lives. That was why idle soldiers like Fortunatus instantly became a figure of contempt to their comrades. That was why they could never again be trusted to serve in the ranks alongside soldiers who actually could commit themselves fully to their comrades.

As a soldier who had traded lives for sleep, Fortunatus had earned the hatred of the Legion. I held that disdain for him too. Although, as he stood firm and unshaking in the presence of the Legate, with only a very deep sadness evident upon his youthful features, I had to at least credit the young lad with a courage normally uncommon to one so young. I was glad for him that, in the face of what was to come; it seemed that he was not going to add cowardice to his crimes.

"Who brings this man before me, and on what charge?"

Sabinus boomed the question out to the Century assembled before him and the brief and coldly efficient formalities of a field trial began.

The unit Centurion stepped out from the ranks and

marched stiffly and with grim face toward the Legate before halting at the side of Fortunatus. The young soldier seemed not even to dare look at his Centurion, for fear of catching sight of the deep shame that he had caused the proud old soldier.

"Legate Sabinus, I Marcus Julius Secundus, Second Spear Centurion of Cohort V bring the prisoner Fortunatus before you and say that the charge is one of gross neglect of duty."

"What evidence supports your charge, Centurion?" growled the Legate.

"Fortunatus has confessed to falling asleep at his sentry post last night, thereby failing to give any early warning of the night attack mounted by our enemies."

The Centurion stood, firm as a rock and chin held high, waiting for the Legate to complete the formalities that would lead to the inevitable sentence.

"Who speaks for this man?"

"None, Legate." Secundus answered.

The oppressive silence was interrupted only by the sounds of the gentle wind blowing across the compound and the somewhat misplaced singing of meadow larks soaring above the scene as Fortunatus' whole Century set their faces silently to the front. They gave not so much as one uneasy shuffle as Secundus confirmed that Fortunatus was on his own now, nothing but a mere stupid young boy who now found himself abandoned by his former comrades in arms.

"Fortunatus." Sabinus lowered his eyes and looked

at the boy for perhaps the first time. "Will you answer the charge?"

"Only to support my earlier confession, that I am guilty of the charge, Legate."

The boy's voice was clear and I felt myself give a slight nod of approval for his courage as he did not crack or waiver under the creeping fear that must have been growing inside him as he approached passing of the sentence.

"So be it." snapped Sabinus. "Centurion Secundus, see to it that Fortunatus name is struck from the nominal roll of your Century and charge your Optio with completion of the service record in the lists of the Legion. Let the lists now read that Fortunatus is discharged with dishonour and that the sentence of Fustuarium was duly passed and carried out this day."

With not one twitch or blink from his comrades, or a swift glance cast in his direction, the last words spoken then by Sabinus ensured that Fortunatus knew that he had lost all honour as a soldier. Holding only the status of a convicted criminal now, he was about to face a punishment befitting his crime.

Sabinus nodded to the Centurion and solemnly gave the order:

"Carry out the sentence, Centurion."

Without a word, Secundus nodded to the two guards flanking Fortunatus and swiftly they unshackled his wrists and began to strip him of his armour, casting it on the floor in an untidy pile at the Centurions feet. It wasn't long before Fortunatus stood stripped of all traces of his former life, clothed only in an unbelted woollen tunic which hung on him like an old sack.

"Fortunatus!" barked the Centurion. "Turn and face your former comrades!"

It was as though the very air crackled with anticipation as Fortunatus, no doubt summoning every last grain of courage he could muster, spun round to face his former brothers in arms. With his back to us now I could still see that he maintained his bearing, although I had no idea what his face may be giving away by now as I watched Secundus step round to stand in front of him once more.

I knew what was coming as Secundus' face set with an even harder scowl than before. I waited expectantly as I watched the sinews of his arms harden as he clamped his grip down on his Vitis. Swinging the gnarly stick back behind his ear, he finally commenced the execution of one of his own:

"Die well, Fortunatus."

The vine stick smashed into the side of the young lad's head with a sickening hollow crack but Fortunatus bore the terrible blow well and fell only to his knees, propping himself with an outstretched arm and fighting to stay conscious. Secundus sent another blow sweeping down onto the crown of his head, finally felling him flat to the ground as the blow itself seemed to signal a headlong rush of men from the assembled Century.

Yelling and wild faced with fury, they descended like a great pack of roaring madmen. They kicked, punched and trampled the disgraced boy until he no longer had the instinctive ability to curl into a ball and shield himself. Instead, he submitted to the murderous onslaught from men who only hours ago would have died for him. Finally, after every man of the Century had joined in the melee and taken their turn to batter the boy towards his bloody and agonised end, it was over. All that remained as the last of the men finally turned their backs and quietly walked off towards their lines was the broken and bloody corpse of Fortunatus, clad in shredded, crimson stained rags and lying next to a pile of armour and weapons that he had once borne so proudly.

Fortunatus had never cried out, nor ever once begged for mercy despite all the terrible pain that he must have suffered. No, I can say in all truth that the lad had faithfully obeyed his Centurion's last order to the letter, he had died well.

"Legate's guard - stand down." yelled Fatalis, as the last of the condemned man's century drifted back to their lines. He pointed to the men at the end of the dissolving crowd: "You lot, get that armour and equipment back into stores and shift that body. I want what's left to be on display when the Legion marches out of the west gate. I don't give two shits whether he's recognisable or not. I want the rest to know what happens when you forget your obligations to your own."

"Poor stupid animal." grunted Aebutius. "Nasty way to meet the ferryman that. I almost felt those hammerings myself. Very business-like though, the way they did him over like that."

"Good riddance to bad rubbish, I say," sniffed Crispus, his tone unconcerned. "It was just a shame he didn't get his before he ended up costing the lives of them other lads last night."

"Well, I for one am glad we won't be here tonight." Zenas said as he made a sign to ward off evil in the direction of the battered corpse that was now being dragged unceremoniously from the compound. "He died condemned and in pain so he's sure to become one of the restless dead now. Take my word for it, you don't want to be anywhere near where the spirit will return to because it's evil now, malevolent. A vengeful Lemur that can visit real harm on you."

"Bah, what a load of old offal." boomed the voice of Batiatus. "Are you still trying to scare the children with ghost stories, you superstitious old woman?"

Batiatus had been standing behind the formation as the punishment was meted out. Once the unit had been dismissed by Fatalis he had obviously seen his chance to renew acquaintances with us.

"They're not ghost stories, Batiatus." Zenas snapped. "Your trouble is you've never had enough respect for the Gods and the spirit world. One day you'll wish you had."

"Now I know you're talking out of your arse, you silly old fart." scoffed Batiatus. "All I know is, if it needs killing then you'd do well to worry about it, if not then bollocks to it because it can't do a damn thing to you."

"You're wrong I tell you." said Zenas solemnly.

"Whatever you say, oh wise one." Batiatus smirked. "Seeing as how you're so well connected to the Gods an' all, you couldn't find out whether they've got any plans to set me up with a fuck fairly soon could you? Only I feel like I'm sitting on a couple of wine skins at the moment and I could do with getting rid."

The resultant laughter began to cancel out the grim atmosphere which lingered from the execution. It only grew louder when, irritated by Batiatus' jibes, Zenas mounted his counter attack.

"For the sake of all the unsuspecting women hereabouts who haven't yet made your acquaintance, why don't you spare them a mauling from your rough old paws for once? In fact, maybe you could skip off round the back of one of those tents and give that prong of yours a good tug or two instead. That way you could just loose your shot harmlessly into the grass. After all, the last thing we want is you contaminating any women with that slop of yours and possibly spawning something equally as ugly and objectionable as you."

We laughed uproariously as Batiatus struggled to formulate a reply in sufficiently quick time to qualify for a witty rejoinder. In the end, stifled of any decent retort, he admitted defeat.

"Ah, Zenas old friend, you have the tongue of a harsh old fishwife." Batiatus smiled wryly as he finally conceded the point. "You cut me right to the quick, so you do."

"It's cutting your balls off that would do more good." Zenas muttered as he concluded the banter.

"Funny you should mention that." Pudens cut in with a distinctly serious tone. "But don't you think we need to be telling our good friend Batiatus about who else just might have ideas along those lines?"

As the usually jovial soldier broached the subject in such an uncharacteristically humourless manner, the smiling stopped and every face dropped. Batiatus stood before us, clearly perplexed by the remark. Slowly, he extended his arms out to his sides, as if to invite some further explanation. With none forthcoming, he quickly voiced the question he wanted answered:

"Well?" he queried. "What's to do then?"

"You tell him, Vepitta." prompted Pacatianus. "After all, you're the one who told us."

Suddenly I was surrounded by expectant faces, none more so than that of Batiatus, as I quickly thought through about what to tell him, and just how.

"Well…" he queried once more.

"It's to do with your old friend Ademetus." I fairly spat the words out.

"Thunder of Jupiter," Batiatus snarled. "Am I to be forever beset by the wretched and irksome hates of this half man?"

I, like the others were surprised by the uncharacteristically flustered reaction from Batiatus as I confirmed about who we were referring to.

Although, once I had regained my thread I continued with the explanation, unaware as yet as to why it was that Batiatus was so rankled by the mention of the Prefect.

"He spoke with me one night while I was on duty in the Legate's tent," I continued. "He made it very plain that he was aware of your friendship with our Contubernium and to be plain, he wants an end to it."

"Oh he does, does he?" Batiatus' face was now beginning to colour up with his rising anger. "So what's the slimy turd saying then, eh?"

"Oh, he's made it very plain," I continued. "Either we distance ourselves from you, or he'll see each one of us broken. It seems that our noble Prefect doesn't want you to have any friends, least of all any in the Legate's bodyguard, I'm thinking."

"All right then." Batiatus drew in a great breath before slowly exhaling. "So what do you lot want to do."

"Still shagging talking to you, ain't we?" rumbled Surus.

Batiatus smiled and nodded his head, laughing to himself before responding.

"That you are," he agreed, his face adjusting to a more serious countenance before he continued. "But I fancy that maybe you won't have to for much longer."

"Look Batiatus," Marinus cut in. "We won't make that choice. Me and the lads we…"

"The choice isn't yours to make." Batiatus cut him

off. "I'm leaving under orders within the hour and there's every chance I won't be coming back."

It was almost as if each of us had been prodded with a sharp pin as we all looked up at once, instantly curious to know just what he meant by that. Almost instinctively we gathered round Batiatus to hear what he had to tell us.

"All of you know me by now." he said. "And so you should also know that I won't give in without a fight. Though the fact is that Ademetus has fixed it that I am soon going to end up in a set-to that I probably won't stand a chance of winning."

"How so, brother?" asked Zenas, real concern written large on his features now.

Batiatus then explained to us how he and his men had come across a reasonable looking fording point across the river the locals called Medway, a couple of miles downstream from Durobrivae. This possible crossing point had a strong current but was quite narrow and should therefore be ideal for amphibious specialists like the Batavians to bring about the surprise flanking tactic that had been agreed in the battle plan. The only real problem with it was that, having monitored the area for a day and a night, Batiatus had learnt that it was frequently checked by large parties of enemy cavalry.

Once Batiatus had identified this opportunity, and the risks it carried, in his report to Sabinus it hadn't taken long for Ademetus to work up a plan to send Batiatus back on a possible suicide mission to secure the crossing.

Ademetus had reasoned that, as Geta wanted to lead the Batavian Auxiliaries and a Cohort of Legionary cavalry in the initial flank attack, the immediate area of the crossing must be secure enough to greatly minimise the risk of losing a Legate in the fighting. Surely then, argued Ademetus, it would be prudent if Batiatus first took his men back to the fording point with a few Turmae of Legionary cavalry to eliminate any enemy scouts in the area as they were the only troops that could be spared from being used in the main attack. He also pointed out that Geta's own scouts from the IX Hispana didn't know the ground so it would be foolish to send them in alone. Ademetus concluded that a successful mission for Batiatus, although risky, would create a better chance for surprise when the main attack force arrived to cross the river.

"So, it doesn't look so good for you then?" Aebutius asked quietly.

"Not really," answered Batiatus. "The enemy cavalry I saw there were always well armoured with good mounts. They looked like they could handle themselves in a fight and there were generally plenty of them. I don't even fancy the chances of the cavalry that are coming with us, never mind my own lightly armoured scouts."

"But he must think you've got a chance." reasoned Crispus. "Otherwise he wouldn't be risking Geta against your success."

"By the Gods man, I credited you with more brains than that, "grumbled Zenas. "If Batiatus fails it'll just mean that Plautius will order Geta not to lead the attack. The crossing will happen anyway, just without a Legate to lead the way."

For a moment there was silence as we all paused to contemplate exactly what had been said. The situation seemed to be hopeless. I felt a sickening knot of anger and sadness beginning to cramp my stomach. Not one of us wanted to lose our friend but not one of us had the power to do anything about it. It was the Gods and the fates who would decide on the life of Batiatus.

"So, enough talk." said Batiatus, breaking the uneasy silence. "I've got somewhere that I and my boys need to be."

With that the old warrior approached each of us and clasped us all by the forearm, giving each a firm shake as he bade us farewell. Each one of us knew there was every chance that it could be for the last time. Finally he stood before Marinus and Zenas, a faintly sad smile on his face.

"You don't do a bad red wine in that place of yours, you know?" Marinus observed. "The white tastes like a family of cats pissed in your amphorae. But the red... not bad at all."

Batiatus gave a short laugh before he shrugged his shoulders and finally turned to say his farewells to Zenas.

"Look after this lot you old sweat, you're soon going to be up to your bollocks in blood and Britons so make sure they've had a good breakfast and buckled their gear tight."

"Don't bother yourself about us." replied Zenas. "Just make sure you ask Mars and Bellona for their blessings. They always seem to favour rough old scrappers like you."

"Mars and Bellona my arse!" snorted Batiatus. "I've got a sharp sword and a terrible urge for a scrap; I don't need the damned Gods."

Zenas shook his head almost despairingly before he clapped his old comrade firmly on the shoulder.

"So long as you've got faith in something, that'll do I suppose."

"And if not." laughed Batiatus. "We nine can all share a game of dice in Hades sometime soon, eh?"

With that he turned and was gone, leaving us to our own private thoughts. It was down to Batiatus what he thought of the Gods but, for myself, I gave a quiet prayer to Fortuna that his luck would hold and we would see him in the world of the living once more. It was only as we turned away, moving back to our tent to make ready for the off, that I caught sight of Fatalis standing at the side of one of the compound tents and within ear shot of what had been said. We made the briefest of eye contact before he turned quietly and walked off down the lines.

CHAPTER 23

Within a very short space of time we had made our preparations to leave the marching camp to press on for Durobrivae. As we began to pull out, each and every man of the Legion had been told to leave via the western gateway and form up in column order on that side of the camp. The order was quite deliberate. In doing so the entire Legion would, by necessity, pass by the pulverised corpse of Fortunatus, which now lay on display just outside the gate on the back of a flatbed cart.

His split, bruised skin and the congealed blood that covered the body had soon become patronised by a small cloud of idly buzzing flies, feeding on the shattered remains, while here and there, the wretched body and the cart that bore it were flecked with the oozing spit of contempt.

There was no notice or placard to accompany the grisly display. In fact there was nothing which might serve to inform the passing men of what Fortunatus had done to warrant the punishment which had brought about such a cruel and brutal end to his life. Nevertheless, each man knew of just what had happened in the Legate's compound that morning and why. As each soldier passed out of the gate and silently viewed the hideously hammered body, they all knew that if they themselves did not maintain iron discipline and commitment to the Legion, then such a fate would be theirs too. It was with that very deliberately planted thought in mind that we set out to cover the last of the distance between the camp and Durobrivae.

The march towards our next objective was made with somewhat less enthusiasm than normal. Prior to the start, we had all been told that the role of the Fourteenth would be to act as a distraction to the large force of Britons that would be arrayed on the opposite bank of the river. Effectively it meant that, during the opening stages of the next engagement, we would not be taking an offensive role.

As our column wound its way through the countryside like a great armoured serpent, we came across scattered settlements and farms, hastily abandoned by the local tribes' folk. We saw at each that everything the Britons could do to deny us had been done. Their buildings had been burned and all tools and stores had either been taken with them, or destroyed and spoiled. Livestock had been driven off and whatever fields had been planted with crops had been either torched or ripped up to prevent us harvesting them later. It was as though we followed in a wake of destruction left by some wrathful demon.

Eventually, we sighted our objective as we crested some high ground and found ourselves approaching the glittering, lazy flow of the Medway. Just beyond lay our objective, the major settlement of Durobrivae. Now, we could match a place to a name and now we were finally able to see just what strength the enemy had mustered to oppose us.

On the opposite bank, a great swarming mass of thousands of Britons watched the arrival of our column. They had seen, and heard, the deliberate display of force as we closed on them at last. We had ensured that our entrance onto the land approaching the river was as conspicuous as possible.

They certainly must have heard our advance long before they saw us as we bellowed out our victory chants and sang songs of our past exploits, all to the blaring accompaniment of our horns and the thunderous banging of our shields. The armour and equipment of the column added its own accompaniment of metallic clanking and jingling as we came into view of the assembled Britons. As the air filled with the threatening melody of war, so too did the ground itself shake under the pounding footfall of over five thousand pairs of feet. I remember thinking to myself, as I had so many times before, that there was nothing on earth to equal the awesome sound of a Roman Legion taking to the field.

As we crested the low hill which had hidden us from view, the thousands of assembled Britons greeted us with a terrific roar. There then ensued a war of noise between us as the enemy hammered rhythmically on the backs of their shields, creating a din like thunder. Rumbling out across the river towards us as they too began their own ritualised war chants.

With characteristic and practiced precision the Cohorts split off into separate formations as we continued the advance towards the great river. Eventually we achieved a standard battle formation of two great rows of soldiers in line abreast, each battle line six men deep. We spanned the slope as we approached the river, shouting and bawling our insults and threats while beating the backs of our own shields in response.

As we closed on the river, the sound of our own shield backs being struck eventually changed from a continuous rumble to a crunching, thumping rhythm that matched our foot fall as we finally pulled up, marking time close to the river bank. Each Cohort was then separately halted and, one by one, each Cohort fell completely silent. Not a sound in the ranks stirred as the Britons on the opposite bank also fell quiet now, puzzled no doubt at why we had suddenly ceased our display.

The early summer sun glittered on the ponderously flowing surface of the broad river. A gentle wind played along its edges and ruffled the tops of the narrow beds of tall reeds, blowing lazily along the banks and causing the various streamers and pennants on the standards to flutter lazily as it passed. Silently, the two armies faced each other as an incredible atmosphere of anticipation, rising tension and excitement pervaded the ranks.

It was Sabinus who then gave each man present something to focus on once more. Slowly, he rode towards the front of our formation and halted on the bank, before turning his mount to face us. In doing so, he deliberately turned his back on the enemy host. Presently, Ademetus and the six Legion Tribunes joined him, they too insulting the Britons in the same way. Slowly Sabinus drew his magnificently crafted Gladius from its sheath and held it low against his thigh. His fabulous armour glinted in the warm sunlight as he raised himself up in his saddle and roared out over our heads;

"Are you ready for a war?"

"Aye, ready aye!"

We bellowed the traditional response three times as Sabinus wheeled his mount around, thrusting his sword out in the direction of his foe. Even the horse itself seemed eager to show its hatred of the enemy as it sent its own challenge to the Britons, rearing up and flailing its hooves in the air while it whinnied out across the water to its foes on the opposite bank. Again, we hammered our shields and howled our curses at the Britons who once more shouted and screamed furiously back at us from the far bank. Eventually though, at a signal from Sabinus, the Centurions silenced us and we were turned about and moved out to where we would establish our lines.

The usual defences were prepared, along with certain refinements to cater for the situation we now found ourselves in. We positioned our lines well back from the river and in clear ground, situated atop a low plateau so that attackers approaching from any direction would always be on lower ground, but also making sure that the huge force of Britons across the river could be fully observed at all times. Closer to the river we quickly erected special artillery towers, upon which were placed our Scorpiones, ensuring we could rain iron tipped bolts down on the Britons if they got too close on the opposite bank.

To bolster this deadly capability, we also set up a dozen Onagers. These ferociously powerful siege catapults could hurl large boulders and a variety of other projectiles into their ranks, as and when required and with devastating effect. Not only had we set up our own Onagers, but we had also seconded other machines and their crews from II Augusta, the main body of which was now out of sight and moving round to the south of us, preparing to outflank the Britons by crossing further upstream.

For the duration of the daylight hours, those soldiers not engaged on preparing defences were moved close to the river in order to maintain a show of force for the Britons, who continued to react to our presence. Their infantry still taunted and jeered us from the far bank, and they had now drawn their cavalry and chariots closer to us. As they postured on the other side, we watched them carefully as they performed their battle rituals. Revelling in the opportunity to show us their considerable expertise, they would flourish their weapons and perform elaborate displays, ever keen to demonstrate to us the extent of their martial skill and fighting prowess. Seeking to cause us to realise just what formidable opponents we now faced.

Their cavalry thundered up and down the bank, both in groups and individually, showing us their great proficiency as horsemen. Once more we were treated to the site of their chariots as they reminded us of just how fast and versatile they could be. There was no doubting the skill and dogged fighting spirit of these men. But, if they had set out to unnerve us with their displays, they may just as well have skimmed pebbles across the water at us for all the good it did.

"Have you seen these boys?" Marinus asked, pointing across the river. "They're brilliant. I'd love to see these lads doing a turn in the arena back home. By the gods, those antics would go down a treat."

"I'll tell you this," added Surus. "They're a bit stupid when it comes to tactics but I get the idea that they know how to put up a half decent fight."

"Oh please! If they were that good at fighting they'd have shown up on the beaches and kicked our all-conquering Roman arses back into the sea." Marinus responded indignantly.

"Maybe so, but the point is that it seems they didn't actually know we were still coming." Crispus pointed out. "If they had, they might well have turned up and spoiled the party. The ancestors of this gang stood against the Divine Julius, you know? Just look at the trouble they gave him."

"Why, what did they do to him then?" Pacatianus enquired.

"Gods man, don't you know your history?" Zenas asked, astonished. "He tried twice to take this land but he never quite managed it."

"Yeah, well, what of it?" replied Pacatianus.

"Well, that's why we're here, stupid," interrupted Aebutius. "If we can pull this invasion off for the old stutterer in Rome then he'll have done what Julius Caesar couldn't. He'll land the Empire with a very valuable new piece of territory."

Too late, we spotted that Fatalis was lurking close by and, having heard the slight on the Emperor, he stalked over and immediately lashed out at Aebutius, striking him hard across the thighs with his Vitis. The hapless Aebutius howled out in pain and fell to the floor clutching his bruised legs as the furious Centurion leant over him and snarled:

"It's just as well that I need all of my men for now, Aebutius. Otherwise, I'd be setting about beating the shit out of you for that remark. The Emperor is your supreme master, who you swore on oath to serve and honour. I don't count name calling as honouring him, and if I hear you spouting off like that again then I'll personally remove your slimy red tongue and stop it flapping forever. Understood soldier?"

Aebutius nodded hurriedly, biting down on his bottom lip and trying hard to stifle groans of pain. Angrily, the Centurion stalked off, leaving us all in a chided silence and with a timely reminder that, if Fatalis utterly revered and respected one man above even Sabinus, it was the Emperor himself.

Eventually, things began to settle down. Both armies made preparation to set in for the night as it soon became clear that there was to be no battle that day after all. Camp fires sent thin strands of smoke drifting lazily across the evening sunset and the comforting aroma of cooking mingled with the familiar sounds of countless pieces of military equipment receiving some last minute attention while men talked and joked. The Britons had settled out in the open and were just a little way up from the bank. They had erected small crude shelters and had fashioned wicker work screens which they had placed along the bank to protect themselves from the random opportunist attentions of archers or slingers. Scores of small fires glowed amidst their encampment and we could hear the sound of their laughing and singing floating over the river towards us.

It seemed somewhat surreal to think that, for now, all was peaceful, with the Britons displaying an almost festive mentality. In fact; neither side even seemed particularly bothered about the other by that time, preferring instead to relax, see out the days end and enjoy the company of their comrades. It was as though, just for now, neither opponent existed in the others world. Tomorrow though, it would be different.

As the many shades of reds and oranges coloured the evening sky, the burnished gold of the setting sun eventually succumbed to dark blue and then finally the blackness of night as the day came to its unexpectedly peaceful end. I sat quietly by our small fire and allowed my thoughts to drift away to those back home in Mogontiacum. I could see Salviena in my mind's eye as clear as if she stood before me. I knew that she would no doubt be performing her nightly rituals of lamp lighting and closing the shutters of that small but comfortable house on the edge of the town. My two boys would be getting their bedtime story, no doubt hearing their favourite tales about the Nymphs and Fauns of the woodland and the mischievous games they played on mortal men.

I shifted uncomfortably as I found myself wondering whether or not Julia's wolves still skulked in the shadows near to my family, watching carefully and waiting patiently for orders from their bitch of a mistress. I knew they had been there; Julia had proven that plainly enough. For now though, even though she had told me what she wanted of me, she had not yet said who, and that at least made me feel just a little easier. Even so, I silently prayed that Salviena had maintained her offerings to the Lares of our house. For in return, they would watch over and protect my loved ones from harm.

I briefly wondered too if she and my sons had given me a thought this night. Did they know what was happening over here? Had they received any news of our success so far? Or, did they perhaps worry that I was already dead? If only Mercury could speed me a message to them this night, just once, just so that I could tell them that I was alive and well and that I was thinking of them…Just so that I could tell them what I should have told them when we left Mogontiacum on that hard winters day. I should have told them then that I loved them all, more than life itself and that one day, I would return home for the last time. No more would I set off for war and leave them far behind. Only the Gods could say what would come to pass. If it was the will of the Gods, then perhaps that which yet remained unsaid would one day come to be the truth.

The thoughts of my family had begun to make me feel maudlin so, reluctantly, I closed my mind to them, turning my thoughts instead to other things. I recalled the tavern we all used to drink at just outside the fortress gates. Hmm, the Inn of the Blind Venus. What a place. I really couldn't imagine Mogontiacum without it. It was a place where I had spent so many good times and I had promised myself that I would return as soon as I was able. I wanted to share good times with my friends again, by eating the cheap but good food, drinking the ever plentiful wine and even ogling the willing and gaudily painted women who paraded their wares there from time to time.

As painful as some of them were, my recollections and thoughts were also a comfort to me. As I sat quietly by the fire I reasoned that it was a fantastic gift of the Gods for a mind to be able to float back home and allow you to be there once more, even if it was only in spirit. As I pulled my cloak tighter around me to ward off the settling cool of the night, I found myself looking skyward and wondering at the dotted lights of countless thousands of stars, twinkling around the crescent of the moon as it hung in the sky. I was certain that it was the same sky that watched over my homeland but now it was from a different viewpoint as I gazed at it from a very troubled and deadly land.

I knew that the Gods of the Britons also dwelt here and watched over their subjects, but they were not like Roman gods. When we came here we had brought our own Gods with us. So, did it then follow that the very Gods themselves would also be going to war with each other in the heavens tomorrow? Perhaps their war would be a divine reflection of the battle to be played out by us mortals. Or did they instead gather together to watch the life and death struggles of thousands of inconsequential people? Would they perhaps be mocking us for our weakness and greed, treating the world instead as their own immense gladiatorial display? Perhaps they were preparing finally to punish us for all of our evils after we had entertained them with our puny power struggles.

Finally, weary with it all, I reached the conclusion that I had done far too much thinking for one night. It was time instead to give in to sleep.

* * * * *

We were awake with the dawn. Throwing on our

armour and moving in our formations down towards the river bank, still veiled as it then was by the low lying mists drifting off the water. The Britons were awake too and had already assembled on the other bank. They appeared only as a random collection of faint and murky shapes at first, moving around fleetingly in the gloomy grey light. Initially shrouded by the thick drifting river mist, they slowly took substance and form as the mist began to evaporate with the quickening of the daylight.

Eventually we stood there, Romans and Britons facing each other once more. We stood in tight packed blocks of soldiers, whilst they stood in a vast line, stretching along the edge of the bank, around twenty paces back from the water with their cavalry and chariots massed behind them. Once the formations had assembled, there was a long and pregnant silence as we stood, each side holding the ground they occupied, each coldly appraising the opposing army.

From their rear formations a single chariot came rumbling forth, its driver moving the vehicle quickly yet carefully through the masses of men assembled in the foremost ranks of the host of Britons. The assembly parted as the chariot advanced through them, finally breaking clear of the throng before halting. Its warrior passenger stood behind the driver in defiant pose, scorn and contempt clearly written large upon his face, even at the distance that separated us.

A man of unremarkable size and stature for his race, he was nevertheless of noble birth. Thick gold torques adorned his neck and wrists and he wore a shirt of iron mail, very similar to the Legionary pattern that some of us wore. A long sword in a stunningly crafted and adorned bronze scabbard hung from a bronze chain around his waist. A red and brown checked cloak hung from his shoulders, partially obscuring the myriad swirling blue patterns that had been painted onto his skin. Unlike his men, he chose to wear his hair in a natural style with his dirty blonde locks tumbling down his shoulders. As was the custom with his kind, he also sported a thick, droopy moustache.

In the end, it was the Briton who broke the silence first.

"Romans!" he bellowed out across the water in coarsely accented Latin, his tone defiant and accusatory. "You will go no further into this land of ours. The ancient realms of our ancestors will not become yours, so take your armies of murderers and thieves and leave. You have my word that if you withdraw your forces from our territories now, then we will swallow our anger and stay our hands to spare your lives. If you do not heed my words and instead try to push further into our sacred mother land then I, Caratacus, son of Cunobelin and chief warlord of the great and noble Catuvellauni people will call upon our Druids to invoke our Gods of war to bring their terrible wrath down upon you. The blood of

Cassivellaunus, he who stood firm and resolute against your Julius Caesar, flows in my veins. I swear on everything sacred, that I will do honour to his shade and protect the land he fought for. It is my vow then, that the only ground you will win this day are the cold graves you will lay buried in!"

As the great army of Britons erupted into spontaneous cheering I thought to myself that these were brave words indeed. But surely, even this rabble rousing Briton could see that after the crushing defeat at Durovernon and despite his superior numbers, it would be us who would prevail, shattering their resistance to claim victory over his people? I did not know it then, but this Briton, this Caratacus, had no capacity whatever to accept defeat at the hands of Rome.

He stood in the midst of his people, arms spread and turning left and right to look up and down our formations, waiting for the reply that would not come until at last, he hushed his men with a gesture and called an end to the suspense once more.

"So be it!" he barked. "Then by all the gods that protect this land know you this Romans, you have all seen your last dawn. The chance for talk has passed. Now I will let loose the righteous anger of my people, my Gods and the ghosts of my kind. Then you will pay in blood for every last yard of soil that you have tainted with your presence."

As he spat the words at us his assembled army erupted once more into gales of howling and cheering. He punched the air with his shield, yelling furiously at us as the Britons started up a barrage of small missiles, pelting us with sling shot which began to fly across the river between us. The front ranks quickly threw their shields up as the deadly hail of small stones and cast lead shot began to strike home. It clanged off helmets and body armour, banging off the faces of our shields and ripping into the flowing waters, disturbing them with an eruption of small splashes as some of the shot landed just shy of the bank area. In an instant we heard the familiar clatter of ratchet mechanisms being wound back as our entire battery of Scorpiones and Onagers were made ready to respond to the slingers volleys and let fly with their own deadly barrage of missiles.

"Mark that bastard in the chariot!" yelled one of the Centurions commanding the bolt throwers, stabbing his finger furiously at the far bank as he shouted up to the crews on the towers and directed them to Caratacus' chariot. "Bring that barbarian scum down and I'll personally pay a month's money to the man who fells him!"

At that, wooden support struts could be heard falling away as the trigger men of the crews tipped the primed and ready weapons off their props and swung them round to bear on their intended target, taking careful and practiced aim on the fleeing chariot. The crews reacted to the incentive in a flash. Almost instantly I heard a repeated 'whack' as each of the machines released the tremendous energy stored up in twisted coils of sinuous rope, sending their deadly projectiles streaking out to the target. My head snapped from left to right as I attempted to trace the path of the bolts as they shot out from the weapons. Hurtling across the river, the fearsome power of the machines was unleashed at last as projectiles took to the air like the bolts of Jupiter.

I watched the chariot as it turned on a tight arc, speeding away from the bank. Caratacus clung onto the framework of the vehicle, facing back to the threat and holding his long shield aloft to protect himself and his driver as the horses were lashed up to breakneck speed. Though, for all the skill of the driver and the swift hooves of the sturdy little horses, they could not outrun the deadly bolts. Within a heartbeat of their release the bolts started to rain down in the area of the chariot. Men began to drop to the ground, screaming out as the thick, iron headed shafts fell all around, biting into their flesh and striking the body of the chariot. Their intended target raised his shield just in time. A perfectly aimed bolt hammered into the iron covered boss of the shield, blasting it from Caratacus's grip and hurling it to one side but ultimately diverting itself away from its intended victim. It ricocheted off the metalwork, tumbling wildly through the air before driving itself into the ground. The chariot finally gained enough speed to pull away from the danger area as, enraged at Caratacus' outrageous good fortune, we shouted hair raising oaths after him and cursed him for his luck.

The initial exchanges had set the tone for the morning as the Britons massed around the bank area and assailed us with slings and arrows, while we responded in kind with our artillery. Their shock had been glaringly apparent when the first of the Onagers had let fly. The immensely powerful machines began to hurl stone in both solid balls and basket loads of sharp flint fragments, both at the mounted warriors and those assembled on the bank, behind wicker screens.

After that, the intermittent noise of the Scorpiones discharging was accompanied by great loud thuds as the thick timber throwing arms of the Onagers shot forward and hit the leather damping pads fixed to their framework, hurling their payload far into the air before it hurtled down on the opposing forces with awful consequences.

The solid stone balls smashed the wicker shields to fragments, throwing great black clods of earth into the air and killing or terribly maiming anyone caught behind them. The flint fragments would hit their marks with equally devastating effect as the razor sharp palm sized stones embedded themselves into bodies and ripped flesh from limbs in great, bloody chunks. Finally, as an added terror, thin walled clay urns filled with finely powdered quick lime were also hurled amongst the enemy by the great catapults. The immense force under which the pots shattered on impact caused the lime to erupt in blinding white clouds of caustic powder, searing the eyes and lungs of anyone caught by the drifting dust.

It was fair to say that, almost as soon as the artillery pieces had been fully unleashed upon the Britons, these awesome weapons had caused absolute chaos amongst their great army. They had ever experienced anything like the terrible damage and carnage that such weapons could wreak.

The Britons soon learnt that it was no longer safe to approach the bank. Instead, they chose to drop back from the river's edge, shouting insults and threats from a relatively safe distance. Now and again our artillery crews would demonstrate to the Britons that they could still be easily hit at over three hundred paces by a well-trained trigger man, all of whom had now gotten their eye in, limbered up as they were by the opening shots they had sent across the river. The crews warmed to their task as they began to fine tune the machines, adjusting the power in the torsion bundles with large iron wrenches. With each successive shot they became progressively quicker at winding the ratchets back to firing positions and setting the bolts into the slides. You could hear the crews joking amongst themselves, picking individual targets as they challenged their trigger men and laid bets as to whether or not the chosen target could be hit. Most of the time the trigger man carried his work out well. A triumphant shout would mean another tally mark was etched on a post of the artillery tower as the crews cheered for yet another Briton felled.

By mid-morning the general situation was little different from when the hostilities had first opened. Although, any Briton displaying wealth or status had by that time learned that it was not a good idea to be in the immediate area of the river bank, given that the Scorpione crews were now picking off as many marks as possible, particularly any clan leaders that they could identify.

It was around that time that we first noticed the Britons milling around excitedly, starting to form a clamouring mass of bodies around fifty paces from the bank. They yelled and cheered, swarming around something that had caught their attention. Soon, the crowd broke and we could just make out a group of men in their midst. As we watched we could see the men lurching around as they were pushed and kicked back and forth. There were about ten or so and by now we could see that they were being viciously beaten with staves and tormented with flaming torches. The unfortunate men gave out awful, agonised screams as the brands were held against their flesh, just long enough to cause excruciating pain, before being removed and applied elsewhere on their bodies.

It soon became apparent that the men were clothed in mail shirts and carried equipment very familiar to us. The Britons, we now realised, had captured a party of Roman cavalry scouts. We all realised with mounting horror that the Britons intended to give us their own unique response to the devastation our artillery had wrought amongst them. Furious shouting rose up amongst our ranks, but we were forced to watch helplessly as the Britons eagerly set to work on the men.

Our Century was arrayed directly in front of the Legate and men were now turning in our direction, exhorting Sabinus to allow the Scorpiones to attempt mercy shots that would end the men's suffering. Sabinus just shook his head slowly, refusing the pleas of the men as the screams rang out across the water.

I looked towards Sabinus once more, unable to understand why he would not permit the crews to attempt shots. Beside him was Ademetus and next to him was the Briton, Adminius. All sat quietly astride their mounts, looking on with faces of stone as the torture continued and remaining resolutely deaf to the pleading and clamorous protests of an entire Legion.

The Britons wasted little time in seizing an opportunity to demonstrate their hatred and contempt for us. They revelled in our furious shouts, taunting and goading us as they continued to degrade and torment their so obviously doomed captives. The screams of the men rang out across the gap between the two forces as the Britons inflicted excruciating tortures on the luckless cavalrymen. We watched, enraged, as their fingers were broken with heavy stones or hacked off. Their ears too were sliced from the side of their heads, all to the delight of the baying mob that surrounded the men.

We roared blood curdling threats of vengeance as

wildly screaming women appeared amongst the mob and actively joined in with the appalling spectacle as the men were roughly stripped of their armour and clothing, before being beaten down into the dirt. As the native men whooped with glee and snatched away trophies of armour and equipment from the humiliated Roman scouts, I never believed that I could feel such outrage and fury as I did when I watched that savage mob waving around the souvenirs taken from their captives. With an enthusiasm totally devoid of pity, they encouraged their women to hack the men's genitals from their still living bodies. They taunted them with their own parts, spitefully waving the dismembered flesh before their bloodied and pain wracked faces, before contemptuously casting them aside on the trampled earth.

Eventually, the screams began to fade as what tormented life the cavalrymen held onto slowly ebbed from them and trickled into the flattened grass. We grew a little quieter as we saw warriors taking up position near to their unfortunate captives, the captors brandishing the men's own Spathas as they prepared to bring an end to the savage spectacle with the captured cavalrymen's own weapons.

Only later did I learn precisely why Sabinus had not allowed the use of the artillery. This was because of the appearance of a man who we had not yet seen from our position but who Sabinus and his party had spotted earlier from their vantage point on the backs of their horses.

As we continued to watch, a Briton who was very much the image of Caratacus emerged from the midst of the howling mob. This was Togodumnus, younger brother to both the enemy chieftain, Caratacus and our so called ally, Adminius.

It transpired that, after seeing the narrow escape by Caratacus, Adminius had requested that if possible, the killing of his brothers on the battlefield might be avoided. This was not due to any brotherly love, I might add, but because Adminius was cut from the same cloth as his brothers. He wanted them both captured instead, allowing him the chance of personally exacting his revenge for being forced into exile by them and having to enlist Rome's aid. Reluctantly it is said, Sabinus granted the request. After all, he would also have needed to bear in mind that the political value of the capture of either of the brothers actually far outweighed the value of their death in battle. He would not therefore allow the artillery to shoot; for fear that a stray bolt intended for one of the prisoners might strike Togodumnus instead.

As we watched in silent anticipation, Togodumnus gestured to the nearest of his warriors to hold the prisoners and then he took a few steps forward until he stood clear of the mob, shouting across the river in thickly accented Latin.

"Welcome home, brother." he yelled out, gesturing sweepingly towards our ranks. "I see you have brought your new friends with you. Father would be proud, I'm sure. What a pity then that he did not live to see this moment."

The dark irony was lost on the assembly but it seemed as though half our army instantly turned to face Adminius who sat his horse, silent and unmoving but with a face almost on fire with anger.

"Did you wish to come and see how your little brothers have made the Catuvellauni even greater, now that we have dispensed with your Roman loving ways?" Togodumnus continued to taunt Adminius. "Your shame is complete now, I see. For not only did you abandon your people and homeland, but you also brought its greatest enemy to our shores, then stood watching while they butchered your own people at Durovernon."

I could see that the effort of not responding to his brother's bile was almost too much to bear as Adminius clamped his jaw so tightly that the sinews in his neck stood proud and his knuckles whitened with the force he used to grip his horses reins.

"Traitor!"

Togodumnus screamed the accusation out across the river as he tore his richly coloured cloak from his shoulders, thrusting a captured sword in the direction of his brother. "Have you nothing to say to the good men of your homeland who stand before you now? Will you not drop to this sacred earth and atone for your treachery? Plead with them Adminius; plead for their forgiveness for killing their kin and handing their land and their birth-right over to Roman filth. Show us your shame, you craven bastard!"

Total silence descended once more as Briton and Roman alike waited to hear if Adminius would answer his brother - his accuser. However, it was not to be and Adminius kept a tight hold of his anger and said nothing.

"If you will not speak then will you fight, brother?" Togodumnus took the blade of the sword in both hands and held it out, as if to reach out and offer it to Adminius. "I will swim the river now and then you and I will settle this battle and fight to the death as champions should. What say you, will you bleed for your new allies, or no?"

We watched and waited as Adminius momentarily sat unmoving before he slowly pulled at the reins of his horse, guiding it round until his back was turned on his furious younger brother.

"Gutless pig." I heard Surus mutter under his breath as he spat contemptuously onto the ground.

"And there it is!" roared Togodumnus. "You turned away from your people once, and now you show your spineless back again. Let us see then if your new-found friends are more capable of dying with honour. In the name of Camulos brother, if you will not oblige me, I will take the head of another to adorn my house, and a braver man than you he will be too. No doubt it will be the Beansidhe who will come and cry outside your house for your mortal soul, while you lay comfortable in your bed. For surely you cannot now be worthy enough to die on a battlefield where only brave men walk?"

With that, Togodumnus spun on his heel and stalked back to where his men were holding the Roman captives.

As we looked on silently, Togodumnus raised the captured blade close up to his face, seeming to carefully appraise it before shooting out his hand and seizing the face of the nearest of the captives. He stared briefly into his eyes before shoving him down onto his knees, forcing his head towards the floor. The prisoner made no sound, resigning himself instead to the rapid approach of merciful death as the sword was raised high in the air. After the briefest pause, the shining blade flashed downwards, towards the man's exposed neck.

With a sickening 'smack,' the blow landed with clean precision and the head of the Roman cavalryman parted from the body and rolled to one side as the corpse slumped fully forward, briefly pumping copious hot blood onto the ground from the freshly cleaved neck. Utter silence prevailed as Togodumnus again critically surveyed the blood-stained Roman blade, seemingly evaluating its ability to withstand and absorb the stresses placed on a sword used for such a task.

Slowly he bent down and picked up the freshly severed head, before raising it in the air along with the captured weapon. Then he impaled the head on the blade tip, parading his new trophy to his comrades who struck up their howling once more and whooped with delight.

Aebutius was standing next to me as we watched the spectacle unfold.

"Cordus." he said quietly, slowly shaking his head.

"What?"

"Cordus." he repeated the name for me. "That was Cordus. Batiatus' lieutenant."

I strained to look harder and closer at the now sallow skinned head. It's mouth opened and closed grotesquely with the movement of the bobbing sword blade, as if attempting to voice some protest at still being raised above the crowd. While the Britons surrounded it, excitedly chanting and thrusting their fists towards it in their continuing demonstration of contempt. Aebutius was right; it was Cordus, now I could see it.

"Blood of Pluto." snarled Surus, adding his own confirmation. "He's right. That is Cordus."

"So what about Batiatus then?" Pacatianus asked the question that we suddenly all wanted answered. "Surely he…"

"Look, look." hissed Zenas urgently. "That Briton - three men to the left of the Chieftain. I'll swear to the god's that's Batiatus' helmet he's wearing. I'd know it anywhere. That piece of barbarian filth must have taken it as a battle trophy."

"Bastard's probably got his head dangling on his horse's harness too by now." snarled Pudens.

"Dis curse him." snapped Aebutius. "I reckon you're

right about that relic of a helmet, Zenas. You're never going to find two of that type these days. Especially in this hole."

The truth was unavoidable and my heart sank as I was forced to accept that, as well as the unfortunate fate that had befallen Cordus, there was now no escaping the fact that Batiatus had fallen to the native war band as well.

"That's it then." said Crispus with a sigh. "I don't know about what you lot think but I don't reckon anybody would get that old thing off him while he still had a breath in his body."

"Stow it." snapped Marinus abruptly. "We're being watched."

I cast a brief glance over my shoulder, only to be caught by Ademetus looking directly at us, a sickly grin written large on his face. 'Bastard,' my mind yelled as I turned away from him and directed my attention to the Britons once more.

As we stood, forced to watch what happened next and helpless to intervene, the remaining Roman prisoners were quickly decapitated and the ritual of displaying the heads was repeated for each until at last, it was finally over. The final act of the barbarous spectacle was played out by their own cavalry, who slung the pathetic collection of ruined, headless and by now totally stripped corpses across their mounts before they rode down to the river bank. Once by the side of the river, the riders unceremoniously shoved the violated bodies off their mounts before laughing contemptuously at us before turning back for their comrades once more. Dumped like so much rubbish, the wretched corpses rolled down the bank and slipped into the silently flowing waters of the Medway, there to drift lazily downstream with the gently swirling current.

As we sullenly watched the last of the pale and bloodless corpses disappear from sight the thunder of hundreds of galloping hooves reached our ears. All of a sudden, we became aware of a great band of enemy cavalry racing off to the north, in the direction of the bend in the river, about a mile and a half downstream from us. Their infantry began to fragment and a large contingent began to swarm off in the same direction, along with a sizeable group of chariots. The euphoria of their vile demonstration of earlier had quickly dissolved. The Britons now seemed to be reacting urgently to some threat. Something perhaps, which had taken them by surprise.

I reasoned that surely it must be the Batavians and the IX Hispana that Batiatus had been sent to pave the way for. Perhaps, even though it had appeared to have cost him his life, Batiatus had succeeded in his mission to keep the fording point open and the flank attack was now taking place as planned.

Only after the battle did we learn that several Cohorts of Batavian Auxiliaries and a contingent of IX Hispana had moved into position beyond the large bend downstream in the river.

It would appear that, before the arrival of the

Batavians in the area, a skirmish had developed between the patrolling Britons and Batiatus' small force which the Britons had crushed. Confident then that they had repelled the attack, the Britons had not been able to resist the opportunity of crowing about their victory and had returned in haste to Durobrivae with their Roman captives. Meanwhile the Batavians, who were experts in the art of fording deep waters in full armour, and capable of emerging from the most arduous of swims ready to fight, had reached the now abandoned fording point. Whilst the Britons had seen fit to play up to our presence, indulging themselves with the gruesome display they had staged for us, the Batavians had seized their chance and forded the river. Outflanked now, the Britons were frantically racing to engage them before the entire battle group managed to cross the river.

The fording of the Medway by the large Roman force had caused pandemonium amongst the Britons assembled around Durobrivae. From my position I could see livestock being hurriedly moved away from the land where the engagement was about to take place. Their herdsmen were pushing cattle and sheep through the back fields in an attempt to deny them to the approaching Roman forces and move them further up river. Nevertheless, it was hopeless. Even now, every Roman on our side of the river knew that they were doomed to failure. We watched as the Britons took the bait and their forces were drawn downstream. Then we cheered loudly as a further wave of momentary panic swept through the remaining force of Britons holding Durobrivae.

To the horror of those remaining defenders, they had discovered that a second flanking force was now advancing on their side of the river, closing in on them from further upstream. II Augusta had skirted our positions in a broad arc the previous day and had moved into position close to their crossing point, without the Britons discovering this. Having forded the river earlier in the morning, they had waited out of sight until word had reached them that the Batavians had completed their crossing. A huge and deadly trap had just been sprung on the Britons and the last thing the defenders of Durobrivae should be worried about now was the safety of their livestock.

For the next few hours, the Britons fought a desperate action on two fronts. They did, I admit, battle their attackers with great courage, making repeated attempts to force back the surging tides of armoured might that threatened to overwhelm them on their two flanks.

Togodumnus himself must have been part of the force that had first set out to defend against the Batavian crossing, for I saw his chariot returning from that direction around an hour later. He reappeared, his chariot tearing along the opposite bank at breakneck speed, along with a now battered looking force which appeared very much depleted from the numbers I had originally seen sallying forth for the river bend earlier.

The chariots were making use of the flat land running alongside the river to speed their progress as they returned, determined now to engage Vespasian's force as it closed on Durobrivae. Almost as soon as they came into view, the artillery crews had spotted them and made their weapons ready. A detachment of Legionary archers also ran down to the bank and waited for their chance to let go a hail of arrows at the approaching Chieftain.

As the chariots and cavalry raced along the bank, almost parallel to our ranks, we jeered and called at them. Hammering on our shields, we drowned out the frantically shouted orders of Sabinus and his staff, all of whom were yelling furiously, attempting to stop the artillery and archers from loosing their weapons at Togodumnus. It was completely hopeless and far too late to even send out runners to stop the various units from shooting. The whole Legion was yelling wildly for no quarter to be spared Togodumnus. They were outraged at what they had seen him do to their comrades and all were determined to stifle the orders that might keep the Briton alive and deny them their revenge.

Too late too did I see Togodumnus snap his head in our direction and realise that, in his hurry to engage Vespasian, he and his war band had carelessly strayed into the killing ground of a host of fearsome weaponry.

Over the din of our calls I heard the wave of artillery being loosed. I watched as the deadly bolts ripped into the fast moving but tightly packed force. The archers too let go their shafts and they soared across the river in a low arc, falling like killer rain amongst the Britons with devastating effect.

Togodumnus was almost level with my formation when the bolts struck. I saw the first of the iron headed shafts rip into the neck of the nearest horse in his team. The animal fell instantly, pulling its mate with it and de-stabilising the whole chariot, tipping it over so that it slammed into the earth in a shower of flying black muck and splintered wood. The driver was rammed into the ground head first and his neck broke instantly as his body hit the earth in a contorted tangle of limbs. Togodumnus was pitched through the air and landed further away as he had been standing up at the time the horse was hit. As he landed, he was instantly struck by another chariot which hurtled past. The impact of the passing wheels must have broken his legs as, once I had regained sight of him, he was floundering and struggling frantically, pushing with his arms in an abortive attempt to rise.

He spun then, screaming out in pain as the first arrow hit him square in the chest, its snowy white fletchings clearly visible as it protruded from his mail shirt. The second arrow struck in an instant and pinned his left hand to his leg. Again, we heard him screaming out in agony, even over our own wild and triumphant cheering.

At that moment, it was as though a great invisible hand had swatted Togodumnus who lurched violently backwards as a streaking bolt from a Scorpione smashed into his face, before erupting from the back of his head. Bloody pink matter and bone fragments sprayed out as it tore onwards, before finally burying itself in the yoke pole of a ruined chariot, leaving the barbarian prince twisted and lifeless on the ground. As I watched death claim him I was given to observe that; nobility he may have been, but his demise was just as miserable and agonised as that of the poorest of foot soldiers.

We stood in reserve for the remainder of the day as the battle raged before our eyes. We had nothing to do but watch as the Britons raced desperately back and forth, frantically trying to repel the Roman forces on their flanks. Every time their forces were pushed close to the bank we would rain storms of artillery projectiles and arrows down on them, forcing them back and denying them any respite. The Britons put up a vicious defence of their side of the river and managed to hold our forces off until just before nightfall. Only then did the blaring notes of Roman Cornus' blast out over the chaotic din of combat. Signalling the Roman forces to pull back to regroup, they set in for the night to rest and prepare for the final attack the next day.

What still remained of the enemy force stayed in the fields just across the river that night. This time though, there was none of the singing or merriment of the night before, just the wretched sounds of men and horses crying out in the blackness of night, giving voice to their pain and torment as they lay scattered all over the far fields, wounded and dying. Their comrades who had managed to survive the fighting without serious injury would also be lying close to them no doubt; battered and exhausted, knowing that tomorrow the killing would begin again.

I lay awake listening to their cries; dread and distant noises which seemed to me as though they were carrying over from another world, from a place of misery and torment where no sane person would ever willingly venture. As time passed, the disembodied moans and screams grew less, but the unmistakeable stench of death and battle steadily began to rise and thicken. It drifted over us like a cloud of foul smelling filth as we took it in turns to keep watch on the enemy positions. Little was said between us, we just ate, drank and slept and waited patiently for the dawn.

The fighting resumed just after the rise of the new day as II Augusta marched back down towards Durobrivae, in a last concerted effort to shatter the remaining force of Britons. The battered and exhausted defenders of the settlement, instead of moving to engage their attackers chose instead to remain close to the settlement. They were making the choice of a standing fight, rather than a running battle. Their depleted numbers and exhausted men would now never be able to sustain the intensity of the highly mobile fighting of the day before, which had cost them so dearly in numbers.

In the early stages of the battle they had fought hard

on two fronts, making the best use they could of their cavalry and chariots. Now, the new day saw them with a battered and much depleted mobile force and with a much reduced number of foot soldiers. They were poorly trained and equipped men in the main, who had stood little chance against the two advancing walls of iron that the Legions had brought onto the field. For all their wild fighting spirit, to which I had to give further grudging admiration, it was plain now that the Britons holding Durobrivae could no longer stand the human cost of another mauling without risking total and utter defeat.

The end had arrived at midday with a shower of light rain. By then IX Hispana, who had pulled back to the river bend overnight to regroup and receive reinforcements, had returned to the fields outside Durobrivae. They hammered at the Britons right flank once more, threatening to squash the life out of the defenders by squeezing them to death between themselves and II Augusta.

Light, warm drops of fine rain fell steadily onto the battlefield as Century sized wedge formations now cleaved their way into the main force of Britons. The rapidly advancing Roman formations bit hard into the forward edges of the defending host. This fragmented them into small disorganised groups that spilled out from between the backs of the charging wedges. Then, they were further ripped apart by running lines of Legionaries that fell upon them, punching out with their shield bosses and stabbing with their swords in a lethal 'one-two' rhythm as they swept up those Britons who had managed to survive the unstoppable assault of the wedges. Soon, native riders could be seen galloping frantically through the remaining packs of Britons. The order to withdraw had been given and now they were hurriedly beginning to disengage and run north.

As soon as he saw what was happening, Sabinus lost no time to initiate the next phase of our role in the assault. We were quickly formed up in column order and marched at speed to the crossing points previously used by II Augusta where at last, we finally crossed the Medway. So far, the rain had not intensified and the river had not risen so we were blessed with a rapid and easy crossing. We emerged on the opposite bank in high spirits and set out at a blistering pace to reach the battlefield outside the settlement, keen to bloody our swords and engage what was left of the defending army.

In very little time at all we had marched to within sight of Durobrivae and formed up just a short way off, waiting for Sabinus to give the order to move us forward in our battle lines. We all knew by that time though, that our chance to play a more valorous part in the epic battle that had been fought here had already passed.

As we stood facing the settlement, the dead of battle lay strewn out across the field before us, sometimes in small heaps, sometimes in ones and twos and sometimes in great twisted mounds of cleaved and battered flesh. Here and there the wounded crawled and lurched amidst the dead, while those who could no longer move gave voice to their pain instead, shrieking, moaning and crying out to their Gods as they lay helpless and abandoned amongst the carnage. The gentle rain now falling on the field had begun to wash the corpses of the grime and filth of combat. Small crimson rivers now trickled through the human debris. Here and there it formed small, muddy red puddles in hoof prints or chariot ruts, before eventually seeping into the soil.

Though this was already rich agricultural land, I had no doubt that the fields of Durobrivae would be fertile for years to come, as it slowly drank of the rich red blood of its own warriors.

Presently, the shouts of Centurions up and down the formations gave warning that the Legion was about to move. Soon after, we were ordered to advance and slowly the XIIII Gemina Legion crossed the battlefield and closed on Durobrivae. Gradually, over the jingling trudge of our advance, a new sound arose from within the defensive palisade surrounding the settlement as the inhabitants of Durobrivae, mostly women and children left behind by the fleeing native warriors, began to wail out in terror at our approach.

The battle for Durobrivae had not by any means been a quick, decisive engagement as had Durovernon; instead it had been a bloody, protracted, two day long battle that had cost the lives of many more Roman soldiers than the previous engagement.

For many of us it was the first time we had actually witnessed our own soldiers being tortured to death before our very eyes. Now our hearts had become cold and hardened to the terrorised cries of the civil population. Now the Britons would learn why nobody should ever dare to stand against the will of Rome. So too would their women learn the awful consequences of mutilating our brothers in arms in such a terrible fashion as they had the day before.

At around a hundred paces we halted. In silence we stood there, waiting for the word from Sabinus that would unleash our fury on those waiting within the great wooden palisade. As we stood poised, the great, heavy timbered gate of the settlement was opened. Emerging from the midst of what sounded like all of the screaming demons of Hades, an old man stepped forth, walking slowly but purposefully up the track towards the ranks of waiting Roman soldiers.

He wore his long silver hair tied back and was clothed only in a simple, undyed, long woollen tunic with a matching cloak. I could see that some form of talisman was suspended around his neck and, even at a distance; I could clearly see that his hands and arms were adorned with a dense collection of swirling blue tattoos. Within ten paces of the nearest soldiers, he halted and leaned on the tall staff of rough-hewn wood that he had used to assist his walk from the settlement. There he waited; looking up and down the ranks at the men before him, a serene and almost benevolent look settling on his features. After a short pause, the ranks parted as Sabinus pushed his way through, nudging his mount forward and riding slowly towards the man, before halting in front of him. The Legion commander carefully appraised the innocuous looking old man as he leaned forward with a neutral expression on his face, resting his elbow on his thigh and waiting silently for the unlikely looking emissary to speak his business.

"Great warlord of Rome." although thickly accented, the Britons tone of voice was conciliatory. It even carried a suggestion of respect as he looked Sabinus in the eye and slowly spread his arms, almost as though he were ready to embrace the Legate. "I am known to my people as Tincomarix, keeper of the holy grove of Nemeton. I stand before you as chief priest to the people who still remain within Durobrivae and I speak on behalf of the peaceful community behind yon walls, who have done naught to harm you. There are no longer any warriors within, my lord; just honest and simple folk, women and children, along with the old and the sick. Surely, you can see that they pose no threat to your great army."

He stood before Sabinus, armed only with dignity and courage as he pled his case for the deliverance of his people. Their very survival teetered precariously on the words he would choose to negotiate with Sabinus now. As I watched the old man plead the case for his people, it suddenly occurred to me that this was no ordinary old man. Tincomarix, I realised with a chilling start, was nothing less than a brother of the reviled order of Druids. Sorcerers and political agitators, these people were now forbidden to carry on their dark practices. Their faith had long since been proscribed by Rome. Here though in this land beyond the sea, here was the seat of their power. Britannia was home to the Druid faith and here, before us now, stood such a man as I had never before seen, or ever thought to come across, until I came here. These people were evil. We all knew that.

There began an uneasy muttering in the ranks as, all around me, others slowly began to realise just what manner of man stood before the Legate now. Quiet prayers of protection were muttered and all through the ranks fingers formed hand signs to ward off evil as Tincomarix the Druid continued to address Sabinus.

"Your victory is complete this day, great lord. Your armies of iron have killed many of our menfolk. The dreadful wailing of the Beansidhe has been heard much in our homes over the last night." he continued. "Will you heed my words now great lord? You have no need to harm the tired old folk and innocent women and children that dwell in yonder homes. I have told you the truth; there are no warriors for you to fight here anymore. Will you now take what it is you need and please great lord, leave us to live and grieve in peace?"

Sabinus quietly regarded the desperate old Druid for a short while before he slowly drew his sword from its scabbard, the blade emerging with a low hiss as he lightly nudged his horse forward. I saw Tincomarix flinch just a little when the gleaming steel blade appeared. Nevertheless, the old man defiantly stood his ground as the imposing mount and armoured rider casually sauntered towards him. The snorting horse halted before the Druid and Sabinus turned the body of the horse sideways on as Tincomarix stood firmly before him, looking up in anticipation of a response. Slowly, the holy man spread his hands wide once more, silently imploring Sabinus to hear his plea and grant his people mercy.

"As to taking what I need," smiled Sabinus. "We are the victors here this day, so this will be done, with or without your say so."

Tincomarix bowed gently in deference, treading with care so that he did not compromise his position, then raised his face once more to listen to Sabinus.

"I will, as you ask, also confer peace upon you and your people," a brief look of relief began to materialise on Tincomarix's face, only to evaporate rapidly as Sabinus continued:

"But, as I and my men have seen the truth of the so called innocence of your women in all of this and knowing full well just what kind of evil deceiver you are, I am inclined only to grant you all the peace of the dead!"

Sabinus' previously benevolent smile changed in an instant to a mask of utter contempt as his words finished in a roar and he lunged out of his saddle, thrusting his blade deep into the Druids throat, before administering a savage twist of the blade. Sabinus quickly shifted back in his saddle as the dying Druids' blood spurted towards him, a sticky, crimson arc spattering his gleaming armour. Eyes bulging with shock and pain, Tincomarix fell to his knees, his staff clattered on the ground as his arms waved frantically in front of him and his fingers clawed at the air, as though clutching out to hold back the ghost that was now preparing to flee his body. A sickening choking, gurgling sound came bubbling from out of his mouth. Then, all of a sudden, he fell heavily forwards, face down onto the rammed earth of the track way.

It was over so quickly. As Tincomarix lay face down in a spreading dark pool, his arms and legs twitched spasmodically as death took a firm grip of him. It was then that Sabinus turned in his saddle and shouted back to his Legion:

"Fourteenth Gemina, many times in the past you have won glory as the children of Mars and Bellona. You have crushed without mercy all who have stood before you, but today you serve the Goddess Nemesis, today you will bring down the Emperors revenge on these foul, deceitful and treacherous people. Now, unleash your terrible fury and see to it that this place never defies Rome again!"

A great murderous cheer rose up from the assembled soldiers. Predatory cries bellowed out from the throats of more than five thousand freshly enraged killers, drowning out the rising, pitiful screaming from beyond the timber walls. With all trace of military discipline now gone, the entire Legion surged forward like an undisciplined mob, descending on the stockade and bursting through the great gates like a great unstoppable avalanche of death and chaos.

I was cheering wildly as I ran. I could hear my comrades whooping all around me as we surged into the doomed settlement, gripped by an irresistible bloodlust. Screams of pure terror rose all around us and rang sharply in my ears. The shrill, penetrating noise of their fear enraged us all even further as we swarmed about the round houses and animal pens, hacking down without pause, the first of the panic stricken inhabitants as we pushed deeper into the confines of the great stronghold.

Every living thing inside that place seemed to be screaming in stark terror, creating a hideous din that filled my head as we began the killing. It was no time at all before the whole place quickly began to take on the image of some damnable place, found only amidst the torments of Hades.

Seemingly innumerable human screams were accompanied by the squealing terror of their livestock. The shrill piercing sounds of pigs trapped in their pens were added to by the panicking bleating and terrified wailing of goats and sheep. Soon, searing hot fires began to roar through thatched roofs. Great flames licked at a sky rapidly becoming choked with a filthy grey smoke, while crashing timbers added to the chaotic din as we ran completely amok.

Everywhere I turned; it was as though the entire

Legion, men of honour and valour, had been transformed into the madmen of the Emperor. Scenes far beyond the ferocity of battle imprinted themselves on to my mind for eternity as all of us descended without check, into a black pit of wickedness. It carried an unmistakeable message to our enemies, better even than the most eloquent of emissaries, exactly why resistance to Rome should not even be whispered of.

My path was blocked to the door of a roundhouse by a group of Legionaries, bawling out raucous laughter. Had it only have been possible to hear them, then one might have thought that they had all just heard the greatest joke of all time, but the reality of it was quite different. I knew exactly what it was that entertained them so as I watched them surround an old man and his wife, setting about them with their swords almost as though they were an armed enemy. They whooped with uncontained glee as the couple fell screaming to the ground. The men rained chopping blows down on them and the lethal blades hacked them to pieces as they writhed on the floor in their terrible death agonies.

Plunging into the smoky, dim interior of another roundhouse, I set about rooting through household possessions, seeking to plunder anything valuable as the occupants endured their fate. Legionaries had already entered the house before me. As I continued my search, my ears were filled with the screams of a young woman who was being held down by a group of madly yelling soldiers, brutally raping her in turn as she shrieked out for her children. I saw her try to reach out a bloodied hand to two of the children which lay close to the scene of her violation, staring sightlessly up at the roof space with their throats sliced through.

As I watched, the remaining child, a girl of no more than two summers, sat screaming in terror on the rammed earth floor, trembling in a pool of her own urine until a slaughter crazed soldier swept her up by the ankles and swung her violently against a timber support, as one would an axe. The dreadful force of the impact instantly shattered her skull and scattered splinters of white bone and pieces of brain matter across the floor, silencing her terror forever as the soldier contemptuously hurled the tiny corpse towards the bodies of her lifeless siblings.

I felt nothing for the people that fell before me. After all, much better that I survive and they perish. Besides, this was the Roman way of war. We had always fought our wars this way. There is no dispute that war needs to be fought with skill and courage, but only a demonstration of supreme brutality will serve to secure complete control over those who ultimately refuse to yield. So I, like any of my comrades, could not allow myself to feel pity or remorse for any civilian population. I knew without a trace of doubt that any one of them would gladly slit my throat, or worse, at the first opportunity that presented itself. Anyone doubting that need only recall the horrors inflicted on our cavalry scouts only yesterday by so called 'peaceful' women. Such women would in time only spawn more enemies and the children that lived now would soon grow to hate us and fight us in years to come. No, they had all freely chosen to oppose us and now they had reaped their reward.

Eventually, as the day turned to a drizzly grey dusk, we finally finished our work in Durobrivae. Having had our fill of killing and brigandage, we drifted off in small groups to set up camp for the night. As we crossed the battlefield once more, we paused only to loot the innumerable bodies of the dead Britons for anything of value. Weary now, I looked briefly over my shoulder and watched the great flames leaping into the air as they consumed the thatched roofs of the round houses. In my fist, I clutched a bag of loot. A small, hairy black pig also flopped lifelessly under my arm. After a day such as this, my appetite was fierce and the taste of plundered meat was always sweet.

CHAPTER 24

Very slowly, I opened my eyes, gradually allowing the morning light to filter in. I groaned miserably with the discomfort of trying to support a head that felt as though it weighed as much as a large Ballista ball. Throbbing relentlessly, it felt sickeningly thick from the drink fuelled debauchery of the previous night.

That had been one of those rare times when the rigid, uncompromising discipline of Legion life had dissolved. The entire force had plunged itself into an abyss of murderous, uncontrolled chaos, soon after Sabinus had unleashed us to sack and burn the helpless settlement before us. We had run amok like a swarm of deranged savages; killing, burning and looting. When our work was finally done and the whole settlement blazed, we had taken the surviving women and forced upon them every conceivable act of depravity.

It had gone on long into the night, until we were all totally spent of any further desire to eat, drink or fuck. Throughout it all, the smell of roasting meat and the lecherous, roaring laughter of raucous men had accompanied the terrible screams of dozens and dozens of women who paid their own unique price for the resistance of the previous two days. The blazing fires had cast unnatural shadows and made silhouettes born of a vision of hell, as every woman still left alive from the great settlement had paid.

And pay they did - over and over again for the torture that their peers had meted out on those hapless cavalry scouts. With the promise of battle unfulfilled, we had needed to release the last of the surging aggression that boiled within us. As far as we were concerned, those women who did not lay butchered back in the settlement owed us that release.

Whilst I will concede that we had utterly debased ourselves with such a display of wickedness and brutality, the aims of the Legate had also been admirably served. After all, Sabinus was determined that the Britons should not continue to defend their settlements in such a tenacious manner. The best way to stop that was to show them the awful price of defiance.

My hands shook and my head spun terribly with the after effects of far too much unwatered wine and strong beer as I pulled myself up from the grass where I had slept off my own excesses. I stood swaying, doing my best to focus on the world around me. My neck and face flushed hot, as a sudden rush of dizziness and nausea swept over me and I was quickly taken by surprise by a rush of sour watery vomit, erupting from my mouth and stinging my nostrils. It gushed onto the grass, splattering my shins with hot drops of bile. The sight of my own puke oozing into the grass made me retch again and a further wave purged my stomach as it hurtled forth, causing my stomach to cramp viciously with the effort of expelling the foetid broth. Eventually I stood upright, grunting stupidly and wiping my mouth with the back of my arm as I took in the scene before me.

The women who had survived the night were now dotted around the field in a random scatter. Those who were not lying curled up and motionless in the damp grass wandered the fields, as if in a trance. Always though, they kept well away from the clusters of sleeping men who lay scattered all around and even more so from those who had just begun to rise. They clutched the remains of their clothes close to their breasts, protecting what little dignity they still had left. Torn, ragged and soiled, their ruined garments barely provided cover for their bruised, filth stained limbs. Last night they were the focus of the undivided attentions of the men, now they were all but ignored by the waking soldiers who had been so keen to pay them such brutal attention the night before. Now they drifted around aimlessly, either sobbing quietly or muttering some unintelligible gibberish as they went.

As was customary with the Roman army in time of war, we had been allowed to plunder whatever we could carry. This we expected as a right. We saw it as our reward for the successes of the campaign so far. It also allowed us to act as brutal messengers for the army commanders. Now it was all finished and military discipline was again taking hold. The duties of the day would be carried out as usual, interrupted only by the presence of these pathetic broken wraiths as they wandered a world that had once belonged to the Britons. Now it was a world which had changed forever, one which was no longer theirs.

Eventually, the shattered women were picked up by the slave traders who shadowed the marching columns. The slavers grumbled disapprovingly as they assessed the damaged goods. Securing what little saleable merchandise they could, they shackled the women in heavy iron chains and strung them out into a few short lines of empty, soulless beings. Those women who shuffled along in the midst of their misery and shame, broken and violated, had little knowledge of what torment could yet still be heaped upon them, beyond the slave markets that awaited them. For once they were sold; their servitude only had the potential to bring them yet more pain and misery. Their future would have every chance of becoming a living purgatory that would last for every day they still drew a breath.

In the coming days, the efficiency of the Roman war machine had been directed to the task of transforming the ravaged settlement and fields as Roman order began to replace native ignorance and backwardness. The dead were stripped of anything of worth, then removed from the field and disposed of by various methods. The supplies and livestock that had been hoarded here by the Britons were inventoried and allocated space in newly constructed granaries, warehouses and pens. Within just two days, the old settlement area had been swept clear of the charred remains of its old roundhouses and stock pens. New buildings were quickly marked out and their foundations and floors laid down as Durobrivae took on its new, Roman identity.

Across the Medway, men from II Augusta worked feverishly to complete the new timber bridge that would allow the carriage of men and supplies over to our side of the river. Men had swum the river with lines and we had used them to haul thick ropes over to our side, before tying them off on great wooden posts driven deep into the earth. These ropes served to guide the floating derrick they had constructed to drive massive, iron tipped oak piles deep into the river bed.

Once the floating platform had started its work the progress of the bridge was swift as the Legionaries on the construction crews got into the swing of their task. One by one the piles were fed out to the floating platform and slid down into the water through an opening in the deck of the platform and carefully positioned under the frame of the derrick. A huge timber block weighted with bags of earth was then repeatedly hoisted above the massive timbers and dropped onto the tops of the piles, hammering them deep into the river bed. When sufficient numbers of piles were in place, carpenters followed, rapidly connecting them with sturdy oak beams to complete the skeleton of the bridge, before finally adding a deck of thickly cut planks.

From dawn until dusk, all that could be heard was

the constant din of construction work. The sound of axes felling trees in nearby woodland drifted across to join in with the rasp of saws as huge quantities of timber was swiftly fashioned into the carcasses of buildings. Constant hammering rang out as nails and dowels were driven home and chisels were used to chop out joints in the fresh wood. Eventually, the first roofs began to appear over the level of the new defensive palisade as old Durobrivae finally disappeared under Roman order forever.

It was during all this clamour of construction that Julia arrived with Senator Saturninus and his entourage. A sizeable timber built villa was already under construction close to the settlement and it would be here that Adminius would be installed to run his kingdom by Roman laws. So, it naturally followed that it would be here that Adminius would continue his Romanisation, to be taught by Saturninus and his staff just how to become a worthy puppet ruler for Rome.

IX Hispana had already pushed north, hot on the heels of Caratacus' fleeing army, as soon as their resistance had crumbled. They were closely followed by the XX Valeria and their battle group, which had been kept in reserve up until that point. Now called into action, the Legion and their support units were fresh and eager to engage the native army. They moved quickly to support IX Hispana in harassing the retreating Britons up to the next great river, the Tamesis. Inevitably, with II Augusta preparing to march out to engage hostile tribes along the southern coast of the island, it was our Legion who had won the honour of providing security to Adminius and the Senatorial party.

* * * * *

"Well, just try and stay well clear can't you?" The question that Aebutius asked of me seemed also to contain the most simple and obvious answer to my dilemma about Julia.

"Would that it was as easy as that." I groaned.

"So what makes it so hard not to then?" queried Pacatianus.

"Have you missed the fact that we are responsible for their safety?" I snapped back. "How in the name of the Gods am I supposed to avoid somebody that I'm meant to protect?"

"Hmm, that's a tricky one." muttered Pudens ironically.

"Bollocks to it, I say." Marinus put in. "Let's just get you talking to her again and then we can find out exactly who it is that she wants doing in."

"And then what?" asked Aebutius.

"Well then maybe we can just do for him and put an end to all this arsing around." came Marinus' matter of fact response.

"Vulcan's balls, man." Surus exclaimed. "Just like that eh? Do you really think that we can just murder some poor bastard and nobody will give it a minutes thought?"

"Why not?" snapped Marinus. "That piece of dog shit Ademetus got Batiatus killed. Everybody knows he sent him to his death and who's done anything about that then?"

"Small point of order there, Marinus." Pudens cut in with a condescending tone of voice. "He just happens to be the Legion Prefect. I doubt Sabinus would seriously consider executing him just because he settled some personal score with a mercenary scout captain. Besides you'd have a hard time proving that one. After all, it was native blades that killed him in the middle of a skirmish, not Roman ones away from battle."

"I don't shagging care." grumbled Marinus. "Batiatus was my friend and he deserved better than that."

Silent up until this point, Zenas then decided to make his contribution to the discussion.

"He was a friend to us all, Marinus. And yes, he did deserve better than betrayal. But in the end, he died honourably and in battle. All we can do now is remember our friend and honour his ghost in our prayers."

The talking stopped momentarily as each of us paused for a brief moment of silent reflection before Zenas picked up the conversation once more and we continued:

"I reckon Marinus has a good enough point though. Maybe it would be best if we could find out just who this nasty little harpy wants dead. If it's possible to do it then we can get on with the job and then get on with our lives again."

"Well that's just rich is that." sighed Aebutius. "We, no less than the Legate's bodyguard, I'll remind you, are actually considering doing for somebody and making ourselves into something no better than some shitty little assassin that works for a few coins. If she finds out we helped him then she will have a hold on us as well as Vepitta. No, you can count me out on that one for a start."

"Now before you go getting all stiff necked on us, just think." snapped Zenas. "Whoever she wants out of the way is not just some miserable animal of any great account. No, what she will want is a big fish and she's said as much to Vepitta. It seems to me that she's an ambitious bitch and she aims high in her aspirations. We need to know just who it is that she's marked out for a visit from Charon. After all, it might do us all some good to know this."

"Whatever it is you're planning Zenas." I interrupted his thoughts. "Just remember, you could be gambling with the lives of my family back home."

"He's right, Zenas." Marinus agreed. "There's much at stake here."

"Find out what she wants Vepitta." Zenas rubbed at his chin thoughtfully. "Your family will be fine - I swear it."

*****

The great, hulking and unmistakeable silhouette of Bucco stepped out onto the track in front of me, framed by the pale glow of a full moon. As before, he had appeared just after I had been relieved from my duties and while I was heading back to my bed.

I halted before him, scowling up at his shadowy features. Though, even in the poor light, I could still detect the vestiges of a smug, self-satisfied grin on his face. Lifting his thickly muscled arm, he beckoned me to leave the path and to pass through a narrow gap in the hedgerow running alongside the track I had followed.

"One day Bucco, when things are more straightforward..." I addressed him in a matter of fact tone. "...You and I really must decide who the better man is."

The grin broadened on Bucco's face as he bowed gently and gestured once more for me to move through the gap. As I passed through the tall hedge he stepped in front of me. I followed him across to a small circular coppice where I found Julia, sat on a fallen tree trunk and gazing into a dark pool at the centre of the trees.

"Could it be Julia, that you are becoming just a little predictable?

Not caring to look up from the reflected glow of the moon in the pool, she responded as she dropped a small pebble into the water. It gave a tiny 'plop' as it disappeared under the surface, sending tiny moonlit ripples shimmering out across the glassy surface of the pond.

"Predictable, my dear Vepitta? How is that so?"

"Because, both you and your overblown handmaiden here seem to be growing fond of creeping around in the dark like cheap thieves, or worse, some treacherous assassins."

As I waited for Julia to respond I took pleasure in the fact that Bucco's smug smile disappeared instantly at the jibe, replaced instead by a ferocious scowl. Julia however, did not rise to the bait.

"Perhaps, if you and Bucco have issues, you may wish to address them once you have carried out your little task for me."

"Indeed, only a moment ago I suggested the very same thing to him."

"Hmm, that would perhaps be something worth watching, I fancy." Julia got to the point. "However, pleasantries to one side, we really must discuss the more pressing matter of business."

"What?" I queried her, my tone heavy with insincerity. "Are we now to skip over the usual greeting and instead move straight for the heart of the matter?"

"I am afraid so, my poor brave soldier." She delivered her response in the same tone as my own. "Much as the notion of another match with you interests me, time is short and I may yet be missed if I linger here too long this night. Still, all is not lost. Saturninus' Egyptian body slave has some very interesting hidden attributes and I'm sure you had your fill of local flesh once Durobrivae fell."

For a very brief moment my mind filled with images of leaping flames and the anguished screams of women before Julia's voice pulled me back into the present.

"Do you wish to know your part in the gods' great game then, Vepitta?"

"Come then." I told her. "Let us see which player it is who will throw the unlucky dice."

"Are you sure you are ready to know this?" she asked in a grave tone. "Once you know, there can be no turning back."

"There was no turning back once you started all this, despite the fact that the intended victim, as you have already indicated, is important enough to damn my honour forever. But that small consideration matters not to you and that aside, you have also made it plain that you have the advantage over me."

"Ah yes." Julia feigned a surprise recollection. "I understand that your family are all well. The youngest in particular, he thrives I am told. What was his name again? Oh yes, young Marcus."

"You made your point clearly enough last time." I snarled. "Don't labour it now."

I stepped toward her in my anger at her veiled threat, only to have Bucco place himself between us, glaring down at me from under his thick brows. I would have been content then to pull my dagger and cut him a new mouth, just below the old one, but it was Julia who instantly broke the deadlock. She quickly stood up from her seat on the fallen tree and looked me square in the eyes.

"Very well soldier, then you should know that the life I seek is no less than your own Camp Prefect. That maggot known as Marcus Donnius Ademetus."

I stood, staring back at Julia, struggling to find some sort of response.

Ademetus - Him! The very idea had never occurred to me and I wrestled with my thoughts, trying to make sense of things in my mind. I had taken an oath to protect this man as well as I would Sabinus. But he, this odious bastard, had threatened both I and all of my close comrades and had eventually succeeded in ending the life of a great friend to us all. My head almost burst with the conflicts that boiled within me now.

"It comes as a surprise then, Vepitta?" Julia stepped closer.

"Why him?" I evaded the question with one of my own.

"What more must you know?" Julia responded irritably.

"You expect me to kill one of the most important officers of the Legion in cold blood and damn my own honour in the process. What evil has he done to you that you should want him dead so badly? I should be told this at least."

"He has given me the life I have today." she hissed. "He is responsible."

"In the name of all of the Gods!" I exclaimed,

spreading my arms wide to better express my exasperation. "You are telling me that you wish him dead because you hold him responsible for your upbringing in the lap of wealth and power? This is madness!"

I slammed my palm into the side of a tree and leant against it, rubbing my forehead, struggling to understand why I was being forced to risk everything for this lunacy.

In an instant Julia was beside me, she grasped my chin and forced my head round so that she was gazing into my eyes as she made herself clear.

"I wish him dead because he stole from me the love of a father I'll never know. And because he blackened my mother's heart with bitterness and grief for a lost love, who she mourns to this day still. I wish him dead because I was not allowed to grow in the bosom of my own family; instead I was accepted into another's family, but always I knew they were not my own blood. The need to see these wrongs put right has gnawed at me for as long as I can remember and I will see justice done, Vepitta. I have sworn it on the unspoken names of dark and terrible Gods, Ademetus will pay."

As she spilled out her thoughts to me I could see then that there was still a heart in Julia, but it was a heart that sought always to hide behind a protective wall of vengeance, hatred and malice. That way nothing could ever hurt it as nothing would ever come close to touching it.

"So, it is to be him then." I spoke my thoughts aloud, shaking my head and still trying to make sense of it all.

"Oh yes, it is he who must die." Julia said. "For it was he, who seeped into my real family like some sort of rot that consumed and destroyed all. It was he who was the cuckoo in my very own nest. But for him, my mother would not have been forced to flee the bosom of her own family. But for him, my grandmother need not have taken her own life to end the shame and pain of losing my mother in such a way. But for him, my grandfather would not now live on as a twisted and bitter old man and but for him, my father would not have needed to give up the Centurionate and would instead have been allowed to marry mother. And finally, but for him, my father may even still be alive today rather than being cut down by assassins sent by he and my grandfather, as he was forced to walk away from a once happy life and a promising career."

As she spoke, for some reason I found my mind drifting back to when we had first boarded the boats for Britannia. In particular, I began to recall a conversation that had taken place on the deck of the Sea Snake, just before we had set foot on the shores of this island for the first time.

"Julia." I asked her quietly. "Your real father, who was he?"

She turned away from me once more and walked to the edge of the quiet pool, gazing wistfully into it before dropping another small pebble into the glistening, moon-washed surface of the water. I stepped over to her side, just in time to catch sight of the track of a solitary tear, glistening in the moonlight, before she quickly brushed it away with the back of her hand. As she watched the ripples spread out across the surface once more she finally answered me:

"My real father was a Centurion of your own Legion. His name was Gaius Vettius Batiatus."

CHAPTER 25

The morning after my unscheduled assignation with Julia, the conversation around the fire at breakfast took on a slightly livelier note than usual.

"Hey you stupid animal, don't speak ill of the dead." snapped Marinus. "Especially when the dead person concerned was our friend."

"Oh, for the love of all the Gods." Surus groaned. "All I said was that I couldn't understand how an ugly old goat like Batiatus could have fathered such a tasty piece as Julia. You know that if he was here that he'd have seen the funny side of it."

"I still think it's a piss poor joke for the Gods to play though." Pudens mused, swigging on a cup of warm diluted wine. "I mean, imagine the daft old bear never knowing he actually had a daughter. And she, after a whole lifetime always thinking that her true father was dead and getting all fired up about things, actually got so close to meeting him before he died. Now that is a pity, and no mistake."

"Hmm, as I recall, they almost bumped into each other that morning we took Julia and the boy riding. Do you remember, Vepitta?"

"Yes." I replied, recalling the morning for all the wrong reasons. "I remember it very well and I agree with Pudens. Even after all has been said and done, maybe it was a shame they didn't get to have at least one look at each other."

"So, why didn't you tell her about him last night then?" Aebutius asked me through a mouthful of bread.

"To what end, brother?" I responded. "That would have been like telling her Ademetus had murdered him twice. She's bitter and twisted enough as it is. The Gods alone only know what manner of reaction that news would have prompted from her. She already threatens my family; I don't think I need to open the door to anymore of her wicked schemes."

"Well, I can't fault her choice of victim." said Zenas. "He's a bad one right enough and if anyone deserved to fall foul of some righteous retribution it's him."

"Are you saying we should sort him out for her then?" asked Pacatianus.

"What I'm saying is that we don't need to do anything yet." Zenas confirmed. "She knows the opportunity won't present itself until at least after the next big battle and by then, unlikely I know, but the Britons might even have kicked us back into the sea. There's plenty of time to wait and see."

"Vepitta, are you sure she will allow you to pick your time?" asked Crispus.

"She said as much." I replied. "She knows there's a big battle coming and that any attempt now might be rushed. She doesn't want a failed attempt because Ademetus would leave no stone unturned in hunting down the perpetrators and that might reveal her part in things; she wants it right first time so she's prepared to allow me to wait for the right chance. After all, what are a few more weeks after all those years?"

"Then wait is what we will do." said Zenas, gazing pensively into the fire.

"Anyway." asked Pudens, grinning cheekily. "While we're all waiting, perhaps you could set us up for the day and give us the full story on whether or not she's as good at rutting as she is at scheming?"

"Oh, for the love of the Gods!" groaned Zenas.

* * * * *

Soon after my meeting with Julia we received orders to move north and join the two Legions on the Tamesis. They now prepared to move from the crossing point they had established on the river, ready for the push towards Camulodunum. That was the power base of Caratacus and his allies and it would be our greatest prize so far.

To Claudius and his Generals, Camulodunum was the most important objective of all. It was both a tribal capital for the Catuvellaunian tribal federation and also a major inland trading port. With Togodumnus now dead, the fall of Camulodunum would be another great hammer blow to the morale of the Britons. Its fall would hopefully reduce the will to resist of the one surviving brother, Caratacus. In fact, so important was the fall of Camulodunum that Claudius himself was rumoured to be bringing his own small army to Britannia to take the surrender of the town.

* * * * *

"Come on then. Let's get it on the shoulder or we'll be deep in the shit with Fatalis if we're not fell in on time!"

Zenas had just overseen the packing and stowing of our trusty old leather tent onto the mule train and was now gathering our Contubernium to join the column. Reacting to Zenas' order, we pulled our equipment together and made ready to march. Shields were sheathed in leather covers and slung on straps over our left shoulders, while our javelins and heavy marching packs were hefted onto our right shoulders. Once each man had shifted his load around and was comfortable, we made our way over to the head of the column. The ever present clanking and jingling of kit mixed with the hum of idle chatter as we took our places, just as we had done thousands of times before. With the whole Century assembled, Fatalis stalked up and down one side of the formation, conducting a mental head count as Mestrius surveyed the other side.

"Right, shut your jabbering, you animals." snapped Fatalis, as he continued to conduct his survey. "We're about to start out on a march here. Not take a cheery stroll down to the damn baths!"

We had only just begun to bear the weight of our

equipment but, in the humid and growing heat of the summer morning, I was already starting to sweat with the weight of full marching order. I rolled my shoulders to position my load more comfortably as we waited to move. Pacatianus stood behind me and reached forward, untwisting my baldric strap and whispering into my ear as he straightened the leather.

"I suppose I'll have to dress you properly then, you scruffy bastard."

Zenas looked back towards us over his shoulder. He grinned and mouthed the words, 'shut up.'

Having finished his head count, Fatalis moved centrally to the column and stepped back so that he could see us all. "Listen up, you men." he instructed us, addressing us one last time before we set off. "We are an easy day's march from our next objective, which is the bridge over the River Tamesis."

"The distance is easy but the day is going to be hot so I will allow us rest breaks every hour so that you can ease your loads and drink your fill. I don't want any spreading out at the stops because much of the land we will end up marching through is dangerous marsh and I'm told the IX Hispana suffered a good few losses to the swamps when they chased the Britons from Durobrivae. Stay close and be ready to give a hand to any man in difficulties. Remember, trained Legionaries are far too expensive to lose to the bottom of a stinking swamp. You are only allowed to die in battle, and, as I have told you before, even then you must have my permission first."

A ripple of laughter spread throughout the Century as the old Centurion concluded his briefing.

"There will be stops along the route where you can replenish your water supplies, so take the opportunity now to have a good drink. We move out in five minutes."

With that, Fatalis turned and walked over to a gathering of some other Centurions at the head of the column while we began to remove the stoppers from water skins and bottles and damp down what was for me at least, an already growing thirst.

"Do you reckon we'll get any trouble on the march then?" asked Aebutius.

"No chance." huffed Marinus. "They've got to get through our lot on the Tamesis to reach us now. They'd have to be bone stupid to try."

"Yeah," agreed Pacatianus. "And it's not as if we're exactly a small force, eh?"

"Maybe not," contributed Zenas. "But it doesn't mean that they won't try. They need to stop the advance force being bolstered up by us if they want to stand even the smallest chance of saving Camulodunum. With the local knowledge they've got, they could probably find a way through the marshes and surprise us."

"Oh, right." Marinus chided Zenas. He took a deep pull from his water skin, swilled it around his mouth and spat the water onto the floor before sloshing the unstoppered skin towards Zenas. "So when did an old kit donkey like you suddenly turn into some sort of tactical marvel then?"

"Just shut your big fat mouth, Marinus!" snapped Zenas. "Maybe you'd do well to remember just who it is who runs the Contubernium?"

Marinus gave a dismissive laugh and, quickly wiping the back of his hand across his mouth, was poised to deliver his retort just as Fatalis returned and barked out his orders, effectively squashing any continuance of the developing squabble.

"Shoulder your loads, you men. Prepare to move north!"

Shortly after the march began, the main formation split into three smaller groups. The intention was to reduce the size of the column, thereby avoiding a large body of troops getting trapped in confined areas of the marshes if we were attacked. Smaller groups would have more room to operate and could therefore mount a more effective defence. Although, in truth, the marshland we were entering was good neither for attack or defence so for now we considered ourselves to be reasonably safe.

As we pushed towards the Tamesis, we came across small isolated homesteads and settlements dotted along our route. Now though, no longer did the occupants stand around, gawping in dumbstruck awe at the great armoured column as we passed through their homeland. Now they fled like scalded cats when we trudged into view. They had learned to be fearful of us now. No doubt they believed that the fate of the people of Durobrivae would also be theirs, and that the passing soldiers would slaughter them all if they stayed. Whenever we saw them making off, we would hammer on our shields and shout and yell, laughing disdainfully as they fell over their own feet in their panic to escape. We knew that they would eventually return to their homes, as they had obviously done so since our pursuing forces had passed this way previously, so nothing was done to the property they left behind. It would serve no useful purpose and besides, it was obvious that they already realised the price of resistance.

Fatalis had been true to his word. Our march had been an easy one, with no need to force the pace as in the previous marches heading out from the landing areas. A party of cavalry had met with some of our own riders and joined up with us to escort us through the marshland. It was they who guided us to the assembly points around the bridge that the Britons had carelessly left intact as they fled the pursuing army.

As we made our way through the treacherous ground, we kept rigidly to the safe routes indicated as we tramped on through acres of thick marsh grass. I could feel my feet springing on the soft, mossy ground and my soles becoming wet from the water that the weight of our passing was coaxing up from below the spongy surface. I was sure I would not be the only one to do so, but in my head I repeatedly said prayers to the spirits of the marsh, asking them to grant that the soft ground would not part under the weight of so many heavily armed and armoured men. With all this equipment we carried, if anyone went under, it was an absolute certainty that they'd never be heard of again.

As we pressed on toward the Tamesis many varieties of birds flew above us. Our noisy progress through the treacherous marsh land frequently disturbed flocks of water fowl as we passed close by the rushes and reed beds that they inhabited. At least their presence meant that there was a plentiful supply of food to hand and where there was water, there were usually plenty of animals and fish. If we were to be camped here for a while, I concluded, at least we would not starve. The thought of food made me suddenly hungry, and I looked forward to the end of the march so that we could pitch camp and eat.

Once we had arrived at the bridge we passed through the encampment of IX Hispana on the southern bank and marched immediately across to the far bank, into the defensive area occupied by the XX Valeria. We were to relieve them on the hostile side so that they could withdraw back across the river to recover from the defence of the bridge. They, and the other forces who had pushed up to the crossing in pursuit of the Britons, had taken the crossing and then fought a defensive action for the best part of two weeks. They were now utterly exhausted. Both the IX Hispana and XX Valeria had defended the northern end of the bridge in turns but the Britons had employed a tactic of continuous raiding. Small parties had constantly harassed and forced the defenders of the bridge to remain in perpetual readiness until our arrival. It seemed for now, that the Britons had learned the wisdom of applying rapid attacks with small amounts of men, rather than engage their far superior opponents in large costly battles which they could hardly hope to win.

Immediately that our Legion had moved into position, it was organized into defensive parties with each allocated their own areas to defend. Rosters were drawn up for the manning of ramparts, day and night, and extra artillery was set up to deal with incoming raiders. Little of the artillery had made its way this far north as yet, so the pieces that we had carried with us in the main column were of vital importance to the defence strategy. Our Century, being bodyguard to the Legate, had nothing to do with these measures. We, as usual, were charged with the protection of the Legate and his staff.

The morning after our arrival, we had been turned out to provide an honour guard. Both of the Legates from the other two Legions in the area and their staff were to meet with Sabinus in his command tent which had been pitched close to the bridge on the south bank of the Tamesis. The tent itself had been pitched away from the defensive lines in order to keep it safe from any large incursions by the Britons.

The morning itself was foul and grey, made much worse by a relentless downpour of heavy rain, falling without let up for much of the previous night.

Conditions around the camp were grim. Men, horses, pack animals and carts had all now to contend with track ways and thoroughfares which had become inundated with foul, sucking mud. The brown muck grew steadily deeper and thicker with each hour of the downpour, making any task twice as hard to complete.

It had soon become clear that the great army that was holding here would have to advance soon, or be sucked down in a quagmire of its own creation. This is why the Legates had decided so quickly to meet, to finally agree their plan for the advance on Camulodunum.

As we stood, formed up in front of the Legate's tent, the army commanders' column rode up before us. At the head of the column rode Gaius Manlius Valens, previously Legate of our own Legion, and now commanding XX Valeria. Fatalis called us to attention and with a metallic crash we stood to order, forming two lines of men to funnel the arrivals towards Sabinus, who waited to greet them under the shelter of the covered entrance to his tent.

As Valens and his officers dismounted, grooms rushed forward and led the horses away in order to make way for Gnaeus Hosidius Geta and his party who were just a few strides behind.

As luck would have it, I was standing very close to Sabinus as Valens and his party approached and hailed their host. Valens was a hard and immensely strong looking man who was well into his late forties.

He had previously commanded our own Legion in Germania while still in his twenties. He was a career soldier, caring little for the idea of putting aside his armour and entering the political arena, as so many army commanders had chosen to do before him. The rigours of war and commanding thousands of men seemed to be his food and drink and there seemed little doubt that he thrived on it.

As he stepped under the cover of the entrance to the command tent he flipped back the hood of his cloak and grasped Sabinus' forearm.

"Sabinus, my old friend." he beamed. "It is good to see you again and looking so well. How is that brother of yours?"

Sabinus clapped Valens on the shoulder.

"I'm pleased to see you too, friend Valens." he responded. "Oh, and my little brother Vespasian sends his apologies for his absence. He asks me to tell you that he would dearly like to share a cup of wine with you, once he has finished kicking the arses of the tribes on the south coast."

As they laughed at Vespasian's message I watched Ademetus step forward and hail the visiting Legate.

"Legate Valens." he cut in, bowing ever so slightly. "It is so good to meet with you again after all this time."

Valens' face seemed almost to turn to stone as he turned and regarded Ademetus as Sabinus gestured towards the Prefect.

"Valens, you know my Camp Prefect, Ademetus, I

understand?"

As Valens looked Ademetus up and down the Prefect seemed almost to shift uncomfortably under his overtly hostile gaze and when Valens finally responded to Sabinus all trace of cordiality had gone from his voice.

"Your Prefect was a young Centurion when I had command of your Legion in Germania." Valens confirmed the manner of his acquaintance for Sabinus as he took a step towards the now ever so slightly uncomfortable looking Ademetus.

"Congratulations to you, Ademetus." The Legate's voice was openly cold and his words clearly lacked sincerity as he addressed the Prefect. "It would seem that your own unique talent has surpassed that of your peers then. Congratulations on succeeding to the post of Prefect."

Without another word to Ademetus, Valens swept past him and called back to Sabinus from inside the tent.

"Hurry up and usher Geta in here so we can all talk properly my friend. Meanwhile, I'm off to raid your wine as I find the view out there somewhat disagreeable."

With that Valens disappeared further into the command tent, leaving Sabinus with a vaguely puzzled look on his face and Ademetus visibly squirming at the thinly veiled snub.

I could hardly suppress the smile that threatened to burst right across my face as I drank in Ademetus' discomfort. Instead I directed my gaze towards Legate Geta and his party who were now dismounting and handing the reins of their horses to the wringing wet grooms who attended them.

"A word with you if I may, Sabinus." Geta boomed as he crossed the ground between them, closely followed by his entourage, huddled in their hooded Paenulae as they protected themselves from the incessant rain.

"Greetings, Gnaeus Hosidius Geta." Sabinus hailed the Legate as he spread his arms wide in welcome and then clasped his arm as they drew close. "Don't tell me you have brought yet more problems for me to deal with, my great friend."

"Now my dear Sabinus, if you were such a good friend as I'd imagined, surely you'd have told me by now where it is that you find such good quality mercenaries." Geta gestured behind him to a figure standing close by with his hood pulled well over his head. "Have him back for now if you must, but whatever you're paying him, I'll cheerfully double it."

As the figure stepped forward to greet Sabinus I tried to catch a glimpse of the face underneath the folds of the cowl but could see nought but shadow. Then I heard a voice emanate from inside the hood that I had thought never to hear again.

"Legate Sabinus, I am hoping that my post still remains vacant as yet?"

"Back from the dead, eh Batiatus?" grinned Sabinus

as he recognised the figure swathed in the cloak. "Welcome back to you. Well, I suppose we can find some gainful work for you to do. Standard contract rate mind you - same as before."

"That is good enough for me, Legate." smiled Batiatus, throwing the hood of his cloak back and gripping the grinning Legate's arm. I, by this point had needed to bring all of my composure to bear to prevent me from dropping to the floor in gales of laughter. As I celebrated the happy return of our great friend, I revelled also in the look of utter shock and dismay that Ademetus had absolutely no chance whatever of stopping from spreading across his features.

Now Ademetus, I thought to myself, now may the gods forever piss on you and your murderous schemes.

Once the entire party had made their way inside the great tent, a few of us had been called in to stand guard inside. As we were called in by Fatalis, I could not help but notice that he was having a hard time of trying not to smile as he directed us to our positions. Then, gripping his Vitis behind him in both hands, he turned to face the commanders before giving the slightest nod and the quickest of winks to Batiatus.

"Now, I must know." Sabinus said, with a wide grin on his face. "How is it my Chief of Scouts managed to trick the ferryman out of a fare, when all of my men were convinced that he had been cut down?"

"Yes, Batiatus." Ademetus cut in, his expression

was by now totally deadpan. "How exactly did you manage to survive?"

"Now don't bother him with your questions, friends." said Geta, shaking his head and waving his hands around as if to hush everyone. "The man still recovers from a bad chest wound, so I'll tell the story for him."

As Geta related the tale, Batiatus stood there, silent and with a mildly embarrassed look on his face as the Legate fervently sang his praises. All the while Ademetus, having slumped down into a chair, just stared vacantly into the bottom of his wine cup.

Geta explained it all, how Batiatus had engaged a much bigger enemy force at the crossing point on the Medway. How he and his men had battled it out in a desperate fight that had seen Batiatus lose most of his men and sustain a serious stab wound to the chest. Once the Britons had pulled back with their prisoners, Batiatus had crawled from out of the river mud he had fallen into and found himself a horse. He then rode to find the Batavian force that was poised to cross the river, fully appreciating that time was of the essence and that the Britons could soon return to secure the crossing once more. Geta positively boiled over with admiration when he told the assembly of Batiatus' refusal to accept medical help, insisting instead that he alone must guide the advance party to the crossing point, then afterwards return for the main part of the battle group. Then, Geta told the assembly as he concluded the tale, and only then did Batiatus finally let go of consciousness and fall from his mount, then to lie unconscious for four days before he finally rejoined the world of the living.

"And there it is, Sabinus." concluded Geta. "As far as I'm concerned, Batiatus' conduct is the very epitome of Roman strength and valour. Were I his commander, I would not hesitate to honour his courage."

Sabinus stepped forwards, slowly nodding his head in agreement at the words Geta spoke. As he approached Batiatus he looked him carefully up and down.

"Has your wound healed enough for light duty as yet?" asked the Legate.

"If I can stay out of trouble for a few days more then I'll be as good as new, Legate." Batiatus answered.

"Perfect." remarked Sabinus. "Then I will have a scribe compose a despatch which will detail your conduct. You can then take that report, along with the rest of our reports for General Plautius and convey then to his camp on the Tamesis estuary where he waits for the Emperor himself to land. I too will write to Plautius to let him know that you are to present my despatch to the Emperor personally. Then we can let Claudius decide how best you are to be rewarded."

The tents interior filled with the sound of rippling applause as Batiatus responded:

"It is far more than I am worthy of, Legate. My thanks to you, I am deeply honoured."

Sabinus smiled at Batiatus before casting a brief

glance at Ademetus who by now was scowling heavily at Batiatus, surveying the living evidence that his scheming had achieved nothing but praise for his bitterest rival.

"Batiatus, you will leave directly after the meeting, once the despatch I spoke of has been completed. I am anxious that you should be given the opportunity to heal properly as I am no doubt going to need your skills again soon. For now though, I'm sending you out of harm's way."

As Batiatus thanked the Legate once more, I noticed that Sabinus did not once take his eyes from Ademetus as he finished what he was saying. Could it be that the Legate was now opening his eyes to Ademetus' true nature?

Within three hours the strategy for the advance on Camulodunum was settled and the visiting Legates and their staff had left for their own camps. True to his word, Sabinus had a scribe complete a despatch for Batiatus and, having handed him a leather satchel full of reports for Plautius; Sabinus bade him to make haste to the invasion commander's camp.

As he passed by me, I cared little for the fact that Ademetus was still present in the tent, and instead shared a few words with Batiatus as he made his way out.

"It's definitely you then." I quipped. "It must be, because you're much too ugly to be a ghost - even a nasty one."

"And you're a cheeky young cock." he replied. "I

can still sort you out with a good thump in the head, wound or no wound."

At that, Batiatus turned his face towards Ademetus, a scarcely concealed grin creasing his leathery face further as he finished his words to me with a clear display of defiance towards the Prefect.

"Besides, surely you must have realised by now, I'm actually very hard to kill. After all, even after the best attempt yet, all they managed to get hold of was that damned old helmet of mine."

The scorn in the short laugh he let out was unmistakeable. I managed a brief glance towards Ademetus who was by now purple with rage. Batiatus clapped his hand on my shoulder and I grinned at him as he paused in front of me, clutching the despatch bag tightly under his arm.

"I told you the God's had their eye on you." I reminded him. "Look at the proof. You fight impossible odds, survive serious wounds and then go and win the job of delivery boy to the Emperor. Where will it all end, I ask myself?"

"Gods my arse!" he grinned. "I told you, a man makes his own luck in this life."

"Maybe so, but it's always good to know that someone is watching your back, is it not?"

"I'll not argue with that lad, so long as the intentions of the watcher are not malicious." he said pointedly as he turned once more to cast a very brief glance in the direction of Ademetus.

"Be on your way, old man." I told him. "When you

return we may share some interesting news with you, but for now, stay safe."

"News eh?" Batiatus responded, choosing to deliberately side step the note of concern in my voice. "Don't tell me that Marinus is finally going to honour his gambling debts. In my condition the shock would fair kill me."

At that he gave a further brief laugh as he turned to leave.

"Fight well, soldier. For I know well that the next battle you are to face will test all of you."

With that, he strode out of the tent and into the rain, flipping his hood up against the continuing deluge before fading into the greyness of the day. As I watched him go I heard Sabinus' voice behind me.

"Ademetus, a word, if you will!"

CHAPTER 26

Within two days of the Legates' meeting, the entire army that had held the crossing point had moved over to the north bank of the Tamesis and begun its march on Camulodunum. Even though the weather remained poor, progress was swift and unopposed as our mighty force bore inexorably down upon its objective.

Along the way, cavalry scouts had made various sightings of small forces of Britons. The encounters invariably came to naught though. The enemy chose instead to monitor our progress, rather than attempt to thwart it. They watched, powerless as we ate up the miles to Camulodunum, every step pushing us deeper into their tribal homelands. I remember thinking to myself then that surely the Britons must now realise that it was futile to continue to resist us? They had not won a single battle against us. Now, depleted and weary as they surely were, they had absolutely no chance of victory. I remember thinking that it must be better for them to bend the knee now, rather than to be wiped from the face of the earth, almost as though they had never even existed.

Our advance finally ended about ten miles short of Camulodunum on a broad, open plain. For the moment, the rain had eased off and there, awaiting our arrival on the top of a vast, gently falling gradient was a considerable force of Roman Auxiliary infantry and cavalry. These units, newly landed from Gaul, were part of the Emperors own contingent that he had sent just ahead of his own arrival. Even at a distance it was plain to see that they had not been idle. They awaited us from behind hundreds of yards of defence works. Great snaking lines of ditches, banks, sharpened stakes and artillery towers which covered the top end of the gentle slope. It was surely a formidable looking barrier indeed to the huge army of Britons who had gathered on the lower half of the plain in one last desperate effort to stop us from storming their great tribal capital.

As we approached our intended battle positions, the Auxiliary forces hailed us with a great shout, echoing out to us across the rolling meadows. We roared back, bellowing out our battle chants as we tramped across the last few hundred yards to our new positions. The damp, early evening air filled with our challenge to the opposing army while they for their part roared their uncontained defiance back at us.

Had the Britons seized their chance to attack whilst we still marched in column order, then they could conceivably have inflicted many losses upon us. Instead though, the Britons preferred to strike up still more of their own vocal challenges as we broke column and prepared to settle down for the night. I will never understand why they chose not to attack at that juncture but, despite their swelling numbers, the Britons elected instead to strengthen their own positions with newly arriving reinforcements, waiting instead for the arrival of the next morning.

Late that evening, as we had just finished our prayers to the small figure of the Genius and prepared to settle in for the night, we briefly reflected on what it was that drove the Britons to push against the odds they now faced.

"I can't believe they still have the will to fight us," said Surus, shaking his head as he pulled out his blanket and arranged it on the floor of the tent.

"Perhaps it is because they welcome death above the prospect of Roman rule," Pacatianus observed. "You've got to admit though that there is something to be said for their courage at least. After all, they still intend to fight us, even though they must know that all is lost."

"Use your head." said Zenas as he carefully wrapped the little figure up in its protective cloth. "This is their homeland. They will fight to the last drop of blood to defend it, as you would yours. I'll tell you this though, I hope Claudius gets everything he wishes for from this sodden shit hole of a land because as sure as you like, this place will cost them and us a lot more dead men before we're done fighting."

There was a brief moment of quiet contemplation as we continued to prepare our bedding for the night and considered what Zenas had said before Crispus subsequently broke the silence with another question.

"Do you think we'll be army reserve tomorrow? Or do you think this time they might let us have another crack at those blue skinned animals down the hill?" he enquired, laying his head on his rolled up cloak.

"Who gives a damn either way?" moaned Surus, his jaw cracking with a huge yawn. "We've marched halfway across the world to chase these damn Britons around. I'm getting tired with all this carry on now and I swear, if I have to wade through much more mud in this damnable country, I'll go mad. It's been damn near a week since my feet were last dry"

"Now look, why you don't shut that fat hole in your face eh?" snapped Marinus. "If anyone's getting tired it's me with all this inane prattle. I tell you Surus, I've got more teeth in my head than you've spent weeks in this place and already you're whining on about being tired? Why don't you turn deserter and take up farming if you're that tired. That might just do us all a good turn."

"You speak to me like I'm some worthless dog again old man and you'll have a few less teeth in your head to be going on with. If I want to make myself feel better with a bit of grumbling that's my affair. Besides, what has it got to do with you anyway, you crabby old bastard?"

Marinus sprang up from the cloak he was sitting on, taking us all by surprise; he lunged forwards, tearing across the tent like he had been shot from a catapult. As soon as I saw him move I jumped for Surus, knocking him to the floor. I struggled to pin the flailing giant down while Pacatianus and Crispus simultaneously rushed Marinus, slamming into his large powerful frame, forcing him away from his quarry. In the confines of the tent, it was utter chaos as by now Pudens, Aebutius and Zenas had joined me in pinning a furious Surus to the ground. Marinus was a big man but Surus was huge and if he managed to get free, only the gods alone would know what terrible violence would erupt.

"In the name of Dis." Zenas shouted furiously, as he struggled with us to keep Surus down. "What is your problem Marinus?"

"Don't you test me, you overblown pile of pig filth!" Marinus was fair frothing at the mouth. He pushed against Pacatianus and Crispus, ignoring Zenas' entreaty and spitting the last word viciously at Surus as he stabbed his finger over Crispus' shoulder. "I'll slip a piece of cold iron into your guts, you miserable fucking animal. Then we'll see who the better man is!"

Zenas shot up and stood between the two with his arms spread between them. As I saw Marinus begin to ease back I felt Surus gradually lessen off in his struggle to break free and stand as both men now focused their attentions on Zenas.

"You," Zenas snapped, pointing to Surus. "You stay down or, big ox or no; I'll sit you back down in a heartbeat if you don't obey!" He whirled round to face the still furious Marinus, even now being pushed back by Crispus and Pacatianus.

"And you!" He snapped, jabbing a finger at Marinus. "What the fuck is wrong with you?

Tomorrow, any number of us could lay dead on that field out there. I don't know what it was that prompted you to do that but do you really think you can threaten to take a comrade's life, just because you've fallen out like a pair of squabbling brats?"

Marinus did not reply, preferring instead to set his jaw and stare murderously at Surus, who Pudens, myself and Aebutius still had pinned securely to the ground.

Zenas seemed frozen in time as he stood, still as a statue, staring at Marinus. After a tense pause Pacatianus and Crispus sensed the threat beginning to pass and slowly released their grip on him. Gradually, the angry expression faded to a look of grudging compliance as he spread his hands and backed away.

"Any more trouble out of you stupid pigs and I'll be speaking with Fatalis and you can take the matter up with him. We fight for each other, not amongst each other. You'd all do well to remember that. Now get some sleep, tomorrow is going to be a hard day."

The remainder of the night before the battle passed without incident and we awoke the next morning to the familiar sounds of the huge camp coming to life all around us. There was a light drizzle in the air and a gentle breeze drifted in from the direction of the distant coast as we stepped outside of the tent and began to prepare our morning meal.

A bar of light grey lit the distant eastern horizon, slowly pushing back the last vestiges of night to reveal dark grey layers of dense, pregnant rain clouds.

They hung ominously overhead as though attempting to fight off the advance of the dawn. The familiar sounds of the morning routine could be heard all around; men coughing and spitting and the rapid 'tap tap tap' of flint strikers being used to light tinder, rekindling small cooking fires which had died down since last night's meal. Here and there men laughed and joked and the familiar clatter of pots and armour being handled could be heard, just like on any other day. As yet, the morning was cool and peaceful, but all of the men in that vast encampment knew that the peace of the early morn was most likely to be in stark contrast against what was to come later that day.

Our very first task that bleak morning had been to seek the favour of the gods for the coming battle and, as an entire Legion; we had formed up in Cohort formations and offered our prayers to the gods, asking for their favour and to guide us safely through the coming hours. Jupiter was ruler of the sky and chief among the Gods. It would be his favour we would attempt to invoke first; beseeching him to strike the Britons with thunder and lightning and inundate them with rain. If our prayers were heard then he would smite our foe with the elemental forces of the sky before they could even engage us. If it pleased him for us to do battle with them, then we prayed that Mars too would give us the skill and strength to wage deadly war against the enemy host. Devotions made to the goddess Victoria would ensure that it was our army that won the day and that the enemy was vanquished, with Rome remaining supreme over all. Every soldier there on that field knew that there was nothing to fear when the blessings of the gods were with you.

After the giving of prayers and offerings we moved up to the forward defences. Already, extra Scorpiones were being hoisted to the tops of the specially built towers, along with great bundles of newly made bolts, providing ample supplies of deadly missiles which the crews would soon send streaking down on the Britons. We quickly began to form battle lines all along the edges of the defences as we moved up. The artillery crews were already beginning to identify their arcs of fire and assess the ranges of reference points in the land before sending out ranging shots, allowing them to calibrate the weapons in order to more easily bring down instantly effective fire when required.

The lethal efficiency of these machines had been proven time and time again through countless years of warfare with the enemies of Rome. The Britons had soon learned of the potency of these dreadfully efficient weapons in our last great battle with them. Now, they would have to face them again, only this time in much greater numbers. They would also have to negotiate the sharpened anti-cavalry stakes that bristled conspicuously along the top of the slope and avoid the deadly little traps that lay in wait before they had even reached the more obvious hazards. Our formations had already been briefed on the clear routes through the fields of spike traps. The Britons would have no such knowledge and so would inevitably fall foul of the waiting surprises if they pushed too far up the slope.

Quick and easy to plant and conceal, hundreds of sharp iron Stimuli lay concealed in shallow pits in front of the wooden stakes. To the unwary foot soldier and cavalryman, they would prove to be crippling and sometimes lethal surprises. Even if the Britons reached the area forward of these, there lay before them a wide expanse of ground, liberally sewn with Caltrops that could easily falter or halt the advance of great groups of men. Like a tiny iron tripod, these small spike traps could hardly be detected in even the shortest of grass and always came as a viciously painful little surprise, easily able to cripple the unshod soldier or embed itself in the soft underside of a horses hoof. Even used on their own, these agonising little traps had been capable of breaking mass charges, causing chaos as whole waves of attackers fell victim to them at the same time.

Confident of the preparation of our defences by then, we waited in our battle lines and watched with interest as a party of cavalry set off from our lines and down the slope accompanied by a delegation of officers. The bright standards streamed behind them in the morning breeze as they made their way towards the centre of the ground between us and the Britons. The great tribal army was, by now, cheering and screaming wildly like some great swarming mob of enraged demons. They drummed thunderously on their shields, ensuring that the approaching Roman delegation was treated to a hostile and unnerving reception.

The Roman party halted at mid distance and held their ground with a display of calm courage, given that they were both a tiny force and also the closest armed Romans to about thirty thousand infuriated native warriors, all baying for their blood and craving possession of their severed heads. I had to admire them for their coolness of nerve as they sat there on their horses, calmly waiting to be joined by the envoys from the baying hoard arrayed before us.

Eventually the sight of riders moving to the front of the mass of Britons indicated that a delegation of their own was now on its way. Presently a group of riders, far smaller than the waiting Roman party, sauntered almost casually up the slope towards their adversaries. The Britons matched their counterparts like for like in their own display of nonchalance for the great assembly of armed might that they now approached.

As they drew closer, I noticed that they seemed to be grouped in threes. A central rider was flanked by two other warriors who bore shields and spears while the middle rider was bereft of armour or weapons save for a long dagger carried on his belt. The group halted and dismounted around thirty paces away from the Roman officers. Six of their number remained behind and held their mounts ready while the remaining number of around twelve made their way up the slope.

A similar sized party of Roman officers dismounted and met their counterparts' midway between the two groups. They then began the talks that would either avoid the need for battle, or plunge us into a large, bloody clash that would ultimately decide who controlled the south east quarter of Britannia.

We waited silently and patiently for the outcome of the talks between the two delegations. As we did so I surveyed the assembled host of Britons who now also stood in relative silence, awaiting the outcome of the parlay. As we stood in our massed thousands amidst the steadily thickening drizzle, my mind floated away from the awing site of the waiting army and from idly watching droplets of water sliding down the backs of helmets. Instead, as I looked around me, I began to wonder just how many of these men would still be standing afterwards if we did enter battle that day, and just what the final outcome would be. All of us, without exception had confidently forecast that it would be our army who would emerge triumphant from the coming battle, but none of us knew just how many of us it would cost to beat these damn Britons this time. That was the question uppermost in my mind then.

"So, do you think they'll fight?" I muttered, addressing the question to nobody in particular but risking the wrath of the officers for talking in the ranks.

"There are absolutely thousands of the bastards." replied Pacatianus out of the corner of his mouth. "I reckon they must outnumber us by at least ten thousand."

"With odds like that, they'd have to be mad not to give it one final try." Crispus responded under his breath, tucking his chin down to avoid being spotted by the officers.

"Who cares whether they want to try or not?" snorted Surus quite blatantly. "Let's just get on with it and flatten the barbarian scum. Food for Ravens is all they are so let's just get on and fight. After all, we all know we're going to hammer them to dust anyway."

"Really? In the confidence of the gods now are we?" Marinus sneered sarcastically. "So, maybe you can also tell us just how many of us will end up as Raven food along with them then, oh great Oracle?"

The question, although provocative in its tone, echoed my earlier thought and once more I found myself taking in the faces around me, earnestly hoping that all of the faces that surrounded me then would still be there at days end.

"For the love of the gods," exclaimed Zenas. "Can't you lot shut your stupid holes just for a bit? You're all like gossiping old matrons, I swear it."

"Eyes up," hissed Pudens. "They've finished with the pleasantries. Here they come."

The two parties of emissaries had eventually concluded their talks and separated while we had been chattering idly and both of the groups were now galloping back to their own lines. The Britons reached their own men first. I could see the riders moving through the great assembly, shouting to their warriors and thrusting their weapons in the air. Very quickly, the whole host assembled on the broad plain below us began to yell and scream and beat their shields with their weapons, thrusting a huge array of swords and spears in our direction. The eerie sound of their Carnyx cut through the air as they raised the great bronze war horns up in their forward ranks, letting out long ululating blasts on them. The almost supernatural sound reverberated around the field like the baleful wailing of a dark spirit, dispelling any doubts that may still have been held as to the enemy's intentions. Without any great surprise to us, it was plain now that the Britons had chosen to fight.

The darkness of the cloud cover that rolled across the sky above us was becoming deeper now and the heavy drizzle that had prevailed throughout the morning had gradually turned into rain. It seemed that there would be no prospect of better weather ahead as we watched the Centurions reporting back to the rear command points to receive final briefings. As they did so, Mestrius moved to the front of the Century and spied us out.

"Zenas, was that your lot that I heard flapping their jaws around again?" he enquired, raising his head up and looking down his nose at us.

"I regret to say that it was, Optio," replied Zenas. "But I did warn them all to be silent in the ranks."

"Then you had better hope that they start to obey orders a little better and that they fight as well as they talk because I get the feeling that this little outing is going to get very rough. Oh, and when we're through to the other side of all of this I think I'll have a word in your ear. Perhaps you could do with a few pointers on how to control this pox stricken gang of idiots. After all, this is the Legate's bodyguard, not some gossip forum for a bunch of piss stinking old washer women. Get them in hand, Zenas. Before I feel compelled to do it for you."

"Yes, Optio!" replied Zenas, shooting us all a look of extreme annoyance.

I instantly regretted starting the small talk in the ranks as the end result of it was that Zenas had now been checked by the Optio, openly questioning his ability to control his own Contubernium and thereby embarrassing him in front of the entire assembled Century. We were professional soldiers and should have known better. As it was, Zenas was a good man and a fine soldier. He didn't deserve to be openly shamed by our lack of discipline, so I resolved to apologise later for it. However, as I stood and mulled over my apology, I soon became distracted by three groups of three riders heading out from the enemy forward lines and galloping hard towards us.

'What now?' I thought. 'Surely, not more negotiations?'

Though as I watched, it soon became startlingly clear to me that these men were not coming to negotiate. No, these men were actually charging us. Just imagine, nine warriors sent to attack nigh on twenty thousand fully armed and armoured soldiers - madness!

I could hear the drumming of the horses' hooves as the native riders rapidly closed on the front ranks of our front formations and I heard their ardent war cries rise full and clear into the rainy air as they closed the gap with breakneck speed. At about sixty paces the riders hurled their light javelins at the formation and ripped their swords free from their scabbards, levelling them at our lines as they rushed in, fully committed now to their suicidal charge.

At that moment the officers of the units about to receive the futile charge could be heard yelling out the order to form an anti-cavalry wall. Craning my neck to look along the front of our formation, I could just see men falling into position at the kneel, locking their shields together as they jammed the butts of their Pilum shafts into the ground, directing the slim iron tips outward to form a bristling hedge of lethal iron spikes. As the charging horses came within range, a wave of javelins hurtled out from the rank behind the locked shields, soaring briefly through the air before punching devastatingly into the group of riders and mounts, felling them instantly amidst a jumble of flying clods of muddy earth, flailing limbs and screaming horses.

Straight after the javelins had done their deadly work I continued to watch with interest as a couple of the horses thrashed around on the ground, trying frantically to stand. I also remained intrigued as to why the Britons had done this pointless thing. Though as I looked on I was further surprised to see the four riders who had survived the volley of flying death leap up and continue their charge at our lines on foot, screaming as though they were possessed by devils and whirling their long bladed swords above their heads as they rushed in.

In the end, I didn't see what happened to the Britons; I just heard the thuds of their impact upon the shield wall and the unmistakeable ring of metal on metal. I heard the shouts of the Legionaries who engaged the warriors and the contemptuous laughing and jeering of the Roman soldiers close to the point of the assault, as the suicidal Britons were engaged and then cut to pieces by the front rank.

Then it was over. A moments silence gave way to a tumult of cheering from back down the slope as the Britons roared out in joy after their slain warriors. I remember that at that time, before I eventually grew to better understand the complex animal that is the warrior Briton, I could not really resolve as to why in the name of Dis they had thrown their lives away like that. Was there some mysterious end that it had served? Still, whatever the purpose of their suicidal charge; not only did it bring the massed gathering of Britons some, as yet unknown cause for elation, it also galvanised our own forces into action.

It began with the immediate return of the Centurions

to their units and was quickly followed by the blast of our own horns and the subsequent forward advance of a large force of Auxiliary infantry, moving to position in preparation for what would be the opening stages of battle. Four Cohorts of Dalmatian light infantry took front position and prepared themselves to draw the Britons out from the assembly area, while two Cohorts of their own light cavalry waited on the flank to support them.

As we watched with mounting anticipation, there was a further blast of horns and the two front Cohorts of Dalmatian infantry then set off at a steady pace, moving down the slope in tight blocks while the other two Cohorts moved up and occupied the vacant forward positions. Presently, they were joined by two Cohorts of Batavian infantry acting as their reserve as the early phases of the Legates' plans clicked into place. As the commanders had expected, it didn't take long for a very large contingent of battle hungry Britons to charge out to meet the advancing force. Thousands of native foot soldiers surged forward and hammered up the hill to the first group of Auxiliaries. The Dalmatians quickly reacted by separating into century sized formations and then counter charged the surging Britons in great wedge formations, slamming into the advance and fragmenting their charge. Fierce fighting raged at the foot of the slope as the wedges were almost engulfed in massive, loosely packed bands of Britons before the second Cohort charged in, moving in running lines and quickly engaging in brutal fighting with the fiercely battling tribesmen.

At the head of the slope, we waited in patient, practiced silence as Auxiliary cavalry almost discreetly filtered across the rear of the Roman front line. One of the cavalry Cohorts made its way across in several small units, only to regroup on the other side and prepare for a charge from the left flank, leaving the other cavalry Cohort ready to move from the right. As the Auxiliary infantry slowly began to draw back from the press, the Britons began to push after them in loose, disorganised groups. Unwittingly they were being drawn up the field by the disengaging Auxiliary formations, caught blindly up in their eagerness to defeat the seemingly retreating enemy.

Horns blew out from the cavalry formations then, and flag signals were quickly exchanged between the two units before they suddenly exploded into a yelling, headlong charge down the slope, swarming down into the mayhem below them. Like a giant pincer, the thundering, thousand strong cavalry charge smashed simultaneously into the pursuing Britons on both sides. The retreating Dalmatian infantry gained valuable time to regroup as the Britons, belatedly identifying the new threat, hurriedly turned their attention to the cavalry.

Horns blasted all along our front. We broke our silence and cheered loudly in support of our forces, banging our shields and crying insults into the air. We cursed the Britons for all we were worth, intending that the roar of our own voices would further distract and dishearten the beleaguered foe, now fighting hard to hold off the surprise cavalry attack.

Suddenly, however, our cheers changed to shouts of dismay as we watched a massive force of enemy erupt from the host assembled below us and charge directly towards the fight. Even at this distance, we could hear the thunder of the hooves and the jingling of horse harness above the guttural war cries. The mounted tribesmen swiftly closed on their quarry and an even more chaotic battle raged amidst a seething, intermingled mass of foot soldiers and cavalry.

We could clearly see from our vantage point on the top of the slope that the great force of native horsemen were steadily encircling the murderous press. Thankfully, it didn't take long for our own cavalry to realise that they would soon be surrounded and slaughtered if they remained where they were. Wisely abandoning the fight, they pulled themselves out of the melee and galloped back up the slope towards us.

As our cavalry fled for their lives, we saw that the Britons had seized the initiative and were now in hot pursuit with their own units of horse, rapidly closing the gap on the rear of the fleeing units. As they drew closer to the Roman lines, the forward Auxiliary units quickly deployed into anti-cavalry walls. With well-rehearsed ease, they dropped down behind their shields to create long rows of densely packed barriers, bristling with scores of spear points. Even before the infantry had deployed their defences our artillery crews had begun to load bolts into their weapons, ready to fell the counter charge with a shower of missiles if the tribal cavalry came too close.

Taken up in the heat of the moment and having got the scent of a quick victory, the Britons totally failed to register the threat that awaited them. Instead they opted to throw caution to the wind and closed rapidly with the fleeing Roman cavalry. As soon as they came within range of our artillery, the crews wasted no time in laying down a withering storm of bolts, loosing their deadly missiles over our heads and out towards the mad onward dash of the Britons. Once more we witnessed the deadly power and accuracy of the bolt throwers as their opening salvo ripped into the wild charge, utterly devastating the forward element of the great, rushing mass of cavalry. Horses pitched and screamed as the charge was reduced to a tangled, chaotic pile and unhorsed riders flailed and yelled as they were launched from their mounts and catapulted through the air. Within a heartbeat of that first wave of missiles punching home, the surviving Britons, stunned at the instantaneous collapse of their charge, turned and fled for their own lines.

By now, the two fresh Dalmatian Cohorts had formed up in tightly packed blocks and the Batavians did likewise as the entire force quickly spread across the field in four distinct rectangular formations, leaving wide gaps between each. Meanwhile, the surviving troops who had fought in the opening engagement quickly moved to the rear to regroup; preparing themselves to be used in a later wave.

All across our front, the order to get ready to move was echoed by the various unit Centurions and Optios as the Auxiliary formation arrayed before us began to advance, slowly closing on the seething force of Britons at the foot of the slope. Fatalis appeared in front of our Century, passing on his last verbal orders. From now on the air was likely to be filled with an even more deafening cacophony of noise that would render most spoken orders ineffectual. Now we would respond mostly to manual signals and blasts of the Cornu, given that a man could no longer easily make himself either heard or understood in the raging chaos of pitched battle.

"Listen up," Fatalis shouted, as he spread his arms as though to gather our attention. "We will follow the Auxiliaries down the hill in extended line and wait for them to engage. They will maintain the gaps you see between their formations in order to filter the enemy through in streams. As they emerge at the rear of the formations, we will engage and destroy them with rolling lines. Understood?"

"Yes, Centurio!" We roared together.

"Two Pannonian cavalry Cohorts are waiting in reserve and will deal with any flank attacks the Britons may try. Meantime, keep it tight and look for the order to fall back and refresh your strength. Remember where the Cornu and standards are and you will know where to look for signals. As usual, shout out any orders you may hear so that the next man gets it too. Now, get ready to move!"

At last, the time for waiting had passed and the excitement of combat and a trepidation born of the experience of battle started to build in me in equal parts as we waited for the final order to move. Then I heard a loud blast from the Cornu which was quickly followed by repeated shouts to shoulder our javelins. At last, we were on the move, trudging slowly down the wet slope behind the Auxiliaries. The waiting Britons jeered and chanted beyond the already countless bodies lying on the field, hammering their weapons deafeningly on their shields, promising bloody murder as we approached.

Marching towards a battle is an experience quite apart from anything else a man can experience. As we pressed on down the slope it was almost as though we were descending into hell as we became enveloped in the stomach churning stench of battle. I have never been adequately able to tell another person just what it is like, other than to say that, once the awful stink of war assails your nostrils, the world suddenly changes around you. Your sense of smell becomes inundated by the thick odours of horse sweat, blood, excrement and the unmistakable reek of fear, just at the same time your ears too fill up with the screams of fury and pain - the terrible sounds of men and beasts in agony.

As with so many other occasions when I had entered a battle, so it was that a familiar change washed over me once more. It was always at this time, just before we joined the fight that my whole body and mind surged with the raw energy of combat. The savage spirit of war coursed through my veins and from that point on, I lived only to fight. This day was no different, as I ground my teeth and squeezed the shaft of my Pilum until my knuckles became as white as ivory. Every step we took drew me closer to an eruption of extreme and uncontainable malevolence which would direct a devastating battle rage on any who stood before me. It was nothing personal – it was war.

By now our minds had closed to the larger world around us. Each of us was entirely fixated on the job of utterly destroying the enemy that waited for us at the base of the grassy slope. Despite the coursing energy that I knew now flowed through each of us, we remained dedicated to our task and maintained an even, steady pace. We looked occasionally to our sides, carefully maintaining the straightness of the line as we marched. We knew from experience that tightly ordered dressings were crucial if the formation was to be effective and if it were to avoid being split by a wild forward charge. This attention to detail was paramount. Above all else in war, despite the unerring capability to fight and kill with practiced skill and ruthless efficiency, the true essence of success in combat is the routine observance of iron discipline.

The rain began to fall harder as we closed the gap still further and I heard yet another great roar rise from the Britons. I saw their reaction to the advancing threat of our battle line. Caratacus had deliberately held his chariots back until we pressed him with an attack in greater strength. Now, with just such a threat presented to him, he unleashed a mighty force of war chariots directly upon the advancing Auxiliaries. As they sped forward from their own lines they were eagerly joined by great swarms of cavalry and foot soldiers, surging forward in one massive, bellowing charge.

Relentless and undaunted, we pushed onwards as the first of the Auxiliaries were hit by the rushing mob and were quickly taken up in fierce fighting. The intense hammering and screaming of battle rolled back up the slope and rang out over our heads as we approached the forward units, all the time watching the gaps between the Cohorts as they filled with charging Britons. As we drew ever closer, scores of chariots burst out from the rear of the Auxiliary formations and bore down upon us with terrifying speed. Again, Cornu's sounded and the order was given to be ready with our Pila and present our shields to the front, preparing to meet the headlong charge.

I swung my shield to the front and raised my Pilum off my shoulder in anticipation of the order to throw. Then, upon hearing the commanding blast of the Cornu, I instantly hurled it out towards the charging mass. I traced its path as it joined a dense wave of other javelins tearing through the air and watched with cold satisfaction as it transfixed a Briton, sending him tumbling from the back of his chariot.

The rest of the lethal storm of javelins struck with terrible consequences amongst not only the chariots, but the hundreds of warriors on foot that had burst through the Auxiliary formations and ran after the chariots. Recovering from the wave of missiles and swerving wildly, the chariots seemed to move as one, like a giant shoal of fish, as they simultaneously swung their left sides to us and rushed along our front. From each chariot, the warrior that was carried on the back then leapt from the vehicle and came screaming towards us in a furious rush. It seemed clear to me then that, just as we found ourselves possessed by the spirit of war and battle, so too did something terrible and yet much more elemental seem to drive on these fearsome tribal nobles. These were the elite of their warrior class. They were hard and wild men who valued prowess in war above all else and who chose to fight either totally naked or, at the very most, clad only in richly patterned breeches as they sprinted forwards into the press.

Their incredible image was one of startlingly impressive savagery, with the flash of gleaming gold and bronze torques adorning their wrists and necks, and their entire skin covered in swirling blue patterns. These men didn't need armour; for it was plain that they coursed with the raw energy of the earth and trusted in that power alone to protect them.

The rumbling thunder of chariot wheels, thrumming

hoof beats and the wild screaming of our foe grew deafening as with a shattering impact, they plunged headlong into our ranks. Relentless in their ferocity, they came on at us, slashing and hacking, stabbing and lunging wildly with spears, or cleaving away with great iron long swords. In an instant, we had gone from a steady advance to dealing with the sudden, violent shock of vicious, close up fighting.

The thrown wave of javelins had done little to diminish the impetus of their assault as the Britons fell on us in droves. My shield slammed back against me as the first of the charging bodies collided with it. I braced my feet, driving out with the shield to knock my assailant back, then plunged my wickedly sharp Gladius into his naked torso. I gritted my teeth, grunting as I drove the weapon home against the weak resistance of skin and muscle. The blade sank deep into the thrashing body and a pain wracked scream pierced my ears. With a sharp twist of the blade and another smack with the shield, my first up-close kill of the battle dropped heavily to the ground. Slithering around on the slimy surface of the muddy field, he was now all-consumed with the agony of the gaping, fatal stomach wound I had inflicted upon him.

Punch, thrust, counter punch, block and stab. The movements repeated themselves over and over again with mechanical efficiency amidst the screaming, frenzied butchery of battle. Relentlessly, we forged forwards, fighting against enraged blue painted demons that swarmed all over us, furiously resisting every last step of our advance. Nothing could stop the slaughter now, not even the intervention of the Gods as the sky grew ever darker with the thickening black clouds, drenching the field of battle with a rain that seemed as though it would never cease. Roman and Briton hammered and railed against each other as a mighty peal of thunder shook the ground and lightening split the sky. Men fell amidst the filth, shattered and bleeding while their comrades fought on, slithering and struggling for purchase in a thickening, bloody sludge as each man there strove to cut their opponents down.

It was then that a massive figure rose before me like an enraged bear. My mind blotted out the rest of the world around me as he and I made eye contact. In that moment, an unspoken decision was made between us that we two would fight.

His tightly muscled and painted physique glistened with the flowing sheen of falling rain, mixed with the splatter of fresh blood. Fine lines of crimson ran in ragged trickles all over his skin, sprayed from the veins of his victims and brother warriors alike, they mingled with the blue of his body paintings and tattoos. His eyes glinted with a terrible spark of fury and hate as, roaring out his battle song, he swung his long sword overhead. The great blade caught my gaze as its polished surface flashed with a wicked glint, reflecting the blue fire of the lightning storm that seemed to tear open the very sky above us. The long sword sliced down in an arc towards my head, water and blood flying from the blade as it cleaved the air. Instinctively, I raised my shield and blocked the shattering chop, ducking under him at the same time and thrusting upwards in search of his stomach. Instead, I felt my blade cramming itself between his ribs and lodging fast. I cursed myself for delivering such a badly placed thrust, frantically twisting and wrenching at the hilt of my sword, trying to rip free the weapon that would keep me alive while I hammered the face of my shield into his powerful body.

As he howled and raged on the point of my blade I would have slammed the shield against him once more to free the sword, had it not been for another of his kind, lunging full into the face of my shield and flinging me backwards with the force of the unexpected impact. My tight grip on the hilt of my Gladius was broken, and I stumbled back, landing heavily in the slimy mud. I felt myself giving way to the first vestiges of panic as I lay, pinned between two corpses, my shield covering but pinioning my body as the half gutted Briton sat atop it, chopping at my face and screaming like a madman. The hole my sword had ripped into his body seemed to have had no effect on him at all as the great sword he carried smashed down once more, chopping into the shield edge and hammering into the front of my helmet. Though the strike was numbingly painful, the brow guard of my helmet saved me from having my brains let out on the field and I struggled wildly, pushing to free my arm from beneath the shield and grab for my Pugio. I was desperately aware that the heavy iron dagger was now my only hope.

For the first time in my life I experienced the awful gut cramping fear that I suppose a victim of violent and bloody death must actually feel. It all seemed so unreal as I became horribly mindful that I was now the one screaming out, not with a cry of battle, but in stark fear. I was horrified that even though I had done everything I needed to kill a man, just as I had done maybe a thousand times before, my opponent still lived. Even with a sword still jammed in a fist sized hole in his rib cage, this superhuman demon was unrelenting in his assault and was about to take my life, leaving me dead amidst the filth of that field.

For a moment, time stood still and a faint sense of shame arose amidst my fear as I felt my thighs warming with the hot gush of urine that I could no longer hold in my bladder. The shock of the unwelcome sensation triggered something within me and I fought back harder, lunging upwards to bite him as me punched at my face and then drew the blade of his sword back for another strike. In a heartbeat I realised that my hand now gripped what it was I so frantically fumbled for. I tugged my left hand free and then lay there, staring upwards as if watching somebody else's hand as it soared upwards, at last, plunging the dagger up, under the ribcage and deep into my attacker's chest.

The scream hardly had time to form in his throat

before the top of his head was cleaved off in one great slice and hit the mud next to me. Then a Roman boot kicked the twitching body off my shield and I heard a voice;

"Get up, or you're dead!"

Fatalis grabbed the neck of my armour and hoisted me up, covering me with his own shield as he lifted the edge of mine. I quickly grabbed it from him and then placed a firm boot on the chest of my attacker, yanking my Gladius free from the torn and now thankfully lifeless body before I spun to face the front and resumed the fight. Everything had happened so quickly that I had no chance to thank Fatalis as he disappeared as quickly as he had appeared. For a few terrifying moments I had spent time with the dead, totally convinced that I would not rise again from the foul mess that lay underfoot. Shaking off a terrible feeling of dread, I quickly resumed my place in the line and tried not to think about the sodden front of my tunic, now cooling uncomfortably in the air and lying heavy against my thighs.

The battle raged on with unabated ferocity. Relentless killing carried on without let up, even after we had been withdrawn and fresh troops had taken our place in the line. Finally, they came to experience for themselves a taste of the extraordinary and unrelenting fighting that raged at the base of the slope. Withdrawing to our rear areas, we carried the badly wounded from the field of battle and delivered them to the large hospital tents that awaited them.

These were grim places, where men suffered the awful pain of combat injuries or succumbed entirely to their wounds. The walking wounded sat outside being tended to by Capsarii who would wash the less serious wounds with sour wine and then dress them with clean linen bandages. The misery of their situation was made all the more worse by the unrelenting rainfall.

A Medicus worked with teams of the orderlies, supervising their work and assessing the seriousness of wounds as the casualties of war arrived in droves at the field hospital. The more seriously injured were taken inside the tents and treated under cover. Agonised screams assailed the air around the tent as men endured anything from having open wounds cauterised or stitched, to the amputation of limbs. In truth, it wasn't somewhere any of us were keen to stay close to, so we tended to leave as soon as we had delivered the wounded, trusting to the Gods that perhaps soon we would see them once more, alive and well.

By late afternoon the rain was showing no sign of letting up and the fighting was still raging. I and my comrades had been told by then that we were due to be sent back into the battle once more. At that juncture the Britons were being cleared off the field by Pannonian Auxiliary cavalry formations, along with their counterparts from the surviving Dalmatorum Auxiliaries. The vast stretch of ground at the bottom of the slope was now carpeted with a great tangle of corpses, slaughtered horses and the scattered wrecks of chariots. But, despite heavy losses, the Britons remained a formidable and ever aggressive fighting force.

Word had reached us that Plautius now wanted the last of the chariots to be taken care of. Plautius knew, however, that he would have to give the Britons some Legionaries as well as Auxiliaries to attack; otherwise they would probably not take the bait. Consequently, he had dispatched a force of four Cohorts, including our own, to lure out and engage the Britons' remaining chariots. Three Cohorts of Batavians would also make up the advance and the whole assault would be supported by Scorpiones mounted on carts, which would be escorted by a small party of cavalry along the right flank. The intention would be for the Scorpiones to engage the chariots when they attacked the main formation. Around twenty of these artillery carts had been moved up in readiness and now waited below the rounded crest of the flank for the Britons to charge.

Once more, we marched down the muddy slope towards the baying hoards of Britons, the Batavians marching on the flanks while the Legionary Cohorts held the middle of the formation, deliberately placed as a tempting prize for Caratacus' chariots and cavalry.

We held the formation together as usual, keeping the extended lines tight and the pace steady as we neared the point at which we thought the Britons would charge. Again my body began to experience great surges of aggressive energy as we drew closer. Once more I gripped the shaft of my new Pilum tightly, determined that I would bury the tip of it deep in the first Briton who got close enough.

As though to herald our approach, the Britons hammered on their shields once more, goading and taunting us as we drew ever closer, until at last the entire mob of them burst forward in a terrifyingly furious charge. Instantly, we halted to form a defensive line and there we stood our ground as the chariots we were after thundered forward at the head of a mixed force of cavalry and infantry. With our shields to the front and our Pila raised on the shoulder, ready to throw, we waited in silence for the Scorpione crews to engage.

"Hold! Hold fast!" I could hear the orders being shouted up and down the line as an intense prickling sensation shot up and down my spine. But for the occasional order to 'hold', our lines remained totally silent as we each fought off our own instinctive desire to turn and run. Instead, we quietly watched the howling mob tear up the slope towards us.

"Make ready. Hold fast!"

In no time at all, the chariots came within throwing range and every muscle tensed in my body, just waiting for the order to throw. As my mind screamed out with the anticipated order I heard at last the distant noise of the Scorpiones discharging their deadly bolts and witnessed their effect as they streaked overhead before ripping into the charging formation. The lethal wave of missiles cut down horses, drivers and passengers alike. The front of the charge turned into a vision of utter chaos as chariots pitched over and horses ran around wildly, screaming in pain and fear.

As soon as the bolts had done their work and the machines were reloading, the order to make ready passed down the line in an instant. Finally it was followed by the order to throw as the surviving chariots were by now around fifty paces out and closing fast. As a collective roar rose from thousands of Roman mouths, waves of lethal javelins took to the iron grey skies and hurtled toward the charging formation. I watched my Pilum fly, as it traced a high arc, before its tip dropped and it plummeted down onto the driver of one of the charging chariots.

The force of the weapon slamming into him knocked him off the side of the vehicle and I yelled out triumphantly, punching my fist in the air as he disappeared under one of the wheels.

However, my joy quickly evaporated as the chariot instantly lost control, swerving into another as they hurtled towards us. I remember raising my shield up to my face as my brief moment of triumph was quickly replaced by dismay as the horses ran in a blind panic towards us, turning only at the last second to avoid the shield wall. The tight turn of the horses sent the chariot slewing round and into a violent roll, crashing and bouncing crazily towards us as it yanked the squealing horses over with it. All I could do was watch in dumbstruck horror, as the tumbling mass of crashing timber somersaulted my way. In that tightly packed formation in which we stood, there was nowhere to go. Instead I closed my eyes, cursed my miserable bad fortune and awaited the inevitable.

CHAPTER 27

The next thing I remember was emerging from the heavy blackness of unconsciousness.

My awareness of the world around me had begun to return slowly and painfully. Pulses of light danced before my eyes and my ears rang as they attempted to attune themselves to my surroundings. Even though I was lying down, my head spun with an intense dizziness and throbbed with a terrible pain that seemed to come from the very core of my skull.

My neck was stiff and sore and I had great difficulty raising my head to see where I now lay. Slowly, my blurred and distorted vision began to settle down and adjust to the dim interior of what I first took to be a large cavern. I blinked hard several times, struggling to force my eyes to focus. Gradually, the loud rushing and whistling noises in my ears began to subside. I picked up more clearly on the sounds of the other soldiers that shared the gloomy space with me. Now I could hear them cursing their pain, or groaning out their misery and discomfort at their injuries. It was then that I gradually came to realise that I was in one of the field hospitals close to the battlefield.

I tried tentatively to raise myself up on an elbow and yelled out in pain as a searing hot agony shot through my right forearm. After lying for a short pause, breathing deeply until the pain subsided, I rolled to my left and gingerly levered myself into a sitting position with my good arm. As soon as my body was vertical my head began to spin violently. I experienced a violent urge to vomit as a wave of dizziness passed over me. Then the awful sensation passed and slowly I began to take in my surroundings.

The floor of the tent was covered with dry rushes and straw. On top of that lay my fellow soldiers, filling the extensive floor space of the tent and laid out in rows on thick woollen blankets, some moving, some not. As my sense of smell continued its return, the thick scent of vomit, blood and excrement filled my nostrils and once again I felt myself starting to retch as the foul stench overwhelmed my sense of smell. The centre of the tent was occupied by long narrow tables, some of which contained medical equipment and large quantities of linen dressings, both clean and soiled.

A soldier lay still and quiet on one of the tables, his pale hands folded across his stomach. As I studied his still, silent form from top to bottom, I quickly realised that nothing more could be done for him. The bottom of the table was dripping freely with blood which had, I imagine, flowed from his veins when the surgeons had sawn his leg off, just below the knee. No doubt the terrible pain and extreme blood loss had been too much for him and he had succumbed. Perhaps he had welcomed the release of death after having to endure the removal of his leg, with nothing more to deaden his pain than the administration of a little opium to dull his senses, while the orderlies took hold of him and pinned him down. I was glad I hadn't had to bear the awful sound of his screams.

"Take this one out lads." a quiet voice said, as I became aware of the Capsarius enter my widening field of vision accompanied by two soldiers carrying a stretcher. He indicated to the still form on the table and watched quietly as the two soldiers gently lifted the dead man. They then placed him on the stretcher, picked it up and moved to the flaps of the tent, carefully stepping between the scattered forms of the wounded as they went.

The Capsarius wiped the palms of his hands on his blood spattered brown woollen tunic. He then picked up a clean scrap of linen, wiping his forehead as he turned, finally noticing me then as I remained sitting upright, watching him.

"Ah, you're awake then." he smiled, stating the obvious in a jovial tone of voice. "How do you feel?"

"You really want to know?" I croaked, as I realised that my throat was bone dry. "I'm thirstier than a horse!"

"Ah, well if it's a drink you're after, my friend, you're going to have to wait. I need to get a Medicus to look you over first."

I groaned in exasperation and tried hard to swallow as the Capsarius left the tent in search of the Medicus. My thirst began to annoy me now that I had become so acutely aware of it, so I tried to occupy myself to take my mind off it. Again I looked at the men around me, searching the faces of my neighbours, wondering if there was anyone else I knew who had also ended up in here. As I cast about the shadowy interior of the tent I tried hard to focus in the dim light, tending to look at the faces furthest from me before I examined those who were lying closest to me. Then, with an awful start I suddenly recognised the soldier lying on my immediate left.

"Oh gods no - Zenas!" I gasped.

I could forgive myself for not recognising him straight away as I took in the awful injuries he had sustained. His face was heavily bruised and grossly swollen on one side, almost completely closing his left eye. A crust of dried blood wreathed his forehead in a broad line where the rim of his helmet had dug into his skin and a thin line of black blood trickled slowly from the corner of his mouth. As I spoke his name, his one good eye slowly opened and he looked towards me. A light smile gradually shaped his dry, split lips and his right hand stretched slowly towards me. I grasped the hand he had offered, squeezing it as I looked on despairingly at what had happened to him.

Silenced by my shock, I could say nothing to him and instead I contented myself with squeezing his hand and trying to smile reassuringly at him. He began to mouth something but I couldn't hear him properly. I leant closer and bent over his face, my own pain unimportant now. I was briefly startled by a low cough which spotted my face with his blood, but tried hard to hear his words as he strove to make himself understood. But I could only make out a low rattle as blood from deep in his chest frothed up in his mouth.

"Zenas, what…Why are….?

To begin with, as I looked upon his broken body I couldn't understand what had brought him to this, then slowly I began to remember the fighting. He had been very close to me in the battle line as the chariot had ploughed into us. Our armour had been removed and I looked over to where it had been piled, close to the head of our bedding. The iron plate armour that Zenas had worn lay just above his bed and was in a terrible state. Much of the metal was caved in all along its left side. Loose plates hung from leather straps which had been ripped free of the securing rivets and the once carefully cleaned and oiled armour was now caked in dried mud from where he had fallen onto the field. I concluded then he must have been hit by the same chariot that I had. Even worse, I recalled with anguish that it was my Pilum that had felled the driver, causing it to veer out of control.

"Oh Zenas, I…."

He squeezed my hand once more and tried to raise his head, finally managing to put together some words that I could actually make out. He smiled weakly and in a dry whisper he said:

"Looks like I won't …be keeping that appointment with Mestrius after all."

His smiled faded and again he coughed as his head slumped back onto the bed.

A wave of remorse engulfed me as I remembered how I had started the undisciplined chatter that got him a reprimand from Mestrius, just before we had gone into battle. I remembered the look of embarrassment on his face and my heart weighed heavy with the knowledge that I was to blame and that it would probably not now be possible to make amends.

"Come on, Zenas. Of course you'll make that appointment. I'll come with you and tell Mestrius that it was I who started the talk."

Again he gave a thin smile as he struggled to lift his head. His mouth began to move again and I strained once more to listen.

"You'll…you'll have to face him…on your own lad. I've got …somewhere else I need to be."

"No Zenas, don't speak like that, I…"

As I tried to give him what I knew would be false words of assurance I recoiled from him slightly as a great spasm of pain wracked his body and he gripped my hand with an unexpected force.

"Time is short…listen." For a moment, Zenas recovered himself and seemed to make ready to force out enough words to explain what it was he wanted to tell.

"Your family, I told you not to worry… They are safe now."

"What…How do you know this?"

Again, his body convulsed with terrible pain as he fought to explain himself. He groaned and gave out a terrible rasping sound from his tortured lungs.

"Look, in my helmet…there is …a folded parchment, I received yesterday. I was going to give it to you after the battle. Something good…from home" he paused to suck some more breath into his failing lungs before continuing. "Take it now…It's the last thing I can do for you."

I looked down at him, unwilling to let go of his hand until he nodded and indicated with his eyes that I should reach for the battered helmet. Reluctantly I let go and reached over, wincing with the pain of extending my body, as I grabbed the helmet and pulled the folded parchment out from its hiding place in the leather helmet lining.

"Read it…while there's still time to… see your face." gasped Zenas.

I quickly read the document as I looked up periodically to check on Zenas. The news that it carried was more than I could have hoped for.

The letter was from somebody called Petronius Crixus, a Legion veteran who lived in Mogontiacum, and was in response to a letter that Zenas had sent to him. As I read on, my heart leapt with joy as I realised that the letter was confirming that Crixus and several other veterans in the colony had acted on Zenas' request to track down the assassin that Julia had sent to threaten my family. It confirmed that one Marcus Flavius Gellius, a stranger in town who had already raised some suspicions within the community, had now met with an unfortunate and fatal accident. Enquiries within the community had established that he had been addressing questions about my family to, amongst others, the military clerks at the fortress. The letter also confirmed that my family knew nothing of the threat and were now under the discreet protection of the Legion veterans. In the concluding passage, it added that I should be assured that there will be no further cause for concern.

I was smiling with relief as I looked down at Zenas who was now doing his best to smile up at me. There was so much I wanted to say to him, to tell him how relieved I was and how much I valued what he had done for me. In the end, I settled for three simple words.

"Thank you, brother."

His smile grew a little wider as he tightened his grip on my hand once more, but then the smile gradually began to fade. His eyes slowly took on, what was to any soldier, an all too familiar, sightless look. His grip loosened and his hand finally slipped down to his side as his lungs slowly let forth one final, rattling breath as his spirit soared free. Zenas was dead.

For what seemed an age I sat next to him, trying to remember all that we had done in his presence and what I had learned from him as a soldier. I had taken up his hand again, feeling it steadily cooling as eventually; I became aware of the presence of somebody behind me.

"The Medicus is here, soldier."

I looked over my shoulder and saw the Capsarius standing there with the Medicus I had seen during the battle. He was the same one who I had seen walking amongst the wounded outside the tent and directing the Capsarii treating the men.

"I honestly didn't think he'd last as long as this." said the Medicus quietly as he knelt beside me and nodded gently towards Zenas. "His innards were damaged by a terrible impact. I fully expected that he would fade in the night. By the Gods, he certainly managed to hold on though. And, do you know, he made sure his hand was on yours throughout the night. Who was he to you, lad?"

"His name was Zenas and he was my Contubernium leader." I said with unconcealed pride.

The Medicus gently nodded his head and placed a hand on my shoulder before he nodded in the direction of Zenas once more.

"Then it looks like he decided to stay around to keep an eye on you for one last time. Just until he knew you were alright."

I nodded sadly as I continued to look down at Zenas' still, silent body.

"Come on, lad." said the Medicus finally. "He's done his bit, just like a good soldier should. I need to do mine now."

Reluctantly, I took myself away from the body and submitted myself to the Medicus' examination, answering his questions and moving my limbs as requested. As the examination continued, I found that I was responding to his requests without thought. But, as for my mind itself, it was still out on the battlefield where we were all last together and I could not help but wonder what had become of the rest of my brothers. Were they alive - or did they lie dead and cold somewhere out on the field?

Eventually the Medicus satisfied himself that I was fit enough to go. He had explained that the injury to my arm was not serious enough to stop me marching with the baggage train, but it would keep me out of action for a while. The muscles had been badly bruised and a heavy gash had required cauterising and stitching. He advised that all I could do now was clean the wound daily with sour wine, treat it with a honey poultice and apply clean linen dressings. It would heal, soon enough.

After promising to keep up with the treatment I returned to my bed space and collected my equipment. However, before I could leave there was one final thing that still needed to be done. I quietly leant over to where Zenas still lay and searched through his belongings until I had found what I needed. Zenas always carried the little figure of the Genius in his armour when we fought and I reasoned that it would need a new guardian now. As I crouched silently by his side I fished around in my money pouch, eventually retrieving a small bronze coin. Turning it slowly in my fingers, I paused to spend my final moments with a man I considered to be both a great Legionary and a true friend. With a melancholy sigh I gently opened his mouth and placed the coin inside before laying my hand over his now still and silent heart.

"There's a coin for your fare, brother," I whispered. "Safe journey, and may the gods speed you on your way."

Quietly, I gathered my things and left the tent.

CHAPTER 28

Though the sky was dull with scudding clouds, the intensity of the light outside still hurt my eyes as, leaving the dim confines of the hospital tent; I eventually emerged to take in the day. I still felt a little shaky and my head throbbed with an oppressive ache. Nevertheless, I was glad to be out of the stale, nauseating atmosphere of the tent and standing once more in clean air. I wasn't too concerned at the lingering pain in my head as I stood, trying to get my bearings and taking in the feverish activity going on around me. My first priority now was to find my unit and rejoin them. But where to start? Things looked so different here now.

Throughout the camp the ground was now like a filthy swamp, churned up by the ruts of cart wheels and heavily pitted from the to and fro of men and horses. Muddy brown puddles filled the scrapes and hollows. Men waded through the sucking mud, cursing their luck at ending up in such a dismal, rain sodden hole like Britannia. What I had noticed almost immediately was that many of the soldiers now moving around the camp were different. I rubbed the back of my neck, pondering the shield insignia's before recognition finally dawned; I'd seen these soldiers in Portus Itius. What in the name of Jupiter was the Praetorian Guard doing here?

For a while I just stood there, trying to work out what had gone on and how long I had been unconscious. After all, nobody had bothered to explain that to me. In the end I must have looked as though I was in need of some help. Before long a grizzled old Legion Optio strode over to me and clapped his hand on my shoulder.

"What's the matter, lad? You don't look as if you're rowing with all of your oars in the water. Are you lost, or what?"

"I need to find my unit Optio, but I'm not sure where they might be now."

I avoided his eyes and continued to cast around the campsite, trying hard to overcome my disorientation and eagerly seeking to spot a familiar face. Maybe I tried too hard to focus on the bustle around me as a dizzy spell soon swept over me. I began to sway before the concerned looking Optio, who quickly clapped his hands either side of my shoulders to steady me.

"What unit are you, lad?" he enquired, with a slightly worried look on his face. "I can see you're XIIII Gemina at least."

"Cohort I, Legate's bodyguard."

"Ah, one of Fatalis' lads then, eh?" he raised his eyebrows as he rubbed his stubbly chin, looking me up and down. "Listen son, it pains me to say it, but your bunch got a really bad mauling yesterday. Truth to be told, a lot of them lads didn't see the dawn this morning."

His comment reminded me of Zenas' death just a short while ago. A wave of intense sadness passed over me as he paused for a moment before lowering his voice, leaning in with a strange look on his face. "So, were you actually in the middle of that lot then?"

The question seemed to echo around in my head as my mind harkened back once more to the Roman shield line and the charging Britons. The thunder and screams of the raging battle filled my ears once more. Once again, I saw the shattered frame of the chariot hurtling crazily towards the formation. After a short, silent pause, I drove the memories from my mind, shaking my head and snapping back to reality.

"Are you alright there?" The Optio voiced his concern once more.

"Do you know where they are now?" I asked, ignoring his troubled enquiry.

"Gone." answered the Optio. "Fatalis took what survived of your boys and moved out this morning for Camulodunum along with the Legate, his staff, the rest of Cohort I and Cohort IV as well. Half the battle group's gone there by now and they should be right on top of the place by this time. What's left of the local boys will be hiding behind their stockade, shitting themselves I imagine. Most of them got hacked to fucking pieces yesterday. I bet they won't fancy a re-match now."

"Fatalis lives?" I sighed, relieved.

"Of course he lives!" laughed the Optio. "Do you know lad, that battle was some of the hardest, nastiest fighting I've seen in many a long year. I said then that anybody who lived through that business with the chariots yesterday was blessed by the gods. I'll tell you this though - terrible though the battle was, it'll take more than a few rampaging savages to snuff that old bastard Fatalis' lamp out. Besides he's never been known to miss out on a chance for glory. And what more glory is there than to actually win the battle in front of the Emperor?"

Suddenly, the explanation for all of the new things I had seen around the camp, including the presence of Praetorians, finally hit me.

"The Emperor. He is here, now?" I asked the Optio.

"Where have you been, boy?" laughed the Optio. "He arrived late yesterday, with two full Cohorts of Praetorians and another bunch of reinforcements. Look around you lad. These are nice, shiny, new boys. They haven't so much as taken a piss in this hole of a country yet, let alone fought a battle here."

"I'm sorry, Optio; I was felled in the chariot charge yesterday afternoon. I have been unconscious until only around an hour ago."

"That's alright, lad!" he grinned "We didn't mind you having a little nap while we did all the cleaning up. Now listen; a baggage column moves out for Camulodunum soon. Why don't you trail along with it and see if you can find your lot at the other end?"

With a genial smile, the Optio slapped me lightly on the back, before turning and walking off through the sticky mud, cursing loudly at the sucking mess as he went. I had to bite my tongue about the 'nap' quip, but I quickly realised that he had not meant any offence by it. Still, I hoped he realised that I would have given anything to have stayed in the line with my brothers though. Now, as things were, I had not the slightest idea whether they were a part of the advance on Camulodunum, or whether they now lay cold and stiff at the bottom of that slope.

It was then that I felt compelled to look upon the great battlefield once more. Curious to see the aftermath of yesterday, I walked over to the side of the camp which overlooked the field and stared out over the falling ground, beyond the now deserted defence lines and down to where the dead lay. There were thousands of them, lying scattered all over the land, cold and lifeless in the mud and gore. Briton and Roman were united now in death; the grim fellowship of those slain in war now transcending any of the cultural and political barriers that separated them in life.

For a while I just stood and gazed out upon the scene. I watched scattered field parties moving amongst the dead, salvaging equipment and beginning the task of removing the vast piles of slaughtered meat from the field. Not even the ravages of the Gods could create such a scene of terrible carnage as that which our war had bestowed upon this land.

The noise of the distant roll of thunder reminded me of yesterday once more, as did the dark and menacing clouds that boiled overhead, full again with the promise of yet more drenching rain. By the Gods, this was summer. Did it always rain in this place? I stood there for a little while longer, watching the rising smoke of countless small fires and of vast funeral pyres, all billowing upwards. They mingled in the air, tainting the turbulent sky with the sickly stench of burning flesh.

There was nothing to be done now. If my friends were dead it was because the gods willed it so. For myself, I could do nothing now but to seek out what was left.

I turned back to the centre of the camp, towards the forming up point for the baggage column that was about to leave. As I walked to join the column, I came across a new picket line of wooden stakes. A wide opening in it was guarded by four Praetorians but my interest was not with them. My eyes focussed beyond the defences and I gasped with shock and surprise at what I saw.

I tried to make sense of what I was seeing, struggling to identify the strange, enormous beasts that stood before me. They were absolutely massive creatures, with thick grey wrinkly skin and two huge white horns sticking out of their ugly faces. And that nose! Like some sort of massive writhing serpent, slithering around on the ground and waving about in the air. As I took the scene in, my mind struggled with the unexpected shock of encountering these huge animals with their great flapping ears.

As I tried to recover my shock and observe them more closely, I spotted that they were chained to great timber stakes that had been hammered firmly into the ground. Whatever they were, they were ours at least.

As I approached the gateway still gazing upon the great beasts, the four guards turned to face me. One of their number stepped forward, holding the flat of his hand out.

"Where do you think you're going then?" he asked curtly.

"Nowhere, I just wanted to know what manner of animal that is." I asked, as I pointed over to the tethered beasts.

Instantly the four of them broke into uproarious laughter and I felt myself reddening with embarrassment and annoyance as they hooted with derision, pointing mockingly at me.

"Those animals you want to know about are only the Emperors pride and joy, you stupid swine!" He informed me superciliously. "They're his own personal war elephants, brought specially from the other side of the world. They're going to put the fear of Hades into these hairy arsed barbarians - and confuse slow types like you, it would appear!"

The Praetorian stood there with a stupid grin on his face as his three companions burst out laughing at the affront. My temper started to rise at his insulting tone of voice. I had to check myself from clapping my hand to the hilt of my Gladius, injured arm or not.

"It was a simple enough question, friend." I snapped

"I have never seen an elephant before today. They're so huge and strange; I just wanted to know what they were."

The Praetorian thrust his fists into his hips while his three comrades fell silent, contenting themselves with sporting foolish grins as their comrade now stared at me coldly.

"Well, now you have your simple answer and that means you can be on your way." he said curtly. "And don't call me friend. Now move on, or you might find you'll need one or two more bandages to be getting along with, you scruffy looking bastard!"

I seethed inside as I fought to control my rising urge to shove my Gladius down his arrogant throat. I satisfied myself with the best spontaneous reply I could manage.

"I suppose it's a measure of a man who only threatens those who stand alone and slowed by wounds." I snapped accusingly, a deliberate look of open contempt spread across my face. "Still, no more than I would expect from an over-polished palace fop, whose worst battles so far have no doubt been won fighting off the attentions of painted whores and Greek arse merchants. Perhaps we will have a chance to talk again, when I am more recovered from my wounds."

With that, I spat at the ground by his feet and turned my back on him, leaving the guard and his companions stammering at my effrontery.

As I walked away I seethed with anger as I asked

myself; just what did these fools expect? Respect for their privileged status, as stay at home palace lackeys? These men were just the kind of soldier who I could never respect. After all, I remember the true nature of their valour when they had not hesitated to butcher only lightly armed soldiers in the town forum at Portus Itius. Maybe if they came out and got their hands dirty on a battlefield once in a while, and shared in the feel of proper combat, perhaps it would lessen the utter contempt that I felt for their kind, for then they too would know what it felt like to be a true soldier.

Having crossed the great camp, I presently joined the column heading for Camulodunum. I passed my time on the march in the company of another Legionary from the Fourteenth, a young lad called Glabrus from Cohort III, serving in the Century of Pantarchus. He had lost two fingers from his right hand and sustained a deep slash along his forearm. Glabrus had stayed in camp overnight, sleeping off the shock of surgery to close his slash wound. They had also removed the two badly mangled fingers, cauterising the stumps while he screamed his head off with the terrible pain, he explained ruefully.

As we marched under the leaden skies, we talked of many things. We both avoided the subject of the last battle, concentrating instead on the simpler, happier things, such as where we hailed from, when we joined up and who we knew. We talked of our own units, though I could not help but voice my reservations to

Glabrus about my misplaced comrades and whether I would actually see any of them again.

"They are your brothers, just as my comrades are mine, I know," said Glabrus, fully understanding how I felt. "If they still live then you will eventually find them, I am sure of it. That being so; we are both soldiers. As such it is part of our lot in life to suffer, though that doesn't always mean with the pain of our labours."

Glabrus bit enthusiastically into a thick, round loaf of bread as we marched alongside the creaking carts. He cheerfully offered me a generous sized piece which I willingly accepted, now that the feeling of concussion induced nausea was gradually starting to subside. As I ate, I watched the chunk of bread he had bitten off, churning round in his crumb ringed mouth as he munched away, giving voice to his thoughts. He accompanied this by ejecting small bits of flying wet bread from his over-worked mouth.

"I have served five years now and I have seen enough good men lost to battle." he continued. "Some of them I knew well and felt close to. To me it seems to be expected, that when we share the life that we have chosen and all that it brings, we can do nothing else but grow close to each other - even if we set out not wishing to do so. When men face such things as we do, it is easy to become brothers. Then the pain of loss will eventually touch us, but always we fight through. There is no shame in grieving for lost brothers, just as long as you make sure that you live on for them too. I'm sure that life is naught but a spark in the great blackness of death, so you must use your time well and become the best warrior that you can possibly be. Then, their spirits will always march with you, and you will never face death in battle alone. Soon Vepitta I will recover the use of my sword arm and then I will rise to be a soldier in your unit. Then I will have properly honoured the ghosts of my comrades. As for you, you will do even more, I'm sure."

I admired Glabrus' take on things. His words more suited somebody older than his own years. Nevertheless, they made perfect sense to me. As he finished sharing his thoughts and concentrated entirely on gulping down great wads of bread, I conceded that I could change nothing. The Gods would see to it that life carried on as ordained. For myself; I would carry on as before, because in that there was no choice. But I would make sure that I did live the rest of my life well and that way my comrades would be as proud of me as I was of them.

Before long, our ultimate goal lay before us. Camulodunum lay sprawled out over a vast stretch of land; it's mass of thatched roofs rising up towards the slate coloured rain clouds that churned above us, threatening to break imminently. The town itself was enormous, ringed by a series of deep ditches and high timber palisades, enclosing the town in their vast protective circle as they stretched round to the great navigable river that the town owed its wealth to.

I could see boats of all sizes tied to wharfs and jetties, extending out like slender fingers into the rain swollen current. Here were the landing areas that received trading vessels from all over the Roman world. The great port had thrived under Cunobelin, becoming an immensely rich capital which swallowed goods by the ship load in return for its own goods, which were in great demand elsewhere in the empire. Hunting dogs, slaves, grain, gold and base metals were traded for luxury items - wine from Greece, olive oil from Asia Minor and fine quality pottery from Gaul.

With its identity and importance as a great tribal centre still intact as yet, the sprawling settlement lay before us, as though it were waiting for the inevitable to happen. Soon, the one time seat of the native war god Camulos, whose power we had shattered in open battle, would fall before the conquering army that had now massed outside its gates. Then, whatever aspirations its former rulers once had for greatness would be over with. Soon, Camulodunum would be a possession of Rome.

Silently, the great Roman force stood arrayed before the vast defences of the town. Still smeared with the filth of battle and yet totally indomitable in their spirit. A huge spread of men and cavalry, they waited expectantly for their Emperor to come at last and claim this rich prize for his own. A wide path extended through the massed force to the very threshold of the town and the massive timber gates of

Camulodunum were now thrown wide open in a very visible and unmistakeable sign of capitulation.

Clearly, the people of Camulodunum had already made a choice. That choice had been to live, rather than to perish uselessly in a hell of flames and appalling violence, as Durobrivae had. The massed standards of the Roman Legions stood tall at the heads of their units. Scores of brightly coloured Vexilla fluttered around in the breeze as the great force stood waiting. Our baggage column had halted just short of the town. Now we began to line the side of the ancient track way, waiting for Claudius to come and claim his great victory over the Britons.

It was not long before we began to hear the approach of distant horns and drums. Their advance carried on the wind to us before drifting down to the assembled forces now massed outside the gates of Camulodunum. The vast, tightly ordered formations of men and horses stirred. They turned to face in the direction of the sounds coming from back up the track way, all of them peering now in the direction of what they knew was the approach of their Emperor. At that precise moment, a great, rolling clap of thunder boomed out, as though even the Gods themselves seemed obliged to herald the arrival of Claudius, fourth Emperor of Rome.

As we looked on, the first part of the Emperor's entourage to crest the hill were the cavalry escorts, slowly riding down the track towards us with their bright, flowing standards raised before them. A full

Cohort of five hundred riders rode forth in their best finery. Their horses too were adorned with gleaming harness fittings and each man wore a set of highly polished armour of silvered scales. They looked truly magnificent. Bright silk ribbons adorned their clothing, fluttering in the breeze as they rode past. The cold, emotionless features of the gleaming metal face masks of their ornate helmets stared impassively ahead as they led the Emperor towards the once great settlement. There, on behalf of the Senate and the people of Rome, Claudius would accept the surrender of yet another people, fallen in defeat to the irresistible military might of Rome.

Then came the Praetorians, so arrogant in their polished finery as they filed past with their chins in the air. They did not spare even one glance for the soldiers that lined the road before them. In return the battle weary soldiers chose not to hail the approach of the Praetorians with a soldiers greeting. Instead they stood silently as they watched them pass. Each man there knew that the Praetorians deserved no accolades. As they stood there, covered in the grime and filth of war, they knew too just who it was that had fought and bled to secure the victory that would finally give Claudius his credibility as an Emperor.

At last, the mighty war elephants lumbered into view and I was surprised to see that the strange looking beasts had been transformed since last I saw them. Now, they were completely resplendent as each bore the burden of a highly ornate, miniature wooden fortress on their massive backs. The huge animals were also extravagantly draped with lustrous, gold trimmed cloth. They positively dripped with fine gold chains and ornaments. In each of the small fortresses on the backs of the elephants, archers held bows nocked with arrows at the ready. The drivers of the beasts constantly pulled at the great flapping grey ears with short iron hooks to steer the beasts. For their part, the elephants strode on, terrifying in their size and, for all the world, seemingly unstoppable. As I looked on I marvelled at the fact that man could even capture such powerful beasts, let alone control them.

Just then the watching column began to cheer wildly as Claudius himself finally rode into view. Riding a beast even more magnificent than its companions, as if that were possible, Claudius sat atop the biggest of the elephants. Its finery was even more breathtaking then the others and I struggled to take in the magnificence of the entire spectacle, the like of which I had never even dreamed possible. Then, all around me, jubilant cheers erupted into the air, greeting the conquering Emperor as he rode along the route.

"Hail, Claudius!"

"Hail to our Emperor, conqueror of the Britons!"

Over and over again, we shouted out the greeting as Claudius steadily drew nearer to where I stood, craning my neck to see over the grubby, filth caked hands of his loyal troops. Hundreds were thrust into the air, waving and reaching out to him as he passed by. As the Emperor neared where I stood I noticed a decorated wagon, drawn by two snow white oxen moving before his elephants.

Four huge Nubian slaves, with oiled skin as black as night, stood on the back. They cast fistfuls of gold coins from great wooden chests, scattering them into the cheering crowds of soldiers that lined the way. The gleaming coins were clearly meant as a gift of gratitude from Claudius, but perhaps they were a token of acknowledgement too, for all the blood his loyal Legions had spilled to win this, the most glorious of days for him.

I could see him clearly now as he gradually came closer to where I stood. Double ranks of Praetorians flanked his elephant as they marched along, their eyes now scanning the crowds of soldiers, searching for any possible threat to the Emperor's safety. Along with everyone else, I was shouting and cheering wildly as the Emperor finally drew level with me. I stared at his fabulous cloak of purple silk, beautifully trimmed with embroidered gold laurel leaves. The white leather undershirt and gleaming golden breast plate tied with a band of purple silk only served to further enhance and compliment the excessive opulence of the decorations on the great bull elephant he rode upon. My heart pounded like a hammer in my chest as; after so many years spent in the service of Rome, I finally beheld my supreme master.

Gold coins showered down around me and after quickly stooping to snatch a few of the precious coins, I sprang up once more to wave and cheer him on like some excited child on a festival day.

I could see his face much more clearly as he passed by; waving sublimely at those he passed. Then, his golden laurel slipped down on his forehead and he encouraged my closer scrutiny as he frowned and fumbled to push it back into place. As I began to cast a more critical eye on Claudius, I noticed that his ears seemed to be somehow too big for his head. I noticed too that he constantly twitched and rolled his eyes. His mouth drooped on one side to create a peculiar looking lop-sided smile and - was he drooling? For the briefest of moments I paused to consider why it might be that such a demi-god should have such apparent imperfections when his image on the coins and the statues I had seen told a very different story. Then the thought was gone and I dropped to the ground once more, snatching at the scattered coins that were now being rescued from the mud by many other filthy, scrabbling hands.

I knew that the value represented by the gleaming gold coins as money could buy me much. But their value as a keepsake, a reminder to me of all I had been through to reach this place, to arrive at this point in time, was beyond price. Perhaps in years to come, when I could finally return home to Salviena and my boys, I would show those coins to my sons. Then, I could tell them the story of just how I had come by them. The thought was both comforting and exciting. I was sure that it would be a story such as they had never before heard in their entire lives. And so, I would live for the day when I could see the look on their faces as I finally told them the tale of how their father had helped win Britannia for Claudius.

By the time I had gotten back on my feet, Claudius had moved closer to the gates of Camulodunum. Now, as he closed with the town and the waiting delegation of tribal Chieftains that waited to offer him their surrender, the moment was almost upon them when they would hand the control of their land and people to Rome forever.

As I watched the Emperor fade into the distance, I quietly opened my pouch and placed inside the precious collection of the few gold coins that I had managed to retrieve from the dirt. Then, gently, I removed a small bundle of cloth from the pouch, carefully unwrapping it to reveal what lay within. As I looked down upon it, the little figure of the Genius lay there in the palm of my hand. Its image was at once comforting and warmly familiar as its tiny bronze face smiled benignly up at me.

"At least while I have you," I shared my thoughts with it. "They are all still with me, in spirit at least."

I smiled, content with my lot, and returned the figure to the safety of the pouch as, taking in a deep, refreshing breath of air; I turned to the north, to finish the short walk to Camulodunum.

Printed in Great Britain
by Amazon